NO HIGHER LAW

Also by Philip Friedman

Grand Jury
Inadmissible Evidence
Reasonable Doubt
Termination Order
Wall of Silence

NO HIGHER LAW

Philip Friedman

First published in 1999
by HEADLINE BOOK PUBLISHING

A HEADLINE FEATURE hardback

10 9 8 7 6 5 4 3 2 1

All characters in this publication are fictitious and any resemblance to real persons, living or dead, is purely coincidental.

British Library Cataloguing in Publication Data

Friedman, Philip, 1944 -
No higher law
1.Public prosecutors - New York (State) - New York - Fiction 2.Fraud - New York (State) - New York - Fiction 3.Jews - New York (State) - New York - Fiction 4. Suspense fiction
I.Title
813.5'4[F]

ISBN 0 7472 1509 X (hbk)
07472 7350 2 (tpb)

Typeset by Palimpsest Book Production Limited,
Polmont, Stirlingshire
Printed and bound in Great Britain by
Mackays of Chatham plc, Chatham Kent

HEADLINE BOOK PUBLISHING
A division of the Hodder Headline Group
338 Euston Road
London NW1 3BH
www.headline.co.uk
www.hodderheadline.com

For Madeline,
who's been there through it all

and in memory of Donald I. Fine

ACKNOWLEDGEMENTS

Once again, I would have been incapable of proceeding without the experience, insight and advice of Dan Castleman, in whose friendship I take great pleasure.

The Treasury law enforcement aspects of the story grew out of conversations with Ron Noble, who provided crucial information and introductions and did his best in the early going to keep me on the right path.

I learned most of what I know about the U.S. Secret Service from Brian Gimlett, whose good humor in the face of my unceasing and sometimes repetitive questions was remarkable.

Niles Goldstein and Baruch Weiss opened doors on a world both familiar and strange . . . and endlessly fascinating.

I am grateful to all of them, as I am to all the people named in the Author's Note at the end of the book.

Three things come when the mind is diverted – the messiah, a found article, and a scorpion.

Talmud Bavli, Sanhedrin 97a

It seemed she'd been in darkness forever. Her flashlight had flickered and died not long after she'd made herself crawl into this horrid narrow hole, telling herself it had to lead somewhere.

The air tasted of death and putrefaction. She could feel the walls and ceiling pressing closer so there was barely room for her to inch herself forward. The rocky ground beneath her was cold and damp, but she embraced it as she went because each time she brushed the ceiling with a shoulder or hip and felt a rain of dislodged earth she was more afraid she would bury herself.

Her outstretched hand warned her of an obstruction, a low place in the ceiling pinching the tunnel almost to nothing in front of her. She probed with her fingers, not knowing if she dared try digging it away. Dirt flaked off it but it wouldn't yield. It seemed too straight and round to be natural. A pipe of some kind, she thought, part of the city's lifelines crisscrossing beneath the streets. She couldn't tell if she could squeeze under it.

Was this finally the end? It seemed impossible that anyone could have gone further, could have kept digging and somehow hauled out the dirt.

He'd told her the tunnel was finished. A way to outflank their enemies, he'd said, but he was afraid that at the crucial moment someone might weaken, so no one knew about it except the few faithful who'd dug it. But he was telling her, *to quiet her fears.*

Suppose he'd been lying. The thought had plagued her since the real tunnel ended, the only opening in its dirt wall the hole that had led her here. Suppose it was a trap – a dead end, a test to see if she was loyal.

And if she wasn't? Memory showed her the reward she could expect: a man defiant in the face of the tribunal that had condemned him, defiant even as they buried him up to his armpits. Unflinching as his accusers looped a twisted length of cloth around his neck and pulled, at the very moment he broke his silence to recite the Shema: Listen, Israel . . .

Fighting to contain her panic, she pressed herself tighter to the tunnel floor, face in the dirt, arms reaching past the obstruction as far as they would go – stretched out flat like an ancient priest prostrated before the Temple altar – trying to find some solid place in the rock and dirt beyond to get a grip on. She took a deep breath of the foul air and then squeezed it all out of her lungs to make herself thin while she wriggled herself under the thick pipe, pushing with her feet and pulling with her hands, stuck at first but scraping through somehow, chunks of earth tumbling down from the ceiling behind her.

She lay there sobbing with exhaustion and fear, dimly aware that there was more tunnel ahead – something about the sound of the dirt still dripping down around her, or perhaps a barely felt tickle of dank air moving against her face.

She started crawling again, no idea what she would find.

2

1

Benjamin Kaplan's beeper went off as he crossed the main lobby of the US Attorney's office for the Southern District of New York, already later than he wanted to be. He stopped at one of the pay phones near the revolving door to return the call, not willing to waste even the moments it would take to go back to the guard desk.

'I need a search warrant right away,' Ian Rogers told him. 'Can you get a magistrate judge on the phone?'

'For Isaacs?' Rogers was supposed to be recruiting a potential informant: emergency search warrants weren't on the program. 'What's the rush?'

'We've got to secure his computers before he can erase the data.'

'That doesn't sound like credit-card fraud.'

The Secret Service agent hesitated. 'Yeah.'

'Tell me.'

'Bogus notes.' The words rushed, as if the agent were unwilling to let them out into the world.

Currency counterfeiting? Where had that come from? 'Hang on, I'll see if someone can handle it.'

He let Rogers dangle and used the other pay phone to call Freddi Ward.

'Why me?' she asked when he told her what he needed.

'Because you're the best prosecutor I have.'

'Not on Friday night, I'm not.'

'It's only a search warrant. Your date can wait an extra half-hour – you're worth it.'

'It's not fair, you know, taking advantage of a friendship.'

'Would you rather I played tough boss?' Into the other phone he said, 'Hold on another minute,' then switched back to Freddi. 'Stop pulling my chain. I've got the agent hanging on the other line, and I'm out of change.'

'Where are you?'

'At the pay phones in the lobby. Both of them.'

'You *are* desperate. All right, but you owe me.'

The subway didn't cooperate with Ben's eagerness to get home. By the time he rushed in the door Vashti had Hannah all dressed up and ready to go: scrubbed pink, blonde hair brushed and gleaming. As he paid the nanny for the week, Hannah tugged at his jacket.

'Daddy? Are we late?'

'No, sweetie, we're just in time.' Stretching it a bit.

'I want to see the dancing.'

'If we hurry.'

'We have to light candles first.'

'Yes, we do. And then we can get our coats on and go.'

Welcoming the Sabbath had become a family ritual for their tiniest of families. Hannah loved the songs, the exuberant dancing in the aisles, the parts of the service their congregation had adapted specially for kids. Ritual and routine were essential for her, a bulwark against the fears that had haunted her since her mother's death three years ago. Not letting work interfere with their Friday nights was the rule Ben tried hardest not to break.

Saturday – clear, and warm for February – they met Freddi at the Central Park Zoo. She bent to hug Hannah, as always with a certain grown-up reserve – 'I keep waiting for her to be ready for boys and clothes,' she'd said more than once. Ben wasn't so eager.

A fifteen-year veteran of the prosecutorial wars, Freddi Ward was famous in the office as a loner, but she and Ben had formed an alliance of two almost as soon as he'd arrived. Freddi joked it was because she'd known right away that, unlike every other straight male in the office, Ben wasn't going to hit on her every time they were alone.

They all trooped up the stone stairway for a good view of the polar bears, Hannah's favorite animals of the moment.

'How'd it go with Rogers?' Ben asked.

'Fine, once he slowed down enough to be coherent.'

The agent had listed as the object of his search all manner of computer equipment, Freddi said: the kinds of things a cellphone pirate like Isaacs might use, but nothing to do with the credit-card fraud Rogers was investigating – not white-plastic blanks, not lists of credit-card numbers. 'A lot of printing-type stuff, though. Any output from a copying or printing device, even inks and toners.'

Bogus notes, Rogers had said. Printing money would be a big step up for Isaac Isaacs, if that was what this was about.

Alan Kest held high the braided, many-wicked Havdalah candle for everyone to see, then turned it over and pressed the flames into a shallow dish of wine. The light sizzled and sputtered out, ending the Sabbath, and they all sang of the prophet Elijah and the hope he would soon announce the Anointed One, scion of the House of

David. Now, and more with every week that passed, the traditional song was filled with a special exhilaration.

When the last strains of the verse had died out and he had wished everyone a good week, Kest mastered the pain in his hip and lumbered to the room at the rear of the house he'd set aside as an office. He settled heavily into the wheeled desk-chair by the computer. He'd thought of himself as a bear of a man, once, an ox, but the pain was making a mockery of all that. It kept getting worse, and the doctors said there was nothing more they could do.

There was a message on the computer from Rudovsky.

'We have located the final parts for the machine,' the e-mail said. 'Delivery in a few weeks at most. The Swiss is still cooperating but I worry about him.'

A few weeks at most!

'Not acceptable!' Kest typed in reply. 'Secure delivery immediately.' He backspaced to take out the exclamation point and put in a 'please.'

The day is short and the task is great, he thought, *the workers are lazy and the profit is large.*

Words as applicable here as to the holy task of studying the Law. But Rudovsky was no scholar. He wouldn't recognize the words from Ethics of the Fathers, wouldn't supply the missing final line – *And the Master is insistent.*

Instead, Kest typed: 'Our own machine will be ready within a week. We depend on you now. As you know our time is very limited, and we have much of importance to do.' Land to buy, houses to build . . . and the cattle, too. Sometimes he despaired of being able to do it all in a year.

He sent the message but it was late now for Rudovsky. Nothing would happen until Sunday morning there, when, with the help of Heaven, Alan Kest would be sound asleep here in Brooklyn, away from his pain for those few hours.

When Ben Kaplan had an exhausted Hannah tucked in for the night, he called his office voice mail. Nothing from Ian Rogers. The agent didn't respond to being paged, either.

It wasn't that unusual. Once agents got their warrants, they had a tendency to go off on their own, following leads and reporting nothing. And Secret Service agents were the hardest to keep track of – always being pulled off cases to protect some dignitary or other.

He checked his voice mail again when he got into the office Monday morning, but there was still nothing from Rogers. Ben tried beeping him again.

It was late Tuesday by the time the agent returned Ben's calls.

'What happened with the warrant?' Ben asked him.

'I can't talk on the phone. Do you have time in the morning for me to come in?'

'What's wrong with right now?'

'There's another agent I need to bring with me.'

'Really. And what's his interest in this?'

A pause. 'He's, uh, working on the case with me.' Whatever the new man's role was, Rogers was nearly choking trying to talk around it. 'Uh . . . look, I've really got to go.'

'Not so fast. You called me with an emergency, and I saw to it you got your warrant, no questions asked. I expect to be kept informed of what you found and where it takes you. And not four days later.'

'Look, I don't mean to be evasive.' Rogers sounded chastened. 'This agent I'm working with now – Frank Lukas – he's been around. He's real good, but he likes to do things a certain way. I promise, we'll tell you the whole story.'

2

Rogers arrived in the morning looking even more tense than he'd sounded on the phone. The agent with him was tall and broad shouldered, carrying just enough extra weight for his middle to tug at his suit buttons. Hanging back, watchful, he was not as easy to read as the younger agent.

'Why don't we sit down,' Ben said, 'and you can tell me what made this search warrant such an emergency.'

Rogers glanced uneasily at Lukas – looking for permission? – then sat down in one of Ben's guest chairs to begin the story. Lukas pulled the other chair back to where it would give him an easy view of both of them.

'It started the way we talked about,' Rogers began. 'George Witty set up a meeting for us both with Isaacs.'

Isaac Isaacs had first turned up when Rogers checked the phone records from Aljo Electronics, the target in his credit-card fraud case. According to the Secret Service databases, Isaacs had already worked as an informant for Secret Service twice before, both times under threat of prosecution for peddling cellphones equipped with stolen account numbers; George Witty had been his contact agent. Rogers had hoped that the phone calls from Aljo meant Isaacs was selling them cloned cellphones, which might put him in a position to learn useful things.

'He wasn't happy to be there,' Rogers reported. 'He bullshitted us for a while – how he just does computer consulting now, nothing illegal, and he never heard of Aljo Electronics.

'"We know you know them," I told him. "Al-Jo. Alan Kest and Joseph Ohry. You talk to them on the phone."

'He suddenly gets this phony lightbulb expression on his face, says oh yeah he does some business with them, buys equipment there, consults about how they can build computers from cheap parts to sell under their own brand.

'I'm telling him how we want to be on his side in this but first he's got to stop holding out on us, and meanwhile George is playing serious bad cop. Finally Isaacs says all right he has something, but not Aljo, these Dominicans who had him reprogram a bunch of stolen cellphones he thinks they're using for drug deals, but it was a while ago, and he's not sure they're in the same place. And so on.

'So I say, "This is Secret Service you're talking to – drugs is somebody else." And George jumps right in and says, "Hey, it's a start. How about some contact numbers for these bad guys, and addresses for their locations and so on?" And Isaacs says, "What do you think, I carry it around?" George doesn't bat an eye, he says, "That's fine, let's go get it."'

Isaac Isaacs lived in a cramped kind of place, the way Rogers told it, a smallish room with grimy windows looking at an airshaft, the space mostly taken up by a couple of long worktables cluttered with computer equipment, ragged stacks of electronics magazines on the sagging couch and a low table. A curtain at one end looked like it screened off an el, maybe where Isaacs had his bed. A short hallway led to what was probably the kitchen and bathroom.

Rogers had stood just inside the door listening to rummaging from behind the curtain, uncomfortable to be there not really invited and without a warrant.

Scanning the room, he noticed something on the desktop near where he was standing, an easel-type picture frame sandwiched between a mini-tower computer and an open laptop. The picture in the frame was cut out of a magazine, a friendly looking woman, naked, lying on a bed propped up on her elbows half sitting, knees pointing in opposite directions so presumably she was smiling for the camera at both ends – except you had to guess about that part because the bottom of the picture was hidden by a hundred-dollar note propped against the frame.

It was one of the new big-head notes, Series 1996, and for some reason Rogers couldn't place right away it held his attention. Funny thing, putting it there like that.

Isaacs came out from behind the curtain and saw them standing there. 'Oh shit,' he said, 'don't close your door, and all kinds of bugs crawl in.' Then, 'Hey, go ahead, make yourselves at home.'

Witty said, 'Well, like you said, you left the door open. And I knew you didn't want us to wait out in the hall.'

'You guys are such assholes, what are you going to do next, beat me up and say I was resisting arrest?'

Rogers could see that Isaacs was pissed off at the whole situation, but his attention was locked on Rogers and he hadn't been able to keep himself from cutting a quick glance over at the hundred propped between the computers. Or maybe he was just self-conscious about the picture.

'Nice to have enough to just leave it lying around like that,' Rogers said, giving the note a pointed look.

'It's my lucky hundred,' Isaacs came back, not quite fast enough. 'I was getting set to have it framed.'

'Kind of funny looking, too, isn't it?' Something to say, keep the attention on the note, because it was definitely making Isaacs nervous.

'What do you mean, *funny looking*?'

'I'm just saying, long as they've been around, the new ones still look kind of phony to me. Like play money.' Pushing it, because counterfeit was what came to mind, unless Isaacs was just worried they'd take it from him.

'I don't know,' the snitch said, 'to me it looks like a hundred-dollar bill.' He turned to Witty, holding up a palmtop computer. 'Here's what you wanted, if you still want it.'

Rogers felt his heart pounding. He had a tingling in his palms and a kind of light-headedness, the way he felt when there was something big going down and he seriously didn't want to screw it up. He didn't know why, not a hundred percent, not yet, he was too far from the note to see if it was bogus and it looked real enough from here, but there was something off in how Isaacs was acting about it, and Rogers knew there was no way on God's earth he was leaving the apartment without that hundred.

'So I start spinning out this horseshit about how I want to give my daughter a hundred like that for her birthday,' he told Ben, 'and how the one on his desk has part of her birthday right in the serial number, pointing to the first numbers I see that could be a month and a day. Oh-eight-one-three, I think it was.

'He starts to say something again about its being his lucky hundred and all, and then he kind of stops himself and says, "Ah, who am I kidding, they're all alike – you want it, you got it, and I hope your daughter gets as much luck out of it as I did.'

'So I give him five twenties for it, happy I have them to give, and I'm thinking, He's good. Good enough to see that if he holds out I'll only get more suspicious, but if he goes along then whatever it is he can claim he didn't know about it. Only he didn't put it together quick enough.'

'Good work,' Ben said, 'getting it out of him that way.' Surrendered freely, not seized, the hundred would have fewer problems being entered in evidence, if it came to that.

'Once I had it I just wanted to get out of there,' Rogers went on, 'but George said could he take a leak, as a way to see what else there was to see. Then he leaned on Isaacs to give him a tour of the drug locations, getting him out of the house so I'd have time to check out the note.'

Rogers stopped, as if he'd come to the end of his story.
'And . . .' Ben prompted.
Rogers looked at Lukas. 'Maybe Frank ought to tell you the rest.'

3

Lukas hadn't moved that Ben could see: leaning back in the chair, almost too big for it, one long leg out in front of him, arms folded across his chest.

He said, 'I happened to be in the office when Ian brought the note to the counterfeit squad, so I got a look at it. I thought it looked interesting, and when we put it into the computer it turned out to be a note we hadn't seen before.'

'Do you get a lot of new ones?'

'A couple of thousand a year,' Lukas said. 'Some of them so feeble you wouldn't believe anybody'd try to pass them, but people take them anyway. The one Ian turned up is closer to the top end, good enough to make this a priority case . . .'

The words were spoken with so little emphasis Ben might have missed them. It was as if Lukas wanted to downplay the case's importance at the same time he was declaring it.

'. . . I took a look at it under the microscope, and they have some of the security features down pretty well. A nice job on the microprinting, and even a decent version of the embedded plastic strip. It doesn't glow but it'll pass muster if you don't use ultraviolet on it.'

'Sounds like somebody put some effort into it.' Though Ben knew it was an outdated image, he still saw high-end currency counterfeiting as a romantic crime – exquisitely detailed printing plates hand-engraved by master craftsmen gone wrong.

'More than usual. The paper's better than you see on a lot of them, and they're using an offset plate – it's not coming off a copier. Though I have to say, you see some good work coming off copiers and graphics scanners these days – like the twenties those kids up at Columbia were putting out. My guess is, this one, they started with a scanner and a computer to generate the negatives for the plate.' Lukas was still keeping his tone flat: just the facts.

'Ian only saw the one example,' he said, 'but for all we knew the guy could have been running the plant that made them. Or anyway doing the computer-graphics part of it.'

'And that was why you wanted the warrant in such a hurry.' Because that had to have been Lukas's doing, not Rogers'.

'Right. We had to get in there before he got back and started getting rid of evidence.'

'What did you turn up?'

'Nothing we wanted. Some cellphone cloning equipment – radio scanners and a chip reprogrammer – and the computers. The electronic-intelligence squad is doing a data dump on the hard drives. A lot of it's encrypted, though. That could be a problem.'

'What are we talking about here?' Ben asked. 'Good? Great? Or do we have a new Supernote on our hands?'

'Supernote!' Lukas all but snorted in derision. 'That was bullshit beginning to end.'

Sure, Ben wanted to say: That's why Treasury completely redesigned the currency. But that wasn't the point here. 'Okay, forget about any Supernote. The question I'm asking is how serious is this? You said "a priority case."'

'And I meant it.'

'I'd like to see the note.'

'It's in Washington. I wanted the forensics lab to take a look.'

It had been most of a week since Lukas first saw the phony hundred, time for a lot to happen: how much was he leaving out?

'Anyway, we don't have to get into this too deep,' Lukas said. 'I wanted to let you know what was up as a matter of courtesy, because it came from Ian's snitch, but I've got somebody I work with over in Organized Crime I've already mentioned it to, so you don't have to worry about it.'

'Not so fast,' Ben said. 'This case is in my office. I'll decide how to handle it.' Lukas was too anxious to minimize this and move it to where he had control. 'I might even keep it myself.'

'It's not really a Major Crimes kind of case.' The Secret Service agent sat forward, bringing to bear the force of deep-set eyes and a broad, menacing brow. 'I can tell you from looking at it, this note is coming out of an organized effort. It belongs in OC, and they've got the experience to deal with it.'

'If you've got a problem with this, have your friend in OC talk to me. Or better yet, there's a unit chiefs' meeting later in the week. I can talk to the OC chief then.'

'Nah, don't bother,' Lukas said. 'I don't want to make this into some big deal. But I'm telling you, OC is where it belongs.'

'And as soon as I'm convinced of that, I'll be happy to move it. In the meantime – you were telling me about the apartment search.'

'Yeah, right,' Lukas acknowledged, expressionless. 'When that came up empty, not even another hundred, phony or otherwise, Isaacs and I had a little chat, but he was playing Mr Know Nothing – he found it on the street and it was such good luck he was going to frame it and hang it up on the wall.'

'You think he knows the note's bad,' Ben speculated.

'I do. And I don't think he expects us to think otherwise.'

'It's a wonder he left it lying around like that.'

'He wasn't expecting company. He probably thought it was cool, liked to look at it.'

'The question is, has he already been on the phone to whoever he got it from?'

'Not a chance. This is a guy who, number one, isn't going to admit he fucked up and, number two, doesn't want to explain why he's got Secret Service agents hanging around his house. He's going to pretend this never happened.'

'Let's hope. In any case, we ought to find out who he's calling and who's calling him, and run it all through the databases to see who they are and how they're related to each other.'

Lukas sat in silence, his eyes on the window over Ben's shoulder. When he spoke there was no mistaking the disdain in his voice.

'The man clones cellphones. You think he makes sensitive calls on his home number? Sure, let's get the records – everybody gets careless sometimes – and a DNR' – dial-number recorder – 'can't hurt either. But eighteen years' experience says we won't learn a damn thing. Better to use a radio scanner on him, but I can't see our getting approval for that from Main Justice, not based on one counterfeit banknote he already claims he didn't know was bogus and never intended to pass. And frankly, the longer we can stay away from Main Justice on this, the better. I say we sit on him some more and make a long list of the crimes we watch him commit, and then I'll go have a real heart-to-heart with him.'

Ben couldn't argue with Lukas's reasoning, though he could have lived without the attitude. But Ben had already won the important point; he could afford to back off a bit.

'Tell me what you need,' he said, 'and I'll do what I can to see that you get it.'

'Right now I only need one thing from you. The Secret Service position on this note is that we seriously do *not* want to publicize it. Not one bit, because it's sure to get blown out of proportion and we don't want the Director, or the new Secretary, reading any bullshit in their morning paper about new Supernotes or threats to the integrity of the currency. So I need your word that none of this is going to get around – not at this office and especially not at Main Justice – nothing at all.'

'I can do that. Not forever, but for now. And I'll have to tell my boss' – Victoria Thomas, the US Attorney for the Southern District of New York, an autocrat universally known as Queen Victoria.

'Not yet,' Lukas said.

* * *

Working with Frank Lukas was going to be a challenge, Ben thought as the two agents left his office. 'He's real good, but he likes to do things a certain way,' Rogers had said. Ben could believe Lukas was a good investigator, but all Ben had seen so far was that if you interfered with the way he liked to do things he'd be real good at making himself unpleasant. It was a battle Ben would have to fight, especially if he decided not just to keep the case in the unit but to make it his own.

Currency counterfeiting wasn't a crime Ben had dealt with in any detail, and he had only a sketchy impression of the Supernote controversy. A little time on the computer told him a lot.

Paper money, it turned out, was a major export commodity for the federal government. The billions of paper dollars that were circulating in foreign hands were a kind of interest-free loan to the US that never had to be repaid – but only as long as people continued to hold the dollars because they had faith in their value. If it ever became the general belief that you couldn't tell real from phony, that faith would disappear like dew on a sunny morning.

Despite the constant efforts of counterfeiters, there had been no real threat until the early nineties, when counterfeit versions of the old hundred-dollar note had begun to appear that were far better than the previous best – good enough to fool Federal Reserve testing machines so sensitive they sometimes rejected *real* bills as bogus. The percentage of high-quality fakes circulating overseas had reached the point where some foreign banks had stopped accepting US hundreds altogether, the good along with the bad. By some accounts, it was the first step toward the destruction of the American hundred-dollar note as a carrier of value, and then – in the most extreme versions – the unraveling of the international monetary system.

No one really knew how many of the 'super' counterfeit notes were in circulation – billions of dollars' worth at even a conservative estimate, mostly out of the country in places like Russia. There were plenty of theories as to where they came from, with terrorist countries in the Middle East the prime candidates.

The Treasury Department had consistently denied or downplayed stories of a single source, insisting that the so-called Supernote was really several distinct high-quality counterfeit notes, the independent product of unrelated counterfeiters, motivated by greed not politics. But what else could they say without contributing to the very panic they wanted to avoid?

More telling than Treasury's words were its actions: the first major change in the appearance of American paper money since a uniform design had first been adopted in 1929. Years in the making, the new notes had involved studies by the National Academy of Science, scads of preliminary designs, Congressional approval, and millions of dollars, not just for design and production but for the massive public relations effort needed to gain acceptance for the new design at home and especially abroad.

The first of the new-issue hundreds had been in circulation over a year now, since late in '96. They featured a much larger portrait of Benjamin Franklin off-center on the face of the note – thus the name 'big-head' – and a slew of high- and low-tech security tricks designed to make counterfeiting the new note as difficult as possible.

Ben didn't know how good Isaacs' note was, but given Lukas's intensity about the case, his insistence on secrecy, and his protest-too-much denials, a new Supernote didn't seem out of the question.

As chief of Major Crimes, Ben had dealt with frauds that ran to the hundreds of millions of dollars, but he couldn't remember a case with anything like the implications this one might have.

4

Not two weeks before, Ben had been surprised by a call from Harry Butler, his old boss, offering to recommend him for a major law-enforcement job in Washington: Assistant Secretary of the Treasury for Enforcement. Now, with a potentially major Treasury case on his plate, Ben called Butler to find out if he'd actually made the recommendation.

'Did you hear?' Butler asked before Ben had a chance to speak.

'Hear what?'

'Oh. Well, I was just getting set to call you.' Butler sounded upset, and it didn't take Ben long to see why. One of the cops who'd been in the police car that had killed Ben's wife had been put back on active duty and had promptly shot a bystander at a grocery-store robbery.

Hearing the news, Ben felt a familiar surge of rage.

'The reporters are already connecting this with Laura,' Butler said. 'It won't take them long to find you.'

'Thanks. I appreciate the warning.'

Three years, and he had mostly walled off the pain, that sunny part of his life more and more like an amputated limb whose use he remembered only in an abstract way, as if it had really belonged to someone else. But memory could still surprise him, leaving him dazed by loss. And he could still see everything that had happened that morning, would always be able to see it with the same awful clarity, always from too far away to help – the patrol car like some awful demon, white with blue and gold stripes, siren wailing and lights flashing as it came hurtling around the sunbright corner, skidding onto the sidewalk, not even slowing, as if they didn't know what they'd hit, or didn't care.

As a way to give Laura's death some small amount of meaning, Ben had used the incident to force new safety and oversight programs down the police commissioner's throat. Now it seemed the effort and the sense of accomplishing something in Laura's memory had been empty self-deception.

'I'd tell you to leave it alone and let things take their course,' Butler said, 'but I know you won't. Just don't let it take over your life again. Call the lawyers if you have to, but let them deal with it.'

Butler was right about how consuming and corrosive it could become. It had been no small feat for Ben to reconcile his commitment to enforcing the law with a world whose right and wrong he could no longer divide clearly, a world so upside-down it counted him an ally of the very men whose heedless cowboy zeal had snuffed out a vibrant life and brought him and his daughter so much grief.

Having apparently failed to change things in one distant city despite having been sure he'd made a difference there, Ben told himself it was just as well the Washington job was such a long shot. According to the organization chart, the Treasury Department's Office of Enforcement oversaw Secret Service, Customs, the Bureau of Alcohol Tobacco and Firearms, and a roster of smaller, highly focused agencies, plus the Federal Law Enforcement Training Center. With a job that gave him a supervisory role in all of those, he'd be in real danger of thinking he could actually do some good.

But that wasn't likely to be a problem. The road to being named Assistant Secretary of the Treasury for Enforcement was full of obstacles, Butler had warned him – not just opposing candidates, some with more experience in front-line law enforcement or administration, but a behind-the-scenes power struggle between Treasury and the Justice Department which was likely to blunt the candidacy of any AUSA, even one with no great ties to the Justice Department's DC power brokers.

Friday, Ben got a visit from an unexpectedly communicative Frank Lukas.

'I didn't want to give Isaacs too much line, so I dropped by last night and told him I knew he knew the hundred Rogers took from him was counterfeit. He said he didn't know what I was talking about, so I told him to stop bullshitting me and for good measure I told him I knew he didn't find it in the street. 'Oh yeah,' he said, 'then where?' So I told him.'

'Just like that.'

'It was an easy call. The only people he's had any contact with who made sense were the ones running the credit-card scam.'

Ben waited.

'Because of the way they all stick together.'

'They?' The Aljo partners were observant Jews, as was Isaacs, but maybe that wasn't where Lukas was going.

'Yeah, *they*.' Lukas looked at him. 'You're Jewish, right? Tell me I'm wrong.'

'Right or wrong isn't the point.' Ben struggled with his anger.

'I know you've got a solid reputation as an investigator' – he'd made some calls, found two schools of thought on Frank Lukas: that he was an asshole, but brilliant, and that he was brilliant, but an asshole – 'but I make cases based on facts, not stereotypes.'

'Think about it,' Lukas insisted. 'Who else would he protect but his own? He gave up those Dominicans he sells clonephones to in a red-hot minute.'

The agent paused just long enough for them both to know Ben had no good response to that, then went on, 'His face told me right away I nailed it, but he wouldn't give me a thing, so finally I said tell me the truth right now or you're going to have agents crawling up your butthole from now until the end of time. And you know what he said? It doesn't matter. "I don't care what you do to me, I don't know anything about those people. And even if I did I couldn't tell you, however miserable you make my life."

'He was sitting there, pale as a sheet, and his knee was going up and down faster than an old-time sewing machine. I said to him, "What do you mean, you can't tell me? You've been selling people to us for years. Is that what this is? You want money? We can arrange that."

'No, he says, that doesn't matter either, he can't say a word. It's against his religion to inform on another Jew – the worst sin there is. That he'd be banished, or worse, and that if he did it more than once he'd lose his place in heaven. Something like that.

'So I asked him how stupid does he think I am? But he wasn't budging an inch. Scared as he was, I had to think maybe he was telling the truth. So I looked at his records and, near as I could tell, in all the time he was working for us this guy never once gave us anybody Jewish. You know anything about this?'

'I never heard of it, but that doesn't mean anything. I'm no expert.'

'Well, right there I put in a call to our rabbi—'

'Your *rabbi*?'

'Yeah. We've got a serious rabbi – long beard, black coat, fur hat, the whole outfit. He helps us out with his people when we've got protection assignments they might be concerned with, anything like that. He said Jewish criminals were a disgrace to the religion and a threat to the community, and it was a religious duty to help root them out.'

'How did friend Isaacs take that?'

'He wasn't buying it from me. I offered to have the rabbi tell him in person, but right away he says, "Yeah, sure, some shill for law enforcement who'll say anything you want and pretend it's Holy Writ."'

'That's not good.'

'I want you to have a talk with this guy,' Lukas said. 'Maybe if it's another Jew asking the questions he'll open up – at least give us a hint of what he's holding back.'

'Sure.' The strained logic of it aside, the request for help from Lukas caught Ben unprepared.

'Right away,' Lukas said. 'I don't want to give him too long to make up stories.'

'I need to be on firmer ground.' Ben measured the fading light of winter afternoon. 'The Jewish Sabbath begins soon, so this isn't the time to get a lot of help from rabbis. Not until late Saturday, the earliest.'

'As soon as you can,' Lukas allowed grudgingly.

'Let's set it up with Isaacs for Monday morning?'

'Okay.' Not happy. 'One thing – much as I don't like it, I won't be there. There's no way he's is going to talk if he sees me, at least not until we get past this business of informing on Jews.'

As Lukas turned to go, Ben said, 'I assume you still have somebody watching him.'

The agent left without bothering to reply.

Ben couldn't believe his own clumsiness. It seemed there were some people he just couldn't get it right with, and trying only made it worse.

He was intrigued by Frank Lukas: a genuine hard-ass, nothing counterfeit about that, and not a stupid one by any means. Lukas might not be making any bones about his attitude toward Jews, but so far he wasn't letting it get in the way. If anything, the Jewish element seemed to be part of the reason he wasn't pushing his resentment at Ben's having kept the case. And he wasn't blindly protecting his turf, either. Not an uncomplicated man.

As for Isaacs' being unwilling to inform on a fellow Jew, the Secret Service rabbi's rejection of the idea, as reported by Lukas, seemed too cut and dried, though maybe the rabbi had just been sparing Lukas the nuances.

Ben, indifferently educated in the religion of his ancestors, had picked up a lot accompanying Laura through the conversion she'd pursued so eagerly. He'd gone with her to her weekly classes on Jewish history and scripture and the basics of observance: attending services and saying the prescribed prayers, celebrating the holidays and observing the dietary laws and the laws of the Sabbath. But he was still mostly ignorant of the literal chapter and verse of the Torah – the Five Books of Moses – not to mention the sixty-plus volumes of commentary and legal debate in the Talmud or the work of the great medieval religious thinkers who had codified the whole vast body of Biblically derived civil and criminal law, of which the laws against informing, if there were any, would be a part.

The first person he thought of to get an opinion from was the rabbi at the synagogue where Hannah so liked to go, but it seemed better to keep that connection in the family, not confuse things by bringing professional questions into it. He thought of trying the Jewish Theological Seminary, not that far uptown from his apartment: maybe someone at the library there.

Then he remembered a ceremony he'd been to recently, an annual memorial service for fallen federal law enforcement agents. He'd gone out of respect for a DEA agent he'd worked a case with as a freshly minted young prosecutor, one of two from DEA who were being remembered for making the supreme sacrifice the previous year, along with three from the Border Patrol and one each from FBI and Customs.

The service, sponsored by the Federal Law Enforcement Officers' Association, had been at St Andrews church, virtually next door to the US Attorney's office. A color guard from NYPD had paraded in and out past a sea of blue blazers and mustaches, to the harsh tones of a police bagpiper. The religious service had basically been a Catholic mass, with a New Testament reading by FLEOA's Protestant chaplain and a reading from Psalms by the rabbi who saw to the spiritual needs of the association's Jewish members. He was a young man, clean-shaven, athletic-looking even in his suit and tie. Ben had been impressed by the directness and simplicity of his reading.

The rabbi's name was Elliot Rosen, the priest at St Andrews told Ben – he chaplained for DEA and FBI in New York as well as for the nationwide, fraternal FLEOA. 'A good man,' the priest said. 'You'll like him.'

'That's a great question,' Rosen said when Ben called him. 'I'm glad you caught me, only right now I'm out the door for Sabbath services. Let's try for Sunday. In the meantime how well do you know the daily liturgy?'

'Moderately.' Mostly from months of morning prayer services, reciting the mourner's kaddish for Laura, as he never had for his father.

'But you do read Hebrew.'

'I can read the letters. Understanding the words is a lot spottier.'

'Ah, the paradox of Judaism in modern America,' Rosen said. 'But that'll do. There's a prayer you should read. Can you get a look at a prayer book?'

'Sure. I'll be taking my daughter to services tonight. Conservative, though, not Orthodox.'

'It's worth trying.' Rosen told him what to look for. 'Check out the translation.'

5

The synagogue steps were jammed with the usual crowd, people waiting for friends, a few getting in a last cigarette before the Sabbath prohibition against lighting any kind of fire, most just hoping to get through the throng at the door and find a seat.

Holding Hannah firmly by the hand, Ben inched his way toward the balcony stairs. He almost collided with an elegant and graceful woman in a dark gray dress, carrying a coat over one arm. As he pulled back to let her pass he glimpsed beneath her rich sweep of thick black hair a high forehead of the smoothest olive skin and an assertive arch of black eyebrow.

His breath caught. 'Judith?'

She turned. 'Benjamin! What a lovely surprise.' Words spiced with an accent compounded of half a dozen languages. 'And who is this beautiful young lady?'

'I'm Hannah,' she volunteered. 'And you're Judith.'

'Yes I am. How did you know?'

'My daddy said so.'

Judith laughed: generous mouth, full lips, bright white teeth. 'Very good. You must be very smart.'

Hannah, Ben was pleased to see, didn't appear overly interested in the compliment. 'We're sitting upstairs,' she announced.

'Oh? Is that a good place to sit?'

'My daddy likes it.' Being this social was rare for Hannah, especially with a stranger. 'You can sit there, too.'

'May I?' A quick glance included Ben in the request.

'If it's all right with Hannah,' he said, 'it's all right with me.'

Or was it? he wondered on the way upstairs. Judith Zilka was his student, after all. On the other hand, she was hardly an impressionable kid.

When they'd met briefly the previous spring at a conference on international financial crimes, Judith as part of a delegation from the World Court, he'd found her compelling, unsettlingly so. It had been the first time since Laura's death he'd reacted to a woman that way – feelings he'd allowed himself only because there'd been no chance to act on them. That was a part of life he'd closed off and didn't know when he'd be ready to reopen.

He hadn't been prepared to have her show up in his office at NYU law school six months later asking to be admitted to the evidence course he taught, much less to be seeing her across a classroom for three hours every Wednesday evening.

Upstairs, there were still a few seats along the balcony rail.

'So many people,' Judith said.

'Yes, we get quite a crowd, even without a special guest rabbi.'

'We? Do you come here often?'

'Hannah and I try to make it every week,' Ben said, suppressing a smile at the unintended singles-bar opening. 'But I haven't seen you here.'

'Tonight's my first time. I came to hear the special guest rabbi.'

'Really? Have you read his books?'

She looked at him with curiosity. 'Have you?'

'All of them. Seeing him here is a real treat for me.'

They were interrupted by the cantor leading the song that welcomed the incoming Sabbath as a groom welcomes his bride. As the voices rose to fill the sanctuary, first a few then more of the people downstairs got up to dance – men and women mostly in their twenties and thirties, looking straight from some brokerage or law firm, along with a scattering of the congregation's older members. The line of dancers, hand in hand, grew as it wound its way up, down and around the aisles. Hannah watched with delight, clapping her hands in time to the singing, making sure Ben and Judith were keeping time, too.

When the singing and dancing had slowed to a close, the congregation's rabbi introduced the evening's guest. Joshua Brauner bounded up the aisle to the raised stage in front of the Torah ark.

He was short and burly and energetic, very different from the august figure Ben had imagined. A plain black yarmulke perched atop his thick head of wavy hair, a shade darker than the reddish brown of his square-cornered beard. His cheeks were ruddy and his bright blue eyes looked, even glimpsed from the balcony, as if they sparkled. He wore a navy-blue suit and followed the Friday-evening practice of ordinary congregants by not wearing a prayer shawl.

The two rabbis conducted the service together, along with the cantor. It was even livelier than usual, full of singing and responsive reading, animated by Rabbi Brauner's infectious energy and his surprisingly rich and full voice.

The atmosphere turned more contemplative during the standing, silent devotion that was the centerpiece of every service. After he'd recited the opening blessings, Ben scanned the beginning of every paragraph for the word Rosen had said to look for, but didn't find it. Rosen had warned him the prayer had been omitted from many non-Orthodox prayerbooks, and he was on the point of deciding this was one of them when he remembered that this part of the service was shortened for the Sabbath, and Rosen had said the weekday version.

Ben found it there right away. The translation on the facing page began: 'Frustrate the hopes of all those who malign us.'

All those who malign us? Could that be what Isaacs was talking about? Even given what Ben had seen of the daredevil swoops and dives of Talmudic reasoning, it was a long way from the prayer book's mild curse to the idea that informing on a fellow Jew would cost you your place in heaven – more than far enough to invite contradiction. Surely Rosen could work up an argument that if you gave *true* information it didn't amount to maligning anyone.

Thinking of Isaacs and this unexpected inquiry into Jewish law he'd prompted, Ben couldn't help remembering how uncomfortable Ian Rogers had been telling him that Alan Kest and the other Aljo partners might be observant Jews.

'Something you ought to know right away,' Ben had responded immediately. 'Being Jewish myself I don't love hearing about religious Jews breaking the law, but that doesn't have any effect on how hard I work to put them away. If anything, I have to watch out for how angry it makes me.'

Anger was what fueled him as a prosecutor. He'd played by the rules all his life and it enraged him to see anyone flouting the law and succeeding – anyone, Jews and non-Jews alike. His words to Rogers had been exaggerated, the better to reassure him.

Or so Ben had thought. But reflecting on it now he saw that it did make a difference to him when the criminals were ostentatiously pious, announcing their holiness to the world by dress and behavior. And all the worse when the religion they paraded was a version of the one Laura had made her legacy to Hannah and that he was still struggling to find comfort in, himself.

He was brought back to the service by the cantor's ringing voice, reciting the kaddish – the same words Ben had spoken daily after Laura's death, a hymn of praise repeated throughout the service, by no means restricted to mourners. With that, the rabbi and cantor yielded the platform to their guest.

Rabbi Brauner paused a moment, his head bowed, then looked up at the congregation and began to speak, in a tone that owed more to conversation than to sermon.

'It's a great thrill – more than I can tell you – to stand here and see you all and hear your voices lifted in praise of the Holy One, blessed be He. I say this, even though this is a Conservative service, and I'm a rabbi from an Orthodox tradition.

'But I celebrate what you do here. I revel in it, because despite our differences we're all Jews, each trying to be faithful to our covenant with the God of our ancestors, the God we sometimes call simply haShem – the Name.

'And that honest effort is what matters, because no person is perfect, and no person fails to transgress. What matters is that you try, that you question, that you learn, and if you fall short at any given moment that you acknowledge it and try to do better.'

Ben looked over at Hannah – she was leaning on Judith, head on her shoulder, making some of Judith's long black hair into a little braid. Judith seemed engrossed in the sermon. He leaned toward her, behind Hannah. 'Everything okay?' he whispered, just close enough to be aware of the scent of her hair, her skin.

'Oh, yes.' She smiled at him and he felt a surge of desire, but almost before the power of it had registered she'd turned to Hannah. 'We're having a good time, aren't we, Hanneleh?'

'Mmm.' Hannah was too busy braiding to respond.

'I look around and I see all of you,' Rabbi Brauner was saying, 'and I think how it was on the average Friday night when I was a boy. A dozen or so old men, the ones who came to pray every day, plus maybe that many more my father's age, the old men's sons, mostly there out of duty, talking as much as praying. And a few kids like me, dragged along by *their* fathers.' The image could have been from Ben's own childhood, though Brauner's telling lent it a warmth Ben did not remember.

'And now, look at this.' Brauner waved an arm at the throng that filled the sanctuary, upstairs and down. 'A thousand of us, welcoming Shabbat – the Sabbath – the holiest day of the year. The day haShem chose to sanctify in the first commandments he spoke to Moses on Mount Sinai. And all of us paying attention, all of us participating in the service. I think we should give each other a round of applause.'

Grinning, the rabbi started to clap. Gradually at first, then with increasing pleasure, the congregation joined in. As they did, Brauner made his own clapping at once more regular and more complex, stamping one foot loudly to drive the tempo, faster and faster, until he held both hands up and almost at once the clapping stopped.

'That was wonderful,' he told them, slightly out of breath. 'Wonderful. And now I want to offer you a gift, the only kind of gift a simple teacher can offer – something new to go along with your singing and your praying.'

He looked around at them. 'First, I want you all to get comfortable in your seats with your hands resting in your lap.' He waited for them to shuffle and shift into place.

'Good. Now, comfortably, let your eyes gaze at your hands and, as you do, repeat to yourself the word "strength." If your mind wanders, bring it back gently, saying *strength* to yourself, and letting yourself see your hands clearly.' He put his own hands on the lectern, cupped in each other. As he did, Ben could see the people downstairs looking at their hands resting in their laps.

To his right, Judith, like the others, was beginning to contemplate her hands. Hannah, too, was playing along, hands held up in front of her face.

Ben looked at his own hands, largeish and square – workman's hands, he'd always thought – and repeated the word 'strength' in his mind. He didn't know whether to keep his eyes on one spot or let them roam over fingers, thumbs, the web of skin between thumb and forefinger . . . He decided to let them go where they would and try not to think about it.

'That's enough for a first try,' Rabbi Brauner said, too soon for Ben. 'But I recommend you do this again, for twenty minutes or so at a time. You'll see as you keep doing it that the abstract word takes concrete shape – it's one way to bring into our lives the deep meaning of haShem's Creation.'

Ben turned to Judith, to share the intensity of the moment and because he couldn't help himself. And turning to her he found that she was looking at him: calmly, as if she had been studying him. For a moment her eyes held his, then she turned again to the scene below.

'I want to leave you with one last thought,' Rabbi Brauner was saying. 'A challenge, if you will. You're doing a great and joyous thing to be here. Do yourself a favor and take it one more step. This week try one new mitzvah, one of haShem's commandments you haven't tried before. Like, for instance, honor the Day of Rest by not doing any work for your business until tomorrow night. See how good it makes you feel.'

At the end of the sermon the congregation's rabbi announced a gathering in the vestry rooms: Rabbi Brauner would be there to say the Sabbath blessing over wine and to greet them all.

'Do you want to meet him?' Judith asked as they headed for the stairs.

'I don't know . . . I think I prefer the view from the balcony to fighting a crowd for the kind of generic hello that's all anyone ever manages at these things.'

'No, I mean really *meet* him.'

He looked at her. 'Why? Have you got some kind of pull?'

'Well . . .' Her smile at this had mystery in it. 'I think . . . you must meet him. You will enjoy each other.'

'Okay.' He was intrigued.

'Come.'

She took Hannah's hand and Hannah reached with her other for Ben's. Ben felt a kind of electricity, as if Hannah were a conducting link between him and Judith. Hand in hand in hand they made their way down the crowded stairs.

In the press of people at the door to the vestry rooms, Ben was forced closer to Judith than he'd ever been. Jolted by the firm round warmth of her hip against his thigh, his body responded in a way that hardly felt appropriate for a synagogue: not even on Shabbat eve – when, the rabbis taught, husbands and wives were supposed to take special joy in obeying the commandments that encouraged marital pleasure.

6

Ben's plan for Saturday had been to go over his résumé, in case they actually considered him for the Washington job, but he decided he'd try instead to follow Rabbi Brauner's suggestion. Once he'd embarked on a workless Sabbath there was really only one thing to do: reread something from the writings of Rabbi Joshua Brauner. He took *The Loneliness of Faith* from the shelf and sat down on the couch with it.

He opened the book, then closed it, unsure he was ready to experience the words in the actual voice of the man he now had met. He sat looking out the window, not registering the traffic streaming north and south in the canyon of apartment buildings, his mind crowded with other images.

The celebration after the services Friday night had been every bit the mob scene Ben had expected, but after the two rabbis had offered the traditional Sabbath blessing over wine, Judith had somehow got Ben and Hannah through the crowd to Rabbi Brauner's side.

Introducing Ben – 'my teacher at law school' – Judith had seemed unusually animated, a flush tinting her cheeks and the base of her throat.

The rabbi had bent first to fuss over Hannah then stood up and stuck out a sincere hand. 'Professor Kaplan.' His bluer-than-blue eyes intent on Ben. 'It's a pleasure.'

'Just Ben, please . . .'

'Good. And you have to call me Joshua. Everyone does.'

'It's an honor – I'm a big fan. Your books mean a lot to me.'

'Really?' He'd seemed delighted, almost like a kid.

Ben couldn't tell how old Joshua Brauner was: the beard was deceptive, probably made him look older, while his plump red lips and cheeks and his youthful skin had the opposite effect. Ben suspected that he was somewhere in his forties, a decade or so older than Ben was, himself. And yet the rabbi had about him an air of certainty that might have become a man twenty years his senior.

Ben had felt the crowd around them pressing close, people eager for their minute. Holding Hannah's hand, he'd made his way to a less crowded part of the room. Judith had stayed by Joshua's side.

Watching them, the word that had come to Ben was cozy: there was a coziness about the way Joshua's exuberance co-existed with Judith's oceanic calm. Yet Joshua sported the thick gold cylinder of a wedding band, and as an Orthodox rabbi he would certainly have to be married. Not that it was any business of Benjamin Kaplan's.

As soon as it was dark, Ben called Elliot Rosen, the FLEOA chaplain, to see when they could get together about the laws on informing. The earliest Rosen could see Ben was Sunday night, he said, 'as long as you don't mind that I'll be coming straight from karate practice. We can have a beer after I get done.'

Alan Kest paused to say the blessing thanking God for bringing them all alive and healthy to this new season. He followed it with the blessing prescribed for seeing a wondrous work of God.

Yossi thought that was funny.

'Why funny?' Kest asked. 'Is this less a work of the Creator because it is also a work of Man, who has these abilities only because the Creator decreed it?'

Work of God or work of Man, the machine was indeed a wonder, though it looked simple, even crude: an aluminum carriage running on aluminum tracks, about two feet by three over all and, except for the industrial laser mounted on the carriage along with a lumpy box of lenses and mirrors that manipulated the laser beam, less than a foot high. A target stage beneath the carriage held a grayish block of extremely hard plastic about three inches by seven that Yossi had locked carefully into place before going to sit at the computer console. Wires ran to the power supply and to the computer that controlled it all. The whole room was shielded so no one from the outside could read the signals the computer radiated.

On the computer screen was a ten-inch-high picture of a number 1 in outline, filled with rows of characters that said 100USA100USA100. Kest and Micah watched in fascination as Yossi played the keyboard and a cursor on the screen began to trace the outline of the 1.

The laser beam itself was invisible. Watching the machine at work all there was to see was a white-hot spot of brightness where the laser was burning a shallow trench in the target, and a tiny wisp of vaporized plastic.

Like the finger of the Creator writing on the tablets of stone, Kest couldn't help thinking.

'Next we do the letters and numbers,' Yossi said to Kest when the outline of the 1 was finished, 'Twenty-one rows all within a quarter of an inch from top to bottom, fifteen letters and numbers to a row an eighth of an inch wide.'

'As the sages remind us,' Kest said, 'everything that the Holy

One, praised be He, created in this world He created solely for His own glory.'

After another hour, he left Yossi and Micah to their work. He could already believe that the engraving they were making was going to be exceptional, better even than the offset-printing plate that Rudovsky had made from the same artwork and used for the most recent tests.

Combine the new engraved plate with Rudovsky's new intaglio printing machine and the end product would be far beyond anything they'd accomplished. Undetectable, the Russian claimed, and the market for them enormous. Kest hoped so, because he had come to understand that there was no limit to how many there would be use for. The more land that could be bought and the more houses that could be built, the more people could join them to prepare for the coming future.

On Sunday night Ben left Hannah with Mrs Brunello, downstairs. A widow in her seventies, she was always glad to see her bambina, though she didn't have the stamina to enjoy the pleasure for more than an hour at a time.

The bar Rabbi Rosen had named was dim and smelled of sour beer and stale cigarette smoke – the kind of working-class place that New York had been full of once but that was almost extinct now, at least in the parts of Manhattan that Ben got to see.

Rosen climbed off a bar stool to greet him. The chaplain was taller than he'd looked reading the psalm at St Andrews, with a wide face and pale hair cut short, wearing a worn leather jacket over a T-shirt and jeans. Muscular arms and shoulders made him look top heavy.

'Did you find it?' he asked Ben after they'd gotten themselves a couple of longnecks and settled in a booth.

'I did. You said it was called the nineteenth blessing, but it seemed more like a curse to me.'

'Yeah, really. *And for the informers let there be no hope.*'

'Informers! My translation said "Frustrate the hopes of those who malign us."'

Rosen laughed. 'I know everybody's afraid they'll offend someone these days, even in prayer-book translations, but that's the lamest I've heard. Some translations say "slanderers," and I thought that was bad. It really means, "And for the informers let there be no hope." And right after that it says, "Let all evil perish in a moment, let all Your enemies soon be cut off." Evil, that's the same – the informers, they're the evil that should perish and the enemies that should be cut off.'

'Oh boy.'

'Yeah.' Rosen grinned. 'You don't think about that kind of thing being in the daily prayers.' His light brown eyes were guilelessly direct. 'You know anything about capital punishment, according to the sages of the Talmud?'

'Not really.'

'You ought to check it out, it's fascinating, full of weird surprises.'

'Like?'

'Like burying the condemned criminal up to the armpits in dung before you do him in.'

'No.'

'Yes. And worse. But what you need to know right now is this – since the second Holy Temple was destroyed there's been no way to impose capital punishment strictly according to the Law.'

'So then informers can't get the death penalty.'

'In the strict sense they can't, except there's one crime so heinous that the rabbis uniformly over the centuries prescribed killing as appropriate punishment for a repeat offender.' Rosen paused to swig down some beer.

'Informing.'

'Right you are. And the one thing you surely couldn't do was inform on somebody as a way to make life easier for yourself – to get out of jail or to avoid a fine or to earn money.'

'And that doesn't help me any,' Ben said. 'Because that's my whole leverage – get out of jail free, collect two hundred dollars.'

'Yeah, but we don't know how much of this stuff your guy knows, if all he said was that informing was against the religion. And there are good arguments the other way.'

They ordered another round and kept talking until Ben remembered, belatedly, to look at his watch.

'I've got to get back.' Poor Mrs Brunello. 'This has been a great help. I've got one other favor to ask – can you be there tomorrow morning when I interview this guy?'

Rosen hesitated. 'How does that help you?'

'I can't interview him alone – I need a witness. And for this guy I think it's got to be someone Jewish, and a rabbi even better, as long as we downplay your connection to law enforcement.'

Rosen thought about it only a moment. 'Okay. I'll have to juggle a thing or two, but I'll be there.'

7

Lukas had set up the meeting in Riverside Park, on the isolated promenade that ran along the edge of the river. It was a gray morning, and blustery, a reminder that winter wasn't over yet. Ben sat on a park bench watching the freighters on the river and the few down-vested men tending their fishing rods.

He was approached by a short, pudgy man in his late twenties wearing a lint-flecked black overcoat and a sagging fedora. 'You Kaplan?'

'Isaac?'

'Yeah. Let's get out of here. I'm cold.'

'Have a seat,' Ben suggested. 'We're waiting for somebody. He won't be long.'

'Better not, or I'm gone.'

Isaacs perched uncomfortably on the edge of the park bench. His complexion was pasty and pale. With the coat he wore a rumpled suit, a white shirt grayed by repeated launderings and an expression of generalized nervousness.

'This is about that hundred, right?'

'And other things.' Not wanting to stress it too much.

'Who's this other guy?'

'I'll introduce you when he gets here.' Ben reached into the brown paper bag next to him. 'Coffee?'

'Nah, that's okay.' Isaacs' knee was already bouncing. 'I'll just sit here and stare at you. That way you can see how it feels.'

Over his years as a prosecutor Ben had seen a lot of phony bravado. He'd learned early that the best response was to ignore it. He put the coffee away and went back to watching the fishermen.

Rosen arrived, dressed as a modern rabbi this time – suit and tie and a tweed overcoat, with a knitted skullcap.

'Another cop rabbi?' Isaacs challenged when Ben introduced them. 'What kind this time?'

'I went to a Reform seminary,' Rosen told him, 'but my practice is closer to Conservative.'

'Ahhh,' Isaacs said in a disgusted tone. 'Reform, Conservative, who cares? It's a different religion.'

'Not really,' Rosen said equably. 'The Torah and the Talmud are the same for everybody.'

'Depends on how you interpret them, though, doesn't it?'

'Why don't we try out some interpretations, see what you think?'

'Good idea,' Ben said. 'But let's get out of the cold first.'

He'd stashed one of the office cars in the parking lot on the hill above them. They got in and Ben got the engine running and put the heater on.

'I'm told that Isaac is worried about a religious prohibition against informing,' Ben opened, turning in the driver's seat so he could see Isaacs and Rosen in the back.

'You bet I am. They teach that in Reform-rabbi school?'

Rosen recited the paragraph from the daily prayers, in what sounded to Ben like flawless Hebrew.

'Right,' Isaacs said. 'So you see my point.'

'But that's not the Law, it's the prayer book.'

'It's in the Talmud, too. The prohibition against informing.'

'Yes, in a way,' Rosen conceded. 'But Jewish law says that we all have to obey the secular law, too. And that's repeated many times in the Talmud. *Dina d'malkhuta dina* – the law of the kingdom is the Law.'

'Yeah, great, but nobody's asking *you* to inform.' Isaacs turned to Ben. 'At least that bastard Lukas had a Hasid to whore for him. I don't know why you're wasting my time.'

'I'm curious,' Rosen said. 'How observant are you? I mean, if the exact letter of the law matters to you, then we ought to look at it very carefully, see where it applies and where it doesn't.'

'Yeah, but my problem isn't how religious *I* am,' Isaacs shot back. 'My problem is – the people Mr Jewish Prosecutor up in the front seat wants me to inform on, *they're* that religious. *They* believe all this a hundred fifty percent. And if they think you're an informer you don't get a chance to give them all that about obeying the law of the land. They're rabbis, too, and by them if you're an informer first you get read out of the religion and then you get the death penalty.'

'Rabbis?' Ben asked. Alan Kest and the others were religious, but Ben had no evidence they were rabbis. Maybe this was about somebody else. 'You mean ordained pulpit rabbis, or just Torah scholars?'

'I mean rabbis, fully certified. And those words this rabbi here just recited so nicely they say three times a day, and they mean it every time – al t'hi tikvah – *let there be no hope*. I'm telling you, if I say a word here they'll kill me.'

'I doubt it,' Rosen said. 'Even in the Middle Ages, when the rabbis started seriously sentencing informers put to death, that was only where it went with secular law. The Jewish court passed judgment, but the king's executioner did the deed. That's not going to happen here and now.'

'Yeah, well they killed plenty of informers in Germany, too – close enough to "here and now" – and I don't think they asked the Nazis to help out.'

'Even so, killing people is a big deal. The Torah says if you save a single life, you save an entire world.'

'Sure, so maybe they'll just cut my tongue out and cut off my hands and feet. They used to do that to informers, too, you know.'

Ben remembered Rosen telling him that bit of history in the bar. It seemed Isaacs knew a lot more than they'd hoped.

'And how long is it since that fanatic killed the Prime Minister of Israel?' Isaacs pressed on. 'You think he didn't claim it was a religious execution? You think the laws on informing had nothing to do with it?'

'Okay,' Ben interrupted, seeing where this had to go. 'Whatever you're afraid of, I have to tell you that the courts in modern-day America aren't impressed by religious reasons not to testify, so I'm going to get you an immunity order and then I'm going to put you in the grand jury and I'm going to ask you questions. The same kind of questions Special Agent Lukas asked you. And either you'll answer them or you won't.'

'That's easy. I won't'

'Then you go to jail for contempt.'

'Beats dying early, with no share in the World To Come.'

'Or we can forget about jail – just get you in and then send you right home after you've appeared.'

'Even better.'

'And what do you tell your friends you said?'

'I tell them the truth – I didn't say bupkes!'

'And you think they're going to believe you? I mean, won't they assume, with an immunity order and all, that if you didn't talk you'd be in jail for contempt?'

'How are they going to know? All that grand jury stuff is secret.'

'You know how rumors are,' Ben said. 'People assume things, and then they talk about them as if they were true.'

'Not *my* friends. Rumor mongering is seriously against the religion.'

'Maybe. But look at that poor guy in Atlanta a couple of years ago, the one they blamed for the bomb at the Olympics. The man was a hero, and somebody leaked it to the press that he was a suspect in the bombing, and the man's life was turned upside down, for no reason. Because everybody believed he did it, even though he didn't. It's shocking a thing like that could happen. I mean, you'd think the FBI, of all places . . .' Leaving it unfinished.

'Well—'

'Not that we've got anybody like that around here. I mean, I don't know Agent Lukas too well, but he doesn't strike me as a man who likes taking no for an answer.'

Isaacs sat in silence – contemplating Agent Lukas, Ben hoped.

'I'm not saying that's going to happen. But I don't have any control over what people speculate, or who they talk to, or if somebody just decides to be malicious.'

'You can't do that to me.'

'Put you in the grand jury? Sure I can, in a minute. The alternative is, talk to me now and no one will know about it at all.'

It took another few rounds of refusal and veiled threat, but the hook was in and Isaacs seemed to know there was no way he was going to wriggle off.

'All right, I'll tell you what I know,' he conceded. 'But this is all there is, and I'm not going to testify or anything. Not in the grand jury – not anywhere.'

'No promises. You know how that works by now. You answer my questions, then we'll see. And if you don't answer . . . well, you know what happens then.'

Isaacs looked suspiciously at Rosen. 'What about him?'

'He's a rabbi, he's not going to tell anybody.'

'Oh yeah, great.'

'Tell me about your lucky hundred,' Ben said.

A sigh of resignation. 'I got it from Alan Kest.'

So it *was* Aljo. 'And where did Alan Kest get it?'

'All I know is what he told me. He got a pile of them in payment for some computer equipment.'

A pile of them! That was going to make Lukas's day.

'Who was the customer?' Ben kept his voice level.

'He didn't say.'

'How long ago did this happen?'

'He didn't say that either.'

'He must have.'

'No. Just what I told you. He thought it was funny. He got them at a big discount on the face value, he said. A briefcase full for a truckload of computer stuff.'

'Was this somebody he'd dealt with before?'

'He didn't say.'

'He must have said something about them.'

Isaacs didn't answer.

'This isn't about your holding out on me, Isaac. I get everything you know, or you get an engraved invitation to the grand jury, and then you can explain all about it to your friends.'

'I'm not holding out! Rabbi Kest and I go back a long time. A really long time. He's like a father to me. He gave the hundred to me as kind of a joke, he said . . . he thought I should have it because I make counterfeit phones. *Used* to,' Isaacs corrected himself quickly. 'I *used* to make counterfeit phones.'

'So you knew the hundred was counterfeit.'

'I didn't *know* anything. What do I know about counterfeit money? All I know is people don't trade briefcases of money at a discount unless it's funny some way, but it could have been marked bills from a robbery, too, or who knows what? All I know is that he made that joke about counterfeit phones, and he said "Frame it, don't spend it." He wasn't expecting me to have nosy visitors from the Secret Service.'

'Tell me about Alan Kest.'

'What's to tell? I just did.'

'I want to know about his business, I want to know what kind of scams he's running. I know you cloned phones for him, but that's got to be the least of it. What's your role in the credit-card scam?'

'I don't know what you're talking about.'

'Maybe I should have Special Agent Lukas ask you.'

'No, listen, don't leave me alone with that guy, okay? You already know everything I know.'

'I need to know more about Alan Kest.' Because now Kest wasn't just a skillful fraud artist, he was the next step toward uncovering the source of the counterfeit currency. 'You say he's a rabbi. Does he have a regular congregation?'

'No but I've been there at the store when he was leading a minyan' – a prayer-group of ten men or more – 'And he gives advice, what's kosher behavior or not.'

'Like what?'

'What to do about certain kinds of customers. If they're argumentative, what's the religious way to deal with them? Also, women customers. If they dress immodestly can you look? If you touch them or shake hands, do you have to purify yourself before you pray or eat, because you know they haven't been to a ritual bath? That kind of thing.'

'What else?'

'That's all I know. You want more, talk to his wife or his kids. Or one of his employees. They're the only people who ever see him. The man works all the time except when he's praying. Works at the store, takes his work home with him, works at home. Except Friday night and Saturday – then it's like work never existed. He prays, he learns, he stays with his family. A deeply religious man. Every day he prays three times, and every time he prays he says for the informers let there be no hope.'

8

Frank Lukas was silent as Ben told him and Rogers about the interview with Isaacs. When Ben got to Alan Kest's alleged briefcase of phony hundreds, the senior agent barely nodded, but there was a new alertness in his eyes and a tension in his body.

'He gave it to him as a joke?' Lukas said when Ben was finished. 'I guess rabbis have their own sense of humor.'

Ben ignored it.

'Nothing about who Aljo's customer was, the one with the briefcase?'

'He claimed Kest didn't tell him. But then, why would Kest tell him any of it?'

'Exactly right. They told Isaacs whatever they told him because it served some purpose for them, and we don't know if a word of it is true. It could be Kest printed the bogus notes himself and he was lying to Isaacs about getting a briefcase-full, or Isaacs is lying to us about it. It could be Kest's customer printed it, if there is a customer. Or it could be somebody else. I'd say it's even odds all the way around. The important thing here is – we've got the next link in the chain.'

'We need to get inside,' Rogers proposed. 'Find out what they're up to.'

'You have something in mind?' Lukas wasn't pleased by the interruption.

'Not a search warrant,' Rogers said, thinking aloud. 'We don't want them to know we're interested in them.'

'We sure don't,' Lukas said.

'We could get an electronic surveillance order. Put in a bug and a camera.'

'How do you propose we justify that?'

'Use the credit-card fraud?'

Lukas snorted.

'There's something to remember,' Ben said. 'Even if we had enough to get a Title III eavesdropping order, our main targets are ordained rabbis. They conduct religious observances in their homes. They conduct religious observances at the business! You have to know how hard it'll be getting authorization to invade that sphere—'

'And to do it we'd have to impress Main Justice with how important all this is,' Lukas put in. 'And that's definitely not something we want to do. But we're not going to roll over and play dead, either.'

'We've already got the phone records for the businesses, and for the bosses' homes,' Ben said. 'Let's go back over those and see what else pops out. We weren't thinking about counterfeiting when we checked them before.'

Lukas didn't say a word.

'You're thinking they use cellphones, with stolen codes,' Ben said. 'All right, but if they do, I'll bet they got them from Isaacs – and he'll know the numbers.'

Lukas looked at him with interest. 'Not bad.'

'You think he'll go for it?' Rogers asked.

'He knows I'm going to have more questions. Sooner or later he's going to dig his heels in, but for now I think he'll cooperate. Cloning the phones is *his* criminal activity, so I won't be asking him to inform on anybody.'

'What about an undercover?' Rogers tried, but Lukas was already going in another direction . . .

'We ought to do a garbage search.'

'Of the businesses?'

'The homes, too.'

I should have known this was going too smoothly, Ben thought. 'I don't think we want anybody near the business, but we definitely don't want anybody near the homes. What do you expect to get there?'

'Didn't Isaacs say his friend the rabbi works at home all the time?'

'Let's say he does. First of all, chances are he works on a computer, so how much useful garbage is there going to be? And second, we aren't going within a mile of a house of worship, not even a part-time house of worship, not without a warrant, which as we've just been saying we would never get and we don't want anyway, for a whole list of reasons.'

'That's why a garbage search,' Lukas came back. 'Garbage is fair game, belongs to anyone who cares to salvage it. And we can get it without their knowing.'

'Then take it off the garbage truck.'

'Compressed in with the rest of the trash?'

'Before they compress it. Have a talk with the sanitation guys.'

'You can't mean tell them who we are.'

'There are other ways . . .'

'Bribe them? Too risky. How do we know they won't turn around and give us up?'

'Look, we really don't want anybody getting caught on Rabbi Kest's property.' This was purely between Ben and Lukas now. Rogers was watching, fascinated. 'What are you going to do, lurk in the apartment-house hallways? Intercept the bags on their way to the basement?'

'These are private houses. They put the garbage out on the street themselves.'

'Private – like, brownstones?' Ben had lived in Manhattan as a law student at NYU and again in the years since he'd returned to New York for the job at the US Attorney's office: Brooklyn was out of his jurisdiction. His limited late-news impression of the Borough of Kings featured rundown tenements and vast complexes of subsidized apartment houses, with a few small neighborhoods of trees and townhouses.

'Not brownstones, regular houses with yards,' Lukas told him. 'Like the suburbs. Nice big houses, some of them.'

Live and learn. 'Then I doubly don't think we want to be going in there. At least in an apartment-house hallway you'd be in some kind of common area, not on the target's very own property.'

'They put the garbage out at the curb on collection days. Outside the curtilage' – a common-law measure of the private area around a house and outbuildings – 'and probably past the property line.'

'Even so. Let's see what we can come up with using the phone records we have and whatever we can generate from the cellphone numbers we get from Isaacs. *Then* we can worry about garbage.'

'I don't like the delay.' Lukas stood up to go. Rogers followed him.

'Life isn't perfect,' Ben said and – again – regretted the parting shot immediately.

Lukas turned at the door.

'*Life* may not be perfect, but that hundred's way too close. So don't talk to me about how I should bide my time.' The agent left without waiting for a response, Rogers close behind.

He gets to me, Ben thought: I can't let that happen.

He checked his voice mail, crowded with Major Crimes prosecutors looking for help with their problems and defense lawyers and FBI agents wanting to talk about their own cases. Catching up with all that kept him busy until it was time to leave for NYU and preach some of what he practiced.

He'd reserved the first part of this class for exercises in problem solving. One of the subjects on his list was the rules relating to search warrants. His argument with Lukas about Aljo was fresh in his mind; he decided to use it as his first topic.

'The core question is – public or private? If you're the subject of the search or the seizure, did you have a reasonable expectation that the place, person or thing searched was private?'

He caught himself looking too often at Judith Zilka, reminded himself he was standing in front of the class, and they were all watching him as they were supposed to.

'Here's a fact situation – garbage. You're definitely going to come across this if you do any criminal work, as a prosecutor or as a defense attorney.

'Suppose you're a prosecutor, and you've got an agent who wants to look through a suspect's garbage. What guidelines are you going to lay down so the search produces admissible evidence?'

As always with his examples from the real life of a prosecutor, the class jumped in and got their own debate going.

When he was sure they saw the issues clearly, he moved on to the magic words of warrantless searching – 'out in plain sight.' He gave them a variation on Rogers' getting the counterfeit hundred from Isaacs, using a salt shaker of white powder that might or might not be heroin.

'At the suppression hearing, what do you argue as the prosecutor? What do you argue as the defense lawyer? Does it matter if the agent just took the salt shaker or if he requested it? What if he somehow reimbursed the owner for it? Actually bought it from him? Paid the fair value of salt, or the fair value of heroin? If the invitation that brought him onto the premises was tacit or expressed?'

The class had even more fun with that one. In the middle of it Ben's beeper went off. It was his home number, with the added code that meant Hannah was sick.

'Time for a break,' he told his students, and took the steps two at a time to the office he shared with another adjunct.

Hannah was running a fever, Vashti told him, but it was only slightly over a hundred, and steady. She'd called the doctor, and he'd told her there was a stomach bug going around and given her some instructions.

'She's napping right now. She took some hot water and honey, but that was all she wanted.'

'I've got another forty-five minutes here, or I can come right home.'

'You stay and teach. She's resting fine. I was planning to stay anyway. Only, don't forget, I'm not going to be here in the morning.'

He *had* forgotten. It was a family obligation, a sister Vashti hadn't seen in years who was passing through: they were going to meet at the airport and spend the morning together. And Hannah couldn't very well go to school sick. He dialed his secretary's direct line and left a message saying he'd be late for work in the morning.

He finished the class as quickly as he could, his mind only half on what he was saying. As the usual horde of after-class question askers descended on the front desk, he held up a hand and said, 'Sorry, I can't stay for questions tonight.'

Judith intercepted him as he pushed through the corridor door into the stairwell.

'This isn't about class,' she said, walking down the stairs with him. 'I have an invitation for you from Joshua Brauner. He's going to be at his synagogue on the West Side on Friday night, and he asks if you and Hannah want to come, and join us all for Sabbath dinner, too.'

'That sounds great, but I really do have to go.' Not wanting to be abrupt, wishing he could linger with her. 'Could you send me an e-mail, or leave a note in my box?'

'Of course. I don't mean to keep you.'

'Any other day . . .'

Alan Kest watched with a mixture of pleasure and concern as the boys crowded around the big cardboard box and pulled it open.

His youngest sons were growing up, and though he'd always wanted to think of them as scholars like their older brothers – off now in Israel, preparing the way – there was no denying their physical energy.

It was impossible not to be pleased watching them at play, especially when it was basketball, the ritual fringes that dangled from their waists flapping wildly as the boys bobbed and weaved and tried to jump like the million-dollar athletes they watched on the rare occasions when they had permission to watch the games.

Watching them fight to open the box, he could see this was special for them. It brought the same glow to their faces as the combat of basketball or – rarely, he had to admit – the discovery of an exciting line of argument in the Law. They'd all had target practice, even the youngest, at ten, but they'd never had their own guns.

The boys unwrapped them admiringly, working the parts, pulling the triggers. They pointed them at each other and made shooting noises, aimed them at imaginary enemies. The one that fascinated them most looked like a cross between a pistol and a rifle. They pushed and pulled to be the one who held it.

Kest lifted himself out of his chair and lumbered over to bring some order to the scene. Then he had them put the guns away, and he blessed them with the words of one of the sages: Be bold as the leopard, swift as the eagle, fleet as the deer, mighty as the lion, to perform the will of your Father in heaven.

* * *

By the time Ben arrived home Hannah's fever had gone down half a degree. He sat on the edge of her bed. Her face was red and her nose was running but otherwise she seemed all right.

'Does anything hurt?'

'Tum.' She held her stomach. 'Hurts.'

'How bad? A little bad, a lot bad, or in between?'

'Hurts.'

'Did you go?'

She shook her head vigorously.

He looked at Vashti.

'No,' she said. 'But the doctor said she might not.'

'It *does so* hurt.'

Deciding that any child who could be so vehement couldn't be too sick, he sent Vashti home.

Ben ate the supper Vashti had left and tried to distract himself with television. Every half hour or so he went in to look at Hannah. She was sleeping, but more restlessly than usual, and when he touched her forehead she seemed warmer sometimes, sometimes not.

Television didn't keep his mind off Frank Lukas and counterfeit currency, or images of Judith Zilka in the third row of his class, watching him from under a spill of dark hair. He wondered if she had a boyfriend, remembered seeing her only with groups of students, both sexes. And she'd been alone at Ohevei Yisroel—

His ruminations were interrupted by a wail of *Daddy!* and the sound of coughing from Hannah's room. He rushed in to find her doubled over on the bed, her face redder.

'What is it, sweetie?'

'Tum,' she wailed, and threw up.

He was afraid at first it might be something worse than a stomach virus, despite the doctor's telephone diagnosis, but a call to one of the moms in his single-parent group confirmed that what Hannah had sounded exactly like what was going around.

She threw up at irregular intervals until well past three in the morning, when she fell into an uneasy sleep. Her temperature the last time he took it was finally below a hundred. He brought a blanket and pillow in from his room and fell asleep on the floor next to her bed.

The phone wrenched him awake from a dream of many Judiths. He staggered up in a shadowy unreality created by the dim orange nightlight and a sliver of day under the drawn curtains, lurched toward the living room, tangling his feet in the blanket on the floor, stumbling loudly. Hannah slept on.

It was Ella, his secretary. 'Agent Rogers needs to talk to you.'

'Where is he?'

'Right here. He was waiting in the lobby when I arrived.'

There was no stopping the man. 'Put him on.'

'We need to talk,' Rogers said.

'I'm listening.'

'In person.'

'I've got a sick kid here. I can't just leave her alone. What's this about?'

Rogers ignored the question. 'Can't your wife stay?'

'She's dead.'

'Oh, shit. I'm sorry. I really am sorry, I mean, I didn't know . . . but is there *somebody* you could get to stay with her?' The agent sounded raw, barely held together. 'We really have to talk, and it can't be on the phone.'

'Just give me a minute, let me get my brain in gear.'

He tried to focus on it: He couldn't ask Mrs Brunello to come up, not with Hannah sick. Vashti was out of reach. His single-parents group didn't include this kind of support. Another occasion to wish Hannah's grandparents weren't thousands of miles away.

'Hang on,' he said.

He checked Hannah. She was sleeping peacefully and her forehead was cooler. He could hope that the worst of it was over.

He got back to the phone. 'You'd better come over here.'

While his coffee brewed he sat on the kitchen stool with the radio for company, not really listening, trying not to speculate what had Rogers so agitated. Letting his eyes close . . . He was pulled back by words from the all-news station, only dimly registered at first. An incident in Brooklyn. Midwood. Something about a suspected burglary and the local security squad, shots fired, someone in the hospital. It was over before he truly started listening: more details when we get them.

9

Rogers arrived harried and wrung out, looking like a man who'd been up all night. Trying to freshen up had only made him look damp.

'What's this about?' Ben asked, pouring coffee for both of them.

'A small problem. We may need some damage control.'

'Not this business in Brooklyn, I hope,' Ben said, mostly to hold this at bay.

'How did you hear about it?' Rogers asked.

Ben's stomach rolled. He'd been hoping, assuming, the connection was in his imagination. 'The radio.'

'Already? What did they say?'

'Not much. Maybe a shooting, maybe a burglary.'

'With luck it'll stay that vague.'

'Let's take our coffee into the living room,' Ben said. 'I want to be sitting down for this.'

He waved Rogers into the easy chair and pushed aside Hannah's family of beanbag dolls to make room for himself on the couch.

'I had a couple of agents in Midwood last night,' Rogers told him. 'It didn't go the way I hoped.'

'How *did* it go?' Bleary as Ben still was, he didn't have to ask why they'd been there. But if it was Lukas's garbage search, and it had to be, why had he sent Rogers to report on it? 'First of all – was anybody hurt? I heard something about somebody in the hospital.'

Rogers looked alarmed. 'I don't know about the hospital. None of my people was hurt that way. There were some shots fired, but nobody was hit.'

'Who fired the shots?'

'Not our people.'

This got worse and worse. The coffee was waking Ben up a little but it wasn't helping the headache Rogers was giving him. 'All right. Tell me what you do know.'

'Well . . . we need to find the source of that note, and soon, and so far we're dead in the water. I was thinking about what you and Frank were saying about a garbage search, and I thought it was worth doing.'

Ben stirred to protest.

'I mean,' Rogers hurried to add, 'taking into account what you said about not trespassing. I understood those were the ground rules, going in.'

Somehow, Ben didn't find that reassuring.

'I got an unmarked van with fictional registration,' Rogers told him. 'Completely untraceable.'

It wasn't necessarily that simple, but Ben let it go by. It was a measure of how unawake he was that he'd even been tempted to interrupt Rogers with objections. The point was to get the whole story.

'I had a team of agents,' Rogers continued. 'Three others and myself, two to grab the garbage and two of us in the van as driver and backup. We did some practice runs, and we drove around the neighborhoods so we knew the terrain.'

'Neighborhoods? Plural?'

'Oh, yeah. We were going to do the business *and* the residences. We did fine at the businesses. It was the residences where we ran into trouble.'

Now Ben could see the picture more clearly: Lukas had pushed Rogers to set this up, and when it went wrong Rogers was left to tidy up. Lukas's name would never be mentioned except in passing.

It infuriated Ben to be put in the position of having to condone this kind of recklessness, even temporarily, but his first order of business had to be gathering information – and, as Rogers had pointed out, damage control.

'It was three thirty in the morning,' Rogers was saying. 'We were parked down the block for a half-hour before that, watching to be sure there was no unusual activity. It looked all clear, so we went.'

When Katselos and Herrera came around the corner pushing their stolen supermarket basket heaped with a bag of empty cans, Rogers thought they looked the part a hundred percent. Up close and in the bright lights of the office, they'd been a couple of agents dressed up in old clothes, but not here, in the middle of the night.

They made their way slowly down the block, poking into the garbage they passed, looking exactly like a couple of mopes trying to find deposit cans and bottles and whatever else they could sell, or wear.

'Fuck,' Hickman said from the passenger seat of the van. 'They going to take all night?'

'You never know who's watching.' Rogers had originally thought of just driving up and grabbing the bags, but if anybody saw they'd know what was up right away. As it was, the two agents were going to be snatching the clear recycling bags full of office paper, not the blue ones for cans and bottles that were actually worth money. Rogers had to hope no one would notice, or think about it.

Hickman was right, though, the two men were taking their time, actually pulling some garbage from other houses so their real target wouldn't be too obvious. Method actors, Rogers thought.

Then they got to the target location, and Rogers had that familiar tingling feeling of not wanting to screw up, because the garbage wasn't at the curb.

Alan Kest lived in a big house, brick with light-colored shutters on its many windows. It took up a corner lot at least three times the size of the midblock lots nearby. There was a lawn and a backyard, with a hedge all around it. Next to the hedge on one side was a driveway to the garage in the back, and there was a sort of narrow alley alongside the driveway, separating the driveway and the garage from the next house. The recycling bags were in the alley, not far back from the street.

When Rogers had seen that on their first drive by, he'd thought of calling the operation off, and maybe he should have, but he didn't feel like explaining to Lukas why he'd wimped out on this part of the deal, even though there were already three big bags of paper from the Aljo store locations sitting heavily in the back of the van.

Herrera and Katselos left the supermarket cart at the curb and strolled into the dark alley after the two bags. Rogers could just make them out in the fringe glow of the streetlight as they each grabbed a bag.

'Come on, fuckers!' Hickman stage-whispered. 'Do it.'

'Take it easy, for chrissake. They've got to make it look good.' Rogers was succumbing to Hickman's agitation, getting worried about how long this was taking.

Herrera and Katselos dumped the bulging bag of cans off the cart and hefted in the two bags of paper. They hesitated, seemingly unsure what to do with the bag of cans.

'Come on, come on,' Hickman was muttering.

Rogers turned the key in the ignition. He wanted to be ready. The engine cranked a couple of times before it caught.

Just as it did, Rogers heard some kind of shout and a man in a black suit and a black hat came running across the street toward the agents, who turned to see what was happening with a definite look of *oh shit!* on their faces.

'I'm watching this guy come steaming up,' Rogers told Ben, 'and I'm figuring, this isn't great but they can talk their way out of it, no reason for me to blow their cover.

'Only the next thing I know there's two more of these guys coming running, and then another two, and they're piling onto my two guys and yelling at them and whaling the shit out of them with clubs or their radios or something.

'So I get the van going and we're there in a second and the two of us jump out of the van, guns out, and I'm shouting "Police!" because I'm sure as hell not going to say "Secret Service" or "federal agents" or anything dumb—'

'Daddy! Daddy!'

Rogers stopped. 'I guess you better go—'

Ben was already on his way to Hannah's room.

'Daddy!'

'What is it, sweetie?' Hurrying to the bed.

'I'm thirsty.'

'Okay, sweetie, in a minute.'

'I'm *thirsty*!'

'Okay, but how do you feel?'

'My mouth tastes funny.'

'I'll get you some water in a minute. How does your tum feel?'

She patted it all around. 'Feels okay.'

'Good.' He kissed her forehead – not feverish – and went to get the water.

She drank the glass of water down and held it out to him. 'More.'

'Okay, you just stay still and I'll be right back.'

She only sipped at the second glass of water. He put it on the night table.

'I'll leave this here, if you want more. Go back to sleep now, and if you need anything just call.'

He bent to kiss her again and she grabbed his hand. 'I want you to stay here.'

'I can't, sweetie. There's somebody here I have to talk to about work.'

'I want you to. Please, Daddy. I want you to.'

She was tired and cranky and he knew they could go on like this forever. 'Tell you what. Let's bundle you up and you can sleep on the couch next to me while I have my meeting.'

'Okay.'

He gathered her up in her blanket and carried her into the living room, settled her carefully on the couch amidst the beanbags and kissed her goodnight. 'We're going to the kitchen for coffee, sweetie, and then we'll come back here and sit with you.'

'I want to give her time to fall asleep,' he told Rogers as he poured fresh coffee for them.

'She's a cute kid.'

'Thanks. You were saying . . .'

'Right. I was . . . at the point where we jumped out. Seeing us with the guns backed these guys off. There were five of them, like I said, and they had radios, and two of them had nightsticks. They were shouting at us and lights were coming on in the houses around, and all I could think was we'd better get out of here fast, I don't want to be explaining this to the cops or the media. So we piled our guys into the van and jumped in and that was that. Except as we were going somebody took some shots at us. Not many, like a couple of short bursts—'

'Bursts?'

'Yeah, I don't know, that's what it sounded like.'

'Automatic weapons fire?'

'Like controlled bursts maybe,' Rogers said. 'A couple of shots at a time. Or I suppose it could have been a couple of people firing close together. I wasn't paying attention to anything but putting distance between me and the shooters.'

'Without the garbage, I assume.'

'Well, yeah. We just got out of there. Left the cart, too. But they were wearing gloves,' he added quickly. 'No fingerprints.'

'Were you on the property?'

'Well, you know, with the fight and all . . . everybody just got pushed further and further from the street, and when Hickman and I went after them, I wasn't thinking about waiting for an invitation . . .' Rogers was sweating, and not because the apartment-house heat was turned up too high. 'Look, I know I made a bad call. We should have moved on when we saw the garbage wasn't at the curb. If we could have grabbed it and been out of there, nobody would have been the wiser, but it didn't work out that way and I take full responsibility. I understand there may be consequences for me. I accept that.'

Lukas could be proud, Ben thought: Rogers was playing this part of it just right. But that didn't change what a mess it was. He headed for the living room so Rogers wouldn't see the expression on his face.

He bent to look at Hannah – asleep, one fist curled up and pressed under her chin. He sat down next to her. Rogers sat in the easy chair, where he'd been.

'You say there were no injuries?' Ben prompted.

'Superficial head wounds and some bruises. Some blood, but it was bandaid stuff.'

'And you got away clean?'

'As far as I could tell.'

'Where's the van?'

'Safely stored away where it won't be found, unless we want it to be.'

'And where are your agents?'

'By now they ought to be at home asleep. I went straight to the office and put in an Office Memorandum about what happened. Garbage run interrupted by local street patrol. Minor altercation. I assume the others'll do the same when they report in.'

'You have no idea who could be in the hospital?'

'Not our people.'

'You keep saying that. So that means it's their people.' He reminded himself to keep his voice down. He glanced over at Hannah. Still asleep.

'If it's anybody,' Rogers said.

'Did you know about this street patrol before you went in?'

'We knew there was an auxiliary police patrol in the neighborhood – nothing very organized, the way we heard it.'

'And you hadn't nailed down its schedule?'

'Our information was that it operated irregularly, if at all.'

'Did you surveil it?'

'Yeah, we did. Last night. There was nothing like that that we saw.'

Ben checked the time. 'It's almost ten. Let's see if there's anything on the news.'

As he got up, Hannah opened her eyes and said, 'Stay, Daddy.'

'I'm just turning on the TV for a minute, sweetie.'

The top-of-the-hour news on NY1 led off with the Brooklyn story: a member of a local street-safety patrol was in the hospital with unspecified head injuries as the result of a thwarted burglary at a home in Midwood. According to police, the burglars, who had been chased off by the patrol, had been described by a 911 caller as three or four Hispanic or light-skinned African American men in their twenties or thirties. The street-safety patrol leader had no comment except to say 'I hope the police catch these animals and put them away.' Several neighbors claimed to have heard gunshots but police would not confirm or deny the report.

'What's this about head injuries?' Ben asked.

'I don't see how,' Rogers looked troubled. 'My guys were there to heft garbage bags. They didn't have anything on them for breaking heads. That was the other guys. The only thing I can think of is they clobbered one of their own in the confusion.'

'That's a lot of confusion.'

Rogers shook his head wearily. He looked tense and drawn, the victim of anxiety and coffee warring with fatigue. 'It was pretty wild out there for a minute or two, and dark. What else could it be? It wasn't us.'

Even supposing Rogers was right, this was still trouble: 'If that's what happened, they're not going to volunteer the information. They're going to keep blaming the burglars. And the cops are going to have to do something.' Because Jewish community leaders were expert at pushing police and politicians, and a prompt arrest was going to be of major importance. 'So who are they going to arrest?'

'Not my guys. They're gone.'

'Exactly. The only people the cops can target are whatever usual-suspect types come readily to hand, and since the usual suspects definitely won't be the people who did it, when the cops come after them they'll probably claim they're being railroaded on racist grounds. And they won't be wrong.'

Rogers looked perplexed.

'My problem here,' Ben explained, 'is we ought to be telling somebody at One Police Plaza we have an interest in this and they should just go slow, not feel so much pressure actually to do anything, so this doesn't get all blown out of proportion. Especially if this guy in the hospital doesn't get better in a hurry.'

'How can we do that?' Rogers said. 'The NYPD's not exactly a leakproof organization. Once the cops know we're involved, so will everybody, including our targets.'

That was true enough. It only made Ben angrier. 'You should have thought of that before you went in there.'

'I already said it was my fault and I'm willing to take the consequences.' Rogers was beginning to sound petulant. 'Right now I'm just worried that if somebody – some cop, for instance – leaks that it was us out there in the street, there goes any chance we have of getting these Aljo people where we can squeeze them for what they know about the counterfeiters.'

'Your supervisor have an opinion about this?'

'I don't know yet. Right after I put in the OM I went over to see you, because I thought we should all be on the same page with this – if it gets out that it was us, or why we were there, it's going to spook the rabbis for sure.'

This was Lukas talking, no question about it. 'They already know there was *some* law-enforcement involvement,' Ben pointed out. 'You said you shouted police.'

'Yeah, and then we hopped in the van and disappeared. Cops don't do that.'

'No . . .'

'And *anybody* can shout police.'

'Right.' Ben rubbed his eyes and drank more coffee.

'And you said yourself they keep talking about burglars,' Rogers said. 'Nobody's going to connect it to us.'

Famous last words, Ben thought: a new flash of anger at Rogers for trying to ape Lukas and his bulletproof bland confidence. 'Just for information's sake, what race are these agents the neighbor reported as African American or Hispanic?'

'One's from Colombia, originally. The other one's people are Greek, but he passes for Latino.'

'You used those particular agents intentionally.'

'It wasn't me. I mean, I put in the request, but it was the ATSAC' – Assistant To the Special Agent in Charge – 'who runs the counterfeit squad who gave out the assignments. And he wasn't going to find anybody who could pass for an Orthodox Jew, not even in a false beard and black fur hat at night. And the rabbi's house isn't so far from where the skin tones start getting darker.'

'You're saying you figured on that – on your guys being taken for homeless people from over there.'

'On the off chance someone spotted them, that late.'

'Sure worked great, didn't it?'

Herrera hesitated. He started to look around, as if he wished there were somebody to give him a hint, caught himself and made eye contact. 'I don't know what Ian was working from. Theo and I got a briefing.'

Amazing. How could they have mounted that kind of operation – part of an investigation they claimed was highly sensitive – with no written plan, no contingency plan, nothing?

But Herrera wasn't the one to ask. Ben let it go. 'This story you told me, that's what's in your report?'

'It's what happened.'

'And when you left the residence were you aware that anyone had been injured?'

'Not except me and Theo.'

'And you said they were shooting at you.'

'Yeah, you bet.'

'Any opinion on what kind of guns?'

'High caliber semi-auto handgun, and maybe an automatic carbine. Small caliber, high velocity.'

'You serious?'

'I've been shooting a long time. And shot at, too. Somalia.'

'Automatic? You're sure about that?'

'It was only a couple of bursts, but I'd say yeah.'

'Okay, thanks. If I need more, I'll let you know.'

'Yeah, right.' Herrera stood. 'And I appreciate all your concern for my safety.'

Ben wasn't surprised they all had their stories fairly straight – Rogers was smart enough to concoct something reasonable, and chances were Lukas had had a hand in it, too. But the story they were telling, true or not, gave him nothing about what had put the guy from the street security patrol in the hospital – probably just as they intended.

He rummaged in his desk for the personal stereo he kept there for the infrequent days he had time to go out for a run at lunch. He plugged in the earphones so he could listen to the news while he pondered what to do.

The incident in Midwood came up almost at once: a quick recap followed by news that the call for police action was being taken up by Jewish community leaders around the city.

This really *wasn't* going away, and that meant he couldn't just sit on it. But before he called the US Attorney he wanted a clearer picture of how the Secret Service was handling it.

He called Tim Ahl, the Special Agent in Charge of Secret Service's New York field office.

'I take it you know about this flap in Brooklyn.'

'Yeah,' Ahl acknowledged, audibly unhappy. 'And I don't want to be quoting chapter and verse on the phone. You want to know what we're doing, right?'

'Right.'

'Well, the short form is – nothing, for now. Down the line I may need to have our Office of Inspection take a look, see if our guys are culpable in any way.

'But that has to wait,' Ahl added quickly. 'We've already got the agents' stories and they're not going to change just because it's somebody from headquarters asking the questions. The missing piece is the other side's version, and there's no way we can interview those people until we're ready to go public. And we can't do that until we know where this bad paper is coming from, and know we can stop it.

'Whether and when to involve the PD is a decision I'm going to make with my headquarters in Washington, depending on how badly this mess in Brooklyn escalates, and God knows I hope it doesn't. But if I do make a call to the PD I'm likely to fuzz it up, maybe in terms of Protective Intelligence – say we were tracking down a threat against, I don't know, the Israeli UN delegation. You already have an idea how important this case is, and I can tell you we're flat out not doing anything that would compromise it. These people can't know they're our targets. That answer your question?'

'Well enough,' Ben said.

'Just so you know,' Ahl told him, 'I'm not delighted with this whole brainstorm. At least the agents involved were man enough to take responsibility. Any case but this one, they'd be in deep shit. But that's got to take second place to getting to the bottom of this thing we're investigating. And let me tell you, we appreciate it over here that you haven't been jumping up and down pointing a finger, blaming folks, the way you could have.'

Ben hung up savoring Ahl's closing: a warning couched in praise. Very nicely done.

Though Ben wasn't happy with Ahl's vagueness about when he would call the police, it was at least a bonus that he was willing to talk about disciplining his agents, and that he knew their stories couldn't be relied on alone. And Ahl's sense of the importance of the case couldn't have been clearer.

All things considered, Ben thought, it seemed reasonable to wait until morning and hope the situation calmed down enough that he wouldn't have to go to Queen Victoria with it.

'All better,' Vashti informed him when he got home.

Hannah came running out of her room. He swung her into the air. 'Is Vashti right? Are you all better?'

The question didn't interest her, but her renewed energy was answer enough.

'You want to watch the news with me on TV?' he offered.

'No! I want to watch Arthur.'

'I have to watch this for work.'

At least it wasn't top of the news. Each time a story started that wasn't Brooklyn he flipped to another channel. With five stations running some form of evening news it was a lot of flipping.

And then, there it was: a reporter on a corner in Midwood, tape obviously shot earlier in the day, talking to a clean-shaven man in a business suit, a knit skullcap barely visible in his curly black hair, who was saying, 'These marauders – outsiders to the community – come into a peaceful neighborhood, hitting and shooting and looking to steal, and we have to defend ourselves. The police are never here for us when we need them. The only way we can defend our homes and our wives and our children is to be out in the street by ourselves, and this means that we are getting our brains beat in. Menachem Siegel – lying in the hospital right now, may he be granted a complete and speedy recovery – is a father of seven children with a modest, loving wife. A scholar, a devout man.'

By eleven, developments in Brooklyn on a slow news day had moved the Midwood incident up to lead story.

Outside the hospital where Menachem Siegel was still under observation, still listed in a stable but guarded condition, milled a crowd from his neighborhood. Once again there was tape of the man Ben had seen on the early news. He was, it turned out, the leader of the street patrol that had tangled with Rogers and his agents.

'We are here to pray for our friend, to provide strength in adversity for his courageous wife and his dear children, to condemn the city government that does not provide protection for innocent people . . .'

As his voice continued, the tape cut to show the wife, a small woman with delicate features, her hair covered with a kerchief, eyes red, a damp hankie grasped so tightly her knuckles were visibly whitened. Grouped around her, the youngest ones clinging to her skirt, were her seven children, a year apart from about ten years old on down – four girls and three boys decked out in their Sabbath best a day early, each holding a candle against the darkness and the unknown evil of the night.

Ben hit the OFF button. If there was more to the report, he didn't want to see it.

* * *

Listening to the radio as he shaved in the morning, Ben learned what he'd missed. The Reverend William Walker of the First African Church of Brooklyn had made an angry statement Thursday to charge that there had been 911 calls describing some of the intruders at Alan Kest's as white.

'On what basis are we hearing code words like "outsiders to our community"?' Walker had demanded, his voice on the radio rich with indignation. 'On what evidence are the police coming into *our* community and rousting our young men based on charges that are completely unsupported?'

As soon as Ben was in his office he called Rogers. 'You been catching the news?'

A silence. 'Yeah, I have.'

'And?'

'And . . .' More silence. 'We're . . . I'm . . .' He was having trouble finding a way into it. 'There's no *and.* There's nothing I can do.'

'They're blowing this up into a community incident, and it's all based on a lie.'

'I can't keep them from lying,' Rogers snapped. 'I mean, shit – the *burglars* were shooting at *them*? Give me a break, here.

'It's not *their* lie I'm talking about,' Ben shot back, even as he thought: He's young, this could be his first real crisis, he must be a mess.

'Look, I'm not trying to be a jerk about this,' Rogers backpedaled. 'I wish it had never happened, but all we can do is let it all blow over and get on with the work of nailing these people and finding out how they're connected to the source of our problems.'

'Let it all blow over? What about these people who are already making this into a racial incident? How does that fit with letting it all blow over?'

'You mean Reverend Walker? The once-and-future mayoral-gubernatorial-senatorial candidate? The guy's a well-known' – Rogers cut himself off, finished with – 'troublemaker.'

'And there's plenty of trouble to be made. I've heard a lot of talk about protecting the investigation, but not enough to convince me we should sit by and watch this turn into a dangerous community conflict, knowing we could prevent it.' He would have to talk to Queen Victoria, after all – and soon.

'All right, I hear what you're saying. Just give me time to talk to Frank, okay?'

Lukas called almost immediately. 'Don't do anything rash. I'm on my way over.'

Don't do anything rash. But what Ben was contemplating now wasn't rash – rash would be to stand by and let this get out of hand, without the authority to make that decision, and without really knowing why.

He picked up the phone and dialed Victoria Thomas's direct line. He got her voice mail.

'It's Ben Kaplan. I need to see you. Soon.' He felt better just having made the call.

11

Lukas arrived dripping wet, wearing a long, waxed duster and a wide-brimmed hat, looking like he'd just stepped off an Australian ranch. 'That's some rain.'

He shed the coat and hooked it behind the door, with the hat over it. 'You'd think we'd get some snow. It *is* fucking winter.'

'Not much longer.' It was the closest they'd come to small talk. Lukas's way of softening him up?

The agent settled himself in a chair, legs poked out in front of him in his usual style. 'So. Ian tells me you're nervous about what you're hearing on the news.' Behind him, water dripped metronomically off the hem of his coat. 'No need.'

Ben didn't wait for the rest. 'I don't want to hear it. The way this is going we're looking at a major racial incident not far down the road. We can stop that. If we speak up now, what happened in Midwood is just an unfortunate misunderstanding. But if we cover it up, we're responsible for whatever happens between now and the day we finally tell the truth. And make no mistake, we *will* have to tell the truth.'

'Look, if I haven't made this clear enough, let me try one more time,' Lukas said. 'This currency counterfeiting is way too important for us to blow the one slender lead we have. That's not just Frank Lukas talking, it goes all the way to headquarters. So the most important thing for us right now is to get as far on this as we can, as soon as we can.'

'You won't catch me arguing with that. In fact, I got those clonephone numbers for you from Isaacs. The subpoenas go out to the phone companies today, and they'll have your name as investigator.'

'Good. We'll follow up.'

'And with any luck it'll tell us something. But that doesn't answer the main question.'

'There's no main question to answer. This is going to blow over.'

'Yesterday I would have believed that. Not now that it's become a race problem.'

'One loudmouth doesn't make a race problem,' Lukas said.

'That's what these people do – they talk to hear themselves, and to pump themselves up with the home crowd. Ninety-nine times out of a hundred, it means nothing.'

Ben couldn't believe what he was hearing. 'You sound like someone who just got off the bus. You have to know how bad things can get here. Crown Heights? You remember Crown Heights? Days of riots? *Kill the Jews*? And how often do we have to be taught that it's never the initial bad deed that gets you, it's trying to cover it up?'

'What then? We just come right out and tell the world what we're up to? Put up a big sign that tells Rabbi Kest we're on his trail? No way, José – that's not happening. You want the truth? The truth is, it doesn't matter if a few . . . *people*' – his inflection left no doubt that he meant *Jews* – 'get into some hassles with their neighbors. Not compared to what we're doing.'

'As you keep saying, without showing me a single thing to support it. I'm going to be very clear. What's been done so far has been done with all respect for the alleged importance of your case. But I can't take the responsibility of concealing this information, not with things threatening to explode the way they are.'

'But you're willing to trash the investigation. You can take *that* responsibility.'

'No. What happens next is up to the US Attorney.'

'I thought we agreed to keep this between us, about the counterfeit.'

'If so, we weren't contemplating anything like this.'

'Right.' The single word was filled with venom. 'And you've already gone to Tim Ahl.'

'Yes I have.' Not flinching from it. 'I had to know how he was handling this, before I could keep it quiet even as long as I have.'

'You didn't take my word.'

'I didn't *have* your word. I had a lame tale from Rogers and Herrera.'

'Those men got shot at. Whose side are you on here?'

'*Whose side am I on?* What's that supposed to mean?'

'Take it however you want.' Lukas made a disgusted noise. 'These people have got automatic weapons. What do you suppose they're protecting if it's not the plant that makes those notes?'

'How about *themselves*,' Ben offered, anger prompting the new thought. 'Maybe they think they're protecting themselves.' From bigoted cavemen like you, he didn't add. 'Ever hear of the Jewish Defense League?'

'I have friends got put in the hospital dealing with those fuckers,' Lukas shot back. 'So don't tell me about the JDL.'

This was getting way off track. 'Look, I'm not saying go public with everything. Nobody needs to know the real reason your agents were there.'

'It won't help to make up a story. The rabbi and his accomplices are going to be spooked anyway.'

'Assuming they aren't already. The time to worry about getting Kest and his friends all raised up and on their guard was when you were contemplating your glorious garbage grab.'

Lukas was silent, his expression closed. For a moment there was no sound in the office except the water dripping insistently off his coat.

'We're not going to solve anything this way,' Ben said. 'I've already put a call in to the US Attorney. How much I tell her depends on you. Play it any way you want.'

'It's not that simple,' Lukas said. 'I can't just tell you everything. Not without permission from headquarters.'

'Then maybe you should make it clear to them how important it is.'

Lukas was silent again. When he spoke, the heat was out of his voice. 'You know how, with Rogers' credit-card case, one reason it went on so long was that the credit-card companies don't like to admit crimes like that are even possible? This is like that.'

'You can't very well deny that it's happening.'

'No, but we have to catch these notes before they get out into wide circulation and the wrong people figure out what can be done.'

'Assuming they're not in circulation already.'

'We'd have seen something by now if they were. And in the meantime, talking about them in public is almost as bad. Because the problem isn't this one note, it's what this note tells the world about what's possible.'

'You're saying it proves the security features can be beat?'

Again, Lukas didn't respond.

'Well, I've said what I had to say,' Ben told him. 'It's past time that I know what makes this case important enough for us to shield agents who may have committed criminal assault, and to stand by while the city risks completely avoidable racial conflict.'

'That's a little harsh,' Lukas said. He pushed out a long breath. 'I'll need some time to see how much I can talk about.'

During lunch, Ben checked the news: Reverend Walker was promising an important announcement before the day was over, and doctors had yielded to pressure from Menachem Siegel's family and allowed him to go home to observe the Sabbath, though they wanted him back first thing Monday for more tests.

With all the turmoil surrounding the garbage search it had been a day since he checked his e-mail. There was something from the lawyer who'd negotiated the settlement after Laura's death.

'City agrees to review training procedures, with public report,' the e-mail opened.

Ben picked up the phone without reading further. 'Is this real?'

'I'll tell you that when I see it happen,' the lawyer said, 'but yeah I think it is. They're pretty upset about this. They're considering the possibility of somebody new to run the program, too, depending on what they find.'

'Good work.'

'The right words in the right ears. They were grateful you didn't make it as bad for them as you could have over Laura, and they don't want to reopen that at all.'

'Just as long as there's nothing in the press.' Chances that it would reach Hannah were tiny, but he couldn't rely on that.

The rest of his e-mail was from prosecutors in his unit, except for one with an NYU Law address. It was from Judith Zilka: the location of the synagogue where Joshua had invited him to services and Shabbat dinner, and a short message: 'I hope you'll let Hannah sit with me and the other ladies part of the time. See you at dinner, JZ.'

He could feel his heart speed up as he read it. He still wasn't prepared to be reacting this way, but he knew that he'd have gone to poetry readings or to hockey games to be with her, whatever it took. The last thing he'd have predicted was that it would be religious services with Joshua Brauner, whose words had been a particular source of peace over the past three years.

When Ben had arrived in New York, newly bereaved, Sam Koenigsberg, the rabbi at Ohevei Yisroel, had sensed his conflict about fulfilling the religious obligations of mourning.

'Even if you say the mourner's kaddish three times a day,' he'd told Ben, 'it won't help you heal if there's no belief to go with it.'

But the kind of belief Rabbi Koenigsberg advised had proved elusive. Ben believed in Laura, and she'd *believed*, in a way that seemed to her consistent with the committed Judaism she'd chosen for herself, but that was as far he'd been able to get.

Saying kaddish in Laura's honor each morning he'd tried to capture some of the sense of a Greater Power that had seemed so effortless for her. But too often he came away feeling uneasy, even angry at the idea of celebrating a Force that, if it existed, had so randomly and cruelly taken a good and harmless life. As the months progressed, he'd faltered in his morning routine, finding increasingly frequent reasons to excuse himself from attendance at prayers until finally it was far rarer that he went than that he didn't.

In his state of guilt and confusion, Joshua Brauner's books – alone among the ones recommended by Rabbi Koenigsberg – had helped him see the possibility of a faith built not on abstraction and theory and myth, but on the concreteness of practice and tradition, of family worship and even an honest day's work honestly done, so that in the last of the prescribed eleven months he'd been able to return to saying kaddish every day, if not as an affirmation of belief then as a statement of grief and love.

The phone rang. 'It's a Mr Morgan,' Ella told him. 'He says Mr Butler suggested he call.'

The name didn't ring a bell, and then it did – Harry Butler's friend, chief of staff to the new Secretary of the Treasury. This had to be about the job.

Nate Morgan had a gravel voice and a clipped, perfunctory delivery. He started with pleasantries about how much his old pal Harry thought of Ben, but the conversation quickly turned into an interrogation: How did Ben like his job? Was he planning to stay in law enforcement? How did he like the administrative work of being a unit chief? Even caught unaware, Ben saw the trap: like it too much where you are, and why do you want to leave? Not enough and what's wrong: you, or the job?

Morgan moved on to the problems of managing a unit full of eager young prosecutors, an invitation for Ben to paint himself as someone good at supervising junior people.

'Actually, I've got a pretty experienced unit,' Ben countered. 'Including four senior trial counsel. Which doesn't make them any less energetic.'

Morgan had more questions about how the unit ran, then switched to Ben's budgetary responsibilities – mostly symbolic – and how he felt about passing policy down from the US Attorney and from Main Justice. Morgan was clearly an experienced questioner, but as a bureaucrat, not a prosecutor, and it was never a mystery what he was after.

He finished with a request for a résumé and Ben's federal employment history and DOJ security questionnaire. 'Fax them today, if you can. And I'll need the names of four people who can tell us all about you. Nobody in your office or at Main Justice. There'll be time for that. We want to keep this closely held for now.'

That was consistent with Harry Butler's warning that this job was a battleground between Treasury and Justice – a product of the changing of the guard at Treasury and the Attorney General's instinct for power vacuums, the danger being that the AG would slip a loyalist into Treasury by getting the President to offer a candidate for the job.

'One other thing,' Morgan said. 'I know you're working on a

Treasury case that's very sensitive, and I want you to know we appreciate the way you're working with the agents. I know Harry's mentioned we have some political issues to face, and he's probably told you too that loyalty is a big, big word here.'

Ben hung up disoriented: this felt more like pressure than a sign they were considering him seriously at Treasury – an attempt to keep him handling the Aljo case the way they wanted him to. And who had been reporting on him? Lukas? Unlikely. From what Ben had heard, Frank Lukas had his defenders at headquarters – his *rabbis* – but he was hardly a team player. Tim Ahl, more likely.

But even if Morgan's call had been a genuine pre-interview, he'd made sure to end it with an unmistakable code word. Loyalty was indeed a big word, and in this case it meant: We want you to play this by our rules, and we're going to be paying attention to how you work with our agents.

12

Ben was still weighing his conversation with Morgan when the phone rang again. Lukas. 'All right – you want to know more, I'll tell you.'

Ten minutes later, he strode into Ben's office. The rain had stopped and he wore no coat. The shoulders of his suit glistened with mist from the storm's foggy aftermath. He settled into a chair, silent, as if to establish that Frank Lukas did nothing against his will.

When he was ready he shifted to pull a wallet from his hip pocket, extracted a hundred-dollar note and dropped it on Ben's desk.

'How familiar are you with these?'

Ben picked it up. 'I don't see a lot of them. I knew about the '96 redesign, and when the case took this turn I did some checking about the new security features.'

'Good. Then I want you to think about something. Of the new security features, which one do you think we placed the most confidence in? The one we really thought wouldn't be breached any time soon?'

We're not playing a game, Ben wanted to say, but there was no need to antagonize Lukas again, not as long as the game led to the information Ben needed.

He didn't think it would be the microprinting in Ben Franklin's lapel and the lower-left-corner 100, or the multiple concentric circles in the background of Franklin's portrait. Or even the watermark portrait. The two features that suggested themselves were the microprinted plastic strip embedded in the paper that was supposed to glow under ultraviolet light, and the special ink on the lower-right 100 that turned from metallic green and gold to flat black depending on how you looked at it – optically variable, it was called. The plastic strip seemed harder, but Ben knew too little about papermaking and the chemistry of printing inks to be able to make a sensible choice. He was about to say as much to Lukas, and then he remembered the agent's original description of the counterfeit note they'd found at Isaacs's: *a decent version of the embedded plastic strip*. So the answer had to be – 'The OV ink.'

'Exactly right. It's a secret formula, made in Switzerland under strict security. A very big deal.'

'Are you telling me these people have got that? They've got a workable version of the OV ink?'

Lukas didn't blink. '*Telling* you? I'm not telling you anything.'

'But you want me to act as if you were.'

'Look, you made a good case that you have a need to know, but the details are still something we're keeping as closely held as we can. There's no way anyone at headquarters or Main Treasury wants even as much as I *have* told you leaking out. Especially not to our colleagues at the Department of Justice. There are people who get overdramatic about things like this' – the agent's face registered clearly what he thought of them – 'and we don't want to give anybody an excuse to hyperventilate about threats to the faith people around the world put in our paper currency, questions of national security, anything like that. Start saying the words *economic terrorism* and right away the FBI is tromping all over your case, and you can kiss goodbye any chance of shutting things down quickly and quietly the way we have to if we don't want serious trouble.'

'They're certainly not getting any ammunition from me.'

'I'm glad to hear it.' Lukas didn't try to hide his skepticism. 'And I'm hoping that you finally see how important this is.'

Important, Ben thought as he watched Lukas's bulk recede down the corridor – if the note Rogers had taken from Isaac Isaacs sported an even passable version of the security feature that the Bureau of Engraving and Printing thought was the least likely to be breached, then 'important' was a pallid understatement. Little as he liked it, he could see why Lukas, and the decision-makers up the line all the way to Main Treasury, might think they had to keep their mouths shut about the garbage run – even if that meant risking trouble in Midwood.

Ben was in a box. He had no more doubt about the timing of Morgan's call – that message was clear, just as Lukas's was. But however much he didn't want to compromise Secret Service's desire for secrecy about the phony OV ink, he still had to follow up on his phone calls to Queen Victoria.

When he finally got in to see her, he started with a quick history of the Aljo case: the credit-card fraud, finding Isaacs, the counterfeit hundred.

'Secret Service's first priority right now is getting to the source of that note. So from their point of view the fraud case becomes entirely a means to that end.'

'You can't fault them for that,' she said, 'assuming it's a serious enough piece of counterfeiting.'

It was a question, but oblique enough to risk side-stepping it:

'They definitely think it is, and I don't have any reason to doubt their assessment. I just wanted you to have the whole background.'

The creases at the corners of her eyes deepened, but she didn't challenge him.

'Let me give you a hypothetical.' He ran down the garbage-run story, camouflaging it as if he were presenting it at the law school.

'That's no hypothetical,' she said when he was finished. 'You're talking about this business in Brooklyn.'

'I am. The house where the incident occurred is the residence of the only lead we have on the bogus note. The so-called burglars were Secret Service agents.'

She sat watching him, saying nothing. She liked keeping people on edge; silence worked for her, augmented by how physically imposing she was: erect and square shouldered, six feet tall plus the two-inch heels she always wore, with a broad forehead and large gray eyes that revealed only constant appraisal of whatever they were turned on.

'You authorized this?' she asked when he was thoroughly uncomfortable.

'When they floated the idea, I told them to forget about it.'

'But they went ahead anyway.'

'Yes.'

'When did you learn about it?'

'Yesterday, when it still looked like it was going to blow over.'

'And you didn't inform me.' No missing the sharpness in her voice.

'I called this morning, as soon as it seemed clear this might not go away. Until then I didn't see the need to involve you. But I did call Tim Ahl at Secret Service, to be sure they weren't ignoring the implications.' He told her about the conversation, emphasizing the SAC's desire to protect the investigation.

She was silent a long, worrisome moment.

'The important thing is, you finally did bring it to me,' she said. 'Now I want the whole story.'

She led him through Wednesday night's events in Midwood a step at a time like the tough prosecutor she was. He was glad he'd grilled Rogers and Herrera, or she'd have caught him unprepared in a way he didn't want to contemplate.

'What a mess,' she said when she had the story to her satisfaction. 'I have to say, though, you were a hundred percent right when you decided to call Secret Service. This is emphatically not our problem. It's theirs, consequences included. And I'm going to call our friend Mr Ahl to make sure he knows it.'

It wouldn't make them happy at Secret Service to be cut loose that way, but maybe Ben would get some points with them for informing Her Majesty about Midwood without giving her any details about the counterfeit note. He pushed from his mind the concern that her *not my problem* freed Secret Service from having to worry about her oversight on how far they let this escalate.

13

When Ben got home Hannah was in a mood, seemingly the result of an incident at school.

'Alicia got her dress all covered with paint and I just wanted to wash the paint off but Bobby G. said I threw water on her, and she started to cry.'

He could imagine the scene only too well. 'Did Alicia ask you to help?'

'No, but it was all yukky.'

'You know, sweetie, sometimes it's better to wait until people ask for help. Did you explain to Janice?'

'Yes but next time we do painting I can't have a partner. I don't care. Alicia's no fun to paint with anyway.'

Whiny and reluctant, she lingered over the Sabbath candlelighting ceremony until he reminded her they were going to see her new friend Judith.

The synagogue's sanctuary occupied the parlor floor of a townhouse just off West End Avenue. It was an unadorned room with a fourteen-foot ceiling, with rows of folding chairs facing a Holy Ark at the rear of a ruby-carpeted stage that ran the entire width of the room and a third of its length, about three feet above floor level. A shoulder-height mechitza partition of gauzy drapes divided the room front to back into a men's side six chairs wide, with five chairs per row on the women's side – unusual equality in an Orthodox synagogue – both sides full to capacity.

As Joshua led the service he walked, skipped and danced from side to side on the stage so he could be heard and seen by both men and women.

Hannah started out with Ben – girls under twelve could sit in the men's section – but before long she scurried off to find Judith.

It was a short service, full of happy singing but with less of the exuberant demonstrativeness Ben sometimes found overdone at Ohevei Yisroel. And Joshua himself seemed different, his energy more imbued with spirituality, less theatrical.

Though the standing-room-only congregation here numbered not much over a hundred, Joshua was every bit as mobbed after the service as he had been as guest rabbi at Ohevei Yisroel.

'Are you're sure there'll be room for us?' Ben asked Judith.

'Of course. And I know Joshua. If there isn't room he'll make some, and everybody will be the happier for it.'

Ben waited at one side of the downstairs room, crowded with round tables set with paper tablecloths, while Judith took Hannah off to wash up.

They reappeared in the company of a pale, slender young woman with a mass of tight brown curls and skin translucent as parchment, to whose ankle-length flowered skirt clung four little girls in matching party dresses. The girls looked about a year apart, from Hannah's age to around two. Judith introduced them. Hannah and the two eldest little girls, instantly immersed in a game only they understood, wound in and out among the adults, giggling; the mother – Suzanne Altman – watched their comings and goings and kept track of her younger two while she made polite conversation.

Ben commented on the crowd around Joshua.

'Oh yes,' said Suzanne. 'We're all so thrilled when he visits. We're in his East Side congregation, but we came over just for this.'

'I don't understand,' Ben admitted. 'I thought this was *his* shul, his own congregation.' Though he hadn't expected it to be so close to where he lived.

'Oh, yes, it is,' Suzanne assured him. 'But it's not the only one.'

'Now I'm really confused.'

'I thought you knew,' Judith said, 'because you'd read his books, but I suppose he's very modest when he gives his biography. Joshua isn't an ordinary pulpit rabbi. He was the principal disciple of the Stropkover Rebbe of blessed memory, a very great sage and teacher. The Rebbe is honored in many congregations, here in New York and as far away as Israel, and Joshua tries to spread himself among them, from week to week. And many weeks he's away on retreat, or visiting another congregation as guest rabbi.' A warm smile. 'Like last week, when we saw him at Ohevei Yisroel.'

'I didn't realize,' Ben said. 'I suppose it was silly of me to think he'd have time to talk.'

Ben saw sudden joy in Suzanne's face. He turned, and there was Joshua.

'Not so silly, I think,' he said to Ben. The blue eyes twinkled with pleasure. 'Suzanne, Shabbat shalom, how are your handsome Mark and your four darling daughters? Is that Sara and Naomi I see peeking out from behind your skirt? Hello girls. Here . . . I have some treats for you' – from the pocket of his coat he pulled two candies wrapped in cellophane – 'if it's all right with your mother.'

'Oh of course, Rebbe, thank you. Girls, girls – Sara, Naomi, come out from behind me and see what the Rebbe has for you.'

They emerged shyly, their smiles as broad as their mother's. The youngest one brought her hand up. Joshua placed a candy in the offered palm and closed the little fingers tight around it. He bent to place a feathery kiss on the fist he'd made and the little girl giggled and darted behind her mother again. This was repeated with her sister, and with the two others who – along with Hannah – had magically reappeared the moment Joshua said 'treats.'

'Hello, Hannah,' he said. 'Shabbat shalom. I'm glad to see you here. Special guests get two candies.'

She stood immobile, eyes on her feet.

'It's okay, sweetie,' Ben said. 'Go ahead.'

She looked up at Joshua. 'I'm not supposed to eat candy,' she said. 'My daddy says it's not good for me.'

Ben didn't know what to do.

'Well,' Joshua said. 'In that case . . .' He slipped the candies back into his pocket, smiling broadly. 'I'm very glad to see you here. You and your father and your good friend Judith.' He cocked his head with interest. 'Yes, Hanneleh, what can I do for you?'

She was holding her hand up to him, fingers curled into a fist like the ones he'd made for Suzanne's daughters.

'Can I have a kiss anyway?'

He roared with delight. 'Yes, of course you can!' He bent to kiss her hand, then scooped her up and raised her high above his head. He kissed her loudly on both cheeks and put her down.

A gentle hand on her head, he said, 'May the Holy One, praised be He, lift His countenance to shine on you always.'

Ben heard murmurs of amen and looked around to see that they had become the center of attention in the crowded room.

Joshua raised both hands, palms out, and spoke to the room. 'May haShem look kindly on this Shabbat observance of ours, and may we all celebrate it with a happy heart. As it is written – worship haShem in gladness, come into His presence with shouts of joy.'

There was another stirring of amens and the room returned to normal.

Smiling still, Joshua said, 'Right this minute, my own heart would be happiest if it had some Shabbat dinner.'

After dinner and the grace after meals, Joshua made the rounds of the room. Ben was momentarily alone at the table – Judith and Suzanne had taken the five little girls off to the ladies' room. Joshua pulled up a chair next to him.

'I had no idea that you had so many congregations,' Ben said.

'I don't know about "so many." But it does keep me busy, and it's a great joy to me that I can help them in their spiritual life.'

'Your books certainly helped me. It can get frustrating and

confusing, trying to find a path that makes sense. Especially raising a child alone.'

'It's a great tragedy when a young woman dies and leaves a small child and a loving husband.'

Ben had no response to that. Joshua shared the silence awhile, then put a hand on Ben's shoulder. 'How about some air? It's good to take a walk after dinner.'

It was a beautiful evening, clear and not too cold. Ben did his best to savor it.

'Has it been a long time?' Joshua asked as they walked.

'Three years.'

'Was she ill?'

'Car accident.'

'I'm sorry. I know there's no real solace, and yet life must go on, in the face of these calamities. We must give thanks to haShem that you and Hannah were spared.'

Unexpectedly, Ben felt a need to say more. 'I was too far away to help,' he said. And then, amazing himself, he said, 'Laura saved Hannah's life,' and choked up.

'So much sadness for so much goodness,' Joshua said and then fell quiet, a comforting presence as they walked.

'I don't talk about it much,' Ben said finally.

'Sometimes it really does help to let it out.'

'But don't I remember reading, "Say little and do much"? In *Tree of Life*, I think. It made a big impression.'

Joshua laughed. 'Well I cribbed it straight from Ethics of the Fathers. And I won't quote the verses I know that talk about the solace of friendship. When you're ready, I'm here.'

After a while, Ben said, 'I will say this much – it leaves you wondering about things like God and random cruelty in the world.'

'Yes – that's the hardest question for all of us. The Creator makes a world that contains both good and evil. We hear many explanations, and people accept them in the name of belief, but the real truth is the explanations we have aren't very satisfactory, because it's not given to us to know His mind and see why these things are so.'

'I'm not sure I can live with a God like that,' Ben let himself say.

'And yet here you are, welcoming the Sabbath and praising haShem. As you did last week at OY.'

'Yes. For Hannah, really.' Again, he was talking about things he usually didn't. 'Laura and I both wanted her to have some sense of community and tradition. Laura especially. She worked hard to finish her conversion before Hannah was born – for herself and so there'd be no doubt for Hannah.' Because Jewishness was a matter of heredity as well as practice and belief, and by ancient law it was passed through the maternal line.

'Children are so important,' Joshua reflected. 'HaShem's gift to us, and ours to Him. But parents matter, too. Can you tell me honestly that you do this just for her and not yourself?'

'I've tried to find meaning in it – and I do respond to the services sometimes, though I don't really know why.'

'Intellectually these things don't necessarily make sense,' Joshua said, 'It's best if you can empty your mind of preconceptions about it, and ideas like fairness and "random cruelty," as you put it. What we can't change we have to accept. There's a passage in Psalms, a prayer of Moses – "Our years pass like a sigh and the best of them are emptiness and pain."'

Joshua paused over the thought, then said, 'None of us starts with understanding. If we're among the truly fortunate we achieve a little of it by the end of our days. By studying, by good works, and by repentance and return.'

Ben said nothing at first, then remembered another passage from one of Joshua's books. 'It makes me think of what you said in *Loneliness of Faith* about emptiness as a starting point. "If you want to fill a vessel of any kind, and you want to put as much into it as you can, the first thing you do is empty it." Something like that.'

'Exactly that.' Joshua clapped a hand onto Ben's shoulder, squeezed with strong fingers. 'I like you, my searching friend – already I feel we're kindred spirits, the rabbi and the professor. So tell me, how can I help you in your quest?'

'You're the rabbi. You tell me.'

'Come to services here tomorrow, if you'd like,' Joshua said as they went down the stairs to the vestry room. 'Judith will be here, too.' He paused on the bottom step. 'Lovely, isn't she?'

'Yes, very. But we're not—' Ben began, then started over. 'She's not—'

'Nothing to explain. She's a fine woman, and she thinks a lot of you. She and your daughter seem to be forming quite a bond.'

Ben and Hannah walked Judith to the house where she'd been invited to stay the night so she wouldn't have to violate the Sabbath prohibition against traveling.

Ben hesitated at the door, wanting to kiss her good night, knowing he couldn't.

'Daddy,' Hannah pulled at his hand. 'I want you to carry me.'

'Okay, but you're a big girl now, so I can't carry you far.'

If you lived here you'd be home by now, he thought, lifting up a Hannah almost out on her feet, balancing her weight on his shoulder.

They said good night. Judith leaned toward him, up on her toes, one hand on Hannah's leg for balance. For a moment his whole being tingled in anticipation, but it was Hannah she kissed.

'Good night, Hanneleh. Sleep well. Shabbat shalom.' She touched a single finger to Ben's cheek and hurried inside.

He watched her cross the lobby, spellbound.

'Daddy!' Hannah shouted in his ear.

'Okay, sweetie.' He resettled her more comfortably over his shoulder and turned to find a cab.

He put Hannah straight to bed, and though it wasn't late got ready for bed himself. It had been an exhausting couple of days and he hadn't fully recovered from his sleepless Wednesday night.

Much as he wanted to maintain the sense of Sabbath peace, he had to know what had been happening in Brooklyn. He listened to the radio as he washed up and undressed.

The Reverend Walker had made his promised announcement, vowing to march through Midwood to the police precinct house, taking his supporters past 'the scene of no crime.' There were the expected calls for calm and moderation. The most alarming news was talk of a major counter-demonstration.

14

Ben wasn't sure Hannah would want to go to services again in the morning, but she was so eager to see Judith she could barely sit through breakfast.

This time she went straight to the women's section. Ben found a place among the men, nodding hello to the ones he recognized from dinner. He felt more a part of the congregation and the service than he'd expected. Once, when he'd lost the place, the man to his left simply handed over his own prayer book, open to the correct page, taking Ben's in return.

After the weekly reading from the Torah, the congregation stood for the return of the scroll to its Ark, a recess in the marble-faced rear wall of the sanctuary, with a traditional satin curtain embroidered in Biblical heraldry covering its carved wooden doors. They sang a song from Proverbs, praise for the wisdom of the Torah.

It is a tree of life to those who grasp it,
and happy are its upholders.
Its ways are the ways of pleasantness, and
all its paths are peace.

For no reason he could name, Ben found the verse tugging at him; at the last line his eyes began to sting . . .

Turn us to You O Lord and we shall return.
Renew our days as of old.

When the Ark was closed, everyone sat, with a great rustling as they all settled in for Joshua's discussion of the week's reading.

'We read a special commandment today,' he began. 'A Supermitzvah, you could say – the commandment of haShem to Moses and the People of Israel regarding the holiest of all days, the Sabbath. This wasn't just given as one of the Ten Commandments, this is a special commandment all on its own.

'The Torah says, "Moses called the whole community of Israel together and said to them, "These are the things that the Lord commanded you to do. On six days work may be done, but on the seventh day you shall have a Sabbath of complete rest, holy to the Lord."" And then Moses said, still quoting haShem, "Whoever does any work on the Sabbath shall be put to death."'

Joshua leaned right to look at the women, left to look at the men, repeating the phrases: whoever does *any* work . . . *shall be put to death*.

'In the days of the Kingdom of Israel, when the Holy Temple still stood and it was possible to impose a death sentence for religious crimes, this wasn't just a way of speaking. If you did any work on the Sabbath you could literally be put to death. *Could be*, not that we know that anyone ever was. Still, to read this in the Torah today reminds us how seriously haShem takes our observing His day of rest.'

He gave everyone a moment to digest that before he resumed: 'This brings me to a subject you might not think was related. We've all heard of the unfortunate incident in Brooklyn and the troubles of poor Mr Menachem Siegel, whose name we include today in our prayers, that he may be granted a speedy and complete recovery.'

Even here, Ben couldn't help thinking: who would have expected reaction to a minor fracas in Brooklyn to be everywhere like this?

'We hear in the news that the Siegel family and their friends have been demonstrating at the police precinct for better police protection,' Joshua was saying, 'along with people from other congregations in that neighborhood. You know how strongly I believe in preserving the safety of the community, but you know, too, that I believe in *self*-reliance. As we are taught by the sages: "Seek not the acquaintance of the authorities." Sometimes it's better not to ask for special treatment, and this is one of those times, because this demonstrating is already causing more trouble.

'I've been told that because of it Reverend William Walker is bringing many of his flock to that same police precinct today to stage his own demonstration. And the march is going to take them right past the house where the incident took place, and they'll stop there to make speeches.

'I also hear that in some congregations around the city rabbis will be preaching that people should go to oppose Reverend Walker. This is where again I have to disagree with people of good will – even people who pray as we do.

'Reverend Walker should be allowed to come and go in peace. If he has something to say, he should say it, and whoever wishes to listen is welcome to listen and everyone else should stay home. I wouldn't urge anyone to go to this event, to protest or for any other reason – not even people who are close enough to get there without breaking the laws of Shabbat.

'And that brings me back to our Torah reading for this morning. In this congregation I don't have to tell you not to go, because all of us observe the full mitzvah of Shabbat a hundred percent. And though we talk often of the spiritual value of transgression and repentance, breaking the Sabbath laws is not something we include in that. On Shabbat we cannot ride, and walking all the way from here to Brooklyn is not a Sabbath jaunt. It's work, and work we cannot do.'

Interesting, Ben thought, that Joshua should feel the need to address the subject. Was it a pretext for a reminder on Sabbath observance, or was Sabbath observance the pretext for a mini-lecture on how to deal with community conflict?

After Joshua led the concluding prayer there was a gathering downstairs to bless wine and bread and share a Sabbath visit. Once Joshua's official duties were done he came over to greet Ben and Hannah and Judith. He surprised Ben by giving him a hearty embrace.

'I'm glad to see you here, my friend. And I've already arranged for you to be at one of our discussion groups, if it's convenient for you.'

'That's great. Thank you.'

It was one of the things Joshua had suggested on their walk – 'You need somebody to argue with.'

'Argue?'

'Absolutely, argue. People today don't seem to realize it's okay to argue about faith and observance, and the love and fear of God, too. To doubt, to struggle with the meaning. That's what the famous rabbis did, that's what students still do today in the great yeshivas. They talk, they argue, they ask. Mostly, they argue. You should, too. And there are plenty of people to argue with – people like you – study groups all over.'

'And have you decided on your new Shabbat mitzvah?' he asked now – he'd stressed that, too: To get the spiritual muscles working you had to start living the commandments. If you did, even with a confused heart, you'd feel refreshed and renewed – 'If you're going to try a new one a week, now's the time to start.'

'We light the candles on Friday,' Hannah offered.

'Very good, Hanneleh,' Joshua said. 'And maybe you can add something new for the rest of this Shabbat.'

'Okay. What?'

'That's for you and your Daddy to decide.'

'No, *you* say.'

Joshua laughed. 'Like father, like daughter. Well . . . how about leaving the television off? Can you do that, for the whole rest of Shabbat, all the way until you can see three stars in the sky?'

'I can. I can do that.' Very proud. 'Radio, too.'

'Three stars. You'll remember?'

'I promise.'

'Good for you.'

'And Daddy, too,' Hannah said.

Strolling in Riverside Park with two couples Judith knew from the congregation, Ben and Hannah and Judith stopped by the low stone wall overlooking the river and let the others walk on. Ben lifted Hannah up for a better view. Judith was at his side, close. He wanted to put his arm around her, draw her even closer, feel the warmth of her head on his shoulder. The intensity of the desire no longer surprised him.

Together, they climbed the long flight of steps that connected park and street.

'Know what? Judith's going to teach me how to make challah,' Hannah announced.

'Really?'

'She said,' Hannah affirmed.

'Yes, I did.' Judith was smiling. 'And we're going to have a lot of fun, too.'

'I didn't know you baked challah,' Ben said.

'Why so surprised? Just because I can argue questions of international criminal law? I was brought up in a Sephardic home, after all, and no matter how enlightened my father was about my schooling, he also believed, like a man of good Portuguese and Moroccan heritage, that I should have the training befitting a well-bred young woman, whose true function and place on earth it is to provide ease and comfort for men.'

'When do Hannah and I have this good fortune?'

'Next week, if it's all right for you – Hannah is so eager, and it happens that Suzanne has invited me for Shabbat dinner, along with whoever I choose to bring, because Mark is going out of town again at the end of the week and she'll be lonely. I know what a careful man you are, and I'm a proper Jewish woman, myself, after all, and this way I'll have kosher chaperones and you won't be alone with a student. How's that?'

He laughed. 'Impressive. But I don't want to impose on Suzanne.'

His hesitation was more than just politeness, and he didn't know what to make of it. A moment ago his fantasy of her had been so strong his body had responded to the mere idea. Now a hint of encouragement had him bolting like a spooked horse.

Could it be that after three years he was locked into his role of bereaved widower and single dad? *Afraid?* Of somehow risking his idealized memory of Laura? Of change, of the emotional challenge Judith would certainly present?

You're being silly, he told himself. Judith was offering to do something generous for Hannah and for him, and it would be less than gracious to refuse. Besides, for all his hesitation, he wanted it more than anything.

When they got to the top of the stairs, Hannah skipped on ahead of them.

'And what's all this about serious meetings in the living room?' Judith asked teasingly. 'I don't remember your telling the class about that aspect of a prosecutor's glamorous life.'

Ben felt a chill that had nothing to do with the weather. 'What aspect is that?'

'Listening to an investigator's problems in your living room while comforting your ailing daughter.'

What had Hannah said? She must have been telling Judith about it during services, in the women's section. Or last night, while he was out walking with Joshua. 'Hannah always sees fascinating things when she's up all night with a stomach virus.'

'No doubt. But an investigator seems an odd thing to hallucinate.'

'Why an investigator?' Playing along because simple denial would only pique Judith's interest, and he couldn't afford that. Too many of the pieces were there: What Rogers and he had said, plus his own immediate and insatiable interest in news about the Midwood incident. Someone half as smart as Judith could put it together, if she wanted to.

'I can't imagine who else it would be than an investigator,' Judith said. 'Other prosecutors can't have problems you have to solve in your pyjamas. Or can they?'

'All hours of the day and night. Not that they they usually bring them to me at home. If anyone did that, I'd bet on its being an old friend with a romantic problem.'

'I didn't know you were an expert,' she said. 'I'll have to bear that in mind if I have anything romantic to explore.' She was teasing again, but there was something more than that in her eyes.

At a loss for a response, Ben was glad they'd caught up to Hannah, who had stopped to watch a trio of Pekingese tethered to a park bench along the sidewalk, frisking and tangling their leashes.

'Here doggies,' Hannah said and bent to pet them.

Judith pulled her back. 'Let's race to the streetlight.' They took off, their coats flapping around their legs.

'I hope that wasn't rude,' Judith said when Ben caught up with them. 'The poor little creatures didn't look any too clean. Their owner, either.'

'Very clever.' But it wasn't the dogs he was thinking about, it was the newspaper their owner was reading. RELAPSE! said the full page headline in huge letters, and under that: BKLYN GUARD RUSHED TO E.R./COMPLICATIONS COULD BE FATAL/MAYOR TO VISIT HOSPITAL.

15

Complications Could Be Fatal.

He had to know what that meant. Important as it was to track down the creators of Isaacs' hundred-dollar note, and to do it in as much secrecy as possible, if Siegel died from injuries that might have been inflicted by Secret Service agents, everything would change.

He waited impatiently for Hannah to be ready for a nap so he could find out what was behind the headline. He couldn't break her Sabbath vow to Joshua, not while she was awake. There was no way she would understand.

When she finally lay down for her nap, he grabbed a pocket radio and some earphones. Hadn't Joshua said, 'Everyone transgresses'?

But before he turned it on he thought, it's only a few hours, and what am I going to do with anything I learn now? The evening would be soon enough.

Waiting, he tried again to imagine the garbage run: Someone had taken it on himself to shoot at the four intruders. Why?

Rogers had already shouted 'Police!' He and the other backup were approaching, fast, with guns drawn. Was that it? Someone who hadn't heard the shout – at a distance from the action, perhaps – who saw the two men with guns?

Still, would that have been enough to prompt gunfire, from those people, in that neighborhood?

Unless there was more provocation than just drawn guns. Unless one of the intruders was beating Menachem Siegel on the head, and the shots were a warning, to stop it.

Why would a Secret Service agent be pounding on Menachem Siegel? That much was easy enough to see—

Rogers and the backup agent coming in a panic from the van. One or more of the security patrol still swinging away at Herrera and Katselos. Inflicting a head wound on Herrera – superficial, it turned out, but head wounds bleed copiously.

You see another agent, somebody you've worked with a lot, blood running down his face, maybe his clothes bloody, too. You grab his assailant, or whoever's nearest, and you club him hard. And again, and *again*. And then you hear shots you know aren't from your side, and you run like hell.

'My guys didn't have anything on them for breaking heads,' Rogers had said. But he and the other backup had had guns, and you could do a lot of damage with the butt of a gun and a good measure of rage.

After her nap Hannah came to play with her dolls on the living-room floor. Ben sat by the window, practicing Joshua's 'strength' meditation in a futile attempt to distract himself from how much there was that he didn't know.

As the afternoon wore on he felt increasingly frustrated, wishing he'd listened to the news while Hannah napped. The Siegel headline had been in the morning paper, news almost a full day old, and by now Reverend Walker had already marched through the neighborhood. Even the mayor had gotten into the act. All because of an incident that was part of Ben Kaplan's case, no matter how skillful he was at convincing himself that decisions about it now were up to Queen Victoria or Tim Ahl. The possibility that the world would soon learn the truth, despite their precautions – made vivid for him by whatever Hannah had told Judith – only increased his feeling that he should be doing something.

At six, time for the local news, the sun was down but there was still faint light in the sky. Close enough, he told himself and reached for the remote.

'Three stars! There have to be three stars!' Hannah yelled, jumping up and down and pointing out the window as the TV screen crackled to life accompanied by the news fanfare.

He went to give her a hug. 'I know, sweetie, but it's hard to see the stars from here. I bet there are really lots by now, and it's very important to Daddy tonight to watch the news for work.'

'There have to be three stars,' she insisted in a hurt voice. She squirmed around in his arms to face away from him.

He let go and turned the television off. 'There. Is that better?'

'Too late!' she said, sobbing. 'You spoiled it.'

She wouldn't eat. When she would stop crying and he'd hope the storm had passed and try to talk to her, she'd say 'You spoiled it' in a small voice, or 'I promised Joshua, no television till three stars,' and start crying again.

He left her alone. When she'd cried herself exhausted and fallen asleep he carried her to bed. He took no comfort in the thought that by tomorrow she would have forgotten, because he knew that would only be how it seemed. This would come up again.

The Midwood Incident, as the newswriters were now calling it, had been pushed from top of the late news by new fighting in the

Balkans. When it came up, after the first commercial, Ben saw what he should have anticipated: the tabloid headline had been exaggerated. Menachem Siegel had been rushed to an ER, and the complications could indeed be fatal, but listening closely Ben had the impression that death wasn't imminent. Siegel was in and out of consciousness, the doctors were worried, but for now, at least, they were taking a wait-and-see approach.

For that, he'd risked upsetting Hannah, he didn't know how badly. Not the first time he'd let professional pressures and anxiety interfere with his good judgment as a father.

With a sour feeling, he watched the report of the march in Midwood. It had passed without major incident, just name-calling and a few fist-fights, though one had been serious enough to get the reporter talking about how close it had come to sparking a riot. Mercifully, whatever guns there were in Kest's comunity, they'd been left home for the Sabbath.

Ben pressed the 'off' button. He could hear himself with Lukas on Friday morning: *If we cover it up, we're responsible for whatever happens between now and the day we finally tell the truth.* It wasn't much solace that the powder keg hadn't exploded yet.

16

Ben was awakened Sunday morning by the sound of sobbing.

Blearily he tried to focus. Hannah sounded upset, not sick or hurt. He caught the time as he swung his legs out of bed: six forty.

She was sitting up in bed, crying. Holding her arms out as soon as he appeared in the doorway.

The story of her nightmare came in bits and pieces as she clung to him, sobbing: a crowded place like a cross between Joshua's synagogue and a cartoon dungeon, dark and scary. Ben was there, and Judith, and Suzanne and her daughters, and kids and grown-ups from Hannah's school, all standing in line.

At the front of the line, she said, was Joshua 'pointing at people, and then the monsters took you away.

'He pointed at *you*,' she choked out, 'and he looked so scary. It was for the three stars. I kept saying it was my fault, but he didn't hear.' She buried her face against his chest.

'I didn't want them to take you away' – he could feel the muffled words vibrate against him – 'only these . . . *things* . . . came and pulled your arms, and I tried to hold on so they couldn't take you.' She held him tighter. When she spoke again he could barely hear the words. 'And my mommy came back from Heaven and said no they can't, either. But they didn't listen to her. And I was hitting them and trying to make them stop, but I couldn't.'

She subsided again into sobbing, and again he rocked her and patted her back.

'It's okay, sweetie, that's not going to happen. No monster is strong enough to take me away from you.' But he was struck by how vulnerable her world must still seem to her, despite the sense he'd had recently that she was healing – her small network of friends and their families so much less a bulwark against loss than he'd hoped.

'But Joshua *said*,' she pointed out when she'd calmed down a little. 'He said if you did anything against Shabbat, then they had to make you dead.'

'Oh, sweetie, Joshua didn't mean that, not really. That's just a story.'

'No it isn't. He *said*.'

'Yes, he did. But you know how big people tell stories sometimes to help you understand things. Only the stories are really make-believe, so it makes it easier to remember.'

'But the Torah is *true.*'

Oops. 'I didn't mean to say the *Torah* was make-believe. Only, there are lots of rules people can't always obey . . .' He was reaching: this was more theology than he was equipped for. 'And the Torah is full of things that aren't the same now as when haShem gave the Torah to Moses long, long ago.'

That diverted them into a discussion of what 'long, long ago' might mean – ground on which he felt more at ease, with the added benefit that Hannah soon grew distracted.

He thought they were out of the woods, at least temporarily, but then she said, 'The police car took my mommy away and now she can never come back.'

Oh Lord. 'Nobody's going to take me away. Not Joshua, for sure.'

'How do you know?'

He put her down and worked up his best mock-serious expression. 'Okay, who's the daddy?'

Dutifully, she pointed.

'And who's the little kid?'

Her forefinger curled around to touch her own chest.

'Okay. And we know that sometimes daddies know more about things just because they're daddies, don't we?'

Grudgingly, she nodded.

'Okay. So's here's what the daddy has to say. *You* kept *your* promise. And I did, too, until the very last minute. Keeping the promise almost all of a whole Saturday has to count for a lot.'

She wiped her nose. 'It does?'

'Yes, it does.'

She considered that gravely. 'But next time we have do it all the way till three stars.'

'Next time we will.' He curbed the impulse to hug her tight and instead stuck out his hand, very official. 'Deal.'

She did her best to get her hands around his, and pumped it up and down. 'Deal.'

She hesitated a moment, then said, 'Daddy, is it Sunday?'

'Yes, it is. And you know what that means.'

'Pancakes!' She jumped off the bed and headed for the kitchen.

Cleaning up after they finished, he listened to the radio: Menachem Siegel had lapsed into a coma. The hospital spokeswoman said only that his doctors planned further tests.

Ben beeped Lukas, then again a half hour later, and a half hour after that.

Hannah was playing with her beanbag dolls, arranging little domestic dramas that included a Little Girl and a Daddy and a Mommy. Ben sat next to her and flipped through local public affairs shows, most of them using the incidents in Brooklyn as a model of the often troubled relationship between African Americans and Jews. One panel was dissecting the anger spreading in the varied communities of Orthodox Jews in and near Midwood, and among the less-observant Jews who were rallying to them. The first flashpoint might have passed, but Ben could see it was far too early to relax about the potential for violent confrontation.

When the phone finally rang Ben half expected it to be Joshua with a penalty for breaking the Sabbath. It was Lukas. Ben had him hold on so he could take the call where Hannah couldn't hear.

'Worried about Siegel?' the agent opened.

'Aren't you?'

'Why? My guys say they didn't hit him, and I believe them.'

'That's such bullshit, Frank.' A good working relationship with Lukas and the others might help him get the Treasury job, but if he didn't stand up for his principles now, he'd never be able to. 'We've been over this once, and things have gotten a lot worse since. If Siegel dies, your agents are implicated in a homicide.'

'Look, you want to be a big hero, get credit for serving up Herrera and Katselos on a plate, and Rogers and Hickman, too, that's between you and your conscience. When the time comes. Not now.'

'You feel no responsibility at all, do you?'

'Sure I do. I feel responsibility to my country and its laws. Not the people who are breaking them.'

'Menachem Siegel, as far as we know, wasn't breaking any of the laws you're talking about.'

'Maybe, maybe not. And if he wasn't, he was getting in the way of enforcing them.'

Like Laura, Ben couldn't help thinking. He said, 'Which he had no way of knowing.'

'This is too important to get sentimental over some guy who should have stood in bed,' Lukas said. 'Whether Siegel lives or dies, we have a potentially serious threat to the security of the country on our hands, much as I don't like to talk in those terms, and the ugly truth is we don't have jackshit to go on. We're up the asshole of an elephant without a flashlight, so we better hang onto the one spark we have.'

Ben was silent.

'Am I getting through? We have the slim possibility that these people have a line to the source of this stuff, and if they get spooked we have nothing. And once our targets get into production – if they're not already – they can put out a whole lot of very convincing paper in a little bit of time. And it's not just what they can produce themselves. If the world finds out these folks can beat this new design so soon after we put it out, how are we ever going to convince anyone that the same thing isn't going to happen again with *whatever* we put out there?'

It was a lot to think about. The official Treasury Department line at the time of the original Supernote scare had been to minimize the implications: currency wasn't that important because the total amount in circulation was a tiny fraction of the total money supply, which included commercial and private bank deposits and various other embodiments of buying power, mostly electronic.

But that ignored the enormous symbolic power of currency. If the world couldn't have faith in the dollars it could hold in its hands, how could it have faith in the imaginary ones? It wasn't just that the US would lose the ability to ship currency overseas in return for goods, services and foreign exchange. The whole foundation of American economic dominance in the world would be shaken. And there were currencies waiting to take over – the German mark, the Yen, even the soon-to-be-born Euro.

17

Monday morning, Ben called Queen Victoria as soon as he got to the office.

'Somebody's got to get out the word that there are reliable eyewitnesses to shots fired from the Kest house, to cool down all this talk of armed marauders.'

'The way I left it with Tim Ahl, I'm assuming he's already had his conversation with the PD by now.'

'I hope so.' The scare he'd had about Hannah's talking to Judith was still with him. 'If this comes out some way we can't anticipate, and we haven't given the police the basic story—'

'Yes, but there's also the problem of police leaks,' she countered. 'Reverend Walker is quoting nine-one-one tapes. That means he's got a line into the PD. Bringing the police department on board is one thing, giving ammunition to aggrieved private citizens is another, especially with Mr Siegel in a coma. The moment his family hears it was an arm of the government in the rabbi's driveway they're going to hire themselves a houseful of hungry lawyers and start filing lawsuits and taking depositions, as you well know. And how long do you think our investigation will stay secret if that happens?'

Our investigation, he noted, pushing aside the reference to Laura. He wondered how much Tim Ahl had said. Whatever was behind it, the US Attorney was clearly taking a proprietary interest in the case.

Lukas was next on Ben's list. He didn't want to get mired in talk of the mess in Brooklyn: he led with a question. 'Have we learned anything from the phone numbers we got from Isaacs?'

'Yeah, we have. Not all the subpoenas are in yet, but almost all the calls we do have are international. Mostly Israel, no surprise. A lot to Amsterdam, that's more interesting. We want to see if that has anything to do with the diamond trade – that's Jews top to bottom, and so far we don't have anything about Aljo being in that business. Also Russia, which could be somebody's cousin or grandma or it could be a mafiya dealer in counterfeit currency. And Colombia. That's really interesting.'

'Wasn't there a case last year, some rabbis in Brooklyn laundering Colombian drug money?'

'Yeah. They ran it through their religious school some way. That's not what I meant, though. Colombia's a major counterfeiting country, the biggest in terms of number of notes seized. The problem for us is, cooperation isn't their strong point. Israel should be easier. We sent the Israeli numbers Kest and the others have been calling to the Secret Service office in Cyprus – that's our liaison with Israel. Let's hope it's not just a bunch of Aljo's relatives.'

'How long till we get some answers?'

'I'm as eager as you are, but it's not up to me.'

'And the garbage?' Ben asked, knowing that if they had anything they'd have told him.

'Nothing obvious. We're checking out the little bit that looks interesting so far.'

So it had been a waste of time, after all. Ben had the sense to keep his mouth shut about it. Nothing he said now was going to come out right.

'I've been thinking that what we really need is an undercover,' Lukas said, picking up Rogers' earlier suggestion. 'Problem is, the only candidates we have are guys a lot more like me than like you, and I don't see our targets talking to a guy like me.'

'I'd be worried they're on their guard in general right now.'

'Because of Siegel? Nah, I bet they really think it was a set-up for a burglary or a home invasion. Anyway, it could take us a while to find somebody who can do this for us, establish an identity, arrange an introduction. By then all that hassle on the lawn is a memory'—

Dream on, Ben thought.

—'So if you have any ideas . . .'

'I might, actually,' Ben said.

When he got off with Lukas he called Elliot Rosen, the federal law-enforcement chaplain, told him the problem. 'So if you've got anybody in FLEOA who's Orthodox, or even lapsed . . Secret Service is best, then some other Treasury Agency. ATF o Customs.'

'You're ruling out FBI and DEA?'

'FBI, for sure.' Though it wasn't Rosen's main constituency, ar way – most FBI agents belonged to their own fraternal organizati not FLEOA. 'And one of the agencies in the Treasury Departm would definitely be best.' Running an undercover from another f office was trouble enough, crossing agencies was worse, cros whole departments of government didn't bear thinking about

'Let me see what I can come up with,' Rosen said.

At lunchtime, Ben listened to the news: Tests on a still-cor

Menachem Siegel had been inconclusive. Doctors suspected pressure on his brain and had scheduled an MRI. They were words too reminiscent of the ones Ben had heard three years ago, when he was waiting out Laura's coma, sitting by her bedside holding her hand hour after hour, convincing himself she knew he was there. He had no idea if seriously observant women held hands with their unconscious husbands, but it was no mystery to him how painful this had to be for Siegel's wife.

Rosen called at the end of the day. 'I have a guy for you. Secret Service, an agent up in Boston named Sid Levy. He says you should give him a call. He was raised Orthodox, and he's been an agent twelve years. His hobby these days is catching and cooking lobsters, but he says he remembers everything from the old yeshiva days.'

The late news told Ben that Menachem Siegel's doctors had found the source of the pressure on his brain and were going to operate. They refused to put odds on his chances of making it through the operation alive. Ben wondered if Herrera and Katselos were watching, too, or Rogers, or Lukas, and if they were, what they were thinking.

Having missed Sid Levy at home, Ben caught him in the morning at the Secret Service's Boston office.

'Rabbi Rosen didn't tell me much, just you need somebody for an Orthodox undercover.'

Ben gave him a quick summary, everything except the garbage run, though he did describe the furor in Midwood. Levy needed to know the incident might have put them on guard, but as long as there was a possibility Siegel might die, Ben couldn't tell him the whole truth.

'Sounds interesting to me. I ought to talk to the case agent.'

'Frank Lukas.'

A pause. 'No shit. *The* Frank Lukas.'

'Unless there's another one.'

'There's only one.' Another pause. 'Okay, have him call me.'

Ben checked the radio for Menachem Siegel's progress over and over, with increasing apprehension as the day passed without word. Siegel wasn't out of the operating room until after four. The hospital spokeswoman reported that the operation itself had been a qualified success, though understandably taxing on the patient, and that the pace of his recovery over the next day or two would be critical.

'Feeling better now that Siegel's out of the woods?' Lukas asked

when he called to report that Secret Service headquarters had given permission for Sid Levy to be temporarily reassigned to New York.

He's hardly out of the woods, Ben didn't say. Instead he focused on the undercover. 'How'd it go with Levy?'

'We'll see. He says he wants you at the first briefing. It's not how I do things, but he's the one who's going to have his head on the block, so I'll make allowances up to a point. As long as he gets us to the source of that note.

'When?'

'Thursday. I'll tell you, though – I'd still rather have friend Isaac doing this than an agent. It'd save a lot of work and a lot of worry. Too bad it'll never happen, the way he worries about his fellow Jews.'

'True,' Ben said. 'But it might not be a bad approach to take, talking to him.'

18

Isaacs didn't rejoice at Ben's invitation, but he clearly saw he didn't have much choice about it. They met him in a motel on West Street too seedy even for the local hookers.

Isaacs was most of the way into the room when he saw Lukas on the bed – long legs poked out in front of him, back propped against the headboard. For a moment, the snitch stopped dead, then he turned away from the agent and said hello to Ben as if no one else were there. He took the chair Ben offered, shifting it so Lukas was out of his field of vision.

'We need to know some more about your friends at Aljo,' Ben told him.

'Is that why you dragged me down here? I already told you, ask them.'

Ben waited, letting silence add to Isaacs' apprehension until the snitch couldn't keep himself from talking.

'When I gave you those phone numbers, didn't I say that was it, the end, period? Why do you keep hounding me?'

'All we want you to do is keep up your relationship with them, and now and then we'll want you to answer some questions for us. That's not hard. And if you don't know the answers right away, just find a reason to go in and hang around, whatever you need to do to get the information.'

Isaacs stared at him. 'Oh yeah. Oh sure. This is a joke, right?'

It took them a while to make him see it wasn't, alternating reason and cajolery from Ben with escalating threats from Lukas until Ben began to worry the agent was genuinely losing his temper.

Isaacs, wearying under the assault, clapped his hands weakly. 'Bravo, bravo. You guys do good-cop bad-cop better than the TV.'

At that, Lukas was off the bed and towering over Isaacs. He grabbed the chair on either side of Isaacs' quaking shoulders and pushed his face within inches of Isaacs' nose.

'Don't sass me, you piece of shit.' He shook the chair back and forth, lifted it from the floor and dropped it, then again, bouncing Isaacs on the seat.

'Frank! Frank! Enough!' It was too convincing to be entirely an act.

The agent pushed himself away from Isaacs, leaving the chair rocking. Isaacs was blanched, spit flecking his chin.

'I told you, keep him away from me,' he wailed at Ben, his voice up at least an octave.

'This is very simple, Isaac,' Ben said calmly. 'We're not asking you to do anything different, just more of the same. All we want is for you to go about your regular business only keep your eyes open for certain things, and tell us about them when you see them.'

'Don't these people have enough trouble already?'

'We all sympathize with Mr Siegel's family,' Ben said, 'if that's what you mean. But that has nothing to do with what we're talking about.'

'You know, when I first heard about that robbery,' Isaacs said, sounding partly recovered, 'about the guys at Rabbi Kest's house, I thought – could that be my old friends from the Secret Service? You know, trying to plant a bug, or peep in the window—'

'What are you saying?' Lukas snapped. 'You making an accusation here?'

Ben held up a hand. 'Let's not get off the track. We're talking about how Isaac can help himself by doing us a small favor.'

'Only I'm not doing it. I'm not setting myself up for a religious death sentence. Not for threats or money.'

'I said this before, Isaac. You're exaggerating. Alan Kest isn't going to kill you.'

'Yeah, well, you listen to me,' Isaacs burst out. 'I'm not going to be the one to find out. *You* want to do it, you go right ahead.' Only the form of Isaacs' bravado was back, his voice was still high and uncertain. 'Maybe your macho friend there wants to do it.' His eyes gleamed with panicky humor. 'Hey, I'll even make the introductions.'

'That's fine,' Ben said. 'It's not as good as what we wanted, but it'll do. We'd be happy to arrange it.'

'What?' Isaacs was staring at him – midway between bewildered and trapped. 'What are you talking about?'

'Just what you said. We know somebody who wants to do business with Mr Kest. You introduce him, you vouch for him, and he'll do the rest. You won't have a thing to worry about.'

'Yeah, nothing except I vouched for him.'

'We're not stupid,' Lukas said. 'Our guy isn't going in there to blow his own cover. Kest won't have a clue.'

Isaacs closed his eyes and let his chin sink onto his chest. He was muttering something – Hebrew, Ben thought, or Yiddish.

'I can't do it,' he said, barely audible.

'Sure you can.'

'I can't.' Eyes still closed. 'What kind of business does he want to do?'

'You tell us,' Lukas said. 'Maybe sell some computers real cheap, or a couple of cases of cellphones. To get things rolling.'

'I can't. I tell you, I can't. What am I suposed to do? Walk up and say "Hey, Rabbi, want some hot computers? Some cellphones, fell off a truck? I know just the guy."'

'There's a way to do this, Isaac,' Ben said. 'And we're going to find it together. The first step is, you've got to think about everything you know about Alan Kest and the business he does, to help us decide how to approach this. And then you've got to think about ways you can learn more. And we'll add the things we know. We'll get it done.'

Isaacs had opened his eyes while Ben was talking. He sat staring, nothing to say.

'Go home,' Ben said. He felt Lukas getting ready to roar and made a small hand gesture to stop him. 'Go home and think hard, and in a day or so we'll talk again.'

'The fuck was that, "go home"?' Lukas wanted to know.

'We've got him. He's hooked.'

'Yeah, right. So you have him hooked you reel him in.'

'He hooked himself, you notice.'

Lukas laughed. 'Yeah, he did. That was something.'

'He'll reel himself in, too.'

'Maybe. Maybe he's like that. He'd fucking better be – this is too important to lose our only inside guy.'

'We're not ready for the next step, yet, anyway. And he's not lost. You can reach out for him any time.'

'That was something, wasn't it, about how he thought the garbage run was us.'

Ben didn't see how Lukas could be so cavalier about it. 'Let's be glad he doesn't give it much weight, or *he'd* be strong-arming *us*.'

Thoughts of the turmoil swirling around the Aljo case – if it even made sense to call it that any more, considering how far it had come from the original credit-card fraud – made it a struggle for Ben to teach his law school students. Yet, preoccupied as he was, he was still constantly aware of Judith watching and listening from the third row.

Over the weekend her presence had been alternately soothing and provocative. And something had changed between them. In the space of a few days they'd gone from instructor and student with a shared interest in the religious teachings of Joshua Brauner to . . . he didn't know what, didn't want to analyze it too closely, especially now.

19

In the morning he had a surprise call from Nate Morgan.

'I'm in New York,' Morgan said, 'and I'd like to see you. Things are speeding up. Can you get away for lunch?'

The last thing Ben felt ready for was a major interview for the job in Washington, but he didn't see how he could avoid it.

'I'll make it my business,' he said.

The Treasury chief of staff looked a lot older than made sense for somebody who'd been Harry Burton's college buddy, Ben thought as he sat down opposite Morgan in a restaurant far from the downtown haunts of law enforcement. Morgan's pale eyes were sunk deep in their sockets, ornamented by tufted gray eyebrows, and his cheeks and forehead were so creased they seemed to carry two faces' worth of skin.

'Well, we've got some ground to cover here,' Morgan said as soon as the waiter was gone. His voice grated even more in person than it had on the phone. 'You're thirty-six?'

'Next month.'

'Too young for Vietnam, too old for Desert Storm.'

'I suppose.'

'No ROTC? National Guard?'

'No.' This was different from the phone interview. This time Ben had no idea where Morgan was headed.

'Have a problem with the military?'

Ben recoiled before he could catch himself. He took a breath. 'There's more than one way to serve your country, Mr Morgan. I've been working for the federal government going on ten years. I'm considered good at what I do. I have law-school classmates who make as much as eight, ten times what the government pays me. I'd say that qualifies.'

'You're right,' Morgan said. 'And you're right to be proud of it.' He paused long enough for Ben to think: maybe this isn't going to be that bad.

He was wrong. The rest of lunch was an uninterrupted assault, everything from whether he paid social security and withholding tax for Vashti, to how he managed to live on his government salary in expensive New York paying full-time help and private-school tuition, to a grilling about his history with mind-altering substances painstakingly detailed one drug at a time. Hardest were the questions about Laura's death and his reaction to it.

'I took some time off,' Ben said. 'I put in for the job in New York, and since then I've been working harder than ever.'

'Effectively?'

'People seem to think so. The unit's statistics are better than they've ever been.'

Morgan didn't comment. 'And being a single parent? Does that get in the way?'

'Not much more than being any other kind of parent.'

Eventually, Morgan got around to sex, but only indirectly: was there anything Ben could think of that might be used to blackmail or coerce him? Or that would embarrass the Administration? the Treasury chief of staff added with a straight face.

'Not a thing,' Ben said. 'I mean, as far as coercion . . . there's always my daughter. But all parents have that problem, don't they?'

Over coffee, Morgan said, 'You're relatively young and you look younger. How do you feel about having people report to you who are decades older?'

'I do it now.'

'Who have served in combat in the military – as you have not' –

So that was the point of his opening salvo.

—'Who have experience carrying a gun as an agent in life-threatening situations, who have been doing that kind of thing since you were in grade school.'

It was a question he'd long ago had to answer for himself. 'When I started as a prosecutor I worked with agents who were carrying a badge and gun before I was even born. I respect experience, Mr Morgan, and I know how to defer to it when that's appropriate. I also know that some people make policy and others have to carry it out. And this country has a long tradition of civilian control of people who carry guns. I think that's very important.'

'How do you feel about authorizing people to kick in doors?'

'I have to be ready to do that now.'

'Only in the abstract. You do white-collar crime – subpoenas and wiretaps. I'm talking about kicking doors not knowing what's on the other side. Authorizing armed raids where an exchange of gunfire is expected.'

'I'll get used to it.' Wrong! he thought, too late, and scrambled to recover: 'In fact, I've already done that. A raid to rescue a major witness—'

'We were talking about your wife,' Morgan interrupted. 'Has the way that happened formed any of your opinions about appropriate law-enforcement response?'

Ben was off balance for only a moment. 'It taught me that high-speed police chases kill innocent people. I don't think that opinion makes me unique.'

Morgan wasn't so easily put off. 'Frankly, Mr Kaplan, one of the reasons we're sitting here is the settlement you negotiated after your wife's death. Your ability to work the system effectively and unobtrusively is interesting to us. But it cuts both ways. To put it bluntly, we have a serious concern that you're gun-shy.'

And screw you, too, Ben allowed himself to think, anger being easier than facing the question. He said, 'Mr Morgan, I understand that those decisions are part of the Assistant Secretary's job. I also expect that I'll be operating in an environment where there are well-thought-out rules of operation and rules of engagement' – and if they weren't well thought out now, he'd do what he could to fix that – 'and that I'll be making my decisions in that context. And while I may not be inclined to choose violent confrontation as a first resort, I also understand that I'll be in the job to implement the policies put in place by the Secretary. And he'll have my signed, undated resignation from day one in case he doesn't like how I do the job.'

'It's gallant of you to offer to fall on your sword, Mr Kaplan, but we don't have the luxury of hiring somebody we'll have to fire later. We need to be sure you're with the program before you come on board.'

Morgan waved for the check. 'No need for you to stick around while I settle up. I know you've got important work at the office – and again, we appreciate how you've been handling that. You'll be hearing from me.'

Ben left the restaurant with the feeling that for most of lunch he'd been a long way from 'with the program.' He consoled himself that at least he wouldn't have to worry about relocating and how it would affect Hannah.

20

To keep Sid Levy away from St Andrews Plaza, Ben and Lukas met him in the parking lot of the sports complex on the Hudson River piers. Levy – Sid the Yid, he called himself – was in his early thirties, medium height, pale with dark curly hair and the stubble of a beard so dark and dense Ben doubted he ever looked clean-shaven. He moved like a dancer but was happy to demonstrate that he could emulate the hollow-chested stance of a scholar or the bouncing or shuffling gait of a man oblivious to the world. Physically he seemed perfect for the job.

Ben liked him at once, but he seemed to have the opposite effect on Lukas, and Levy seemed wary of the senior agent from the beginning. Their conversation was a mix of pedigree questions and sparring about work history and connections in Secret Service, in increasingly combative tones.

'Frank, you have some pictures for us?' Ben interrupted.

'Yeah.' Lukas pulled a stack of eight-by-tens from his briefcase – Alan Kest going in and out of his store. He was a big man, shaggy, some age between fifty and seventy, Ben thought. In some of the pictures he seemed slightly bent, or leaning to one side.

'Arthritis, one of our surveillance guys says,' Lukas told them. 'I have the partner, too.'

Joseph Ohry, outside another store, was rotund, more walrus than bear. His round face sported only a wisp of beard, and a black fedora covered what Ben guessed was a bald head. He looked younger than Kest, in his early fifties, at most.

Lukas gave Levy a quick rundown on the men and the businesses and the credit-card fraud that had opened the case, gave him an envelope of the case reports he'd need to read. 'Just remember the thing that matters here is the counterfeit currency. Our snitch said Kest talked about a briefcase full of these notes, and we've got to find out where he got them without letting him know we care.'

'Okay,' Levy said after he'd taken a while with the pictures. 'Here's the way I see it – we know these guys are serious about religion, so I'm going to be putting myself on the line in a world full of technicalities and special meanings, and I'm not going to have the time to explain every little detail. I want somebody Jewish as a contact.'

'We've got some Jewish agents in the office,' Lukas said, 'but not in the counterfeit squad right now, and I can't be extending the line of communication that way. I run my own operations.'

'I bet you do,' Levy said.

'Maybe we're overthinking this,' Lukas said to Ben.

'Maybe we don't need a Jewish undercover.'

'I think we do,' Ben said. 'There are going to be major issues of trust here, and Jews are *clannish*, remember?'

'I'm okay with Ben,' Levy said. 'He brought me into this.'

'What does he know about running an undercover operation? I can't cede my authority to him, either.'

'I'm not saying you should. Somebody has to handle the Secret Service end of things.'

'I don't do fetch and carry,' Lukas said.

Levy turned away from him with a look of disgust. 'Just one thing when you're working all this out,' the undercover said to Ben, 'I remember enough to go in there as your basic Modern Orthodox, but I don't have a prayer of faking anything more specific – like Satmar or Bobov or any of the other Hasidic sects.'

'Modern Orthodox should work fine,' Ben said. 'We don't really know where on the spectrum they stand. Somewhere to the right of Modern, but they don't look Hasidic, either. But maybe that's something you can use.' Thinking about the passion he'd seen at his own congregation for renewal of the faith and the proliferation of outreach at all levels of Judaism – even the way Suzanne and Mark and the others he'd met through Judith seemed to gravitate toward a newcomer. 'If you can express some curiosity about their beliefs and their practice, a desire to learn, that may be a way in.'

'Good idea,' Levy said. 'As long as they're not too insular, that could help a lot.' He turned to Lukas, wordless.

'Right, I get it,' Lukas said. 'Just let's keep clear who the case agent is.'

'Yeah, no problem.' The undercover shook Ben's hand and walked off toward the bowling-alley entrance.

Ben's impression of a welcome extended to newcomers was reinforced at the study session Joshua had invited him to try.

The discussion, in the Greenwich Village apartment of one of the group's members, was about how to deal with a situation in which obeying religious law might involve an affront to human dignity. The foundation of the Talmudic debate seemed to be a division of all activities into those that sanctified God's Name and those that profaned it.

'A *profanation*, in this context, is any violation of Law,' the discussion leader said, 'and the text quotes Rabbi Judah as saying,

"Where a profanation of the Name is concerned, no respect is paid to a teacher." But how do we understand that?'

The commandment at issue was a Biblical prohibition against wearing a garment made of mixed linen and wool – and the remedy for an unwitting violation, according to the sages, was to take the garment off the moment you discovered its forbidden nature, even if you were in public. Or to snatch it off your teacher's back if you saw that he was inadvertently wearing the prohibited cloth, an idea that prompted heated debate.

'Imagine for a moment that any profanation of the Name could result in a kind of spiritual death,' the leader said, summing up. 'Then you'd definitely be willing to disrespect your teacher to help him comply with the commandments. Just as you'd keep him from jumping off a bridge, even if it meant treating him roughly and disobeying him in the face of the great duty of respect and honor that you owe a teacher – more respect than you owe your own father, because, as the Talmud says, your father brings you into this world, but your teacher gives you wisdom so you can enter the World To Come.'

To Ben's surprise, Joshua arrived as the study group was breaking up. He greeted everybody warmly by name, had personal questions for all of them. He saved Ben for last.

'How'd you like it?'

'It was great. A lot of arguing, as you said. It reminded me of my class at NYU, in fact. Just on an intellectual basis, it fascinates the lawyer in me.'

'This is just one level, people learning to wrestle with issues of faith and observance. We've got all kinds of groups, right up to serious Talmud study in Hebrew. Even intensive retreats for special students. I've got one coming up – three days and two nights of study and meditation out in the country.'

Ben could feel how much he wanted to be a candidate for Joshua's three-day retreat, to be *special* enough. The intensity of it alarmed him. 'That sounds fascinating.'

'We'll have to let you try it. Meanwhile, let's move you to a different group for next time, give you a taste of the more mystical side.'

'Whatever you think.'

'Judith was telling me the other day how much Hannah enjoyed the children's services.'

'She did, but there was something I wanted to ask you about.' Ben told him about Hannah's reaction to the idea of the Sabbath death penalty.

Joshua listened sympathetically. 'I'm sorry she was upset,' he said. 'Children can take these things much more seriously than we realize.

I'll be happy to talk to her if you want, but it sounds like you handled it very well.'

'I hope so. I worry about her. She can be very emotional.'

'Considering all she's been through – both of you – you seem to be doing a great job. I hear she's become great friends with Deborah and Dina, and Suzanne's two little ones, too.'

Ben couldn't help smiling. 'I guess I don't have any secrets.'

Joshua grinned at him, full of sudden joy and mischief. 'Not from this rabbi you don't.' Serious again, he said, 'I'd like to make a suggestion about Hannah, if I may.'

'Please.'

'She's said some things to Judith, and in Deborah's house as well, that she doesn't have a good time in school where she is.'

'She's had some difficulties.'

'*We* have a school, you know,' Joshua said. 'Kindergarten through fifth, all English subjects taught fully, plus art and music and gym. It's an excellent school, the teachers truly care, the classes are small.' He stopped himself. 'Forgive me, I don't usually do advertisements like this, but . . . one way to avoid the kind of overreaction you told me about is to make sure the little ones have the right background.'

'That makes sense.'

'You have to decide for yourself how much you want to let her explore her spiritual impulses, but if you do want to open that door for her, then providing an enriched environment – other children and other adults – will help her and take some of the burden off you. And we pride ourselves on teaching the religious subjects at a level appropriate for how old they are, and so they don't frighten their parents too often by playing religious police.'

Ben laughed. 'That's your best advertisement so far.'

He thought about it on the way home. He could hardly deny that Hannah was having trouble at school: today she'd had another run-in with Bobby G., fighting over building blocks this time. The improved attitude her teachers had claimed to be noticing not long ago seemed to be ebbing away. And it was true that she behaved better with Deborah and her sisters than with anyone else, and seemed happier with them.

When he got home he looked in on Hannah, sleeping peacefully, one little fist pressed to her chin. He looked closer – she was sucking her thumb. He watched her awhile, full of the frustrating desire to make her world right. He was glad he'd had the chance to talk to Joshua. Looking into a new school for Hannah was probably a good idea.

When he'd begun taking Hannah to services, educating her, he'd seen immediately how good it was for her to be immersed in a broader family, a caring community that offered the solace of regular practice and ritual. But until now, until Joshua, he hadn't thought of it as his own returning.

He'd never seen himself as observant. 'Honor the Sabbath, to keep it holy,' the Torah said. Honoring it was something he could manage. Keeping it holy, in anything approximating strict practice, had always seemed more than his oscillating belief would support. And yet now he was letting himself be pulled in that direction. Because of Joshua? Because of Judith?

Maybe, he thought, the one who really needed a warm community and the solace of shared practice and ritual had all along been himself.

21

Sid Levy wanted to meet Isaacs right away, to give himself time to learn about Kest and to modify his cover – David Gershon of Boston, shady broker of odd-lot merchandise – if that looked advisable. They all met at a coffee shop uptown on Broadway, Isaacs' old Secret Service rendezvous.

The two men shook hands, Isaacs warily. Sid said a few words in Yiddish. Isaacs stared, then answered with what sounded like a question. Sid's reply was apparently surprising enough to get a laugh out of Isaacs.

'Where'd you get this guy?' he said to Lukas.

'He's my brother.'

'Yeah, right,' Isaacs said. 'You should have told me before.' He slid into the booth next to Ben with an exaggerated exhalation of weariness. 'Let me guess. This means more work for our hero Isaac.'

'We want you to introduce him to one of your friends.'

'This is the guy?'

'He is.'

Isaacs said something else to Sid in Yiddish. This time the agent's response was longer, and it didn't make Isaacs laugh. Isaacs had some more questions before he was satisfied.

'All right,' he told Ben. 'I suppose he's plausible. And he seems to have the sense not to push it too far. So why am I introducing him? I mean in this fictional world you want me to live in.'

'Why depends on who you're introducing him to.'

'Bravo. So, who?'

Lukas said, 'Alan Kest, unless you've got another candidate.'

'I can't do this,' Isaacs said abruptly. 'They're going to know it's funny. I never did it before, now all of a sudden I know people who want to be in business with them?'

'We've got to get him in there,' Lukas said. 'It's the only way you're going to get off the hook.'

'A powerful argument,' Isaacs acknowledged. He fell silent and when Lukas started to speak snapped, 'Shut up and let me think.' To Ben's surprise Lukas did.

'Okay,' Isaacs said. 'It can't be somebody who wants something

Rabbi Kest has, it's got to be somebody who *has* what he *wants*. Then I'm doing him a favor, not the other way around. If I say to him, I've got a guy here, wants to get in on your deal, what does he need that for?'

'Good thinking,' Ben said quickly, to keep Lukas from pointing out it was no more than what they already knew.

They kicked ideas around, settled on Lukas's suggestion that they use computers seized by Secret Service's electronic intelligence squad as something Sid could offer for sale as a first deal: 'Nothing crooked, just a lot of almost unused high-end computers for cheap.'

'How soon can you set that up?' Ben asked Lukas.

'My part of it shouldn't take long, a week at most. The question is, when can our man be ready.'

'Midweek next week or not much after,' Sid said. 'If Isaac thinks so, too.'

'Maybe,' Isaacs said. 'But I'm not introducing anybody until I'm a hundred percent it'll pass inspection.'

'Sooner is better than later,' Ben said. 'But Isaac's right, we can't be too careful. And we don't want to spook them by pressing too hard.'

'Do you have to?' Alan Kest's wife asked him. 'He's only a boy.'

'He disobeyed. He endangered us all. This is long overdue.'

'He's barely fourteen years old,' she said. 'And you gave them the guns yourself.' The anguish and the accusation in her voice cut deep. It made him angry.

'Consider what we're doing, how important it is. They could have ruined it all by their recklessness. He's the eldest – he's responsible.'

'He thought he was protecting you.'

Kest took his wife by the shoulders. How tired she looks, he thought: why haven't I noticed it before?

'We have to do this together,' he said, and quoted: '"And his father and mother will take hold of him and bring him out and they shall say, This is our son, he will not obey our voice." *Our* voice. It has to be both of us.'

'And if I don't want to be part of it?'

'It's for his own good. The sages tell us, a rebellious and incorrigible son is judged on account of what he may end up to be.'

His wife sighed. 'Why are we the only ones who do things this way?'

'We don't measure ourselves by others. For them, the Law is forgotten.'

'But not by us – oh no! We keep the covenant.' She sounded

indignant, but he knew she had given in. He kissed her lightly on the forehead. She had given him four strong sons, but she was still a child herself in many ways. She could be forgiven her outbursts.

She went to get the boy. He came, slowly but without protest, silent, his eyes straight ahead.

Kest assembled his other young sons and the three men who would serve as judges. They led the boy down the stairs to the basement and Kest tied his hands on either side of a column.

Kest took a leather strap and doubled and redoubled it as the Law required, bound it at the middle to make a handle.

He laid it down and went up to the boy and put his hands on the boy's shirt and ripped it off him. The boy winced with the pain of the cloth digging into him as it tore, but he didn't cry out.

Kest couldn't look at him. 'How many can you stand?' he said, and he thought: my son, my son.

The boy didn't answer.

'Eighteen, then,' Kest said. 'You're too young for more.'

He picked up the whip he'd made. It felt curiously insubstantial.

His son cried out with the first blow, and again with the second. Every time Kest brought the strap down on the boy's naked back the boy screamed, and Kest felt a sharp pain in his own hip. Good, he thought, let it hurt me as well.

By the eighth blow the boy was bloody and sobbing. He no longer had the strength to scream.

Kest was sweating, his hip a ball of pain. He was barely aware of the scene around him.

Kest raised his arm the ninth time and heard his youngest son say, 'Papa look. Dovy made in his pants.'

Kest put down the whip, as the Law decreed.

'Enough,' he said. 'Time to clean up.'

22

Ben got home later than he'd planned to find Hannah all dressed up and waiting eagerly for her baking lesson. He splashed water on his face and changed his shirt, then hustled himself and Hannah downstairs and into a cab.

Judith answered the door at Suzanne's even more tempting than he'd envisioned her – an apron protecting her dress, her cheeks pink with kitchen heat, tiny beads of dew on her forehead and upper lip.

'Sorry we're late—' Ben began, but she waved it away.

'Come, Hanneleh.'

The kitchen was large by New York standards, with room for a small table and chairs. On a counter along one wall was a marble bread board and on that a small mound of fresh dough, its glistening surface a creamy white.

'We have to hurry,' Judith said, 'because the bread has a lot to do before candlelighting time.'

Ben watched as she gave Hannah an apron, helped her dust her hands with flour, and got her started braiding a miniature loaf from inch-thick ropes of dough. Judith's own hands flew over the remaining dough, making new ropes, braiding them into compact twisted loaves, interrupting herself to help Hannah when she faltered.

'See? That wasn't hard, was it. And it's just like a little challah. Let's make a nice H-for-Hannah on top with strips of dough, and then we can put it on a baking sheet.'

She arranged her own miniature loaves carefully side by side. 'Okay, now yours.'

She guided Hannah's hands. 'There. All ready.'

'Can I put it in the oven now?'

'First we have to let the yeast inside the dough make it nice and round and fluffy.' She draped a cheesecloth over the baking sheet. 'This is to keep the goodness inside, and so it doesn't get all dry.'

She opened the oven. 'And look what's in here . . .'

Two other baking tins, each with a beautifully braided full-size loaf already golden. 'I had to start these before because big ones take longer.'

Hannah, every bit as glowing now as Judith, her face smudged with flour, turned from the oven with a huge smile. 'See, Daddy? I'm making a challah. Just like Judith.'

Suzanne and the girls, who'd been playing in Deborah and Dina's room while Hannah had her first experience as apprentice baker, come out so they could all light candles together before they went to services. The image of Judith and Hannah praying together over the candles stayed with Ben through the Sabbath services and the walk home. Then it was time to sanctify the wine. Suzanne insisted Ben say the kiddush prayer, brushing away his reluctance.

He read the passage from Genesis marking the first Sabbath, and the blessings of thanks for the wine and the hallowed day, and they all said amen. There was an ornately embroidered cloth over the bread. He lifted it to show two loaves, one large and one small – the small one marked with a letter H.

'See Hannah, there's yours,' Judith said.

'No it's not.'

'It has an H. Don't you remember?'

'Mine wasn't pretty.'

'Maybe it was prettier than you thought.'

Ben said the blessing, cut the large loaf and passed pieces around the table.

'This is delicious,' he said. It was – as good as any he could remember. 'We should try Hannah's, too. Or do you want to save it because it's your first ever? You could put it in the freezer.'

Hannah looked down at her plate.

'I think we should eat it,' he urged. 'That way everybody can see how delicious yours is, too.'

Hannah, eyes still down, shook her head. 'It's not.'

'Not what?'

'Delicious.'

'I bet it is,' Ben said. 'Can I try it and see? I'd really like to.'

'Okay,' she said, barely audible.

He tore off a small piece and tried it. 'It *is* delicious. Here, you try.' He gave Hannah a piece.

Tentatively, she tried it. Ben hoped she wouldn't spit it out, the way she sometimes did. She swallowed it without comment, but Ben thought he saw the hint of a smile, and she held out her hand for more.

After dinner, Deborah and Dina took Hannah to their room, Sara and Naomi trailing after. The grown-ups sat in the living room.

Ben couldn't resist asking Judith about Hannah's challah.

'It wasn't really hers,' Judith said. 'I baked it earlier. I was afraid you might arrive too late for even the smallest challah to rise properly and bake before Shabbat. I don't like to fib like that but I was afraid she would be very disappointed.' She smiled. 'As transgressions go, it's not a big one. I won't get many points for repenting.'

They talked about kids and religion and disappointment. It was Judith who brought the subject around to school. Deborah and Dina went to the elementary school run by Joshua's congregations.

'They love it,' Suzanne reported, 'and I do too. It would be great for Hannah.'

Ben had plenty of questions, and Suzanne was happy to answer them.

'Hannah and I should go,' Ben said finally. 'We've imposed long enough.' He stood up.

'You stay right where you are. I didn't invite you here so you'd have to travel on Shabbat. Hannah is going to sleep in the girls' room, that's all arranged. And you can stay on the couch, it folds out. Judith is sleeping in my bed, and I'll sleep in Mark's bed and we'll all be comfortable.'

She left the room without giving him time to argue.

'She's a force of nature,' he said to Judith.

'Yes, she is, and I don't advise you to oppose her.' She stood, took a step toward him. 'Is it so terrible, to spend some more time with us?'

'No, it's . . . This whole evening has been wonderful. Just watching you and Hannah in the kitchen . . .'

'It was special for me, too.'

'You seem to have a way with her, with Suzanne's girls, too. Better than a lot of mothers I've seen. But you don't—' He caught himself. 'Or do you?'

'Have children of my own? No, I don't. But I *was* a mother, in a way. My own mother didn't spare much attention for us, so I took care of myself and my three sisters. The odd thing is, I was the second youngest. Two sisters older and one very much younger, but I was the one who cared for the others. They called me *petite maman* – little mother.'

This was a new perspective. Everything else he knew about her – childhood in Morocco, school in France, law degree from Oxford, well-bred manners and elegant clothes – all spoke of a life of economic ease. 'Somehow I can't visualize you as struggling,' he reflected aloud, then hastened to add: 'I don't mean to pry.'

She ignored the disclaimer. 'We weren't without resources, if that's what you mean. We even had a governess, but the poor woman was at a terrible loss for how to deal with us four, so I ran the household. And because Mother wished us to be self-sufficient there was little we could expect from her in the way of comfort or support. For the others, providing that was my job, as well.'

'And who provided it for you?'

She shrugged. 'It seems like such a long time ago, and far away.' She was silent a moment. 'I can't begin to tell you how much pleasure I take in being with Hannah. It's as if in her I see myself as a little girl. I only hope you don't think I'm . . . intruding.'

She was standing very close, he thought.

'No, not intruding. I worry about . . . your being my student, sometimes' – as good a catch-all for his fears and misgivings as any – 'and then I tell myself I'm being silly, as long as this is about you and Hannah . . . and what can be wrong with that?'

'Nothing, I hope. I so enjoyed seeing the pleasure she took in our lighting the candles together.'

He could see it again, and the three of them tonight on the way to services and the way home, and that first Friday evening they had shared by the happy accident of Joshua's speaking at OY . . . Hannah leaning on Judith, Judith almost as close to him as she was now, close enough to inhale her scent.

And now she truly was close, the hollow of her hips radiating warmth against him, her hair fragrant, soft and silky under his hand as he bent toward her and she lifted her face to him, her lips brushing his, searching—

'Daddy! Daddy!'

They jumped apart as Hannah burst into the room. 'You have to stay over.' Rushing toward them and wrapping herself around his leg. 'You have to. Then we can wake up in the morning all together – Hannah and Daddy and Judith.'

Ben lay awake immersed in remembered sensation – Judith's lips brushing his, the smell of her skin, the heat of her body.

Eventually he fell asleep. He was awakened by five giggling little girls bearing juice, and coffee from an automatic brewer. Judith was mercifully out of sight.

They all went to Sabbath morning services together, then he and Hannah started walking across Central Park toward home. It was a sunny day, warm, a tantalizing hint of spring.

About halfway across, he could see that Hannah was too tired to make it. He bent so she could climb aboard piggyback, but he wasn't going to make it, either, if he had to carry her the whole way. At Central Park West he put her down and flagged a cab.

'Nap time,' he said when they got home.

He sat by the window in the living room, looking out at the city. There were two limousines in front of the church across the street, a white one and a black one. Balloons were tied to the white one. A wedding? They had a nice day for it.

He thought about Judith. Tried to get past playing the kiss – almost-kiss – over and over . . . Remembered how awkward he had felt seeing her in the morning and the way she had banished the awkwardness with a smile and a discreet touch on his sleeve.

'I hope you slept better than I did,' she'd said lightly.

And that had been all, that and a few quick glances, at once conspiratorial and amused. She was much better at this than he was.

Or was he imagining it all, reading meanings where there weren't any? But that moment in the living room had been real. And she had been as much a part of it as he had.

Real or not, now was the time to keep it from going further. For his own sake and for Hannah's. If he got romantically involved with Judith now Hannah would know it, and experience had taught him to beware of anything that seemed to take him away from Hannah.

23

Monday morning Ben had breakfast with Frank Lukas and Sid Levy. The undercover had spent the weekend hanging out with Isaacs, learning what he could and getting comfortable with his cover identity.

'Isaacs is still skittish about all this,' Sid reported. 'But he's going to do it, and he knows that if he screws up he's the one who gets it in the neck. So I think it's going to be all right.'

'Have you gotten anything useful out of him?' Ben asked.

'Some feel for Kest, but not a lot else. I don't think they use Isaacs for much beyond what they know he knows how to do. One thing, though – I think your idea about making points on the religion side is right. And being I'm from out of town, it makes sense I might be looking for a congregation.'

'Good,' Ben said. He looked to Lukas, who'd been listening without comment.

'Whatever works.'

'Okay,' Sid said. 'Isaacs is calling Kest to see if he can bring me by the store tomorrow to say hi.'

'We'll be there, in a surveillance van,' Lukas told Ben. 'There's room if you want to come.'

'Sure,' Ben said after a moment's hesitation. Playing agent was usually a bad idea for a prosecutor, but this was different. He was, in a way, Sid Levy's case agent. And if he had any chance at all for the job at the Treasury Department's Office of Enforcement, it might be a point in his favor to have been out on a recent operation with Treasury agents.

They straightened out the details, then Sid went off to make sure Isaacs made his phone call.

'Anything more happening with the garbage?' Ben asked Lukas as they got into the Secret Service pool car.

'We're still following it up.'

'And the foreign phone numbers?'

'Too soon for that.'

'I thought you were in a hurry. It's been a week.' But Ben knew he was pushing things.

'I'm not saying I'm happy about it. I called Cyprus this morning to put some pressure on them, and our guy out there promised to light a fire under the guy he talks to at the Israeli National Police. But you know how that is – like pushing the wrong end of a wet noodle.'

'And the other countries where we have phone numbers?'

'It's like I told you, the Israelis are big-time cooperative as these things go. Most countries figure they have more important crimes to worry about than who's counterfeiting some other country's currency. Even US currency.'

'What about the ink? Anything about that?'

Lukas shot him a hard look and occupied himself getting them out into traffic and on their way downtown.

'I'm assuming the car isn't bugged,' Ben said.

Lukas grunted, unamused.

'The Swiss are convinced it has to be an inside job,' he said, 'based on how close the chemistry of the ink is. They've started checking their people out, but the first cut is everybody looks clean – no Jewish employees, and the ink-chemistry people have all been there forever and no one's ever questioned their loyalty.'

'And if it's not an inside job?'

'Then we're dealing with somebody very good at chemical reverse-engineering. All the more reason to find out who these people are as soon as we can, before they start spreading the wealth.'

At the office, Ben sat through one of Queen Victoria's interminable unit chiefs' meetings. When it was over she asked him to stay and give her an update on the Aljo case.

She sat in her usual skeptical silence after he'd told her about Sid Levy. He knew better than to fill the void.

'I have some news for you,' she said finally. 'I hear that Reverend Walker is about to go public with two men who claim they witnessed shots being fired from the rabbi's house. I let Tim Ahl know about it, and he talked to the police. It's been agreed that the police will announce they have a significant lead and they're sure now the people on the rabbi's lawn weren't from the neighborhood, and they weren't African American.'

'That's good, if it takes the heat off. As long as the PD can withstand pressure from both sides to follow their significant lead to a quick arrest.'

'I think they expect this to make it all go away. I doubt the rabbi will want to push the police any more. They *were* doing the shooting, after all.'

But it wasn't just 'the rabbi' who was up in arms about it, Ben didn't point out. And what would happen if Siegel had a relapse?

'Something else,' she said. 'Johnny Harper is leaving us. I want you to take his job.'

Harper was one of the three deputy chiefs of the office's criminal division; his departure had been rumored forever. It was a promotion for Ben, but not one he was eager for.

'When?'

'Not till next month, but I want you to start making some case-intake decisions right away. Ken' – chief of the criminal division – 'will give you a call to get you oriented.'

'Thanks. I appreciate the vote of confidence.' Ben thought of telling her he might be leaving, too, in not too long. But despite the lunch interview with Nate Morgan he still couldn't believe he had a real shot at the Washington job, so he let it go.

'As far as this keeping you out of the courtroom,' Queen Victoria said, 'we can make some adjustments for that. For starters, you can keep this currency-counterfeiting case, if you want.'

He accepted it without comment. There was no rule saying that silence worked in only one direction.

'There's no need to settle everything right now,' she said. 'Talk to Ken, get used to the idea, then we can worry about the details.'

The surveillance van Lukas was using was a converted pickup truck with an enclosed bed. Its fiberglass canopy had smoked windows all around. Inside, it was fitted out with low benches along the sides, and bullet-deflecting ballistic blankets velcroed over the windows. Electronic equipment racks lined the forward end and two small video cameras were hung from the roof, where they could be swiveled to look out any of the windows. Illumination was a dim red light that made Ben think of submarines in the movies.

There was room enough for Ben and Lukas along one side. The tech sat across from them and gave Ben a tour of the equipment while they drove to the location and got in position. Once they were parked, the tech peeled back one of the ballistic blankets and pointed a camera out that window. He turned on a ten-inch monitor that nestled in the middle of the equipment racks and fiddled with the controls to bring in a sharp image.

The Aljo Electronics display window looked like any of the personal-electronics stores that were everywhere in the city, the tourist traps indistinguishable from the true discounters. By the angle of the picture, they were parked about four car lengths away from the entrance. Ben watched the street scene flowing by, fascinated by the mere fact of being an invisible watcher.

Lukas's cellphone warbled. 'They're coming,' he said.

Voices began to crackle from the audio system. Lukas pointed at the screen. 'There.'

It was Isaacs and Sid, walking briskly down the street, talking to each other. Ben didn't understand what was being said, realized after a few words that they were speaking Yiddish, as they had when they met.

They disappeared into the store, but the sound of their conversation continued – partly English, mostly Yiddish – as they introduced themselves and asked to see Alan Kest. Judging by tone and rhythm, everything seemed to be going all right. Then without warning the sound cut off.

The tech fiddled with the dials. 'Nothing. Either they killed his transmitter or they went into a shielded room.'

'Interesting that they have one,' Lukas said, his voice brittle behind the calm façade.

'We going to do anything?' the tech asked urgently.

'Not yet,' Lukas said. 'So far I don't see any reason to worry.' That was always the question – if an undercover lost contact unexpectedly, at what point did you kick the door down and pull him out?

'How long do you think they'll be?' The tech was clearly nervous about this.

'Could be ten minutes, could be an hour.' Lukas's coolness sounded hollow to Ben, a shell over whatever he was really thinking.

After twenty-five minutes Ben's shirt was soaked with sweat. He wanted to think it was being cooped up in the back of the truck, not concern about what might be happening in the store.

Then, as abruptly as it had died, the sound system came to life again. Three voices – Isaacs, the undercover, and a slow bass rumble that had to be Alan Kest.

Ben watched the monitor, waiting for the undercover to emerge from the store. He was surprised to see all three come out, still talking. Alan Kest looked like his pictures, broad-beamed and bearish in his white shirt and dark trousers, favoring his left hip noticeably. The only odd note was a black cowboy hat that made him look like a shaggy version of General Grant on the eve of Vicksburg.

The three men shook hands, and Kest went back into the store. Isaacs and Sid said a few words to each other and parted.

'That's it,' the tech said.

'Let's make sure he gets clear,' Lukas said, and repeated the instruction by cellphone to Rogers, who was their backup. 'See if anybody's interested.'

They followed Sid for a few blocks – the monitor showing an image from a camera in the truck's cab – then passed him and went around the block to let Rogers pick him up. Three blocks later, Rogers drove past him and they slid in behind him again. Playing leapfrog this way, they ended up at a subway station. Sid headed downstairs to the train.

'Looks okay to me,' Lukas said. 'I didn't see anybody following him. Let's head back to the barn.'

24

In the morning Lukas had more news.

'You know that cowboy hat Kest was wearing? Well it seems he's got a friend in the cattle-ranching business.'

'Rabbi Kest?'

'That's what the phone numbers are telling us. There's a whole bunch of calls, mostly from Kest's home number, to one Sheldon R. Busby, lives outside of Lubbock, Texas, president of S.B. Ranch Corporation and Scientific Breeding Associates.'

'This is for real?'

'It's not that big, as ranching companies go, but it's no Mom-and-Pop operation, either. The Scientific Breeding operation was incorporated eight years ago, and our folks in Texas tell us they have a good reputation for using high-tech breeding methods. From everything I hear it looks a hundred percent legitimate. And it makes no sense at all.'

'Friend? Relative?'

'We're checking, but I don't think Mr Busby is a major employer of religious Jews, and the calls are all to the central business switchboard. We're paying special attention to Kest's incoming calls to see if we can trace it backward.'

'Weird.'

'You bet. And we picked up something else interesting that got overlooked when this was just credit-card fraud. You know that the rabbi has a second home, up in Rockland?'

'No.'

'Centerville, New York. It's some kind of religious community across the river, about an hour up. And when he's up there Rabbi Kest has a lot of contact with one Joel Solomon, proprietor of Centerville Sports.'

'What's a lot of contact?'

'Sometimes once a visit, sometimes twice, three times a day.'

'Calls to the store?'

'And between the residences. And guess what they sell at Centerville Sports.'

'Basketballs.'

'And baseball gloves. And guns. Joel Solomon d/b/a/ Centerville

Sports is a federally licensed firearms dealer. Not exactly what you'd expect in a religious community. Do Jews hunt?'

'I doubt it. You couldn't eat what you killed, and killing God's creatures for fun . . . No, I don't think so.'

'So who's buying guns up there? And why?'

'You think that's where the guns in Brooklyn came from? From the pattern of conduct it sounds more like they're friends, fellow congregants, something like that.'

'We'll see. I have a call in to a friend at ATF. I want them to pull a standard compliance check of the dealer's records, see what they come up with about our friend Kest as a customer. I'd like to know how big the rabbi's arsenal is – at least the legally purchased part.'

'You're not worried about alerting them?'

'It's a routine check for ATF, and I'm telling them to be real careful. It shouldn't ring any alarm bells.'

That afternoon Ben had his first meeting with Ken Potter, chief of the criminal division, about beginning to do intake work on the cases that were coming into the office.

He and Freddi had been unable to figure out why Queen Victoria would want to promote him away from his strengths.

'Can you remember a single deputy division chief who had a decent reputation in the courtroom, or for running good investigations?' he'd asked her.

'One or two, but it's rare,' she'd had to concede.

Mostly, deputy division chiefs were people too good at case management to lose, but who were better off kept away from judges and juries. The only theory Ben and Freddi had come up with was that Her Majesty had a protégé she thought was ready for a unit chief's job, and Major Crimes was it.

'Mr Morgan called,' Ella told Ben after the meeting with Potter. 'He left a voice mail.'

Ben skimmed through his messages until he heard the harsh voice of Nate Morgan: 'Secretary Nelson has an unexpected opening in his schedule tomorrow. He'd like to see you.'

Just take a breath, Ben told himself, and returned the call. 'I think I can arrange to get away. What time?'

'Nine in the morning.'

Ouch. 'All right.' It was the only possible answer: Morgan didn't need to hear about his family-logistics problems. 'Nine it is.'

He called Vashti and had her put Hannah on the phone.

'I have to go away for tonight, sweetie. Do you want to go to Justine's for an overnight?' Her best friend among her classmates, and his best friends among the parents – people he could easily ask this kind of favor.

'No!' Hannah said. 'Deborah.'

'But we just went to see them on Friday, for Shabbat.'

'I want to go to Deborah's.' Her take-no-prisoners voice.

'Okay, I didn't say no. I'll call and see.'

He felt uncomfortable imposing on Suzanne twice in less than a week, but she couldn't have been more gracious.

'One more little girl I don't even notice around here. Four, five – it's the same. I'll be happy to have her.'

He told Ella he'd be leaving early and taking a day for personal business. Then he walked down the hall to Freddi Ward's office, knocked and let himself in, closing the door behind him.

'I just got a call from Washington. The Secretary wants to see me at nine in the morning.'

'Good for you. Wait—When? Tomorrow?'

'Yes, tomorrow.'

'Well, then, we'd better get to work.'

They did mock interviews in as many styles as they could think of. Ben was even less prepared than he thought. They kept at it until as close as he dared to the last Washington shuttle.

When they stopped she sat in silence a moment, regarding him with interest. 'You know what, Kaplan? There's something different about you.'

'Me? I looked the same when I shaved this morning.'

'You've lost that look of ultimate seriousness and gloom. First I thought it might be this Washington thing, but that's only part of it.' She studied him, long fingers raking hair absently back from her forehead. 'You're in love, aren't you?'

He could feel the redness rising in his neck and cheeks, the hand-in-the-cookie-jar grin tugging at his mouth.

'You *are* in love.' Shaking her head in exaggerated wonderment. 'Who?'

'It's really not . . . There's nothing . . .' He was searching for a way to put it. 'Nothing happening.'

'Nothing *happening*. But that's just the physical details.'

He sighed, an admission half to her and half to himself. 'Right.'

Her turn to grin: 'Tell!'

'Not yet.'

'I want to meet this woman,' she informed him.

'But there's nothing—'

'I still want to meet her. Maybe I can save you from a terrible mistake. Or maybe I can give her a good, hard push.' She looked at him again, more carefully. 'I'm wrong – right? It's not her, it's *you* that's not happening?' She threw a paper clip at him. 'Get out of here, Kaplan. Don't come back till you've earned my valuable concern and assistance.'

Ben had been pleased to find a hotel right on Fifteenth Street opposite the US Treasury building. As soon as he'd checked in, he went across the dark, empty street to scout out the entrance he'd be using in the morning. Then, in his hotel room, with room-service soup and sandwich on the coffee table in front of him, he went over the rules he and Freddi had made for this just hours before.

He quickly began to feel he was working too hard at it – that was one of the things Freddi had drummed into him: remember to relax. He finished eating and took a hot shower, then grabbed a beer from the minibar and tried to watch television. Surprisingly, what distracted him wasn't the interview less than ten hours away, it was the cattle breeder and the gun dealer Frank Lukas had added to the Aljo puzzle.

25

Ben was out of bed before the wakeup call. He did some quick exercises on the theory that if he got his heart pumping some oxygen might make it to his brain, then he took a long, cool shower, his mind going again to the Aljo case, wondering if the Treasury Secretary would bring it up and how much to say if he did.

He shaved carefully, not wanting to go to the interview a mass of nicks, and fussed with his hair until he realized what he was doing and laughed at his own image.

He practiced saying hello to the mirror and checked out various attentive listening expressions. Giddy? he asked himself. He was rescued by room service bringing his breakfast.

With his coffee – enough, not too much – he recited the mantra Freddi Ward had proposed: He's just a person, he's worried about keeping his job, you know more about law enforcement than he does, you're good at what you do.

'Sure I am,' he'd told her when she'd suggested the last one, 'but so far what I do hasn't included being Assistant Secretary of the Treasury.'

It was a clear day, and everything looked uncommonly vivid to him. In the dark he hadn't realized how grandly imposing the Treasury Building was, with its block-long row of towering Ionic columns – a Greek temple grown large beyond Attic dreams, stark white against the late winter sky.

Fifteenth Street sloped sharply downward from Pennsylvania Avenue, so the base of the columns was a full story above the sidewalk at the south end of the building. Glass doors framed in dull brown metal had been inserted into the stone wall, an ugly intrusion of bureaucratic reality. Mounting the broad steps from Fifteenth Street, Ben could see through the grimy glass to a metal detector and an X-ray conveyor belt that looked like they might have been transplanted from the local unemployment office.

He was scanned and then directed through a closed door to a reception station that lived up to the building's monumental exterior. Marble, brass and old wood, it sheltered two members of the Secret Service's Uniformed Division. He handed over a picture ID, careful to select his driver's license, not his Justice Department ID. The man sitting at the entry window typed him into the computer, gave him an intrigued second look, and directed him to the Secretary's office.

From the standard-issue elevator, Ben emerged into a vast hallway under a ceiling twice the height of the ones at the Southern District of New York, with strips of intricate molding ornamenting the tops of the walls. Along the corridor, magisterial stairways were flanked by marble columns.

My boy, all this could be yours some day, he couldn't help thinking. He tried to see past the grand scale of it all to the cheap modern office partitions and government-issue furniture, to remember that this was just another government job, and it would be the work and the people that mattered after the initial thrill of the setting wore off.

For all the surreal vividness of his surroundings from the moment he'd left the hotel, the interview itself passed like a fever dream. Afterward, Ben had only the vaguest idea of what most of the questions had been or how he'd answered them.

He remembered most clearly being interrupted by a phone call.

'Sorry,' the Treasury Secretary had said. 'It's the Fed chairman. This'll just be a minute.' Phone at his ear, he had swiveled his high-back leather chair so Ben couldn't see his face.

Ben had used the moment to let his eyes go to the window over Secretary Nelson's shoulder, to the view he'd been resisting since he came into the room. Framed there, like something from a postcard or a movie, was the White House, just beyond a short stretch of lawn. The folks next door.

Ben had thought: This is me, Benjamin Kaplan, sitting here with the Secretary of the Treasury and looking out the window at the White House. Being interviewed for a job that will have the occupant of this office and the resident of that house asking for my opinion about law-enforcement policy.

He had come back to full consciousness standing in the outer office. The secretary who was gatekeeper of the inner sanctum was watching him. He smiled at her and turned to walk the length of the room to the door out.

He couldn't hide completely from the knowledge that he'd badly blown at least one major question. Asked what he'd do if confronted with a rumor of Presidential or Vice-Presidential wrongdoing, he'd focused on checking out the informant and verifying the information. A good answer for a prosecutor, but not for a high cabinet official, whose first questions ought to be: Why is this on my desk? How does it affect the agencies I'm responsible for? And who should really be dealing with it?

Nelson had spent a lot of time on the issue of law-enforcement oversight. Ben thought that if he'd done well on anything it had been that, though he'd been a little vague about preserving deniability for people like the Secretary, who often didn't need or want to know the details of the problems their subordinates were handling.

He'd been trying to rescue himself from that one when the intercom warbled. Nelson had picked up the phone and listened, hung up without a word.

'I'm going to have to cut this short,' he'd said, his mind already elsewhere. 'Thanks for coming in.'

In the corridor, Ben realized he had no clear idea where he was going. Alexander Hamilton, gazing serenely off into the distance from his perch on the wall, was no help.

Ben pointed himself in the direction he remembered coming from and walked down the stone-floored corridor trying to feel at home with the tall portraits of former Secretaries. It was too soon to have any coherent idea about when he'd be here next, or whether.

I could do that job, he thought on the plane back to New York: I could be enthusiastic about it. The lunch with Nate Morgan had had a similar effect on him, though nowhere near as powerful. It was as if this interview – not just imagining himself in the job but responding to Secretary Nelson's questions and concerns right there in view of the White House – had made it all real and tangible in a way it hadn't been before. And Nelson had hinted at having difficulty getting an Under Secretary confirmed, had suggested that the new Assistant Secretary might be running the whole office by himself. 'For a limited period,' but still . . .

Lukas had beeped him while he was in transit. He returned the call as soon as he hit the office.

'We're getting closer,' Lukas informed him. 'It turns out Alcohol Tobacco and Firearms is already working a case in Centerville – a ring that steals firearms shipments in transit from the manufacturer.'

'Is the gun dealer – Solomon – involved?'

'They're not sure. They're thinking maybe as a fence.'

'Any connection to our targets?'

'That's what I want to find out. Right now, I'm guessing it's all one thing and the guns aren't being stolen for resale, they're for their own use.'

'What for?' Ben asked, though he knew what Lukas would say.

'To protect their counterfeiting plant. My main worry right now is that ATF's poking around up there enough to put our targets on guard.'

'How far along is the ATF investigation?'

'They've opened an active case in General Crimes. Can you roll it into ours some way, so we can keep it from getting out of control?'

'I'll see what the status is here.' Ben didn't expect any problems moving the case. Queen Victoria wouldn't want some junior prosecutor in General Crimes in a position to screw up the Aljo case any more than Ben or Lukas did. Still, until that was taken care of it might be smart to put off telling her about Washington.

He climbed the stairs to his second-floor classroom at NYU thinking about guns and rabbis. Lukas might have a powerful reputation for his investigative instincts, but they had no evidence yet that the pieces all went together, much less that Kest was actually running a counterfeiting plant. Ben wanted to know more.

It was just as well being distracted this way, he thought. It muted the tension of having Judith in his classroom.

He watched the class file in, in twos and threes, finding their way to their seats, fussing with their backpacks and their laptops, gossiping. Judith's chair stayed empty. He wondered if she had reconsidered her rashness and was avoiding the class to let the memory fade.

Some students came down to the front of the room to ask him questions. He was abrupt with them – not his usual style – and saw one of them react with an almost comic take.

'Sorry,' he said, 'I'm preoccupied right now. Try talking to me after class.'

He pulled the textbook from his briefcase and let it drop onto the lectern with a thud – his way of announcing that class had begun. 'Okay,' he said, 'let's talk about some more exceptions to the Hearsay Rule.'

The door opened and Judith came in. He watched her find her seat, waiting for his pulse to slow. Finally, he found his voice and began, telling himself the class would think his paralysis had been silent reproach for the latecomer.

26

In the morning, Ben stopped on the way to the office to meet with Sid and Lukas to go over plans for Sid's next meeting with Alan Kest. The computers were ready for delivery – only nine where they'd planned fifteen, but all of them fully loaded, with a CPU that wasn't yet obsolete.

'Not exactly an impressive first showing,' Sid grumbled. 'But I suppose it'll have to do. If I didn't know better I'd say somebody was trying to sabotage me.'

'This is a just a calling card,' Ben jumped in to say before Lukas could respond. 'Try to stress quality.'

'Easier if the quality were better.'

'Next time we'll have a stronger selection,' Ben assured him, 'even if we have to go out and buy the stuff.'

They did a quick run-through of the emergency rescue procedures Lukas had worked out.

'A waste of effort,' Sid said. 'They're not going to hijack me for nine computers. Not these nine computers.'

Ben couldn't keep his mind on the case-intake files he found waiting on his desk. He broke early for lunch and stopped by Freddi Ward's office. She was on the phone, chair swiveled toward the window, looking out. The light framed her chiseled features, backlit her mane of hair.

'Hello stranger,' she said when she'd hung up.

'Hardly a stranger.'

'You are if you don't count the time I spend coaching you for your secret ventures.'

'Not so secret any more.' Not since he was vetted for the meeting with Secretary Nelson and passed into the building. 'Everybody in Secret Service knows by now, or will soon.' He wondered if Lukas knew already.

'Our good Queen Victoria doesn't take kindly to having her employees sneak around on her, as I recall. You ought to tell her before she hears it from somewhere else.'

'Good point.' The General Crimes unit chief was due in his office after lunch to talk about the ATF case in Centerville. He'd have to risk waiting until after that.

'Are you going to tell me how it went?'

'That's why I'm here. And to say thank you and buy you lunch.'

He took them further afield than usual, to a bright, high-ceilinged restaurant that at night drew a crowd of uptowners trying for a downtown edge, but was relaxingly empty at lunch.

She looked around. 'Washington must have really gone well.'

'I'm not the one to ask.' He told her about it. With Freddi, he didn't have to leave out his excitement seeing the White House out the window, and his growing enthusiasm for the job.

'Have you talked to Harry Butler about it?'

'This morning. He says they're down to me and one other serious candidate, and a lot depends on the interviews.'

'And?'

'He hasn't heard.'

'Sounds like good odds, anyway.'

'Maybe. The timing couldn't be worse, though.' He couldn't imagine letting go of the Aljo case at this point. 'I'm worried about Hannah,' he admitted. 'It'll take me away from her. I won't be able to come home every night at six like clockwork' – earlier on winter Fridays – 'And I'm worried about disrupting this comfortable world we've spent three years creating. It's taken her so long to feel even a little bit safe.'

'She'll adjust,' Freddi said. 'She's almost six. They're so resilient at that age.'

'The expert speaks.'

'Hey I have some nieces, you know.' She looked at him. 'I bet you're worried about yourself, too. You'll need a whole new support system.'

Freddi was right, he saw. He had established a pattern of living here, if not exactly what people called a *life*. And there was his new connection with Joshua, and the feeling of community he was beginning to develop. And Judith. What about Judith? The unresolved intimacy of their Friday night and Saturday morning had kept her in his mind ever since. Even now, thinking of it made his mouth tingle where her lips had touched his.

'I know what it really is,' Freddi divined. 'It's your new love interest.'

He flushed. 'Caught me.'

'Well . . .'

He told her everything about Judith he could think of. She listened in uncharacteristic silence.

'I was right,' she said when he was done. 'You *are* in love.' She raised her iced-tea glass. 'Here's to really living your life.' They touched glasses.

'When I was in high school,' she said, 'I had a big sixteenth birthday party, and my boyfriend gave me a silver key ring from a famous jewelry store, and attached to it was a small silver disk. On one side it said *Safe* and on the other side it said *Alive*, and the idea was you could have one or the other in life but not both.

'I kept the key ring a lot longer than I kept the boyfriend, and I lost the key ring a long time ago. But I still have the idea, and I think it applies here. As the shoe people say, just do it.'

She raised her glass again ceremonially, then lowered it.

'With one exception,' she amended. 'I do think you need to be careful how public you are, for now – for the law school, and for the Treasury job.'

He laughed. 'You make it sound so simple.'

'Well, I'll admit it may take some doing, moving it along and keeping it quiet at the same time.'

'I have some news, too,' she said later, picking at her salad. 'I had a chat with Her Majesty about transferring back to Organized Crime.'

'That *is* news. I thought you'd burned out on all that.'

'Just the Five Families part of it. And I need a change.'

'I didn't know you were unhappy.'

'Not yet. But just between us chickens, I'm not about to work for the creep who's replacing you as unit chief.'

Walking back to the office, she said, 'You know, I was so tickled that someone finally broke through that shell of yours that I forgot my first and most basic instinct. I don't want you to do a single thing more until I've met this woman and given you the high sign.'

He protested, but he knew he'd have to give in. And there was even a good way to do it.

'How about coming to Sabbath dinner tomorrow? It's short notice but it's getting to be almost a tradition for Judith and Hannah, and with chaperones we can do it at my place, assuming Judith can make it.' He noticed Freddi hesitating. 'Your date is invited, too, if you think he'll survive all that domesticity.'

She laughed. 'I'll tell him it's an anthropology expedition.'

As soon as they got back, Ben called Judith and left a message inviting her to Friday dinner. Then he sat down with the General Crimes unit chief and the Assistant who'd been assigned the ATF case in Centerville.

'It started with a missing shipment from a firearms manufacturer,' the Assistant told him.

The package had been fine as far as the freight company's regional terminal, where the company separated local from long-distance. Tracking numbers had traced it from there to the airfreight terminal, odd because the delivery address had been well within the area the freight company defined as local – truck delivery, no need for an airplane. From there the package had disappeared.

The theory was that someone at the regional terminal had put on a new address label, but for some reason the original tracking numbers hadn't been obscured, so the package had stayed in the computer until it got to the air-freight terminal and somebody there had covered the tracking numbers or more likely substituted new ones.

'ATF went to work on who had access to the crate at the two terminals, and then they tried to find anything that might connect anyone on the access list from terminal one with anyone on the access list from terminal two. The best they could do was a pair of part-time workers on the loading docks – one at each terminal – who both once lived in Brooklyn and now live in the same town out in the suburbs. Centerville, NY. Rockland County.'

'Okay. Then what?'

'The database turned up a federally licensed firearms dealer in Centerville, and he *also* had once lived in Brooklyn.' The Assistant made a face. 'Him and two-plus million others. But when they ran a check of the firearms dealer's local customers in Centerville, they turned up a guy with the same last name as one of the freight loaders, turns out to be his cousin. That's when they brought it to us. They wanted subpoenas for the phone records of all the people involved. Some of the records have come in, and I assume ATF is following them up; the others are still being awaited. That's where it stands, as far as I know. The connections make it look like the guns may be going via the cousin to the gun dealer for resale, but we need a lot more before we can be sure that's even what's going on. It's not a case I expect to be ripe for indictment any time soon.'

'Okay, great. Thanks for coming in. I need to say a few words to your unit chief, he'll let you know what's happening.'

He told the unit chief he wanted to combine the case with a related, ongoing case in Major Crimes and asked him to have the Assistant collect the case materials, write up a summary and deliver it as soon as he could.

That done, Ben put in a call to the ATF case agent to give him the news that the case was being moved and ask him to come in with an update on his progress.

He camped out at Queen Victoria's office until she could see him. He led with the new developments in the Aljo case. He could tell by how attentively she listened that she was as intrigued as he was, not just by the connections that were turning up but by the gaps that remained. She agreed immediately that ATF's Centerville case had to be merged into Aljo.

'That's the kind of decision you'll be making yourself as deputy division chief,' she said, 'though I suppose for appearance's sake if it involves one of your own cases it's smart to have Ken or me sign off on it.'

It was the kind of decision he'd be making as Assistant Secretary of the Treasury, too, it occurred to him: Which of two Treasury law-enforcement agencies should be lead agency when they each had been working on cases that turned out to be different legs of the same beast?

He made as short work as he could of telling her about his interview for the Washington job. Mercifully, her annoyance seemed tempered by the realization that it could be useful to have an ally at Treasury's Office of Enforcement.

27

Joshua's study sessions were cancelled that night so everyone could celebrate Purim, the holiday marking the Biblical Queen Esther's defeat of a plan to annihilate the Jews of ancient Persia. Joshua had urged Ben to bring Hannah to the party at his school. 'She can see her friends, and maybe I'll get a chance to show you around.'

The school occupied the townhouse next door to Joshua's West Side synagogue. When they arrived, the party was already in full swing, in a gymlike room that took up almost the whole top floor. In the Purim tradition, the kids were all in costumes – many Queen Esthers among the superwomen and witches and high-fashion models. Some of the boys had come as Queen Esther's uncle Mordecai or as the King. There were even a few contrarians dressed as the archvillain, Haman.

Hannah looked for Deborah, found her in a group of little girls in variations of Hannah's own royal costume – all wearing crowns and carrying scepters.

'Are you Queen Esther, too?' Deborah asked.

'No! I'm Queen Vashti,' Hannah said with great pride.

'So am I,' Suzanne said, herself quite regal. 'I like how she stood up to the king.'

'My *nanny* is Vashti,' Hannah announced. She'd been exclaiming for days over the discovery that a character in the Biblical drama had the same name as the woman who took care of her. Ben had noticed it when he first hired Vashti but never asked about it, just assumed it was a common Persian name.

He was looking around for Judith, not seeing her.

'She's not here,' Joshua said, coming up out of the crowd, robed as either good Mordecai or evil Haman, Ben couldn't tell which. 'But I'm glad you are. If you can wait awhile, I'll give you that tour.'

When Joshua could get away, he led Ben downstairs to see the school's classrooms and cafeteria, all the while enthusing about the school's teachers and its academic program. They ended up in a small teachers' lounge furnished like a cozy living room.

'Let's sit down, take a rest,' Joshua proposed.

With evident relief he sloughed off his robes. Underneath he was wearing jeans and a white T-shirt. His compact body was even more muscular than Ben had guessed, with the lumpy shoulders and barrel chest of a wrestler or a weightlifter. Ben thought of Elliot Rosen – Rabbi Terminator, they called him at FLEOA, for his karate black belt and his fascination with danger – and wondered if athletic rabbis were some sort of trend.

'Do you wear that under your ceremonial robes, too?' Ben asked.

'It's a throwback to the habits of my youth,' Joshua said, smiling, 'when I learned the spiritual value of physical work.'

'Is that part of training to be a rabbi?'

Joshua laughed. 'Hardly. It was part of my own days of spiritual questing – not exactly the same as yours but not wholly different, either. That's one of the reasons I respond to you the way I do – your struggle in life means something extra to me because I recognize it so well.'

'I wouldn't have guessed,' Ben said. He tried to read the face hidden by the brown beard and the aura of spiritual command. Saw blue eyes full of energy and knowingness, pale cheeks, plump red lips. 'You look like you've always known just where you are.'

'I've always felt I had a special affinity for the Law. But as a boy it was confusing because I wasn't happy about what I saw around me.'

'Like the synagogue you described in your talk at OY'

'Exactly. It passed for true observance and belief, but it was false.'

'It sounded just like the one I went to as a kid. But it had a different effect on you.'

'Not really. It pushed me away, too. So I went to Israel and worked on a farm. Went into the desert and fasted. Joined the army. When I was ready I came back.'

'And then what?'

'I looked for the real thing. Eventually I heard about this obscure but very learned rabbi from the Old Country, not exactly Hasidic but not straight Orthodox, either. Rebbe Yaacov Moshe Friedlander. So I went to his prayer hall and saw him and heard him speak, and I knew that was where I wanted to be. I wanted to go up to him afterward and ask how I could learn his teachings and become a member of his congregation, but I didn't think I could even get close – there were all these men around him, security guards, precisely to keep people like me from bothering him.

'I was standing there, knowing I had to talk to him somehow, and he looked over and saw me and made a gesture for the others to let me through. And he said to me, "You have come here to learn."

'I was speechless, all I could do was nod yes. Because I could just as easily have been there to ask him to pray for my sick mother.

And he said, "If you are sincere, I will teach you." That very day I became his disciple, and I was still learning from him the day he died, more than twenty years later.

'Many times since that first day I've asked myself, How did I know to keep looking? And how can I help others find the right way for themselves?'

'Is that why you wrote your books?'

'Yes, because I saw that this was a time when people were ready for a return to Judaism and Jewish practice, and they needed guidance. Why be Jewish? Why be observant?'

The old post-war answer – that to diminish the number of Jews in the world was to grant Hitler a posthumous victory – had long ago lost its power, Joshua said: In the last moments of the century people were coming back to Judaism from Buddhism, from all kinds of New Age practices and beliefs, from pure atheistic or agnostic secularism, because they were unsatisfied with their lives and they remembered or sensed that the old traditions offered the possibility of peace, safety, joy.

'But between that insight and the true reward is a lot of hard work that has to be undertaken for its own sake, not because it offers answers.'

'That almost sounds like a pitch for blind faith.'

'Just the opposite. I'm saying that even the wisest of us can never truly understand the mind of haShem, so you shouldn't feel that you need to form some image of what God is – certainly not right away, and maybe not ever. That's a point I can't make strongly enough – the questions never end, but you don't have to hurry for the answers, especially to the really big questions. For someone like you the hardest thing may be accepting that the intellect is not the best way to approach God.'

'You're right. It's not clear to me what there could be besides understanding on the one hand and blind faith on the other.'

'There are many ways to see. You have to be open to whatever appears, however it becomes visible to you. It's true that your vision can be sharpened by study, but much more than that by practice, by following the commandments. And the heart of everything is to be steadfast in that.'

'Okay, that seems possible,' Ben said. 'But if practice is the foundation of understanding, and everything flows from that, how do you reconcile Sabbath-observant Jews who are transgressors in their daily lives?'

Joshua sighed. 'I admit it's a paradox – sometimes good Jews can seem to be bad people. You must see a lot of bad people in your work. Even bad Jews.'

The startled reaction Ben couldn't quite suppress made Joshua laugh. 'It's from Judith. She tells me that besides a professor you're a prosecutor of white-collar criminals, and that you're very important in that work. That you have a very high rank. True?'

'Yes.'

'How did you come to be doing that? I mean, not "I went to law school and clerked for judge so-and-so." What inside you gave you the fire it took to do that, and do it so well?'

'I like the work, the challenge of it.' For some reason, the question made Ben uneasy. 'I like thinking I make the world a cleaner, better place, safer for the law-abiding citizen.'

'Yes, but *inside*, what does it feel like there?' Joshua's eyes were locked on Ben's, the intensity of his interest almost palpable. 'It's so very important for you to understand the spiritual dimension of it.'

Ben was still struggling with his uneasiness, but Joshua's focused attention was impossible to resist. Besides, Ben told himself, if you're looking for guidance you need to surrender at least a little to the methods of your guide.

'I want to get the bad guys,' he said. 'I see good, honest people struggling, and then I see crooks of every stripe prospering, and it makes me angry. Furious. And, doing what I do, I can change some of that. I can make sure that some of the crooks don't prosper.'

'It really does make you angry, I can see it, it almost makes you glow.'

Ben laughed. 'I don't know about glowing, but it does make me angry.'

Joshua said, 'There's a concept – a mystical concept originally, but you hear it a lot now – tikkun olam. It means repairing the world. When we talk about repairing the world we think about doing the mitzvot, about good deeds, and about teshuva. But getting the bad guys is a part of it, too, and sometimes' – with a twinkle – 'a little anger is good fuel for repairing things.'

'Seeing what I see every day,' Ben said, 'it's easy to get angry. When people get away with criminal behavior it's a mockery of everyone who trusts in living honestly.'

'Like you.'

'Yes. I really do believe in honesty and fair play.'

Joshua regarded him thoughtfully. 'Can I suggest something?'

'Sure, go ahead.'

'Is it possible that in hating the transgressor the way you do, you're hiding from yourself that you're also jealous? That the transgressor within you wants some of those same things but can't have them? And at the same time another part of you also hates that *internal* transgressor, every bit as much as you hate the one you prosecute.'

Ben wanted to protest, but he heard truth in what Joshua was saying and was intrigued as much as he was repelled.

'If it's there,' Joshua went on, 'your spiritual development demands that you recognize it and come to understand it. You need to *know* the part of yourself that wants to try everything, to have everything – know it, live with it, and accept it – in order, ultimately, to master it. To keep it from mastering you.'

'I don't know . . . I never thought of it that way.'

'Then you're ahead already,' Joshua said. 'Because the first step in all spiritual progress is to break the mold of previous thought.'

28

Friday morning Ben met Sid and Lukas at the dry fountain overlooking the 79th Street boat basin. A fine rain on the edge of freezing gave them privacy.

'Kest's a character, that's for sure,' Sid reported. 'He's, what, sixty-three on his driver's license, and the arthritis makes him seem older, and he's got this genial-grandpa manner, but you can see he's thinking every minute. I bet, the chips are down, he's one tough bastard.'

'How is he with you?' Ben asked. 'Any danger signals?'

'Not so far. He wants to do more business. Made me promise again the computers weren't hot, though. I told him hey, I lucked into a law firm that went belly-up from expanding too fast, I have all the paperwork if you want to see it. So he just dropped it.'

'He believed you?' Lukas wanted to know.

'Not for a minute.'

'Anything about how you're spending the weekend?' Ben asked.

'As a matter of fact, yes. I told him I had a congregation near me. That it wasn't my style, but good enough. "You have to come have Shabbat by us sometime," he said, and I said, "Great, I'd love to."'

'What's next?'

'I told him I could get some laptops. He wants to see a sample.'

'Fast work,' Lukas said. Ben thought there was a hint of censure in his tone.

Sid heard it, too. 'I don't think it's too fast. I played it the way I felt it. I think it's okay.'

'Let's hope.' Lukas didn't sound convinced.

'Something else you should know about,' Ben told the undercover. 'These people may be dealing in guns. You ought to keep your eyes open for anything like that.' He told what he knew about the ATF case in Centerville. 'We don't have much on it yet, so anything you can add is going to help.'

'It's a secondary issue for now,' Lukas put in. 'The important thing is to get close to Kest and find out what you can. This is still about currency counterfeiting.'

* * *

Ben and Lukas watched Sid walk off into the rain, then they headed down into the underground garage. Ben expected an argument from Lukas about how they were dealing with Sid, but there was nothing.

On the way downtown, Lukas said, 'Those Israeli phone numbers? We heard from Cyprus. The Israeli National Police are interested, too. They want to know what we're after. It seems some of those folks are known to them. People with links to Russian mafiya types.'

'That's interesting.'

'More than you think, maybe. Russians in Israel are among the top sources of counterfeit US currency.'

'Really?'

'Really. And this adds a new element to some things we found in the garbage from Kest's store. There were a couple of bubble-wrap envelopes from Israel with "books" written on the Customs declaration, and you could see they'd held something book-shaped. Which could have been books. Or it could have been bricks of counterfeit notes.'

'In the garbage? Thanks for keeping me up to date.'

'You want me to tell you about things before we know what they are?'

'Considering the disaster that garbage run turned into, I'd think you'd want to advertise every possibility, by way of justifying it if nothing else.'

'This was just a couple of envelopes from Israel until the fax from Cyprus.'

'You think Isaac's bogus hundred came from Israel?'

'It's looking possible,' Lukas said.

'Then what happens to your theory that Kest is buying guns to protect the counterfeiting plant?'

'That's possible, too. Just because I like to connect the dots doesn't mean I only see one picture.' Lukas looked at him. 'That's what you thought, isn't it?'

Ben didn't answer.

'You've got to watch that,' Lukas said, pulling up to drop Ben off in Foley Square. 'You can get in trouble jumping to conclusions about people.'

After work, Ben took advantage of the lengthening days to get in a quick shower before candlelighting time, in the hope that the rushing water would wash away some of his pre-dinner-party anxiety. While he dressed, Hannah put out the fresh-baked challahs that Judith had dropped off earlier. The table was already set by Vashti for five.

The food was on the stove keeping warm, thanks also to Vashti. Everything was ready but the wine, the best-pedigreed kosher wine he'd been able to find, a classified Great-Growth Bordeaux. He'd just pulled the cork on the second bottle when the doorman rang to say Ms Ward and friend had arrived.

Freddi's date – Russ, no last name offered – was like a lot of her beaux: pleasant, good-looking, younger. As usual, Freddi seemed completely in control. While Ben was greeting them and taking their coats, the doorman rang again with Judith.

Before Ben could complete the introductions, Hannah took Judith's hand and said, 'Want to see my room?' Tugging her down the hall without waiting for an answer.

They all followed on an excursion that featured Hannah's room, Hannah's bed, Hannah's drawings, photos of Hannah, even Hannah's bathtub alligator – the full tour of Hannah-land.

Ben was getting everyone seated for dinner when Hannah rushed off with a shout of *wait!* and galloped back a moment later carrying a silver picture frame Ben was afraid he recognized.

'This is my mommy,' Hannah said, handing the picture up to Judith. 'Only she's in Heaven.'

'She's very pretty,' Judith said, breaking what seemed to Ben like a stunned silence. 'Thank you for showing us. But now we have to pay attention to your daddy so he can say kiddush.'

She handed the picture to Ben. Not wanting to leave the room, he found space for it on the sideboard.

He was upset enough to stumble on the Friday evening blessings over wine and bread, but once he was past that – and a glass of wine – everything smoothed out. Hannah sat next to Judith and kept up a constant line of patter but made no further scenes right up to the point where food and excitement got the better of her and she put her head down on the table and went to sleep.

'It's not the company,' Ben assured the others. He carried her into the bedroom and helped her into her pajamas and bed.

When he got back to the dining room, Freddi and Judith were locked in a debate about the jurisdictional reach of international war-crimes tribunals. Ben knew well Freddi's merciless sharpness, and she wasn't holding back. Judith's voice was softer than Freddi's and her delivery more measured, but she was no less tenacious in argument.

Russ finally called a halt. 'How about some mercy on a poor ignorant guitar player?'

After dinner, Freddi and Judith insisted on clearing the table together, making many trips with long pauses in the kitchen, laughing about something.

'Good guests don't overstay their welcome,' Freddi said when the dishwasher was loaded. 'Let's go, Russ my boy.'

It was the moment Ben had been eager for, yet dreading. What would Judith do? What did he want her to do?

'Coats in the bedroom?' Freddi asked. 'I should remember, shouldn't I? It's the wine. Good wine.'

'I'm glad you liked it. Coats are in the hall closet.'

'So they are. But you know what, I think I left my purse in the bedroom. Come help me look for it.'

'That was subtle,' he said quietly as they crossed the living room.

'Well, I'm too sated with food and drink to be clever. She's terrific. You don't deserve her, you reclusive misanthrope. Don't let her go.'

She reached the bedroom door and turned around.

'What about your purse?'

'It's in my coat.'

Judith and Russ were standing by the front hall closet, Judith drying her hands with a dishtowel while they talked.

'Okay,' Freddi announced, 'we can let these nice people be by themselves now.'

'I'll come down with you,' Judith said, heading for the kitchen. 'Just let me get my things.'

'Are you sure? Russ and I aren't the greatest company at this hour. And you'll want to say good night to Hannah.'

'I'll only take a second, and Ben will come with me so I can say good night to him, too.'

On the way to Hannah's room Judith said, 'Thank you for inviting me. I had a wonderful time.'

'I'm glad you could be here. It's over much too soon.'

'Yes it is. I hope there'll be more.'

He wanted to touch her – affection, not sex, he told himself. Just to touch her hair or her shoulder. But he felt ungainly and awkward.

They stood close to each other in the doorway looking at Hannah.

'Daddy?' Hannah was in the state of semi-sleep she sometimes woke to when he looked in on her. 'Kiss g'night?'

'Sure sweetie. Judith, too.'

They went over to the bed and Hannah tilted her head for them to kiss her, then fell instantly asleep.

'I like your friend Freddi very much,' Judith told him as they headed back. 'She's so intelligent and amusing, and she has a good heart.'

'She likes you, too. I suppose you know she was checking you out.'

'That was clear from the start. She's very protective of you. I think she's getting ready to marry us off.'

'Well . . .' There was a clever response to that but he had no idea what.

'I'm surprised that you and she haven't been together romantically,' Judith said. 'She's very beautiful, and not that much older than you. Or am I mistaken?'

'No, you're right, we haven't . . . It's . . . we met at the office, for one thing, and it was right after my wife . . . died. There wasn't any possibility. And we got to be friends right away. Good friends. And that's how we like it.'

'It sounds very nice. The way I was brought up, I didn't learn about having that kind of friend.'

'No time like the present.' It seemed like a safe thing to say.

'Sorry to be so long,' Judith said to Freddi and Russ.

'It's okay,' Freddi said. 'But you don't have to—'

'Time to go,' Russ interrupted pointedly.

Ben walked them all to the elevator, which arrived far too quickly.

29

Back in the apartment, so recently full of conversation and laughter, he felt abandoned and adrift. He picked up the few glasses and plates that had missed the general cleanup, brought them into the kitchen.

One of the glasses had a lipstick imprint on the rim – Judith's. He explored it with a fingertip, resisted the silliness of touching it to his own lips.

The loneliness of the party giver, he thought. He didn't even get to hope he'd get lucky and not have to go home alone. He was already home – and he was always alone. Except for Hannah, his one solace, his one true love.

This is dumb, he told himself: you had too much wine, it's making you maudlin.

He started washing pots and pans, his mind on the moment with Judith in Hannah's doorway, then their walk back to the living room. Why had Judith said what she did – *I think she's getting ready to marry us off* – and then immediately switched to the question about Freddi and him as a couple? Was she testing something? His reaction to the word 'marry'? His availability?

Over the sound of running water, he heard the doorbell. Rushed to the door, barely taking time to turn off the kitchen faucets, heart going like mad. Dumb, dumber, dumbest: *it's not her.*

'Who's there?'

'It's Judith. I forgot something.'

He pulled the door open, expecting the three of them, the elevator waiting to take them back down.

Only Judith. The elevator door closed.

He stood there in a state of . . . 'Come in,' he remembered to say.

As she came in he closed the door. 'Are they waiting downstairs?'

She didn't say anything. She was looking into his eyes, motionless.

He felt flushed all over, and chilled. His chest was rising and falling slowly, his inhalations very deep and – he realized – in rhythm with hers.

Nothing changed for a long time. Each breath, each blink of his eyes was attenuated. A drop of sweat rolled down his spine. With it, a shudder of apprehension – it had been so long . . .

In a corner of his mind were movie images of new lovers tearing off their clothes in a frenzy. This was different.

He lifted a finger to touch her cheek. As he did, she caught his hand lightly, her eyes not wavering from his.

She turned his hand to kiss his palm. He felt the warmth and softness of her lips, the tiny wet touch of the tip of her tongue tracing his lifeline. The warmth of exhalation on his skin.

His free hand cupped her cheek, stroked her hair, drew her closer so he could inhale the scent of her skin and breathe soft warm air onto the slope of her throat, into the delicately graceful curves of her ear.

His hand moved over the smoothness of her cheek and neck, pushed up into her rich thick hair, fingers tangled there tightly as finally he pulled her mouth to his.

And then the frenzy, after all. Clothes were an almost malicious barrier, growing new clasps, hooks, zippers everywhere to thwart and tantalize as he rushed to see smell taste hear touch all of her in a state that balanced the most vivid sensitivity with the blindest oblivion.

He felt her hands on him, deliciously cool, her arms, the pressure of her legs, heard her voice, incoherent, demanding.

Then, abruptly, she was clinging to him, arms and legs so tight around him he couldn't move.

'What's wrong?' he said.

'We have to stop,' she said between harsh breaths.

'All right,' he said, aching for her. 'Whatever you want.'

Her grip loosened. 'It's not what I want. But we must stop.'

She rolled away from him and gathered her clothes to her in sudden modesty. He made himself look away while she hurried to the bathroom to dress. Quickly he got up and pulled his own clothes back on, jarringly aware of Hannah just down the hall, the possibility of her coming in. Not knowing what to make of this, his head too abuzz to form clear thoughts.

When Judith came back they sat on the couch. She spoke in the same soft voice, her head down, tracing patterns on the couch with a fingertip.

'I shouldn't have come back.'

'I'm glad you did,' he said.

'I so wanted to be with you.' Her finger touched the back of his hand. 'But we have to talk.'

'Should we exchange vows of good health?' he asked, forcing a smile. 'I'm ready.'

Medical history was an easy subject for him: for three years now he'd been a poster boy for abstinence. He didn't want the details of her history, just an assurance that everything was all right. But he could tell that being careful wasn't the only thing on her mind, and he said so.

'I've never wanted to be with someone the way I want to be with you,' she responded, 'but it has to be right. I can't do it casually.'

'There's nothing casual about this for me.' He couldn't help feeling hurt by the suggestion. 'I haven't thought of being with anyone since Laura died.'

'I apologize. I didn't mean to imply you were treating this lightly.'

Sitting next to him, she was immobile, both her hands holding one of his. 'There's so much,' she said. 'So much we don't know about each other.'

She traced a line on his palm where she had kissed him, her head down, a curtain of dark hair obscuring her face.

'Your wife, your beautiful wife,' she whispered, barely audible. 'So sad for Hannah, and for you.' A tear fell on her fingertip and trickled onto his hand.

He lifted her face so he could kiss the wetness on her cheeks, then he drew her to him. He was aware only of heat and the rhythms of her breathing.

After a time they began to talk. About Laura, and Hannah, about his fear of putting Hannah through another loss . . . And about Judith – so different from Laura, he thought: dark to her light, a deep clear pool to her quicksilver brook . . .

'It's so important to me, if I'm going to be with someone, that he understand what I believe,' she said, 'and be comfortable with it. And yet my own beliefs and practice are changing every day. Joshua has opened new doors, brought me closer to full observance than I've ever been, and I still have a long way to go.'

'And I have even longer,' Ben said. 'But I'm learning. And I'm enjoying it, though I'd be surprised if I ever get all the way to full observance.' And he didn't want to feel blackmailed into it.

'I'm not asking that. Just that you respect and honor what I chose to do. And what you do shouldn't be because you want to make love to me, that's not what I mean.'

'Until now, it hasn't been.'

'You're angry. I don't blame you.'

'I'm not angry, I'm frustrated. Not that way,' he hurried to add, then laughed. 'Well, that way, too.'

She leaned over to kiss him gently. 'Both of us.'

They talked more, about childhood disappointments and youthful escapades, books they loved and movies they didn't, the things they might have talked about on the dates they'd never had, until they could barely keep their eyes open.

'Will you stay?' he asked her.

'I can't. You know that.'

He did, though his reasons weren't hers. Even now, he was worried they'd awakened Hannah, that she would call out to him or come out into the living room to investigate the voices or to get a kiss or a glass of water.

'But how will you get home?'

She laughed, a response to the distress in his voice. 'I'm not going home, remember? I'm staying with friends around the corner.'

'Of course.' She'd hardly be riding in a cab or handling money: violating the Sabbath – punishable by death, as Ben had ample reason to remember – had to be far more culpable than unmarried sex. He didn't even know where the prohibition against fornication might be found, or if there was one. Adultery, yes, but that was different. And didn't he remember something from the Bible about betrothal by having sex, if both parties were available for marriage?

Whatever the religious-rules status of what they'd almost done, in the secular world it could only mean trouble: complications, heartache, the risk of pain . . . yet despite all that he already burned to see her again, even before she was gone.

30

He was dead asleep until Hannah coaxed him into the day.

'I made cereal,' she informed him. 'For you, too.'

This was a rare event, only the second time since she'd been given permission to take her own cereal on Saturday mornings if Daddy was sleeping late.

'Okay, I'll be right there.'

He washed up quickly and put on a robe: his morning shower could wait. It would only wake him up, and wakefulness didn't strike him as a desirable state: he wanted to cling to the fading wisps of the night before.

He sat down next to Hannah at the counter in their narrow kitchen. His bowl, unsurprisingly, was brimful of milk, the white surface barely broken by a small island of wet flakes, a few others drifting forlornly like boats cast adrift. Hannah had otherwise done a reasonably neat job, though the paper towels she'd used to sop up the overflow remained a damp white lump at the back of the counter.

Hannah was intent on her cereal, making swirling patterns with her spoon in the mush. Without looking up, she said, 'Was Judith here last night?

Oops. 'Sure she was. And Freddi was too, and Freddi's friend. We all had dinner together.'

'Noooo. Last *night*. I was in bed and I heard you and Judith.'

'When we came in to kiss you good night?'

'After that.'

What tangled webs we weave . . . 'Well, she came back to get something she forgot, and we sat and talked for a while. Maybe you heard that.'

'Maybe,' Hannah said, and went back to making patterns in her cereal.

As he cleaned up the dinner-party mess Hannah tagged along, playing helper. And she had a serious subject to discuss.

'I want to go to Deborah's school.'

'Don't you like it where you are?'

'I hate it.'

Dumb question. 'The school year's almost over.'

'I want to go now!'

'You don't know anybody there.'

'Do so! Deborah.' Triumphant.

'That's only one.'

She reeled off a list of unfamiliar names, friends of Deborah and Dina's no doubt, kids she'd met at their house and he didn't know where else.

'They learn different things from your school.'

'I know. They have Hebrew. Deborah says it's easy.'

Hebrew. Though he knew kids were supposed to pick up languages best at an early age, he wasn't sure how he felt about it for Hannah, whose attention span was not the best. Especially with a different alphabet, words running right to left . . .

But she *was* unhappy where she was. And it wasn't as if by leaving she'd be disrupting some complex academic program. This was kindergarten they were talking about.

Alan Kest waited until they'd sung the grace after meals and the Sabbath songs that went with the long 'third meal' that occupied much of Saturday afternoon before he walked across the room to sit down next to Isaac.

'It's good to see you here,' Kest said. 'And your mother, how is she?'

'Keine ayin hara, she's feeling a little better, rabbi, thank you for asking.'

'We don't see you so often on Shabbat anymore. You don't visit her?'

'During the week. There's a minyan near me in Manhattan I go to for Shabbat, now.'

It made Kest sad to think that Isaac – whom he still remembered as a lonely little boy with a huge thirst for learning – was losing contact with a proper Torah life, and that he felt he had to lie about it. Kest blamed Isaac's too-close contact with the wrong kind of people, the drug dealers and the others from the nations of the world that he conspired to break the secular law with. 'Keep far from an evil neighbor,' the sages said. 'Be not a partner with an evil person.'

Not that it was Alan Kest's place to judge. Didn't the sages also say, 'When you assess people, tip the balance in their favor'? And Isaac still had an impulse to do good for the people who had been helpful to him.

'I like your friend that you introduced me to,' Kest told him. 'He has a good mind and an appetite for learning. I think I'm going to keep doing business with him, not that a person should talk about such things on Shabbat.'

He waited for Isaac to say something, but he didn't. He seemed distracted, even nervous. Reflecting on it, Kest thought Isaac had been behaving oddly for weeks now.

'I'm always glad if I can do you a favor,' Isaac said belatedly. 'You've done so much for me, all my life.'

'I had great respect for your father, of blessed memory, and you were a smart boy, with a good Torah heart. It was a pleasure to help you learn.' All history now, Kest thought sadly. 'Talking of favors, you remember that souvenir I gave you a few months ago, the little piece of paper?' Some instinct kept him from naming it directly, and not just because of the Sabbath.

'Piece of paper?'

'You know, the printed one. Green, with numbers in the corners, and a picture . . .'

A long silence, and then Isaac smiled. It looked as if wires were pulling on the corners of his mouth. 'Oh, sure. I like having it to look at. It makes me think of you.'

'You still have it, then? You kept it, the way I said?'

Isaac's stiff smile wavered. 'Sure. Why wouldn't I?'

'Good, good.' Kest patted Isaac's bobbing knee. 'Because that's a favor I would ask you – to give it back. For right now, I need to have it.'

'You do?'

'Yes, please.' Just asking for it made Kest feel better. Having it out in the world was not a good idea. 'You could maybe bring it by the store, sometime soon?'

Ben brooded about Judith all afternoon, increasingly convinced their timing was terrible, that before they went further he had to figure out how to approach this with Hannah, and what direction his life was going in. Though he didn't know exactly what he was going to say, he watched the sky for stars or anyway enough darkness to feel safe calling.

She beat him to it. 'Hi,' she said. 'How was your Shabbat?'

'Different.'

She laughed – a warm, inviting sound. It gave him chills. 'So was mine,' she said. 'In a nice way.'

Though he'd decided to say, 'We have to talk some more,' what actually came out was, 'Can I see you?'

'I hope so. That's why I called. Do you have any time tomorrow?'

'In the afternoon. I can leave Hannah with a neighbor for an hour or so. Maybe we can get a cup of coffee or go for a walk in the park.'

'It's supposed to be another nice day. I'd love a walk in the park. And then Hannah could join us after we've had some time alone.'

'Sure.' They picked a time and he hung up, relieved to have put off saying things he didn't really want to say.

He slept fitfully, tormented by predictably erotic dreams, including an odd one in which Judith stood in his office undressing and he was sure Joshua was there, too, watching from one of the guest chairs – but every time he'd look over, the chair was empty.

He woke up groggy, burned his hand making Hannah's breakfast pancakes, burned the first batch of pancakes, too. Scraping the mess into the trash, he thought, No wonder they write songs about this.

As he reached Riverside Drive he could see Judith standing on a bare scarp of rock atop a long hill just showing its first hint of the coming season's green. Her black hair glistened in the sunlight; the shadow of her strong brow shrouded her eyes.

He was glad to see her, more than glad, elated. He wanted to relish that awhile – there would be time for serious talk.

She turned as he crossed the street to the park, smiled, raised a hand. She took only a few steps in his direction, waiting for him to cross the sidewalk and a patch of grass to the rock where she stood.

She reached out a hand for his, tilted her head up to him. He kissed her gently on the corner of her mouth.

'Hello,' she said, that same rich voice as her laughter on the phone.

'Spring is coming,' she said.

'Soon.'

They were in a part of the park where a broad walk ran between a vista of the river and a long strip of hilly woods, the woods bordered by a high wall of dark gray stone. People strolled alone and in pairs, walking dogs and pushing strollers, mobile slalom markers for the inline skaters.

Wordless, Judith tugged on Ben's hand to lead him uphill into the narrow woods, kicking at the remains of last fall's leaves like a kid. He followed, compelled to match her silence. She angled over toward the wall where it was at its highest, stretching three people tall from the bed of mulching leaves to where the dark stones bordered Riverside Drive as it ran along the high ridge above them.

She drew him back against the stone wall with her, used the lapels of his jacket to pull him closer. He could smell the warm fragrance of her skin mixed with the sharpness of late-winter air.

'A little bit of privacy,' she said.

He bent his head to kiss her. Her lips were soft and tasted of an unfamiliar spice, tantalizingly reminiscent of Friday night.

The kiss lasted a very long time before he lifted his head to look around. The people on the promenade didn't seem to have noticed anything happening up here.

'I thought of you all day yesterday,' she said. 'Of us, together.'

'I did, too.'

'And today was worse. I don't know why I stopped us.'

All the sensations of Friday night engulfed him in a rush. They kissed again and he felt her body press against his. His hands traveled over her back, strayed to her hips.

She reached down, caressed him. He didn't resist.

'Kiss me again.'

'Not here. We can't—' It had been so long . . . so long. And all that time he'd made himself believe it didn't matter.

'Kiss me.'

'There are people—'

He could feel himself responding, his judgment clouding. Safe or alive, he could hear Freddi say, and Joshua: you have to know the transgressor inside you. Dim voices under the roaring in his ears.

She moved her hand, her eyes not wavering from his, as if she were willing him not to look away. Slowly, she lifted her skirt between them and drew his hand to her. Leaned against him, her mouth ready for a kiss he couldn't withhold.

He kept himself aware of the outside world just long enough to believe there was no one near, that from a distance they were just romantics sharing a kiss, their busy hands concealed between them by their bodies and their clothes and the long gray shield of the wall.

'I can't believe we did that,' he said as they walked back through the park.

'I can.' She was smiling fiercely. 'I'm glad. I'm just sorry we had to stop again.'

'Yes. Me, too.' Trying to be light about it. The rational side of him said it wouldn't help anything to encourage this, and yet he couldn't bring himself to say anything negative. He made himself try. 'We shouldn't be doing this, though.'

'Why?' She seemed amused. 'We're both healthy, and pregnancy isn't a problem.' She was on the pill for some medical reason, she'd told him Friday night. 'Not because of NYU, surely? There's no reason for them to know. Besides, you're not exploiting me. I've wanted us to be together since the minute I learned you were teaching at the law school. I had a mad crush on you those few days in England.'

'A year ago.'

'Yes, a year ago. And I used to fantasize we'd meet again and be passionate and reckless.'

He stopped and took her in his arms. 'I think I must have been dreaming of you all this time, too, only I wasn't letting myself recognize it. And then seeing you – it's been so hard in class, trying not to stare all the time.'

She grinned up at him. 'I know. I could tell. I just kept thinking, be patient, we both want this even though he doesn't know it yet.' She laughed. 'The last thing I expected was that we'd be brought together by religion.'

Hannah's delight at seeing Judith was an arrow in Ben's heart. He watched them play, full of love for both of them, unable to stifle an unease that bordered on dread.

You're being crazy he told himself. What could be bad about this? He couldn't protect Hannah from emotion forever, from the risk of loss or being left, and there was no reason to suppose this would end badly, or end at all – a thought he recoiled from immediately.

Judith called him to join them. 'I'm teaching Hannah a new card game, and we need a third person.'

He went over and sat with them, willing himself to be as unconcerned as they were. This wasn't a crisis, it was just a pleasant Sunday afternoon.

31

As he started across the concrete bridge toward the lumpy, cocoa-brick building that housed the US Attorney's Office, Ben heard someone calling him. He turned, saw at first only the usual morning stream of paralegals and secretaries and lawyers. Then he noticed a man leaning against the parapet – stocky, in a blue jogging jacket and a baseball cap with the brim pulled low over his face. Isaacs?

He beckoned, then turned away and walked quickly toward the arched passageway under the Municipal Building. He paused once to look back, kept going. Ben followed him to a bench in City Hall park.

'We've got trouble,' Isaacs said, face almost hidden by the jacket's standup collar, his knee bobbing.

'What's wrong?'

'Kest wants his hundred back.'

Oh shit. 'What'd you tell him?'

'What do you think – "Sorry, Rabbi, I gave it to the Secret Service?" I said, "Sure I have it." So now you've got to give it back to me.'

'Why? Did he say why?'

'What difference does it make, why? I've got to give it to him.'

'How did he seem? Was he accusing you of something?'

'Will you just get it for me, please. Or else he's going to kill me for sure.'

'Not a chance,' Lukas said, leaning back in the guest chair in Ben's office as if to distance himself further from the idea, legs poked out in front of him. 'You know we can't let it go. The only way we can do that is if we bust Kest the minute Isaacs hands it back to him, then try to flip Kest. And that's not happening.'

'It may be a choice between that and losing the lead entirely. Because Kest is going to know something's wrong the minute Isaacs says he doesn't have the note for him. And if that happens we have to pull Sid out, too.'

'Who says we do? What's Kest going to know? It got stolen, Isaacs spent it, who knows what happened to it?'

'That's awfully risky, even assuming Isaacs can pull it off,' Ben said.

'Worth trying, given the alternatives,' Lukas countered. 'And maybe we can have our cake and eat it, too. If we can record the conversation, and Kest says anything that shows knowledge the note was counterfeit, we've got something to use when we're ready to move on him.'

'You don't seriously think you can get Isaacs to wear a wire.'

'Don't you mean *we*?'

Isaacs didn't want to believe they weren't going to give the hundred back to him.

'This can't be happening. I did everything you said. Didn't I just introduce your undercover guy for you? And this is how you treat me?'

'We appreciate what you've done,' Ben acknowledged, 'but there's no way we can give up that note. All we can do is help you protect yourself.'

'Yeah, great. By getting you more evidence, and doing even more to betray a man who took me in when I was a kid. It never ends, does it? You squeeze and squeeze. There's a *limit*, but you don't understand that.'

'This is a problem we have to face together, Isaac. We're willing to give you whatever support we can. But we can't do it on our own. You have to work with us on this.'

'I can't. I can't keep doing this. I'm telling you there's a *limit*.'

'That's *my* limit,' Lukas said, up out of his chair. 'I'm going to arrest you, you little prick, throw you right in jail. Then you won't have to worry about returning anything to anybody.'

'Jail! What for?' Panicky. 'What did I do? I didn't do anything.'

'You think we haven't been watching you? You just cruise along, doing your same old same old, right in front of us. We take names, Isaac. And you know what comes after taking names? Kicking ass.'

It went on like that until Isaacs was too worn down to continue. All the petulant bravado went out of him at once.

'All right,' he conceded: 'But I can't just go and tell him I lost it or I spent it.'

'Somebody stole it from you,' Lukas proposed. 'You want, we can arrange to have you mugged, going to see him.'

Isaacs stared. 'Anybody ever tell you you're crazy?'

'That's enough, Isaac,' Ben interposed before Lukas could blow up.

'You guys know the people who print the real money,' Isaacs said abruptly, a gleam in his eye. 'Why can't they make one like the one I gave you? So I'd have *something* to give him. How hard can that be?'

Lukas rolled his eyes.

'Actually, that's not such a bad idea,' Ben said. 'You say he never told you it was counterfeit?'

'Hinted, is all.'

'Suppose we give you a *real* one for him.'

'What are you talking about? Won't he know? The serial number or something?'

'Probably.' And not just by the serial number: there were other designators that most people didn't even notice – letter-and-number combinations that identified the plate the note was printed from. 'But it would be a lot easier to convince him that you got it mixed up with a real one than that there's an innocent reason why you just don't have it.'

'How?'

'How about – you were comparing them to see if you could tell the difference, and the one he gave you was so good that somehow you got it wrong which was which. You guarded this one carefully and spent the other one. You can be as horrified by the mistake as he is.'

'*I* don't know,' Isaacs said, but Ben could see the idea appealed to him.

They spent the rest of the afternoon role-playing until they were satisfied Isaacs had it down, but no matter how much Lukas badgered him, he wouldn't agree to wear a wire. In the end, he accepted a transmitting beeper – mostly, Ben thought, to get Lukas off his back.

'I don't know about this,' Lukas said when he and Ben were on the way back to the office. 'Kest has that shielded room in the store. If they go in there we get zip.'

'I'd think you'd be more concerned about putting Kest on his guard. If he found Isaacs wearing a wire, that'd blow us out of the water completely. And what about a scanner? If he's worried enough about transmitters to have a shielded room, isn't he likely to have a scanner that would pick up the fact that Isaacs was transmitting?'

'He might.' Lukas was silent awhile. 'We've got a new beeper with a digital recorder in it. It doesn't hold much, but I'll see if I can break one free.'

Lukas called him later.

'It's all set up with Isaacs. He's bringing Kest the hundred at closing time tomorrow. We'll be following him to make sure nothing goes wrong. Come along if you want.'

'I'm assuming it won't be much different from the last time.'

'Unless it goes bad.'

'If it does, I don't want to be in the way,' Ben said. And he wanted to be at home with Hannah in any event. The week's schedule had already included too much time apart.

'Sure,' Lukas said. 'Maybe that's a part of your education you'd rather wait for.'

That sounded as if Lukas knew about Ben's visit to Treasury.

'I think this time I ought to let you do your job without having me along playing tourist.' There was a chance that Lukas would think he was gun-shy, as Morgan had put it. On the other hand, a reputation for letting agents do their job wasn't a bad one to have, and so far he'd shown himself all too willing to interfere. 'Not that I won't be eager to hear how it goes.'

'You'll be the first,' Lukas said in a tone Ben couldn't read.

'Good. And we ought to set it up so Sid can meet with Isaacs, alone, and get his own read on the situation.'

'You think I can't—' Lukas started to snap, but cut himself short. 'Right,' he said. 'We can do that.'

'Anything new from Cyprus or Switzerland?'

'Not today. I'll check with them again tomorrow. Meanwhile Ian and I are going up to Centerville to take a look around.'

32

Centerville, as Lukas and Rogers described it, was an odd amalgam of century's-end Americana.

'Once upon a time, it must have been a nice quiet town out in the country,' Rogers reported. 'There's still some of that feeling left, but now the highway's been widened and it's strip-malled on both sides, plus a big factory-outlet center. The weird thing is, when you get back in off the main road, it's all religious people living there. Jews, where we were looking, but not far down the road there are all these old churches, too, and signs on the barns that say Jesus Saves.

'The Jewish part looks like two main neighborhoods. In one you see a lot of long black coats, and black hats with fur brims, and long beards. Then a couple of blocks away they dress more like normal, except they all look sort of the same, like they all shop at the same store. And they all seem to know right away who belongs there and who doesn't. We were driving along streets like any street you'd see in any suburb, except there were all these people out walking. Kids walking to and from school, mothers with strollers and maybe a couple of bigger kids, men walking together, all of them talking eighteen to the dozen. And they'd look at us. Look at the car and look at us. Men in cars, too – a couple of them followed us for a while. Seemed like they were all wondering what the hell we were doing there.'

'There's no way we're going to park a van on the street out there and watch what's happening,' Lukas said. 'We'd get made in a hot minute.'

'What about Sid?' Ben asked him.

'Maybe he can get up there through Kest, but that's not happening overnight. I'd say our best bet is pole cameras' – remote-control video cameras rigged to telephone poles or powerline towers – 'I already put in a request for the equipment – we should have it tomorrow, the next day. The big question is going to be where to put them. It's almost a shame to use one on Solomon's store, but we've got to.'

'Why a shame?'

'It's only open four hours a day, four days a week, so it's mostly dead time. We'll have to hope the traffic we do get means something.'

'How good a look did you get?'

'Pretty good. It's in one of the smaller shopping areas along the highway, and the store's not much bigger than a postage stamp. It has camping stuff in the window, and a pair of skis for effect.'

'Was it open when you were there?'

'Yeah. We took a chance on Ian going in to take a look.'

Rogers said, 'They made me as an outsider right away. I don't know if they thought I was from the churchgoing part of town or what, but I could feel it as soon as I came in. There was a girl about eighteen or so with a shirt that buttoned up to the neck and down to the wrists. She kind of stared at me, then ducked out through a door behind the counter, and a minute later in came a guy maybe fifty or sixty, tallish, with a pointy white beard, in a white shirt and dark pants with one of those skullcaps, asks if he can help me like he thinks the answer's no.

'I asked did he have one of those fluorescent camp lanterns, and sure enough he did. New stock, too, the box was clean, no dust. I bought one and asked him did he know anything about campsites nearby, or where I could find some place to do rock climbing. "Exit eighteen," he says, and he gives me my package and goes into the back. Like I'm supposed to know he means the Thruway.'

'Not exactly trying to build business,' Lukas commented.

'Did you see any guns?'

'A rack of rifles and shotguns on the wall behind the register, and two display cases of handguns. The usual accessories. I didn't want to make too big a deal of taking inventory in that part of the store.

'And something else,' Rogers said. 'While we were up there we checked out the addresses we have, for Kest and Ohry and Solomon and the other people on the phone records. They're all in the regular-clothes part of town. In some cases, around the corner from each other, or next door. The street names and house numbers don't tell you much, but when you're out there you can see that almost all the houses are within a few blocks.'

'That cuts both ways,' Ben said. 'I still want to see something that makes these people more than just friendly neighbors. Maybe the ATF case will do that for us – I'm seeing the case agent this afternoon – but let's get those pole cameras up and running, so when it comes time to push for phone taps and bugs we can show how hard we've tried to get the information by less intrusive means.'

'As fast as we can.'

Andy Ciampa, the ATF case agent on the Centerville firearms investigation, was medium height and muscular, with the aggressive stance and wary eyes of a man formed by the tough neighborhood of his youth. He wore a dark-gray turtleneck with a wine-red, double-breasted sportjacket that bulged slightly under his left arm.

'There's something major weird going on over there,' he said in answer to Ben's question about Centerville. 'This is a highly armed community. Solomon, the FFL' – federal firearms licensee – 'does a real good business with his neighbors. These people've all got shotguns, rifles, you name it. All legal, paperwork all in order, nothing we can do anything about, but it does make a pattern. And then you add in this stolen shipment that we have reason to believe went into the neighborhood and you've got something to pay attention to. Plus we checked back with this same manufacturer who lost the shipment from the freight terminal, and also with a couple of other firearms manufacturers in the same general area of New England, and they all have a higher than usual incidence of packages missing that passed through this one terminal since our subject started working there. Not a pretty picture.'

'You think it's a systematic, planned diversion?'

'Yeah, I do. The guy must have been tired that one day, to leave the tracking numbers showing like that when he put on the new address label. We think there's two of them working together, and one diverts to the other, and also lets him know when something good's routed out his way. And subject number two being at the airfreight hub, a lot of good stuff goes his way. It saves him some time to get a heads-up when it's coming in, makes it easier for him to divert.'

'And he doesn't have to take anything, or carry it out with him.'

'Just slaps a label on it and hey, it's on its way wherever he wants it to go. Only my guess is mostly they put it inside a clean box first, so there's no manufacturer's name, there's no bill of lading that identifies it as what it is, nobody's going to look at it twice. And if they're not greedy, don't do it too often, nobody's going to put two and two together for a long time.'

Just like the credit-card scam. 'What stage are you at with it?' Ben asked him.

'We checked the phone records we got and there's definitely telephone contact between the freight loader and his cousin in Centerville, and plenty of it, right around the time the package we know about got diverted. We've been surveilling all three of them, with pole cameras in Centerville – that's not a place our people are going to go unnoticed. It's all Jewish, a bunch of different groups. I suppose you know about that.'

'Some. I'm glad to hear you've got pole cameras up. How long?'

'About two weeks. The frieght loader's been to see his cousin,

cousin came to see him once. They both have garages, and they both drive their cars inside the garage when they come to visit, close the garage door, don't open it until they leave. No way to know what they've got in the trunk, coming or going.'

'What're you planning next?'

'We were thinking about running a sting on our freight loaders, then seeing if we could flip one of them. Now we've got the FFL, Solomon, turning up in a Secret Service case some way, and they're saying hold off to see if it's all connected. But I hate to let it all slip through our fingers based on some hunch.'

He sounded jazzed up enough about the case to make Ben wonder. 'What aren't you telling me?'

'Sorry?'

'What you've been telling me – I'll find most of that in the case file.'

'Yeah.' Wary.

'What'd you leave out? There's always something – a snitch, something. I understand you want to stay a little ahead, but this is Major Crimes now, not General Crimes.'

Ciampa looked uncomfortable, but it didn't take him long to decide which way to jump. 'The only thing – we aren't sure enough yet to put it in the case file . . .'

'That happens.' Letting him save face. 'Tell me.'

'We've got an address in Centerville allegedly receiving unlabeled, mislabeled shipments of firearms and destructive devices, completely unregistered—'

'Based on?'

'A source.'

'I need more than that.'

'A freight-company guy who delivers in the neighborhood.'

'This is unlabeled or mislabeled shipments?'

'Right.'

'Different from the ones you think the freight loaders are diverting.'

'Right.'

'How does he know what's in them?'

'Sometimes you get a box with a major ding in it, or the tape comes loose, so you get a look inside, or you judge by what it weighs and how it feels. This delivery guy sat on what he was seeing a long time and then finally he decided to do the right thing. Which is good, except Lord knows how long this was all going on before he discovered it, or after, or where they've had time to move the stuff to since it came in.'

'How much did he see?'

'Not as much as we'd like, but enough. Empty hand-grenade

casings in one shipment, and then a while later a crate of firearms that from his description sound like semi-automatic assault rifles, maybe AR-15s, the kind you can convert to basically an M-16 full-auto military submachine gun.'

'And the delivery address is in Centerville? In the same part of town?'

'Definitely the same part of town,' Ciampa said. 'A block over from the freight loader's cousin and two blocks the other way from Solomon, the FFL.'

'Okay,' Ben said, 'What we need now is for you to sit down with the Secret Service agents who've been working the case that led us to Solomon, so you can get each other up to speed, see if we can connect this all up. And they'll definitely want to have a look at anybody you caught with the pole cameras.' Thinking: What *is* this? What – excluding a holy war – does a religious community want with all these guns, especially illegal guns?

Not that a minor holy war was impossible: an ongoing factional dispute in an Orthodox Jewish community farther upstate had been in the news for years – there'd been stonings and other assaults, and a home for pregnant women had been burned to the ground. And there'd been a history of sometimes violent antagonism between the Jewish newcomers who'd consolidated their neighborhoods in to the new town called Centerville and the parishioners of all those churches Rogers had noticed, who'd been there for generations and felt pushed out by an invasion of people with alien beliefs and customs.

33

Wednesday morning Ben met Frank Lukas and Sid Levy for another of what were becoming regular morning meetings. They drank bitter coffee at a dark little café in the meat-packing district that marked the northwest corner of Greenwich Village.

'That was a good call, having Isaacs tell me about Kest and the hundred, just the two of us,' Sid told him. 'He's a slippery guy. I wouldn't want to be relying just on what he was willing to say in front of Frank, and he sure didn't get much on that little recording thing he was carrying.'

'Just as long as you're satisfied it's safe for you.'

'Who ever knows? But, yeah, I think Frank's right about that – this isn't the time to pull out.'

'At this point, Sid's our only real shot,' Lukas said. 'We're not going to get much more from Isaacs. Even assuming Kest swallowed the substitute-note story whole, and that's a lot to assume, he's still going to be careful around Isaacs.'

'That's for sure,' Sid affirmed. 'Isaacs told me Kest warned him about how bad it was to inform on a Jew to the non-Jewish authorities. And reminded him of the value of repentance.'

'I didn't hear that,' Lukas said.

'See what I mean? There are things he holds back.'

Ben said, 'I don't like the sound of that, about informing.'

'I think it's just a precaution,' Sid said. 'If I remember my religious law, you can't be convicted of a crime unless you've first been warned not to commit it. So this sounds like Kest was drawing a line in the sand – don't step over this from now on.'

'And offering Isaacs a chance to confess.'

'Yeah, but Isaacs isn't going to do that.'

'I still don't like it,' Ben said. He *really* didn't like it. But he didn't feel in a position to insist on pulling Sid out. It was all well and good to be one of Sid's contacts, but Lukas had been right that Ben had no first-hand experience of this kind of operation – and in this situation he was doubly wary of providing evidence for the theory that he was gun-shy.

'All right,' he said, 'we'll leave it sit is for now. But let's make sure your meetings are somewhere Frank can monitor them and pull you out if things show any sign of going sour.'

'Sure. Fine. I mean, look, I'm not saying I won't have to be careful. I think Kest is going to be on his guard for a while, now, and I need to be aware of that. But, hey, that's part of the job.'

Ben wasn't expecting to see Lukas again until the next morning, but he came by just after lunch.

'I went back to see Mr Isaacs,' the agent said. 'After all that about Kest freezing him out, I wanted to ask him what he knew about Joel Solomon.'

'Is Solomon on his phone records?'

'No, but this is Isaacs – he could be using any kind of phone – so I went and asked him, and sure enough he used to know the man. But the gun store surprised him. "It must be somebody else," he said. "The Joel Solomon I knew was a rabbi." Another rabbi, would you believe it? And not just a rabbi in name, like Kest. This one's got his own temple he preaches at, right there in Centerville.' Lukas shook his head. 'I said it before and I'll say it again – I don't get it. All these *rabbis* . . . Money, sure, but guns . . . I keep trying to think how that would work in the Church, a gun-dealer priest.'

'Maybe not so odd if the priest was Irish.'

Lukas pounced on it. 'You think that's what it is? Old-country politics? Something to do with the Arabs?'

Holy war Ben had thought only the day before, but he hadn't really been serious. Still . . . 'At this point there's no reason to count it out.'

Every reason not to, in fact. Holy Land politics had been conducted with imported weapons and money for millennia.

'Speaking of that,' he said, 'what's the news from Israel?'

Lukas smiled – a rare sight. 'We may have another piece in the puzzle. It seems the Russian that gets the most calls is somebody the Israelis have had their eye on for a while.'

'Oh?'

'They say he was a bigshot gangster in the old country. Very fast rise – based on some strong-arm stuff, but mostly he was a manipulator, not one to hit somebody over the head if he could do it some other way. And it could be he's had some dealings in Lebanon, too, not clear what exactly, but one rumor is he was trying to work a private deal with an alleged counterfeiting plant in the Bekaa Valley. Probably bullshit, but he's a guy worth looking at. We're trying to get more on him from the Israelis.'

'If I remember correctly, your intrepid dumpster divers came up with some packages from Israel that looked like they might have contained books.'

'Right.'

'And you were saying it might have been bricks of counterfeit notes.'

'And this makes that a lot more likely,' Lukas said.

'Maybe it's time to have Customs to put a watch on shipments from Israel to the addresses we're watching in Centerville.'

'The Brooklyn addresses, too.'

'And Brooklyn,' Ben agreed. There was still something off between him and Lukas, but at least they'd begun to work together fairly well. 'I don't suppose those packages had a reliable return address.'

'Not unless they're suicidal. If the package gets intercepted you don't want anybody tracing it back.'

'If we're talking about false addresses, that basically means covering every shipment from anywhere in the country.'

'Things are hard all over,' Lukas said. 'This is worth however much work it takes.'

'What about the OV ink?' – the forbidden topic – 'It would make a difference if we could connect this Russian with that.'

'No real news there. The Swiss are tracking down anybody who left the company in the last five years, anybody who might have worked on the OV ink himself or who might have been friendly with somebody who did, but they haven't given us anything about their progress.'

'So you've still got at least two working theories – Kest is connected to whoever's making the notes here, and the guns are related to that somehow, or the notes are coming from Israel, something to do with this Russian. Assuming, that is, Kest is anything more than what Isaacs said he was – somebody who sold some computers for a whole bunch of counterfeit currency on a one-time basis.'

'I don't think there's a chance of that last one. Rabbi Kest is in this up to his eyeballs.'

'And what about the cowboy hat and the cattle breeder? Where does that fit?'

'Beats me. That's the one piece that makes no sense at all. I was hoping you could help with that – some Jewish thing.'

'Nothing comes to mind.'

The question, frivolous as it seemed, was in the back of his mind when he called Elliot Rosen to thank him for recommending Sid Levy.

'No thanks necessary. I'm glad to hear he's what you needed. Anything else I can do, let me know.'

'You know, there is one question. What would an Orthodox rabbi in New York be doing with a Texas cattle breeder?'

Rosen laughed. 'You're kidding, right?'

'No. I mean, I don't know how serious it is, but it is part of my case.'

'Maybe he's planning a designer line of kosher beef.'

Ben's turn to laugh. 'That makes as much sense as anything.'

Ben spent the rest of the day avoiding case-intake work and beginning to organize his Major Crimes files for his successor. All he could think of was that in a few hours he'd be with Judith again. All his misgivings had dissolved the first time he heard her voice on Monday. He'd called to say he'd been in the middle of ordering flowers for her when he realized he didn't know her address, and he didn't think it was a good idea to get it from the registrar at NYU.

It had been Judith's idea that they take advantage of spring break to see each other. He'd asked Vashti to stay late, telling her he had to be at the law school anyway, even though he had no class to teach.

The address Judith had given him was on an East Side street not far from the UN. Among the prosperous-looking townhouses on the block were several with the brass plaques of UN missions.

Next door to one of them, Ben mounted the stoop of a townhouse and was surprised to be faced with a heavy, carved wooden door and a single buzzer and intercom speaker in the doorframe. He'd been expecting the usual mostly glass lobby door and a row of apartment buzzers. He double-checked to make sure he had the right address before he rang.

Judith came to the door looking fresh out of the shower – her face scrubbed naked, hair wrapped in a towel, wearing only a short robe of dark blue silk tied loosely with a sash. Trying to catch his breath, he followed her through a narrow entrance hall hung with coats and umbrellas and into a parlor-floor living room with fourteen-foot ceilings. Along the left wall a stairway climbed to the next floor.

'No coat?' she teased.

'*I* took a chance.' It was a raw March day with rain in the air, but right now it felt like summer to him. 'And now I feel overdressed.'

'We'll fix that.'

He shifted his armload of flowers so he could put one arm around her and draw her to him. He marveled at the softness of her body and the heat it radiated.

She kissed him thoroughly then pulled away, laughing. 'This time we don't have to hurry. Or stop.'

'I just . . . can't wait.'

She kissed him again. 'Not long. I want to put these beautiful flowers in water.'

They walked through the living room. Books and papers were strewn helter-skelter on the couch and chairs. Through an archway was a dining room with a large round table similarly cluttered, the only blank space occupied by a laptop computer.

'Excuse the mess,' she said. 'I'm working on my seminar for the Global Law School program.'

In the kitchen, a wall of glass looked over the backyard garden. She found a vase and filled it with water.

'There's a student from Nigeria who's very clever. She got a two-minute ovation after her seminar last week, and I'm determined to get that much and more – standing.'

'I'd love to be part of that audience, if it wouldn't bother you to have me there.'

'Maybe I should give you a private performance instead.' She took a bottle of champagne from the refrigerator.

'This place is amazing,' he said, taking it all in while she got them glasses and opened the bottle. 'Is there more upstairs?'

'Three more floors. And a separate apartment downstairs.'

'Is it yours?' He'd assumed she was financially comfortable, but not like this. The house had to be worth millions.

'Oh no,' she said, handing him a glass of wine. 'I'm borrowing it from an old school friend. House-sitting I believe it's called.'

'An enjoyable way to live.' He lifted his glass. 'To enjoying life.'

'Yes,' she agreed. 'To enjoying life.'

It was an evening of firsts for him: not just the first time they made love, but the first time he saw her fully naked and at leisure, so he could look and touch and look until the unaccustomed frankness of it was more than he could maintain; the first time they made love a second time; the first time they showered together.

He laughed about that. 'You just took one of these.'

'Not quite *just* . . .' She lathered him vigorously.

'Hey! Tender parts.'

'Not so tender a minute ago.'

'And won't be again soon if you keep that up.'

She kissed him, tasting of clean running water, and turned her back.

'You do me.'

'I just did. Twice.'

'Oh, my,' was her response. 'You're worse than I am.'

He took a cab across town, replaying the evening in his mind. Even after their adventure in Riverside Park, he hadn't been fully prepared for Judith's openness and intensity, or for the power of his response.

When it came to sex he considered himself neither especially naive nor especially experienced. He'd had a couple of unbuttoned years in his late teens and at college, with increasing wariness as AIDS became more of a terror. Before Laura he'd had serious relationships with two women – one a shy law school classmate who, even as she clutched his body to hers in the extremes of pleasure gave no more evidence of it than a shudder and a sigh; the other a fledgling newscaster with a bouncy, unthinking lustiness. With Laura everything had been sweet and loving, not without experimentation and laughter, but almost always touched with a tenderness that in retrospect almost seemed wistful.

This was different. Very different. It had a . . . completeness . . . that he'd never experienced before. They'd had the time – and he, the awareness – for him to feel the true pull of it, and in the aftermath he felt both energized and, if he was to be honest with himself, a little frightened.

34

Ben joined Lukas and Rogers at Secret Service's World Trade Center offices to watch Ciampa's pole-camera video tapes on the big TV monitor used during press conferences, the four of them gathered in the front corner of a darkened room meant for hundreds.

'This is a dupe of some individual frames, ones with people in them,' Ciampa explained. The cameras had been set to shoot single-still frames every four seconds, as a way to minimize the need to change tapes.

The image – like a fuzzy black-and-white photograph – showed a ranch-style house of white siding and brick. It was set on a moderate-size lot, landscaped with young-looking evergreens and flowering bushes that were just budding.

Ciampa identified the first person to appear as the homeowner, the go-between cousin of one of the freight loaders suspected of diverting firearms shipments. With him were his wife and five children. After that, shots of three different men arriving and leaving, no one they could identify. By the time-date numbers at the edge of each frame, each visitor stayed five or ten minutes. One was carrying a skinny rectangular package when he left.

'Could be long guns,' Ciampa observed. 'From how he's carrying it, it looks fairly heavy.'

As the day progressed two women arrived with small children. There was a shot of the kids out in the yard playing.

'Very domestic,' Rogers commented.

The kids and their mothers left. A series of frames showed a car pulled up, the driver on his way to the door, then waiting to be admitted. He was a bear of a man with grizzled hair and beard.

'We know that guy,' Lukas said.

'Alan Kest,' Ben said almost at the same moment.

Ciampa stopped the tape.

'This is our main target,' Lukas told him. 'Does he stay in there long?'

'Yeah, if I remember right.' Ciampa flipped quickly forward to a shot of Kest on his way out. The timing numbers were more than an hour after his arrival.

'I wish I could hear what they had to say to each other,' Lukas said.

'We need to get inside one of these places.' To Ciampa he said, 'This guy whose house it is isn't a rabbi is he?'

'A rabbi? What are you talking about? I mean, he's Jewish—'

'It's a joke,' Ben said.

'Maybe it's finally time to try for an electronic surveillance order,' Lukas proposed, 'We've got the gun crimes to go on, now.'

'It's still a stretch,' Ben said, 'until we have more evidence they're actually doing illegal business in this location. Being somebody's cousin and entertaining a rabbi, even a suspicious one, doesn't make the grade at the Justice Department.'

'Kest may be more than just a suspicious rabbi,' Lukas said when Ciampa had left. 'I got a reading on him from FinCEN' – the Financial Crimes Enforcement Network, Treasury's lead agency in fighting international money laundering – 'and they found a third house he owns, besides the ones in Brooklyn and Centerville. In Israel. A place called Kiryat Yaacov, if I have it right. According to the map it's up in the north, not so far from Lebanon. He also has three foreign bank accounts, two in Israel and one in Leichtenstein. So it looks like at the very least he's a rich rabbi.'

'Or a nominee for somebody.'

'Either way, I wonder what kind of money he put in those foreign accounts. Stacks of US hundreds, maybe?'

'What about this . . . Kiryat Yaacov? Is it a place that shows up on the phone-number list? Or on what you found in the garbage?'

'No, but I don't have any addresses from the Israelis. All I got was some profiles on the people they thought could be involved in counterfeiting or related crimes. Like the Russian. Lev Rudovsky.'

'I think it might help if your Cyprus office asked their Israeli friends for the phone-number locations. Not just the addresses, the neighborhoods. A map, if you can get it. I've got the feeling there's a lot of geography in this case.'

Back at the US Attorney's office, Ella had a message for him that he'd stopped expecting: Nate Morgan wanted him to call.

'Congratulations,' Morgan said. 'The Secretary's decided to send your name to the White House personnel office as his first choice for Assistant Secretary. You'll probably be hearing from them at some point, and we're going to be starting your FBI and IRS clearance procedures immediately. We've put all that on the fast track, because we'd like to get all this wrapped up as soon as possible.'

Ben got Harry Butler on the line as soon as he could.

'Thanks for the warning.'

'I didn't want to steal Nate's thunder. I'd say congratulations, but this is just the beginning. Assuming you get past the FBI and the IRS, there's still the possibility Justice will convince the President to put up a candidate for the job, and then there's getting past the Senate.'

'That's okay. I'm not in a hurry.' Understatement of the week. Now that he might have it, the Washington job seemed all trouble: losing the Aljo case, losing touch with Joshua and the increasingly compelling world of spiritual community he was leading Ben into, maybe losing Judith, too, an intolerable thought. Worst of all was the possibility that the job would cripple his ability to be the kind of father he wanted to be to Hannah. Yet he couldn't imagine letting go of it. 'Do you really think I could run into trouble with the FBI?'

'Nelson's candidate for Under Secretary sure did, and at a time when there was no obvious second choice. That's one reason they're so anxious to get someone in as Assistant Secretary – to fill the power vacuum before the AG finds a way to.'

Ben had the uncomfortable feeling he was being shuttled from square to square in a game he didn't understand.

'Is this really worth the bullshit that goes with it?'

'And a lot more, if it comes to that. It's a life-defining opportunity. Never mind the things you can do in the job – influencing policy, advising the President. Whatever other job you want, any time in your life, you go in having been Assistant Secretary of the Treasury. A major officer in the executive branch of the United States government, one of the top law-enforcement officials in the country. Is it worth it? You tell me.'

'I apologize for my moment of doubt,' Ben said, and almost meant it.

At home, there was a message for him from someone named Yitz, who'd called with the address for the evening's study session. Ben felt too preoccupied with the world for the mystical inquiry Joshua had promised this time, but Hannah was already off on an overnight play date, and he wasn't expecting Judith until later, so he decided to go.

The springboard for the session was a Talmudic opinion that a transgression committed for its own sake is greater than a commandment performed not for its own sake. Ben saw at once that these people knew more about the Law than the ones at the other session he'd tried. Everyone seemed familiar with Biblical texts, and a few were comfortable quoting from the Talmud.

They progressed from the basic idea of acting out of pure intention to a more general discussion of sin and error. The Stropkovers taught a view of most transgression as part of a cyclical process that led through repentance to the repair and rebuilding of the world, but when Yitz began to describe a mystical Adam clothed in a spiritual garment that included all the souls of humankind, Ben's mind wandered.

He was brought back from a reverie of Judith by a half-heard remark about how Adam's sin had transformed the mystical Adam and plunged all the souls into the realm of evil with him. The speaker was a small man with a dense black beard that almost covered his cheeks, and he was continuing despite the fact that the others were glaring at him with obvious disapproval. 'What about the power of evil embodied in Adam Belial?' he insisted: 'How do we deal with that?'

'Why don't you just go pray with Rabbi Stern?' a sharp-faced woman snapped at him. 'That's his kind of talk.'

The rabbi's name produced hissing from the others, and rapid spitting noises – proof against demons, Ben guessed.

'Enough of that,' Yitz said severely, and launched into a review of the more traditional concepts they'd been discussing.

At the break, Ben asked about the reviled Rabbi Stern.

'Not important,' Yitz said, dismissing the subject with a wave of his hand. 'Something from our past. He's nobody you need to worry about.'

On the way home to meet Judith, Ben was bothered by the brushoff. The whole incident seemed inconsistent with everything else he'd experienced among the Stropkovers.

'There's something bothering you,' Judith said after they'd kissed hello.

'Am I that transparent?'

'A kiss can tell a lot.'

'It's nothing, really. I heard something tonight that sounded' – already feeling he was being silly about it – 'call it surprising.'

'At work?'

'At the study session.'

'Then you have to at least give me a hint.'

'Something about a rabbi who seems to be out of favor. Very out of favor.' He described the reaction, left out his question to Yitz.

'That must be Asher Stern. He's the only one I know of who'd produce a reaction like that.'

'Do you know anything about him?'

'I know that some people have claimed Joshua didn't actually receive the Rebbe's blessing, even though the others who were present at the time have confirmed it. Rabbi Stern's supporters claim the blessing was intended for him. He was the Rebbe's son-in-law.'

'Sounds like Jacob and Esau.'

'Except that Joshua didn't go to the Rebbe wearing the wool of a sheep on his arms. Nobody was deceived. I find it rather disturbing, actually, that people are willing to distort the truth about such an important matter. But you should really ask Joshua what happened. You'll have to wait until after the weekend, though, because he's away on a retreat.'

The retreat. He and Joshua had joked about it, and Ben had – in his mind, in his fantasy – placed himself there. Joshua hadn't, apparently, and Ben wasn't prepared for how deeply that stung him.

He'd thought of himself as having formed a special bond with Joshua. Hadn't Joshua treated him that way, him and Hannah both, making much of them whenever they were around, blessing Hannah alone among the many children at that first Friday night? He'd even said as much, just a week ago – your struggle in life means something extra to me. But maybe that was how he talked to all his new . . . recruits.

'Are you all right?' Judith asked him. 'You seem distressed.'

'No, it's just . . . He mentioned the retreats to me once, and I was kind of hoping I could go.'

'Next time, I'm sure. It's likely he'd already decided on this group by the time he got to know you. They have to make the arrangements well in advance.'

'Of course. Why didn't I think of that?' He pulled her to him. 'It amazes me how close I feel to you,' he said. 'In no time at all.'

'Not so. We've been building up to this for a year and more, if you count the time when it was still a fantasy.' She kissed him. 'Or, if you believe the legends, since the angels first introduced us in Heaven before we were born.'

'I like that one. It's the only thing that begins to make sense of how I feel about you.'

They stood there, pressed to one another, and he thought: who else is there that I can talk to and feel safe this way?

They went to bed and made love. He was having trouble believing that she didn't have to leave, that Hannah wouldn't come bounding out of her room to interrupt them. He wanted to spend the whole night appreciating Judith, but sleep pulled him away.

'Are we having Shabbat tonight?' Judith asked over their morning coffee.

'If you can stand seeing me again.'

She kissed the corner of his mouth. 'I'll pretend I'm having a good time.'

At the door he said, 'We'll have to be careful, around Hannah.'

'Oh?'

'I think it's too soon for her to know we're . . . involved, this way.'

She hesitated. 'All right. Father knows best' – smiling – 'Isn't that what they say?'

35

Alan Kest stopped talking while his wife brought them a tray with cookies and tea. She put it on the coffee table and left the living room as quietly as she had come.

Kest poured tea and passed the cookies. 'Pareve,' he said – neither milk nor meat, a neutral element in scheduling their eating for the day.

The Israeli said, 'I say this friend of Isaac's is a liar. If he prays in Boston, I didn't find the congregation. Nobody there heard of any David Gershon.'

'We can ask him where,' said Dov Winkler, the Israeli's friend.

'And what will we learn?' Kest asked. They spoke in English because the Israeli had no Yiddish and Kest's grasp of modern Hebrew wasn't good enough for important subjects. 'We will learn that his name isn't David Gershon, or that he isn't from Boston. He's a criminal. Do you expect to get his right name?'

'He has ours,' the Israeli said, as if that meant something.

Kest didn't like the smugness in his tone, didn't like a lot about Ari Benzvi, the young man he thought of as the Israeli. Only twenty-two and already nothing was beyond him, no one too learned to contradict. *Do not disdain any person*, Kest had to keep reminding himself, *do not underrate the importance of anything*. And with the Israeli it was necessary to make additional allowances – he was the Rebbe's great-grandson.

'Yes, he has our names,' Kest acknowledged. 'I don't think there's harm in that.'

'We need to get a closer look. To see how much truth there is in him.'

'As you please.' There were better ways to learn about a man's heart than sneaking around after him or trapping him in lies, but Kest saw only futility in trying to explain that to these self-important boys.

'What did you decide to do about Isaac?' It still made Kest sad to think Isaac had turned disloyal, and to contemplate the consequences, but he knew it couldn't be ignored forever.

'We planted a microphone,' the Israeli said. 'He has too many telephones to listen to all of them. This way, if he says anything in his apartment, we have it on recording tape for as many witnesses as we need. And he's already been warned, so God protect him if he does anything now.'

It was a distortion of how the Law was supposed to work, but that was typical. The Israeli had a devious intelligence of a secular sort but despite his blood he had neither head nor heart for the Law.

Friday afternoon Ben got a call from Sid, wanting to meet. Ben called Lukas to set it up with him.

'I had a conversation with my contact in Switzerland this morning,' Lukas said on the way. 'You remember I told you that the Swiss were checking into people who'd left the company?'

'Did they find someone?'

'It looks that way. A chemist who worked on the OV ink and quit about three years ago then just last year left the country. And guess where he went?'

'Brooklyn?'

'Israel.'

'Israel? What, a Swiss Jew?'

'No, that's the weird part. The guy's pure Swiss beginning to end. Solid German Swiss at that. Dieter Kolb. His father was a major banker in Zurich for half a century.'

'And they don't know why he picked Israel?'

'Not that they're saying.'

'This half-century that his father was a banker – did it include the Big War?'

'I assume.'

'What kind of banker was he?'

'Didn't occur to me to ask.'

'It might be interesting to know.'

'Sure.' Skeptical. 'Meanwhile, I told Cyprus to ask the Israelis to locate the guy and see what he's up to.'

Late afternoon in the meat-packing district everything was closed and shuttered. The undercover met them at a deserted loading dock. He was in character, wearing a black suit and white shirt, no tie, with a black fedora. He looked like he could use a shave and sounded in a hurry.

'I was talking to Kest about laptops and things took a new turn. He shows me a news clip about how this old-time OC family is dealing with having Dad in the joint and Junior running things on the outside. That got us started on criminal organizations, and he brought it around to where he was asking my opinion, basically, on crime networks and how they communicated with each other.'

'Has it gone anywhere from there?' Ben asked.

'A little. He's been hinting at the idea of needing somebody who can negotiate for him with the nations of the world, that Isaacs isn't up to the job. And he's been pumping me for what Isaacs told me about him.'

'How are you playing it?'

'Mostly, I'm talking around it. But he has to assume I'm all about stolen merchandise, so I gave him that much – that Isaacs had basically said he was in the market for whatever I had to sell.'

'The business about Isaacs is a little worrying,' Ben said. 'But if he's asking you then maybe that's a good sign, as far as how he feels about you.'

'There's more,' Sid told them. 'He's invited me to his house for Shabbat with his family. I think it's some kind of test and if I don't go I'll never get closer to them than this.'

'What does that mean, invited you for Shabb—?' Lukas gave up on the strange word. He seemed mostly content to let Ben have the stage with Sid, at least for now, and play helpful assistant, himself.

'For one thing,' Sid said, 'it means I'm completely out of touch for twenty-five hours.'

'I don't like that,' Lukas said. 'What if it's a trap?'

Sid made a face and turned to Ben. 'You understand, right? If I do this, there's no halfway.'

'No halfway to what?' Lukas wanted to know.

'Sabbath observance,' Ben explained. 'You can't do anything that's associated with work. You can't carry anything outside the house, including in your pockets, and you can't switch anything electrical on or off.' To Sid he said: 'I'll bet Frank can get you a tracking device to wear in your shoe or somewhere.'

'I could wire you up, too,' Lukas said. 'They're not going to make you undress.'

'You kidding me? All this between now and a half hour before sunset? And I've got to be in Brooklyn by then. I barely had time to make this meeting.'

'You sure it's safe?' Ben asked and knew as he heard the words that they just emphasized his inexperience at this.

'If it looks bad I'll split.'

'Carry a gun, at least,' Lukas said.

'How do I do that?'

'Put it in your bag with your toothbrush and your underwear,' Ben said. 'You're supposed to be a bad guy. If somebody finds it, it'll just help your cover story. And it'll make us all worry a little less.'

Performing the rituals of Friday evening with Hannah and Judith,

Ben couldn't help thinking of Sid, off performing similar rituals in an atmosphere of tension and danger. Here, the greatest tension came from being near Judith, aware of her more intensely than ever yet forbidden by his own decree to show it by word or gesture.

Saturday he played with Hannah and tried not to let worries about the undercover bring work into his Sabbath. The day of peace was rapidly becoming something he wanted to protect. Joshua had been right that the satisfactions of observance bred a desire for more observance.

Unable to shut Sid from his mind, he allowed himself the justification that his concern was human, not professional. The minute it was dark enough for the undercover to be done at Kest's, Ben called Lukas. 'Anything?'

'He just beeped me. We haven't talked yet, but he's okay.'

'Great.' He felt the tension drain from his body.

He watched a video with Hannah, an animated feature they'd seen at least a thousand times before. By the time it was over, she was exhausted. As he was tucking her into bed she reached up and put her arms around his neck and gave him a kiss.

'I love you, Daddy,' she said.

'I love you, too, sweetie.' There was nothing pro-forma about it – he loved her more each day, enough to break his heart. He nuzzled her cheek. 'Mmmm deelicious.'

She held onto his neck. 'Daddy?'

'Yes, sweetie?'

'When are you going to get us a new mommy?'

Oh. He kissed her cheek again and took her arms from around his neck so he could sit on the bed next to her.

'What makes you ask that, sweetie?'

'Jeannie's mommy asked me.'

What's wrong with people? he thought. Why do they inflict this stuff on little kids?

'*Are* you, Daddy?'

'Would you like to have a new mommy?'

'I like Judith a lot.'

'I like her too.'

'Can she be my mommy?'

He leaned down to kiss her cheek again. 'Oh, sweetie, it's not that easy.'

'Doesn't she want to?'

'I'm sure Judith loves you very much, but loving you is only part of it. There's a lot of grown-up stuff that has be worked out before anybody can be a new mommy, even somebody who loves you.'

'Don't you want her to be my mommy?'

'I think she's very special,' he said, and then: 'I also think it's time for sleep, and we should talk about this more tomorrow.' To his surprise, he got away with it.

In the morning they had pancakes, and the subject of mommies didn't come up.

Sunday afternoon, Joshua called.

'Benjamin! I'm sorry to have missed you this Thursday but I'm glad you went to Yitz's study session.' He was as full of energy as Ben had ever heard him. 'Wasn't I right? Wasn't it much better for you than the other one?

'It was great, but I'm not sure I'm up to their level.'

'Nonsense. You're a smart man, you can process what you're hearing and make a contribution to the group even if you can't recite a page of the Talmud by heart. Or a sentence. Yet.'

'I appreciate the vote of confidence.'

'It's earned. And I want to tell you, I'm full of ideas from this retreat I'm just back from. What a great experience. Next time I want you to be there with us, no excuses' – as if Ben's not being there this time had been his own idea – 'not even for your important job.'

'I'd be pleased to go.' Despite his hurt at being left out, or maybe because of it, he could feel the tug of Joshua's enthusiasm.

'We have to get together,' Joshua said. 'I really want to talk to you about all this.'

'Sure. When?'

'No time like like the present.'

36

At Ben's request Joshua didn't arrive until after Hannah was in bed.

He was running over with anecdotes about the retreat, about the pleasures of long meditative walks in the woods on the leading edge of spring, the first buds just beginning to appear.

'And next time I'm determined that you'll be there. We always do this around the equinox, and you'll see when you come, that haShem's world is even richer at the very end of summer.'

'I'll look forward to that.' And if he was working in Washington, he'd find a way. 'I'm only sorry it's so far in the future.'

'So am I, and I just got back. I always learn so much when I go away with students who are serious. There's a saying of Rabbi Hanina – "I've learned much from my masters, and more from my comrades than my masters, but from my students I've learned the most." Speaking of which, how was the study session?'

'Actually, there was one thing that came up that I wanted to ask you about.'

'Sure.' Joshua adjusted his skullcap with exaggerated care. 'The rabbi is *in*.'

Ben laughed, harder perhaps than was called for. Cleared his throat.

'Well . . . There was talk about a rabbi, a disciple of the Stropkover Rebbe, may he rest in peace, who – if I've got it right – denies that you're the Rebbe's heir. And just hearing his name upset the people at the study group.'

Joshua's expression had grown more serious as Ben spoke. He took a moment before he answered. 'It gives me great unhappiness that we have strife and discord in what was once a close community. But as you know I'm a great believer in the power of teshuva, and I still believe we'll overcome these differences.'

Joshua closed his eyes and put his fingertips to his temples. He sat that way awhile before he opened his eyes again. Ben thought he looked tired.

'I told you the last time we talked how I came to be a disciple of our Rebbe,' he began, in a tone stripped of emotion. 'Once he'd accepted me as a student, I was with him night and day. Of course, he had other disciples, men who had first studied in Stropkover schools when they were so young their teachers would put honey on the Hebrew alphabet letters to make the learning experience sweet. One of these was Asher Stern, who many said was the Rebbe's most brilliant student. Even as a teenager he was already teaching men much older than he. When I came to study with the Rebbe, Asher had just been chosen to be the husband of the Rebbe's elder granddaughter. Asher was in his twenties, and Miriam was nineteen, and beautiful. Very beautiful.'

Joshua sat back, gazing at some remembered scene, a smile not quite forming at the corners of his mouth. 'Miriam had a sister, younger by a year or so and not so beautiful, but with a wonderful spirit. As I spent more and more time with the Rebbe, it was impossible for me not to have thoughts about Ruth, because she was often there to look after her grandfather. And I knew it was a mistake. I knew I was jealous of Asher, and I feared that, however much I truly cared for Ruth, I was also making a kind of trophy of getting the hand of the Rebbe's other granddaughter – a measure of whether I meant as much to him as Asher did. I knew this could not lead me in a good direction.'

'What did you do?'

'I told the Rebbe about it.' Joshua grinned at Ben's reaction. 'Surprised? Well, I revered the man. I thought he was the wisest man on earth. And I saw this as a flaw in myself, that he could help me understand and repair. So I told him. And you know what he did?'

Ben waited.

'He laughed!' Joshua grinned wider, shaking his head. 'Why? Because he'd been waiting for weeks, months, for me to say something. He'd had a kind of bet with himself, and by my volunteering this information he'd won.

'Because he'd come to see the situation as a test for me, though he hadn't planned it that way. He had noticed how I looked at Ruth, and how she looked at me, and he had seen that no good could come of it. But he wanted me to recognize the problem myself, and he wanted to see how I'd deal with it.

'He told me that he had found me another house to live in, to put temptation away from both me and his granddaughter. "Because I do not know if she is as strong as you are," he said. And that made me both happy and unhappy, because it told me that she was interested in me, but that her interest in me didn't please him, and that therefore we'd never fulfill our desire for each other.

'I consoled myself that his opposition wasn't because of any character flaw in me, it was because I'd become Sabbath observant only as an adult. And many fathers don't want their children – of either sex – marrying a ba'al teshuva, as we're called – someone who's mastered the process of returning, or repenting, as some would say. Because they think of us as having been out there in the world and tasted its pleasures. So we tend to end up marrying each other. Which is what I did, ultimately, and I'm very happy with my Rivka, my jewel, and our four children, thanks to haShem for his bounty and may He keep them safe.

'In the meantime, Asher Stern had fathered the Rebbe's first great-grandchild, and the Rebbe had arranged a marriage for Ruth with the son of a rabbi in Israel whose father had come, as the Rebbe had, from the north of Slovakia.'

'And she went to Israel?'

'Where she is to this day, in a town called Kiryat Yaacov, north of the Sea of Galilee, not so far from the Golan Heights.'

The town's name distracted Ben for a moment: Wasn't that where Alan Kest had a house?

Joshua noticed his reaction and smiled. 'The name's not a coincidence.'

'Really?' Ben was startled, trying to cover it.

'It's named after the Rebbe' –

Oh.

—'The town was founded by Stropkovers.'

'Is it still a Stropkover community?' Ben wasn't sure the name was the same – Kiryat meant town or something like that, and there were dozens of them, Kiryat This and Kiryat That – but his curiosity was piqued.

'Not a hundred percent. It's a popular part of the country, and with so many immigrants from Russia, and everywhere else, it's a mitzvah to welcome strangers. But Ruth and her husband are still there, and their six children.'

Ben didn't want to call any more attention to his interest in Kiryat Yaacov, so he changed the subject: 'Did you find . . . Rivka? . . . soon after that?' He didn't recall Joshua ever mentioning his wife before, and she hadn't been in evidence at any of the services Joshua had officiated at.

'Rivka, yes. My jewel, her price beyond rubies, a wonderful woman,' Joshua said, beaming. 'Everyone says she's a saint and I don't deserve her. And they're right, but I've got her, so I thank haShem every day for my good fortune. But no, it was almost five years before the Holy One, Blessed be He, granted me the great gift of meeting my wife. By then the Rebbe had sent Asher to be the spiritual leader for a Stropkover community that was forming a short distance upstate, in a place called Centerville' –

This time, Ben's reaction didn't show.

—'where families were going who wanted some fresh air and to be away from the city's problems. Asher became the Rebbe's surrogate there, and the Rebbe encouraged everyone to treat him as they would treat the Rebbe himself. And I? I stayed in Brooklyn and studied, and lightened the Rebbe's load when I could. And sometimes when the Rebbe would want his family around him, he would call Asher back from Centerville and I'd go out there in his place.

'And then about five years ago, with no warning, the Rebbe had a stroke.

'By this time, some of the Rebbe's oldest and closest followers had begun to speak of him as a kind of modern Elijah, who it is written will herald the coming of Moshiach – haShem's anointed one whose arrival sets the stage for the World To Come. I didn't think it was smart to encourage this talk, especially because many thousands of the Lubavitcher Rebbe's followers all over the world were already proclaiming *him* the actual Moshiach. I didn't think we should get into a shouting match with them about whose Rebbe was going to inaugurate the Messianic Age.

'The Rebbe survived, but he couldn't talk very well. We had to devise ways to help him communicate, and to understand what he was trying to say. Some people seemed better able to do that than others and, for whatever reason, haShem chose to give that ability to me but not to Asher.

'This went on for more than two years. Almost from the beginning, Asher started acting in the Rebbe's place in Brooklyn, and there was another rabbi doing Asher's job in Centerville' –

Solomon? But by Roger's account there were at least two different groups of observant Jews in Centerville. Solomon could just as well be from one of the other groups.

—'The Rebbe was unchanged for a long time, a little better a little worse, and then one day I had to to warn people it might not be that way much longer. Asher got very worked up about my being the Rebbe's interpreter in what might be his last days in this world. Asher had some other men come and stay in the room with us to monitor what was going on, and he called in a new team of doctors.

'But it wasn't the time for doctors. The Rebbe's neshama – his soul – was ready to leave his body and return to the heavenly realm. He wanted to hear Vidui, the confessional prayer – he was beyond saying it himself. It was Saturday and it was getting dark. He was exhausted, fading, but he was hanging on to see the Havdalah ceremony that closes the Sabbath and separates it from the rest of the week. I was sure it was symbolic – closing this life for him and separating it from the next.

'Everyone went off to make preparations, leaving only me and the male nurse who saw to the Rebbe's medical and hygienic needs. And the Rebbe spoke to me. Spoke coherently for the first time in almost two years. In Yiddish, he said, "My child, my son, I wish to bless you." And with great difficulty he pronounced the first part of the priestly blessing, "May the Lord bless you and keep you, May the Lord lift up his countenance to you . . ." And then he said, "I cannot carry my burden any further, yet I must not put it down. I give it to you. Prepare for Moshiach." And then he was silent again. In a minute, Asher and the others were back, hurrying to perform the Havdalah ceremony, because they saw how weak the Rebbe looked.

'We lit the special braided candle with many wicks. Asher held a small bowl of fresh spices – they couldn't take the time to put them in a spice box – and put a pinch under the Rebbe's nose for him to smell, and we sang the blessings and the song of praise to Elijah, the herald of Moshiach.' He paused, eyes glistening, cleared his throat.

'You know,' he said, 'there's a tradition that we each get a kind of extra soul to celebrate Shabbat and it returns to heaven at the end of Havdalah when the candle is doused in the wine. So it was that the Rebbe's own soul rose from him at that very moment, escorted heavenward by all of our special Shabbat souls.'

He lapsed into a momentary silence.

'And that should be the end of the story,' he resumed, 'except that Asher didn't believe it when I said the Rebbe had handed on his burden to me, even though there was a witness who saw everything and heard everything. Asher said that if the Rebbe addressed me as his son, he must have thought he was talking to Asher, who is his actual grandson-in-law, and not some stranger. Stranger! As if I hadn't sat at the Rebbe's feet for twenty years.'

'And it was enough to split the community?'

'Oh yes. Because he, or his followers, didn't let it rest at an accusation that I was mistaken. They said I was malicious, that I lied to gain power for myself and to do harm to Asher, who was justly the Rebbe's heir. In the most extreme form of the slander, some even say I hastened the Rebbe's death. I find it incredible that anyone could think such a thing, much less say it, but they do. To speak no evil of anyone is one of the most important of haShem's commandments, but . . .' He spread his hands and shrugged.

'So you can see,' he resumed, 'anyone who believes Rabbi Stern's version of events will obviously have nothing to do with me. And the people who believe me must also believe that Rabbi Stern is engaged in unjustifiable libels, and so they want nothing to do with him.'

37

Joshua walked with Ben when he got up to check on Hannah. She was on her side, her feet tangled in her blanket, fist to her mouth.

'A beautiful child,' Joshua said.

They stood awhile, watching her sleep.

Passing the kitchen on the way back to the living room, Ben said, 'I'm being a poor host. I don't think I'm up to washing your feet, but I can offer you something to drink. Wine or beer, or whatever.'

'I'll take a beer. When I see wine I always think there ought to be a ceremony.'

Joshua said the appropriate blessing, without ceremony, and Ben said amen. They carried the bottles into the living room.

'It must be very difficult for you,' Ben said, 'knowing you're being maligned that way.'

'Yes, every day I endure the knowledge that this man is spreading slanders about me. I desperately want to fight against this, not just for myself but to protect the ones Asher is misleading. But I can't say a word, because the prohibition against loshon harah – evil speech – applies even when the bad things you're saying, God forbid, are the truth. And that's what matters most.'

'And that's why no one talks about him.'

'Yes.' Joshua fell silent. Then, abruptly, he lifted the beer bottle to his lips and tilted his head back. Ben could see the Adam's apple bob under Joshua's red-brown beard as he chugged down the rest of his beer. He put the bottle on the coffee table and belched lightly.

'Enough about unhappy things. I hear Hannah's going to be visiting our school.'

'Suzanne's daughter invited her.' Hannah's school was closed for spring break, but Deborah's didn't break until Passover, two weeks away. 'She's very eager.'

'She'll love it. Don't be surprised if she wants to stay the rest of the term.'

'Nothing she does surprises me anymore. Another beer?'

Joshua hesitated. 'Sure, why not? All that talking is thirsty work.'

'There's something else that I wanted to ask you about,' Ben said when he returned with a pair of fresh beers. 'Not so personal and serious.'

'I'm happy to help if I can.'

'Red heifers.' Rosen had called and left a message about a Biblical ritual he thought might be a clue to Alan Kest's interest in genetically engineered cattle.

'Red heifers! I see I have a student with a taste for the obscure.' He drank some beer, settled himself in the easy chair and told Ben about a Biblical requirement that all who served in the Holy Temple be purified from any contact with the dead.

'The ritual itself is a great mystery, but it's there in the Torah. The purification involves drinking a potion mixed with the ashes of a properly sacrificed, absolutely perfect heifer, with only red hair and without any blemish. But what brings you to such thoughts?'

'Someone mentioned it to me, about the red heifer, and I just got curious about it.'

'It's been in the air,' Joshua said. 'They thought there was one born in Israel last summer, the first one since Temple times. It caused a great fuss until it grew white hairs in its tail.'

'I was wondering where things like that fit, in the Rebbe's teachings.' An innocent enough question, Ben thought. But if Rosen was right about why Alan Kest was dealing with a Texas cattle breeder, it would be interesting to know where Asher Stern – sometime resident of Centerville – stood on the question.

The question of the Temple led them to a discussion of the belief that only God should decree a government of Jews in Jerusalem. 'And that's not until the time of Moshiach,' Joshua said, 'or even until the World to Come, which – as you may know – is different from the Age of the Messiah.'

'Is it? I assumed that once the Messiah comes, that's it.'

'That's what most people think. Actually there are several theories of how This World comes to an end, but virtually all of them feature a messianic era when there's a return to Eretz Yisroel – the Land of Israel – and also a rebuilding of the Holy Temple, which is where your red heifer comes in. Because not just the priests but the architects and the construction crew have to be purified. Anyone who has anything to do with the Temple.

'That's one of the ways we know the Messiah is here – the Temple is rebuilt. And there's also a belief that there's a potential Messiah in every generation, just waiting for the Children of Israel to be worthy enough for him to come forward.'

'And this is all part of the religion.'

'It's not a part most people pay attention to, and that's how it should be. There's a saying of Reb Yokhanan ben Zakkai, one of the great sages of the Talmud, that if you have a seedling in your hand and you're about to plant it, and someone tells you, "Come, look, the Messiah is here!" you should first plant the seedling, then you can go out and greet the Messiah.'

'So Stropkovers aren't out beating the bushes looking for a red heifer.'

'I know *I'm* not. And, honestly, if someone brought me one, I'd be more scared than excited, because right now any overt signs of the Messiah are dangerous to us.'

There was a new seriousness in Joshua's tone: this was no longer angels dancing on the head of a pin.

'Why dangerous?' Ben asked him.

'Because of the the craziness in the society. Because by some bizarre logic people have decided the millennium is coming. They don't seem to know or care that the New Testament millennium is the predicted thousand-year-long reign of their Jesus, and not the thousandth *anniversary* of anything. Not that this year 2000 is a significant anniversary, either. Certainly not of the birth of Jesus, no historian or theologian thinks that anymore. But never mind history or logic – for more and more people this so-called millennium is a time to preach apocalyptic violence, and especially violence against Jews.'

'We've seen that before.'

'Yes, over and over. There's never a time when somebody isn't tying salvation to the destruction of the Jews. But it's gotten much worse all this century, and especially the closer we get to this millennium nonsense.' Joshua was up and pacing, with a kind of fury to it. 'Did you know that one of the biggest televangelists in the country is already preaching that the Antichrist is walking the Earth among us? And he's preaching that this Antichrist is a Jewish man?'

'A mainstream clergyman?' Ben was incredulous.

'Oh, yes. It's not a fringe opinion. There are plenty of ministers who are pro-Israel only because they believe a Jewish government in the Holy Places is a sign that the Final Days are upon us. Days when *their* righteous people will be sucked up bodily into heaven, and the rest of us will be annihilated in apocalyptic wars and sent down into the Pit. Jews first. Or what they're pleased to call *false Jews*.'

'False Jews? Us?'

'Yes, *us*.' Joshua stopped, filled with an intensity greater than any Ben had seen in him. 'It's straight out of their Bible. The Revelation of St John the Divine, chapter two, verse nine.' He struck a pose and began declaiming with a fulsome hellfire sonority. '"I know the blasphemy of them which say they are Jews and are not, but are the synagogue of Satan."' He relaxed, but only a little. 'And that's just the starting point. I'm telling you, annihilation is not too strong a word.'

Could this be some part of what was going on in Centerville – the Jewish Defense League theory writ large? 'Sounds like we should be preparing for the worst.'

'A few are. It may be a tragedy that more of us aren't.'

'Was that the Rebbe's point of view, as well?' Thinking not of the Rebbe but of Asher Stern.

'It's not a question of this one's teachings or that one's. For Jews to be frightened about this is just common sense.'

Serious as Joshua was, Ben couldn't help smiling. 'After what you were saying, I wouldn't have expected you to be crediting Asher Stern with common sense.'

'Was I talking about Asher Stern?' Joshua stood up. 'I should let you get about the rest of your evening – we've both got to get up in the morning. We'll do this again.'

38

Monday, Sid Levy met Ben and Lukas in the meat-packing district again, in a restaurant meant to look as if it were in Paris.

'It went fine,' he said. 'I was kind of rusty on the rituals and I worried they might get spooked, but I think I got by. Good thing we didn't play any high-tech games though, because I had to take a dip in a mikvah. Turns out the men all go there before services on Friday.'

'A who?' Lukas said.

'A ritual bath. It's mostly for women, restoring their ritual purity after their period. Growing up Modern Orthodox, I didn't see it as something for men, but Kest says it's pretty common, especially for men who have a lot of contact with the non-Jewish world.'

'This is public?' Lukas asked.

'Yeah, and no bathing suit, either. No way to wear a wire, or anything else.'

'You think Kest accepts you?'

'So far. I'm meeting with him again Wednesday to finish the laptop deal. We ready for that?'

'Count on it,' Lukas said.

'I want to offer him some more stuff after that, but I don't want to push too hard. I'm meeting people, I'm getting to be one of the crowd. A couple more of these Sabbath visits, assuming they invite me—'

'We've got to find a way to monitor you,' Lukas interrupted. 'I still don't like the risk.'

'It's not worth making a big deal about. These people aren't doing anything remotely related to business on the Sabbath, especially not anything violent. It'll just take a couple more, like I said, and it's the only way I'll move up to the next level.'

'There's a name I just came across,' Ben said. 'Asher Stern. Rabbi Asher Stern. Mean anything?'

Sid shook his head. 'Haven't heard it. Anything special?'

'Just a name I heard,' Ben said. 'Probably no connection. You've got more important things to think about.'

'Another rabbi?' Lukas didn't sound surprised. 'Where does this one fit?'

'I'm not sure he does. I heard his name over the weekend in the same sentence as both Centerville and the town in Israel where Kest has his house.' He'd verified that much.

'And where'd you hear that?'

'Confidential source.'

Lukas looked at him, but offered no challenge.

Ben said, 'I've been thinking about what you said about this having to do with Israel and the Arabs. It's something we have to watch out for, but I don't want to get distracted by it until we have better evidence that's what it is.'

'We've got guns and money – assuming they're not building a criminal army you have to think politics. Although we also just got some word that gives some of this a religious twist.'

'Like what?'

'The cattle breeder out in Texas is kind of a nut that way. Belongs to a fundamentalist church that's getting itself all set for big doings when all the zeros turn over on the calendar. And our Texas people tell me there's talk around that he's been doing business with some religious Jews, making a deal for some kind of cattle that are described in the Bible.'

'That fits with what I got.' Ben tried to explain the little he understood about the red heifer as a necessary condition for rebuilding the Holy Temple.

'I don't know,' Lukas said. 'I'm lapsed, myself, but used to be I took communion every week, and I bought the whole wine-and-wafer thing a hundred percent, so I've got a pretty good idea of what folks are willing to let themselves get talked into. But what you're talking about now is off my scale. Good for them if they believe it, but I don't see where it fits with printing money or stockpiling guns.'

'I don't, either,' Ben said. 'Except that maybe they're using the money to pay for the guns and the cows, but that still doesn't tell us how the guns and the cows fit.'

'And if that's all it is, why not do it like any other cult and recruit a couple of millionaires? Printing money is kind of the long way round the barn, especially money that good.'

'With what we have so far, we're just going to confuse ourselves if we start talking in terms of a cult. These may be religious people committing these crimes, but I don't see where it goes any further than that.

'Call Mr Morgan,' Ella told Ben when he got back to the office. 'It sounded important.'

'The Secretary wants you to start coming down as a consultant,' Morgan told him. 'Full time, if possible.'

Full time! The last thing he wanted right now. 'I'm really tied up in that case we've talked about. Important things are happening.'

'I want to hear about that, but I have to tell you – the Secretary wants you down here, getting your sea legs.'

'You don't even have my FBI check yet.' An educated guess, though he knew it was well underway – he was having to reassure people who were calling to say the FBI was asking about him. 'Or IRS.'

'No, we don't,' Morgan conceded. 'Why – are you expecting trouble?'

'Not for a minute. But I also can't just walk out on my boss, and you're not even ready to move ahead.'

'If we can't start getting you up to speed until *after* the background checks come in, we're losing that much more time.'

'Let me talk to Victoria and see what I can do. But I think we'll have to be content with a day or two a week for now.' He was far from ready to be pulled off the Aljo case this way – not now. And his concern about the US Attorney was genuine: it wasn't smart to treat her cavalierly.

'How often do they want you?' was her first question.

'Full time.' He said it straight out because he thought that was the best way to get her to react. He was pleased to see her eyes narrow.

'Are you formally nominated yet?' she asked him.

'They don't have my FBI check done. Or IRS.'

'Then why full time?'

'They must be expecting me to get clearance any minute.'

'There's too much for you to do here. And what about your little girl?'

'If you can't spare me full time that's not even an issue.'

'And I can't.' With the barest hint of a conspiratorial smile.

'How about two days a week,' he proposed.

'A day and a half.'

'I'll see what I can do.'

'Don't bother,' she said. 'I'll call them myself.'

There was a fax from Lukas waiting for Ben at his office – a payoff for his intuition about the importance of geography in the Aljo case – addresses of the people in Israel being called by the Aljo targets. What jumped out at him was how many of them were in Kiryat Yaacov.

Kiryat Yaacov wasn't a purely Stropkover community any more, Joshua had said. So all this contact with people there was – like Centerville – just another piece of circumstantial evidence, not yet proof the Aljo targets were Stropkovers.

It was a fair bet, though, that the Rebbe's grandson-in-law had been the town's first spiritual leader and might well still be. The man who had married Joshua's first sweetheart. Asher Stern's brother-in-law.

Ben wanted to call Joshua and ask him more about Rabbi Stern and his teachings. He'd said Stern misled his congregants. Just about Joshua and the Rebbe, or about doctrine as well? Did Joshua know if Stern had strayed far from the Rebbe's teachings? What about the red heifer? Joshua hadn't said the Rebbe didn't believe in the ritual or its centrality to rebuilding the Temple and welcoming the Messiah, he'd just said he, Joshua, didn't want to see one any time soon.

There was bound to be a lot Joshua could tell about Asher Stern and his followers before crossing the boundaries of evil speech, but Ben was uneasy about making an informant of a man he looked to for spiritual guidance. The possibility of a religious prohibition against informing only made it worse.

Maybe someone else could get the answers. He called Elliot Rosen.

'Have you ever heard of an Orthodox group that followed a Reb Yaacov Moshe Friedlander? The Stropkover Rebbe?'

'Hasidic?'

'I don't think so. Probably some Hasidic influences, some other esoteric twists, but more in the direction of Modern Orthodox, from what I've seen. That's what I'm trying to track down – their practices.'

'I don't know about them myself, but I know somebody who probably would.'

Ben came home to find himself attacked by an overexcited five-year-old. Hannah had decided they were playing tag, which by her rules meant her running out of a hiding place and giving him as hard a wallop as she could, shouting 'You're it!' and running away, giggling.

The reason for her agitation, it developed, was that she'd had a good time at school with Deborah, made new friends and wanted to keep going there. And anticipated that her father might not be so willing to have her make the change.

'I don't want to go to my old school. I hate it. I hate Bobby G.' The list of things and people she hated went on, getting louder as it went.

'Okay, okay,' he said when he thought she could finally hear him. 'Let's just talk about it, okay?'

'Okay.' Pouting, arms crossed.

'You didn't tell me about the teacher yet.'

'Mrs Geller. She's nice.'

'I thought you liked Janice.'

'Mrs Geller is nicer.'

And not just Mrs Geller but everything else at Deborah's school was better than the one Hannah went to now. She even liked the Hebrew letters posted around the room.

'Do you get them mixed up with English letters?'

'There's one that looks like a C, only backwards. And a funny one like a giraffe with a long long neck. But Mrs Geller said I don't have to learn them.

'Did you have prayers, too?'

'Yes. For eating, and washing hands. Like candles, on Shabbat.'

'A little bit. But this is every day.'

'Mmm hmm.' Not interested in the details. 'I want to go there. You said I can.'

'No, I didn't.' He tickled her. 'You're a silly.'

She giggled. 'Stop. Stop.' Giggling madly, squirming out of reach. 'So are you.'

'I tell you what. This is only your first day. Let's see if you still like it so much after you've been there some more.'

Ben lay in bed, kept awake by thoughts of the case and Washington, Joshua Brauner and Asher Stern and their roles in each other's lives and in his, even whether it was all right to let Hannah go back to Joshua's school in the morning.

He had to face the fact that he wasn't likely to be carrying the Aljo case to a conclusion. Even if he didn't get the job in Washington, if the case really had a Stropkover connection he'd almost certainly have to get off it before it went to court, because any defense lawyer who wasn't brain dead would look at Ben's relationship to Joshua and Joshua's rivalry with Rabbi Stern and – depending on how close Stern was to Kest and the others – cry vendetta, harassment, misuse of prosecutorial power.

But that was months away. The more pressing question was whether, if Kest and the others were Stropkovers, that meant he needed to withdraw before that. Not because of the schism between Stern's faction and Joshua's, but because of the ties that might have existed before the break.

He found the whole situation easier to think about in a non-Jewish framework: Suppose some potential defendants worshiped at a church whose one-time assistant pastor had moved on to be pastor of a rival church the prosecutor was about to join. And – assuming there was any connection at all – during the pastor's days at the previous church he had probably known some of the bad guys, in the way that an assistant pastor 'knows' his parishioners.

Was that reason for the prosecutor to disqualify himself from supervising the investigation? To keep his daughter out of the church school or find a new church for himself? Probably not, though Ben could see arguing it either way, depending on the details. For now, he thought, there was no reason for him to assume the worst. He needed more information.

Before he left for the trip to Washington in the morning he checked in with Lukas about Asher Stern.

'We're going over the phone lists we have,' Lukas told him. 'So far, no hits. Kest and them don't seem to be calling him, not on any line that's in his name.'

'Let's see if he's calling them.'

Lukas had found addresses and phone numbers for Stern in Brooklyn and Centerville. Ben wrote them down. 'I'll get subpoenas right out for his phone records, and we can apply for a pen register and a trap-and-trace.' Geography again. 'Can you check proximity of the addresses, see if Stern's their neighbor?'

'Already did. The map shows him a couple of blocks from Kest in Brooklyn. Centerville, we can't tell exactly because we don't have a decent map. But it's the same end of town.'

Again, not proof that Kest worshiped with Stern, but in a community that went to Sabbath services only on foot it was another strong indicator.

'You're awfully interested for it's being someone you don't know is connected to this,' Lukas said.

'Not really.' Ben didn't want to get into questions of how far up the religious hierarchy knowledge of the crimes might reach. 'The truth is, it's probably one of those tips that leads nowhere, especially if we don't have any sign they're communicating.'

39

Ben's first consulting days at Treasury offered a bonus – the chance to steal a night with Judith. Much as she wanted to fly down with him, he was unwilling to tempt fate, or taunt the FBI, by arriving in her company. It was going to be daring enough to spend the night in her hotel room.

His time in Washington was fully scheduled. He bounced around the Treasury building meeting people, after a pro-forma interview with the presidential personnel director. Lunch was with various career people in the Office of Enforcement and the lone surviving political appointee, a Deputy Assistant Secretary.

After lunch, Morgan showed him the office he'd be using as a consultant and that would be his if he got the job. He didn't know what he'd expected. Certainly not this.

It was on the fourth floor of the Main Treasury building in the corridor above the one that led to the Secretary's office. It had an anteroom as big as his office at the Southern District, with two wooden secretary's desks and in the far corner a massive old steel filing cabinet with a huge lock on it.

'Don't get excited,' Morgan said. 'Two desks, but only one secretary.'

'Assigned?'

'No, you'll get to choose.'

The office itself was at least as big as Victoria's, but the double-height ceiling and white walls made it seem even larger. An antique-style leather couch and chair made up a sitting area in one corner, and a huge old wooden desk he thought might qualify as a real antique commanded a view of the room and out the windows to the south.

'I'll let you settle in. You've got about ten minutes till your next appointment.'

Ben saw Morgan to the door and closed it behind him. Paced around the office, feeling like a cat staking out territory. He stopped at the sitting area and looked out the window at the green swathe of the Mall and the Washington Monument two blocks away. Not the view of the White House that the Secretary had, but he could live with it.

He felt himself getting used to the office, to the idea of the job, even in the few minutes he had. It was dangerous to let himself feel like that, he knew. There were still things that could go wrong, ways it would affect his life he was not yet ready to contemplate.

He was dizzy with meeting new people by late afternoon when he again had a few minutes to sit quietly in his office. His office! Again he felt the danger of getting too attached to all this. The people he'd met so far seemed smart and responsive. Politics wasn't his strongest suit but he had the impression these were people he could talk to.

There was a knock on his door.

'Come in.'

It was Mary Harrell, the politically appointed Deputy Assistant Secretary for Enforcement. 'Am I disturbing you?'

'Just taking a break between meetings.' He stood up, waved her to the sitting area, feeling a little like Lord of the Manor.

She sat carefully, back straight, hands folded, feet crossed at the ankles. He'd already assessed her at lunch. Sharp but laid-back – she hadn't said much – mid-thirties, about his own age, well presented in a navy skirt and jacket, white blouse, more conservative than some of the other women.

'I think you're going to find the job challenging,' Harrell said, 'especially if you come on board before they have an Under Secretary.'

'It's odd being suspended between the two places like this,' he said. 'I know there's good reason for me to start working down here soon, but I also have real obligations to wrap up where I am.'

'The currency-counterfeiting case?'

'Among other things.' Interesting that she knew about it, and knew it was his.

'They're trying to keep quiet around here about how important it is, but my feeling is, it's scaring some people,' she said. 'I think it's given them a comfort level that you're handling it, and you have ties to Treasury. They wish you could have more time on it.'

'I wondered about that, actually.' He didn't know what her agenda was, but it clearly included positioning herself as someone willing to give him the inside story. 'Considering how hard they're pressing me to be here.'

'There's a lot going on here, bureaucratically,' she said. 'We need somebody solid in the office.'

He waited, watching her with what he hoped was a look of expectancy – the eager pupil.

She shifted on the couch, leaning forward a bit, then began to fill the silence with explanation: 'We're expecting a challenge from the Justice Department for some of our jurisdiction. There's still a lot unresolved about domestic terrorism and how to deal with it, but the FBI already looms pretty large in that area and they want to make it their own – and that's going to impact Secret Service and ATF. Customs, too, because we're worried about terrorist weapons that come into the country. And that's just the beginning. For now they've stopped talking about merging ATF into FBI, but that only brings up some other craziness, like a move to take Customs out of the Treasury Department and make it part of a separate cabinet department along with INS, or even move it to Justice. Nobody's happy about any of that.'

He waited a moment but that seemed to be all for now. He said, 'I appreciate your coming in.' He wasn't sure if he wanted to keep her close or at a distance – in the guise of being helpful she seemed to be trying to co-opt him, and draw him into areas where for now he had no authority. He'd have to be careful. 'I'll look forward to our working together some more.'

Judith was waiting for him at her hotel.

'That's better,' he said when they broke from their clinch.

'Hard day?' she asked.

'I've had more fun. But I think I like this place.' He told her about his office.

'My. Doesn't that sound grand,' she said, pushing her multi-layered accent in the direction of the British. 'And properly so, as befits a man of your impressive talents.'

He pulled her to him again. 'I've got other talents I'd like to impress you with.'

'As you already have.'

He kissed her. 'I'd better call Hannah.'

Hannah was even more excited about school than she had been the first day. It was a while before he could get in a word. The message was clear: She loved it and she wanted to stay, a demand she wasn't shy about insisting on, despite his repeated assurances they'd talk about it more when he got home.

'Is Judith there?' she asked out of the blue.

He thought of saying no, knowing the truth would add fuel to the 'new mommy' campaign, but his rule was not to lie to Hannah even when the chances of being caught were nil.

'Yes, she came to visit me.'

'Suzanne said.'

'Oh.' Perfect.

'Can I say hello?'

'Sure.' He handed Judith the phone. 'There's a young lady here who'd like to talk to you.'

'She's a tiger,' he said when Judith was finally off the phone.

'I think she's wonderful.'

He kissed her. 'The way to a man's heart – praise his little girl.'

'Oh?' Archly. 'Is *that* the way?' She grabbed for him.

He ducked away. 'Fresh.' From a safe distance he said, 'I've got a business call to make, first.'

'Well,' she said, 'I ought to have a shower. I've put in a hard day working on my seminar paper.'

'Right. I noticed the fancy shopping bags.'

'Well, I had to take some time for shopping, too. It's not as hopeless here as I'd feared.'

'Get anything interesting?'

'Just this.' From one of the bags she drew an item of silky black lingerie that seemed to be mostly lace.

'That *is* interesting.'

'A thong teddy, the shopgirl said it's called. Would you like me to try it for you?'

'If you want to.' Pretending not to care.

She threw it at him. 'I'd appreciate more enthusiasm than that, if you please.'

He laughed. 'I promise as much enthusiasm as you could ever want.'

He listened to the drumming of the shower while he waited for Lukas to answer his beep – envisioning the water cascading over Judith's body. He had to shake himself clear of the image when his cellphone rang.

'I think we've got our break,' Lukas said. 'You wanted to know about the guy who took delivery of the assault rifles and grenades.'

'Right.'

'Well, the guy who owns the house is just another of the people who live out there. Clean as a whistle. But it turns out he has a boarder who's an Israeli national and who looks to have overstayed his student visa, and it also looks like he signed for at least one of the shipments. Name of Ari Benzvi. We're verifying it now about his status. I was talking to Andy Ciampa and we agree it wouldn't be too big a stretch to impute receipt of those weapons to this Israeli so-called student, and that puts him in big trouble. I think we want to pick him up and talk to him. Not yet, but when we're ready he's our guy.'

'Sounds good. What else? Anything on the pole cameras?'

'Haven't seen today's tapes yet.'

'And Sid? Is he delivering the laptops to Kest?'

'Postponed till Thursday. We couldn't get the merchandise assembled in time.'

Ben didn't comment. 'I'll be back late tomorrow. Let's talk then.'

He hung up and turned around to see Judith leaning against the bathroom doorframe fresh from her shower, modeling her thong teddy. 'Wow!'

She turned slowly. He marveled.

'Done being a lawman?'

'Why? Do you have something in mind?'

'Don't you?'

'You bet. As soon as *I* shower.'

She stuck her tongue out. 'In that case I'm putting on a robe before I catch my death.'

'How was your talk with Hannah?' he asked her as he dried off. 'Did she bore you to tears about school?'

'Well . . .' Judith said, drawing the word out mischievously, 'she asked me to be her new mom.'

He flushed, almost stammered: 'Uh . . . you have to excuse her.'

'Oh, of course. I know how badly she must need a caring woman in her life who isn't a paid nanny, any woman at all. And who can blame her, poor chick?'

'That's not what I meant. It's you she wants. It's just, she doesn't understand that even when grown-ups like you a lot it doesn't mean they want to be your mom full time.'

'Oh, I wouldn't mind. I think she's a very special little girl.'

He could feel his face burning. He wanted to make a joke of it, say something like, is that a proposal, but he knew it would come out wrong. He settled for wrapping his arms around her and pulling her close.

'Let's wait and see what state I'm going to be in.'

'Is that figurative or literal?'

'Both. And I've always assumed you were going back to England when you were finished at NYU. Or to The Hague.'

'That's what I'd planned, but that was . . . well, that was before I'd been at the law school very long, and you know how experiences you have during your education – even post-graduate education – can change your outlook.' Teasing.

'I guess I do.' They were actually talking about this. Not directly, but still . . . talking about it. It scared him.

He woke up before the alarm went off, hyper-aware of Judith in the bed next to him, trying to hold onto wisps of a dream that seemed important. Judith again, and Joshua . . . He couldn't remember. But he did remember something else, whether prompted by a dream or not he couldn't say. Isaacs had talked of Alan Kest as being like a father to him. It had gotten lost in the shuffle, but now that Ben remembered, he wanted to follow it up. Isaacs would certainly know if Kest was a Stropkover, and he might even have some idea how much the non-religious part of Kest's life depended on Rabbi Stern and his teachings.

Wednesday at the Treasury Department was a lot like Tuesday. Meeting people, listening to presentations.

He'd asked for a tour of the Bureau of Engraving and Printing. They took him right down on the working floor with the huge intaglio presses – presses in the most literal sense, squeezing the paper between two rollers with enormous force so the image was embossed into the paper in relief.

Intaglio printing was one of the principal features that separated real money from the vast bulk of counterfeit, because of the huge effort and expense involved in buying or building a machine that could impress a high-quality intaglio image into the paper, as opposed to the flat surface image produced by even the best offset printing. So far, the Aljo notes had been offset printed but – as Lukas had already pointed out – if the counterfeiters were in position to ramp up to intaglio, detecting their work was going to be vastly harder. In a practical sense, virtually impossible.

Ben stood there oblivious to the din of moving metal, watching the enormous yellow presses at work, envisioning them transported to a place he could not identify, served by a crew whose faces he could not see, as the first broad sheets of paper were squeezed out between the rollers glistening with fresh black and green ink and on each bill a metallic sparkle of gold-green-blue-black . . .

'What did you mean when you said that Alan Kest was like your father?' Ben asked Isaacs on the phone Thursday morning, after they'd worked through the informant's predictable reluctance to talk at all.

'You're looking for my life story, maybe you ought to buy me dinner, like a date,' Isaacs taunted.

'We can get together if that's what you want.'

'A *nice* dinner.'

'Sure. But tell me a little. Whet my appetite.'

Isaacs sighed – for dramatic effect, Ben was sure. 'My father died when I was twelve, and my mother's always had trouble with her health. Mostly, I had an aunt bring me up, but Rabbi Kest gave me a job, loaned me college money, gave me advice.'

'You're a Stropkover, then.' A shot not quite in the dark.

'Oh, no. Not me' –

Not me. Not: What's a Stropkover?

—'Anyway, what do you know about Stropkovers, or any of that? I didn't take you for an expert on obscure sects.'

'I think it helps to understand people, knowing what they believe.'

'Is that what you're up to, understanding people? Could have fooled me.'

'How's Sunday for dinner?'

A long hesitation. 'Sunday? Sure. Why not. Maybe I can teach you something.'

Ben had too much case-intake catchup work to do for him to join Lukas debriefing Sid about his latest meeting with Kest. Lukas came by at the end of the day to fill Ben in.

'It went smooth as glass,' the agent reported. 'Sid said there was more talk about a long-term relationship, and Kest needing some kind of intermediary with the world. Makes me wonder what Isaacs has been doing for him that he hasn't bothered to tell us about. I was thinking we ought to pull him in again, help him see the value of full disclosure.'

'Let's wait on that.' Ben wasn't sure how much to tell Lukas. 'I'm following something up with him.'

'Alone?'

'What we need from Isaacs now is information, not evidence. This business of the cattle breeder and the red heifers has me wondering how much the religious part of Kest's life plays in this. I'm thinking Isaacs can help us with that, if I catch him off guard.'

'Is that what your Rabbi Stern is about?'

'Maybe. Let me see if there's anything to it before we start building theories.'

'Sure. I wouldn't understand, anyway.' The agent had seemed more accommodating lately. Ben assumed it was because of rumors about the Treasury job.

'Sid wants to do another Sabbath visit. He says they invited him again.'

'If it's going as well as he says . . .' Ben ruminated. 'What do you think?'

'I still don't like being out of touch that way. I'm giving him a little emergency transmitter. It's nothing like foolproof, but in Brooklyn at least we can be in close, catch the transmissions if he needs us. Centerville would be something else. But, yeah, I think he should do it.'

'Let's do it, then. Anything else new?'

'More people visiting each other up in Centerville. That's one friendly town.'

That triggered a thought for Ben. 'We ought to set up a camera by Solomon's house of worship.'

'Way ahead of you. It's there.'

'Good. Great. What about this Israeli who signed for the assault rifles and grenade casigns . . . ?'

'Benzvi.'

'I was just beginning to think this wasn't political, but with that in the equation—'

'I put in a call to Cyprus about him. They tell me the Israeli National Police don't care much about the Mideast-politics theory. They're thinking if it's the whole community stocking up on guns it's more likely some kind of domestic Jewish-power thing.'

'Interesting idea.' Not saying I told you so. 'That could mean the guns have nothing to do with the financial crimes, after all. If the counterfeiting plant is in Israel, they're not protecting that.'

'It's still an awful lot of guns.'

'Maybe they're paranoid about their churchgoing neighbors.' Ben didn't want to get into Joshua's worries about millenarian madness – or anything about Joshua. 'There's been violence up there in the past.'

'If Sid can get as close as he thinks,' Lukas said, 'he'll be able to tell us if that's what it is.'

That evening there was a gathering of kindergarten parents at Joshua's school. When Suzanne suggested he come along he wasn't sure whether to go. Isaacs' initial response on the Stropkover question had been ambiguous, but Ben couldn't avoid the thought that he was trying to put these people's friends, or former friends, in federal prison.

No one at the gathering tonight would even know that was possible, he told himself. And he was eager for a better sense of the school in action, to supplement the tour Joshua had given him at the Purim party.

He was glad he went. He was impressed with the teachers and the atmosphere of cooperation that seemed to connect staff and parents, and Hannah was delighted to play with her new friends again while the grown-ups talked. By the end of the evening she had an invitation for a Shabbat overnight.

When the meeting broke up, Joshua stole a minute with Ben. 'I know we were talking about your coming to the retreat in the fall,' he said, 'but we're having a mini-retreat this Shabbat and we've just had a couple of cancellations. Can you and Judith join us? It's overnight, so you'd need someone to stay with Hannah.'

Ben laughed. 'What's this, a conspiracy?'

Joshua responded with an exaggerated face of incomprehension.

'Never mind,' Ben said. 'Hannah's all taken care of. I'll be glad to join you.'

40

Joshua's Sabbath retreat was held on the East Side, in the small synagogue where Suzanne and Mark were regular congregants. There were nine couples, some he recognized from the parents' meeting at the school. Joshua opened with a rumination on the unknowability of the Holy One:

'And Elijah began his discourse by saying, "Master of worlds, you are One – but not in the sense of a number. You are exalted above all the exalted ones, hidden from all the hidden ones, no thought can grasp You."'

When the long passage was done they sang the traditional songs welcoming the Sabbath and danced a ring dance even more exuberant than the ones Ben had watched so many Fridays from the balcony at OY. Despite his initial uncertainty about the steps, he found himself swept up in the mood of it. Judith, holding his hand, was flushed with pleasure. It was odd to see strictly observant men and women holding hands in public, but no one seemed even a little self-conscious about it.

After the prayer service they went downstairs and had a Friday night dinner, not unlike the one Ben had enjoyed at the West Side synagogue, with an abundant supply of good red wine. They followed the food with grace after meals and Sabbath songs lustily sung.

Ben was feeling the wine and the fatigue of a long and trying week, but dinner and praying and singing were preamble to discussion groups about the meaning of the mystical passage that Joshua had used to begin the evening.

After the discussions Joshua led them out into the world, inviting them to contemplate the Deity as they went – a meditative journey through streets that glistened with rain that had fallen while they prayed and ate and sang. A police car passed as they walked, siren wailing, its roof-lights streaking the pavement with red and white – for Ben, a piercing reminder of love and loss. He watched his breath puff out in front of him as he walked, doing his best, as Joshua had instructed, to visualize in the fugitive white clouds the letters of the Divine Name.

At some point after they returned and again broke into groups for reading and discussion Ben realized that Joshua had no intention of letting them sleep. He felt a surge of anger – he was exhausted, he needed his rest, and he was an adult, here to learn, not to be bullied.

He was about to say as much when Joshua called them all together again.

'Most of you have been to one of these mini-retreats before and know the value of unbroken study for an entire Shabbat, and how just when you are at the extreme point of fatigue your mind opens in new ways. I offer that experience to all of you, but if anyone wants to sleep, there are beds in the guest rooms upstairs.'

Ben looked around to see how the others were reacting, and Judith was there beside him.

'How are you doing?' she asked.

'I'm holding up. You?'

'I feel wonderful. I have you and Joshua and the Divine Presence all at once and in the same place.'

After that he could hardly let himself take refuge in fatigue. He almost nodded off more than once, but he stuck it out. Toward dawn, Joshua went around the room, talking to everyone individually, briefly to some and to some at length.

To Ben he said, 'The true Jewish life is family life, and families have a father *and* a mother.'

'Hannah's mother is dead.' Ben said flatly. And then, amazingly, he began to cry.

Joshua opened his arms. Ben clung to the broad, solid shoulders as the crying washed over and through him.

He cried a long time, body shaking with the force of it, his initial embarrassment at making a scene quickly dissolved by the tears. Joshua held him, rocked him, patted his back. Eventually he had no more tears. He felt empty, bottom to top. Hollowed out.

'You need to start life again,' Joshua said. 'You need to break the grip of your grief or you'll be strangled.'

'I don't understand,' Ben said. 'I thought I was moving on. I thought I was all right.'

'I think you *are* moving on, and I think this is an important step. You need to be open to love and wholeness. More than that, you need a wife. For Hannah, certainly, but more than for Hannah you need a wife for your own sake. A companion for your soul.'

Ben listened, still feeling empty.

'I've been watching you and Judith these past weeks, and I've talked to her,' Joshua said. 'She'd be a perfect wife for you. She loves Hannah. And any man would count himself blessed to have wife of such intelligence and beauty. Not to mention her good Torah heart. You should be grateful to be loved by a woman who has the strength that Judith has, the strength to be in awe of haShem and to devote herself to creating harmony between her physical self and her spiritual self, doing her best to inhabit both her body and her soul completely and joyfully.'

Ben couldn't suppress a memory of how thoroughly and joyfully Judith inhabited her body.

Joshua poked him in the arm. 'I don't just mean sex.'

Ben stared. Again he thought: What does this man know?

'I'm not trying to embarrass you. I just want you to see past the obvious. This is an exceptional woman and I think you're an exceptional man. But you also have to realize that marriage is like being born. Which is exactly the opposite of starting over.'

'What do you mean?' Intrigued by the paradox.

Joshua said, 'We learn from the mystics that the soul starts out on high, in a peaceful place, and then at birth it comes down to earth to inhabit a body and is swept into the raging flood of material experience. That's why a baby cries when it's born – because formerly the soul experienced Godliness, but now it only experiences gross physical reality.

'And just as the soul descends from above into the materiality of the world at birth, in the same way both the soul and the body become mired even deeper in the world after marriage. There is a home to build, a family to provide for, all the necessities of life are multiplied. But this is compensated for by the soul's intimate connection to another soul.

'You've already been married, you've had this second birth that attaches you to work and to the need to provide for your family, but also connects you to another soul and another body . . . and tragically plunges you into grief and despair if you lose that other person. It's a terrible thing when a soul so cruelly and abruptly loses the comfort of the companion it relied on.

'The Prophets tell us, and so does Koheleth' – Ecclesiastes – 'that it is more pleasant not to be born than to be born. But we who are already here don't have that choice. And the best solace we have for the pain and the seeming injustices of reality is our soul's connection with the soul of the person to whom we cling as one flesh while we live our material life.' He gripped Ben's shoulder with strong fingers. 'It isn't healthy for your soul for you to be a widower alone with a small child. Or for your body, either.'

They had a light breakfast and passed most of Saturday in prayer and study. There were more discussion groups, and another meditative walk – this one longer. At its end Ben's fatigue seemed to have fled, replaced by a sense of lightness and clarity.

After the walk Joshua had them maintain the traditional separation between men and women, even when in the afternoon they gathered for the religiously mandated third Sabbath meal. There were cold foods and again, as at Friday's dinner, abundant wine, as they sang again in celebration of the day of rest.

They said the afternoon prayers as the sun left the sky, the last sunset before the clocks were turned ahead for daylight saving time. As darkness encroached, the men and women prepared separately for Havdalah, the closing ceremony.

When it was time for the blessing over spices, instead of passing a traditional spice box Joshua carried around a small silver bowl.

'We do this in memory of Reb Yaacov Moshe, may he sit at haShem's right hand forever, who for his last Havdalah in this world performed the mitzvah of smelling the spices from an open bowl.'

He came first to Ben, took a pinch of the white-flecked brownish powder, balanced it on the end of his forefinger.

'This is special,' he said. 'Because it's your first time with us.' He held his finger to Ben's nose and mimed a healthy inhalation.

In that instant, looking into Joshua's eyes, Ben felt a suspension of his connection to ordinary time and causality. A part of his mind recognized the appearance of drug-taking within the ritual, recognized the likelihood of his own paranoia in the thought, and the difficulty of refusing to participate.

You hate the transgressor in yourself, he remembered Joshua saying, and remembered the shock of recognition that had caused. And even as he let himself embrace his own deep desire to go beyond rules and convention – to return to the time almost forgotten when the world was a place full of new experiences to be explored, none more appealing than the ones that promised danger – he knew that in this case transgression committed for its own sake was beyond him. If he did this now it would be to avoid embarrassment and to please Joshua.

He said the prayer praising haShem for creating fragrant spices and sniffed gently at the air above Joshua's finger – just enough to smell cinnamon and cloves. Turned his head to sneeze.

'Gesundheit,' Joshua said. 'And best wishes for a good week.'

Joshua carried the bowl around the room, giving each man a chance to say the prayer and sniff the spices. Most of them looked, Ben thought, as if they were taking snuff or genteelly snorting some designer drug.

Joshua said the final prayers and doused the candle, sputtering, in wine. In a loud voice he said, 'A good week, everyone.'

As if in response to the greeting the women rejoined the men. There was laughter – the men and the women – and then rhythmic clapping and someone had a violin and someone else a clarinet and they were playing happy music that Ben vaguely recognized, and some of them danced.

He was lifted by the music but he stood where he was, feet rooted to the floor. In a haze of sleeplessness and wine, his head felt infinitely separated from his body.

Then Judith appeared, across the room, in a long dress of white silk, with a garland of flowers in her hair and a veil over her face. Joshua had told him about this, a symbolic marriage of the People Israel and the Sabbath bride – had offered him the honor of participating as the groom. He hadn't been sure: flattered and gratified to be chosen, yet apprehensive. Now he was glad he'd said yes.

They led her to him and put her hands in his. And the music was faster and happier, and the others were clapping in rhythm and stamping their feet as Judith danced him round and round.

They were standing under a canopy, suronded by smiling people, and Joshua was saying words for Ben to repeat, and then Judith was walking around him many times while everyone chanted a prayer and again clapped in rhythm. Joshua put a glass under his foot and he broke it. His eyes didn't leave Judith, her body tantalizingly obscured by the clinging dress, her dark hair a canopy over her shoulders like the canopy over their heads . . .

Then the others surrounded them and congratulated them and led them to the stairway.

They walked slowly up to a bedroom that smelled welcomingly of spice. Judith undressed him and led him to the bed. His desire for her felt almost abstract: he had a sense that if he waited everything good would come to him. He watched while she unzipped the back of the white dress and slipped it down off her naked body, then came into the bed with him. The touch and scent of her skin broke whatever bonds were holding him and he devoured her.

They awoke later and found each other again. This time they were slow and gentle and when they finally joined it was beyond anything he could remember. He paused, holding himself still, and looked into her eyes.

'Happy?' she said.

'Ecstatic.'

She moved just enough to intensify the sensation. 'And they shall become one flesh,' she said.

He let himself move again, slowly, looking into her eyes as she looked into his. It was almost too intense. Something about the willed awareness of each other made real all the clichés about the eyes being windows on the soul. He fought the instinct to retreat to mere physicality by closing his eyes or looking at her body or at both their bodies.

'Marry me,' he said, not knowing where the words came from.

41

He slept, dreamt – disturbingly. Woke. Judith was next to him, asleep. He slept again, awoke worried about Hannah. Judith was gone. He got up and dressed, still dizzy and light-headed. Walked out of the bedroom and made his way downstairs to the recreation room where they'd had their third Sabbath meal and then the wedding ceremony.

Joshua was dozing in a chair. His eyes opened as soon as Ben came into the room.

'How are you?'

'You tell me,' Ben said.

'You're fine.' Joshua was smiling warmly. 'It's still Saturday night. You need some more sleep.'

'Where's Judith?'

'She went off to get Hannah and bring her home. Suzanne's there now, so there'd be someone she knew.'

'Thanks.'

'Before you go, I want to apologize.'

'I don't understand.'

'For not preparing you better. You seemed surprised by how full and complete the ceremony was. And about the Havdalah ceremony as well.'

'I had a moment there where I wasn't sure about the spice bowl.'

'What? Drugs?' Joshua grinned. 'No, just the traditional spices. Cinnamon, cloves, cardamom. And the wedding was only symbolic, if you were concerned about that. It's only real if there's a written contract.'

Ben reflected on how real the consummation had been, but he didn't say anything.

'Sometimes I'm too mischievous for my own good,' Joshua said. 'And usually the groom is someone who's been part of our more advanced group for a longer time and has seen these weddings before and knows what to expect. Next time I get you into one of our special rituals I'll be more careful.'

Ben was too tired and disoriented to pursue it. 'You're right, I need some sleep.'

* * *

He took a taxi crosstown. Suzanne let him in.

'Hannah missed you, but she got too tired to stay up,' Suzanne reported.

'Thanks for coming.'

'No thanks necessary. Congratulations.' She kissed his cheek.

He stared, confused. There had been no real wedding, so why the congratulations?

'On being one of us,' she explained.

So he'd been right to think that playing the groom implied some acceptance into Joshua's inner circle. In retrospect he saw the ceremony with unnatural clarity. He wondered how much of the rest he had dreamt. Not his proposal to Judith, that was real. But what about the part where Joshua – and had there been others? – came into the room to congratulate them? A dream, surely: he'd had other dreams where Joshua was a presence, usually unseen, in something that involved Judith and sex. At this point he couldn't tell what was real and what wasn't, and thought he should be grateful for that.

He woke up late Sunday morning with his head pounding and his stomach upside down.

Hannah was bouncy and full of energy. He tried not to snap at her even though making the Sunday pancakes was almost more than he could manage.

The experience of Friday and Saturday stayed in his mind. He saw himself over and over in the moment of wanting to leap unquestioningly into the unknown and not quite being able to accept the possibility of pure transgression. But later, with Judith, he *had* let go, not into anything he wanted to think of as transgression but into a full enjoyment of all and everything he wanted, an act done as purely for its own sake as any he could remember. Maybe that was the secret to embracing what was offered – truly wanting to.

Joshua was right that it was bad for him to stay single. For him and for Hannah. And Judith would be a great mom, he was sure of that. He'd wanted to go slower, wanted to be surer . . . had wanted not to confuse Hannah or frighten her by changing the structure of her universe too quickly. But that was the same kind of holding back, of editing himself, failing to trust wholeheartedly his own desire to act . . .

Marrying Judith suddenly seemed inevitable, and once he'd accepted that he couldn't see any reason to delay. Amazing that he'd had to act it out symbolically to see how much he wanted it.

And how would Judith feel about it? From all that Joshua had said and all that had happened it seemed reasonable to assume that she wanted it, too. But it was as well for now that she wasn't here, so he could digest it all and see how he wanted to deal with it.

He napped, woke up missing her. He picked up the phone to call but somehow he couldn't dial the number – not the first time or the second. The third time he dialed but left only his name.

The sun was going down by the time she called.

'Hi.' Tentative.

'Hi, yourself . . .'

'Are you okay?' she asked him.

'A little stunned.'

She didn't say anything.

'Come and visit,' he blurted. 'Stay the night.'

'What about Hannah?'

'We have to start sometime.' It really was what he wanted.

He got off the phone feeling surprisingly good, and then remembered that he had dinner plans with Isaac Isaacs. The weekend had driven it completely from his mind. Could he get away with postponing it? Probably not. He'd have to call Judith, hope she'd understand, come over anyway. He wouldn't be that long and she could stay with Hannah. They should start spending more time together.

The phone rang. He grabbed it. 'Miss me already?'

'Not so you'd notice,' Lukas said.

'Right.' Only feeling a little bit like a jerk. 'What's happening?'

'Friend Isaac got bombed.'

'What!'

'In Centerville. A small device, but big enough to cost him a leg and most of one arm. He's alive, I don't know how.'

This wasn't happening. Not now. 'Where is he?'

'They took him across the river, a big hospital in Westchester with a good trauma unit.'

'Has anybody talked to him?'

'The doctors say maybe tomorrow if he lives.'

'Will he?'

'Hell, I'd say he should have died on the spot. Tough little mother.'

'I want to go up there.'

'No point, not yet. If he wakes up, sure, we'll need you. You talk to him best.'

'You call Sid?'

'I thought he'd rather hear it from you.'

'Okay. The bomb?'

'ATF's working on it. The State Police brought them in on it right away.'

'They've got to make this a priority case.'

'They know that – nobody wants to see people start knocking off federal informants.'

Ben beeped Andy Ciampa. 'What can you tell me about the bomb?'

'The bomb itself? Nothing much, not yet. The state cops got there in a hurry and somebody must've been reading to them from our investigation guidebook because they did a decent job of preserving the scene. We've got a team there now gathering evidence.'

'Was it a grenade?'

'Like those M-21s we think they took delivery of? No, from what we've seen it was a blast device, not shrapnel. The kind of thing where you want to get the guy who's holding it and not a lot else.'

'Let's make sure it doesn't end up in the take-a-number-and-wait-your-turn line at the forensics lab. We need answers yesterday.'

'You bet—'

The doorbell rang.

'Hannah can you get the door please? Sorry, Andy, you were saying . . .'

'Just, I'll stay after them at Forensics.'

'Good. Let's stay in touch.' Ben could hear the commotion at the door as Hannah and Judith greeted each other. 'I'm going up to the hospital as soon as there's any chance I can get in to see him.'

He hung up and turned to see Judith, cheeks pink from a chilly early-spring breeze. She was carrying a garment bag and had an excited little girl hanging from one arm. Ben took the bag, left the little girl.

'Hi,' he said. 'Welcome.'

'Hi.' Judith turned her face up for a quick kiss. 'I was telling Hannah you'd invited me for a sleepover play date.

'Did you, Daddy, did you?'

He picked up Hannah and kissed her. 'That I did.' It came out flat.

'Something's wrong,' Judith said.

'Work. I just had some bad news.'

She put a hand on his arm. 'What?'

'Somebody got hurt.'

'An agent?'

'A witness.' Upgrading Isaacs a little.

'Hurt badly?'

'Mmm.' He didn't want to say more in front of Hannah. 'You know what?' He forced cheeriness into his voice. 'We need to find a place for Judith's clothes. Hannah, you want to help Judith hang up her clothes?' He hadn't thought about where.

'How about the front closet?' Judith proposed. 'Is there room?'

'I have room,' Hannah announced proudly. 'You can stay with me.'

'Okay. Let's go look.' Judith held out her hand and the two of them went off together.

He beeped Sid, stood by the phone willing him to call. Mercifully the phone rang almost at once.

'Yeah?' the undercover said, no introduction.

'Bad news. Somebody tried to kill Isaacs.'

Silence, then: 'How?'

'Bomb.'

'Shit. You know who?'

'Not yet. But you'd better watch yourself. If they got him, they may be after you.'

'There's been no sign they don't buy my act.'

'Even so. No in-person contact with them until we figure out what's happening.'

'I think it's an overreaction.'

'So is murder by bomb. Stay away for now. I'll let you know as soon as I know more. And give Frank a call. He worries about you.'

They went out for kosher Mexican food not far down Broadway. Hannah and Judith were having a good time, playing a word game. They tried to include him but quickly saw it wasn't worth the effort.

Back home he checked with Lukas. Protection was in place at the hospital – state cops. No change in Isaacs' basic condition: he was in the recovery room following the emergency surgery that had sewn up the parts of him that remained.

'They say it's a miracle he's still alive. He lost a lot of blood, and they're worried about internal damage. He could start bleeding in there any time.'

Ben tried to join the banter between Judith and Hannah but failed dismally. Judith seemed to understand and did her best to take up the slack. Their own conversation would have to wait.

They made love quietly and slowly, Ben constantly aware of Hannah in the next room. He slept fitfully. He wanted to think it was because in the dark he could sense the warmth of Judith's body and the scent of her skin. But he suspected the real reason was that he blamed himself for not realizing how dangerous the Aljo case was. Despite the warning signs, he'd persisted in thinking of it in white-collar terms.

Lukas called him as he was about to leave for the office in the morning.

'Isaacs woke up for a while. He's unconscious right now, or asleep, but they think he'll be resurfacing off and on. If you want to go up, Andy Ciampa's up there waiting to talk to him about who gave him the bomb. But I think he'll be more willing to talk to you.'

'Thanks.'

He called the US Attorney to give her a briefing.

'You want anybody to go up with you?' she asked him.

'I don't want to confuse him with too many new faces. I'll use the ATF agent as a witness.'

'Whatever works. I'm sorry about this.'

'Thanks. It looks like these are bigger bad guys than we thought.'

All the way to the hospital, driving through a steady drizzle under a sky that had turned bleak, he tried to convince himself it wasn't his fault.

And all the way to the hospital he heard Isaacs predicting that Kest was going to kill him. 'If I say a word they'll kill me,' he'd protested, and: 'I'm not putting my neck in a noose.' And Ben remembered his own smug reply: 'I can't believe religious people would be killers.' And even the ridiculously declarative, 'Alan Kest isn't a killer.' As if Ben Kaplan knew a damn thing about whether Alan Kest was a killer or not.

Pulling into the hospital lot he saw TV-news vans clustered near the entrance, decided to park the official car where it wouldn't be noticed. No surprise: a bombing in the suburbs was big news any day of the week. He threaded his way past the reporters hanging out in the lobby, trying to look like a typically disoriented civilian visiting a sick relative, ID'd himself to hospital security as discreetly as he could.

Ciampa met him at the nurses' station. 'He's conscious. Pretty doped up, the docs say, but he's awake.'

'Tell me what we know about how it happened.'

'He was in a diner outside Centerville, on the main highway. He arrived with another guy, who was carrying a black bag. Descriptions of the bag vary – computer case, attaché, overnight bag. Made of leather or vinyl or canvas. The man was in his twenties, medium height, build and complexion, wearing a leather bomber jacket and a baseball cap. They both ordered coffee and bagels. At some point the other guy went out to the car. The waiter heard him say something as he left about being right back. It was after the lunch crowd, and it had been a slow day anyway, so there weren't many people. We think Isaacs must have decided to go to the men's room. He put the bag under the table, probably so it wouldn't be sitting there in plain sight. Either the other guy set a timer when he left or he triggered it from outside. Isaacs had stood up and turned away when the thing blew. He was very lucky.'

'Anyone else hurt?'

'The waiter may lose a hand, and he's got some broken bones. One patron seriously injured. Some people scratched and bruised and some cut by flying glass. And a bunch of damage to the restaurant.'

'At least it wasn't any worse.' Two bystanders seriously injured – try telling *them* it could have been worse.

'Well, like I said before, they weren't trying to knock over the World Trade Center,' Ciampa said. 'It was a small device. Assassination, plain and simple.'

Standing in the doorway of the hospital room, Ben had to steady himself. Nate Morgan had been right, this kind of thing wasn't part of his experience. Isaacs' amputated leg was evident in the way the blanket sagged below his left hip. That his left arm was gone below the elbow was painfully visible. His head was swathed in bandages like Wile E. Coyote after another encounter with a device from Acme.

'Who's there?' His voice was a raspy whisper.

Ben went to stand near the bed, on Isaacs' good side. Ciampa stayed in the doorway.

'It's Ben Kaplan.'

Isaacs turned his head so he could see. 'Goody,' he said. He tried to moisten his lips with his tongue, a slow and unsuccessful process. He waved his hand toward the nightstand. 'Water.' Almost a croak.

Ben filled the plastic water cup and started to hand it to him, noticed that his intact arm was bandaged down to the fingertips. Leaned over the bed and held the straw to Isaacs' lips.

Isaacs sipped, then sipped again, then nodded for Ben to take the cup away. This time he had less trouble licking his lips.

'Ah,' he said, 'better.' He rested a moment, then said, 'I *said* they were going to kill me.' The words came slowly and with effort, but they still had a measure of Isaacs' accustomed vinegar.

'It doesn't seem to have worked.'

'Not yet.'

'Who did it?'

'Who you think?' Bitter.

'Isaac, this isn't what I had in mind for you. You have to know that.'

'You don't care. None of you.'

'I care about getting whoever did this to you.'

'Sure – they got your snitch.' Grimace of pain.

'I tell you what. We can joke about this all you want *after* you tell me who did it to you.'

'Bastard. Worse'n Lukas.'

'Who did this to you Isaac?'

'Kest.'

'Why?'

'Why? Because they like me.' He dissolved in weak, shaky laughter that transformed immediately into uncontrolled coughing. His face began to turn red. He made feeble gestures with his bandaged hand that Ben didn't immediately understand were for the nurse-call button.

Ben pressed it. 'Get someone quick,' he said to Ciampa and followed him out into the corridor.

A nurse came running. Intercepted by a state cop.

'Come on! He's choking.'

It was another moment before the cop waved her on and she ran past Ben and disappeared into Isaacs' room.

'What was that?' Ben said.

'We have to check their ID. It's just when there's a so-called emergency that the bad guy gets by.'

When the nurse left the room she gave Ben a hard look. 'What'd you do to him?'

'Me? Nothing. He told a joke and laughed at it himself. That got him choking.'

'You waiting to go back in?'

'If I can.'

'Two minutes. And no more jokes.'

Isaacs looked, if anything, livelier than before the coughing spell.

'Do you know for sure it was Kest? Kest himself?' Ben asked him.

'You never quit.'

'I told you, I want to get whoever did this to you.'

'Kest's orders.'

'Who gave you the briefcase?'

Isaacs smiled feebly. 'You ought to be a cop.'

'Who?'

'Dov Winkler.'

'Who's he?'

Silence.

'He works for Kest?'

'Dov Winkler. Ari Benzvi.'

Benzvi – the Israeli student who'd signed for the assault weapons. Ben took out a notebook. He repeated the names and spelled them for Isaacs to be sure he had them right.

'Dov gave you the briefcase. What did Benzvi do?'

'Built . . . bomb.' Struggling to speak, now.

'How do you know?'

Isaacs made a face, barely visible behind the bandages.

'Okay, that's okay for now.'

The nurse appeared in the door.

'Time's up.'

'I'll be back,' Ben promised and turned to go.

'Kaplan!' Isaacs breathed.

Ben turned back.

'You know a rabbi?'

Ben thought a moment. 'How about Rosen?'

'Your cop rabbi?'

'He's mostly a chaplain. He counsels people who are hurt in the line of duty. Like you.'

'Like—' He spluttered. 'Don't make me laugh.'

'Somebody else?'

Long silence. 'Rosen.'

42

Crossing the plaza behind the Municipal Building after he dropped off the office car, Ben looked over at St Andrews church and for a moment wished he could light a candle and pray for intercession on Isaacs' behalf, and believe. But the Hebrew prayers he knew were about mindfulness – stopping to appreciate and acknowledge the daily wonders of Creation.

He would have prayed, if he knew how, for Isaacs' health, but not for forgiveness for putting him in harm's way, despite his repeated warnings. Ben's transgression had been against Isaacs, not Heaven, and it was from Isaacs that forgiveness had to come first.

He called Rosen and then went up to the eighth floor and waited until Victoria could see him. She maintained her usual silence as he told her about the visit to Isaacs.

When she spoke, it was to ask, 'Do you know how they got onto him?'

'I don't see how it could have come from here. And Isaacs isn't the most discreet person in the world. We may never know what he said, where. It makes me worry about our undercover, though. Isaacs introduced him, so if they tried to blow Isaacs away, how do they feel about somebody he vouched for?'

'Are you pulling him out?'

'I don't see any alternative. I hate to do it, but it's too big a risk to take.'

'How's the investigation going?'

'It's coming together.' He filled her in on what was happening. 'We've got criminal activity that runs from financial crimes through currency counterfeiting to firearms violations. And we've got enough now, with Benzvi as the link, to be fairly sure it's all connected, though there are still plenty of pieces missing.'

Her Majesty sat in silence again, her eyes appraisingly on Ben. 'You'd better start sharing the wealth. This would be more than I'd want you to be handling alone as deputy division chief, anyway. It's worse if you're going to be in Washington most of the time. Whether you get that job or not.'

He'd known it was inevitable, but that didn't mean he had to like it. 'Do you have somebody in mind?' Hoping she didn't.

'Not yet.'

'I think it should be somebody senior from Major Crimes or OC. There are going to be RICO counts.'

If he was going to have to share the case – and probably surrender it sooner than he'd like – he wanted somebody to work with he knew and trusted. Definitely not Lukas's pet Assistant in Organized Crime.

'How about Freddi Ward,' he suggested. 'She's got strong experience in both kinds of cases.'

'I'll think about it,' the US Attorney said.

Elliot Rosen picked him up at the office in a sedan painted to look like an Israeli flag. 'I apologize for this,' he said. 'It was all I could get on such short notice.'

'I'm amazed it's legal.' The white with blue was the same color scheme the NYPD was beginning to use on its cars.

As they struggled up the West Side in the vanguard of the afternoon rush, Ben answered Rosen's questions about Isaacs. On the highway north, Rosen changed the subject.

'I talked to one of my colleagues at JLSC' – the Jewish Life Study Center, Rosen's day job – 'about the Stropkover Rebbe. You sure picked somebody obscure.'

'Could he tell you anything?'

'Not much. You were right about the Hasidic influence. They started Hasidic but they've been moving away from that for at least three generations. There are always a million questions of how the old teachings apply in modern times: How much mysticism, which sages to prefer. Emphasize prayer, emphasize the commandments. Worry a lot about preparing for messianic times or ignore it – that kind of thing. It leaves a lot of room for customizing.

'From what my colleague's been able to learn – and he's an expert on this kind of thing – Rabbi Friedlander extended his father's heavy emphasis on Kabbalah and other esoteric mystical texts. And he established nested circles of belief and practice, so that only the most advanced students engaged in the most rarefied practices, or even knew what they were.'

Ben thought of Joshua's retreats, and the Sabbath wedding ritual that had been a kind of initiation for him. No one had ever talked about circles of belief, but the idea fit.

'Did your colleague say anything about a rift in the Stropkover ranks?'

'Most of what he knows is from the name-calling around the time Rabbi Friedlander died. The truth is, nobody's paid much attention to the Stropkovers. It's too small a group to matter much, and the inner circle is too tight for there to be many leaks. All there really is, are rumors.'

Isaacs was asleep when they arrived but he woke up almost at once. Ben brought Rosen in, then left them alone.

'How's he holding up?' Ben asked when the rabbi came out almost half an hour later.

'Spiritually or physically?'

'I mean, does he seem strong enough to talk to me?'

'I'm not the one to ask. He's awake but he's tired.'

Ben looked around, didn't see a nurse or doctor to ask, went in to see for himself if Isaacs looked ready for some follow-up about Dov Winkler and Ari Benzvi.

Isaac's eyes were closed but Ben couldn't tell if he was asleep. He moved closer to the bed.

'Nice guy,' Isaacs said, startling Ben. The informant's eyes were still closed.

'Yeah, he is.'

'Needs practice' – long pause – 'with dying.'

'Let's not talk about dying.'

Isaacs made a rattling sound Ben took for a laugh. 'Scared?' His eyes opened to slits.

'You're going to make it, Isaac. You're too mean to let them kill you like this.'

Isaac said something that sounded like 'Dream on.'

'You up to talking about Dov Winkler and Ari Benzvi?'

Isaacs' body jerked, a kind of all-over wince.

'You okay?' Ben fought back panic. He needed Isaacs.

'Another rabbi.' Isaacs let his eyes close. 'Orthodox.'

'Sure. Tomorrow.'

Isaacs was silent for so long Ben thought he'd fallen asleep. Ben leaned over him to see, jumped when he said, 'Who?'

Ben hesitated. Orthodox rabbis weren't his long suit.

'No Stropkovers.' Isaacs said. He stiffened, gasped. Looked around wildly. 'Shit. Something wrong.'

'Should I get a nurse?'

Heavy breathing. 'I'm okay.'

'I promise I'll get you a good rabbi,' Ben said, pressing ahead now even without a witness in the room. 'But I need to hear more about Dov and Ari.'

'Too many' – struggling – 'Stropkovers.'

'Are Stropkovers involved in this? Kest? Asher Stern?'

Isaac's eyes widened. He was breathing hard again. This time it was longer before he spoke. 'Get out . . . get . . .' He gasped. 'Oh, shit!' His body stiffened. 'Nurse!' he gargled, his face twisted.

Ben reached over and grabbed the call button, pressed it hard and long then ran out into the corridor.

'Nurse!'

Two of them were coming running. This time the state cop let them pass.

'What's wrong?' one asked on her way by.

'He's in pain,' Ben said. Last time, he'd made Isaacs choke. He seemed to be carrying a hex. 'Bad pain.'

He stood in the doorway watching them work. He wanted to ask how bad it was but wasn't about to interrupt.

Rosen came to stand next to him. 'He okay? I heard a commotion.'

A doctor rushed by them and closed the door.

'I don't know if he's okay,' Ben said. 'Something's definitely wrong.'

Rosen looked stricken. 'We said Vidui, and I think he's feeling all right spiritually, but I'll tell you, this isn't my favorite part of the job, if this is what it means to be Rabbi Terminator.'

They decided there was no reason for Rosen to stay. Ben sent him off with thanks and went back to Isaacs' room.

The state cop had a chair tilted back against the wall next to Isaacs' closed door. 'Necessary medical personnel only,' he said.

'What happened?'

The trooper shrugged. 'All I heard was they're trying to get an operating room. It doesn't sound good.'

A pair of orderlies hustled a gurney down the corridor and into the room, then hustled it back out with Isaacs on board accompanied by a nurse wheeling the IV stand and two doctors bringing up the rear, all headed for the elevators.

Ben fell into step with the doctor he'd met on his morning trip. 'What's happening?'

'Vital signs are way off. I don't know what the pain was but we think he's hemorrhaging somewhere, so we're going to take a look.'

'Is he conscious?'

'Why?' the doctor snapped. 'Have some more questions?'

Ben sat in the waiting room, trying to assess what had just happened.

He'd been struck by Isaacs' apparent horror at the idea of Asher Stern. And he could stop wondering if Alan Kest was a Stropkover. 'Too many Stropkovers,' Isaac had said, almost his last words.

Ben tried to make sense of Rosen's rumors about the old Rebbe, but it was all too esoteric, featuring practices allegedly drawn from the most successful of the serious false messiahs, a compelling charlatan who had deluded himself and hundreds of thousands of followers in the seventeenth century. The only piece that seemed relevant was that for the Stropkovers the Rebbe didn't operate on the Hasidic model of an autocrat who regulated the everyday lives of his congregants. 'They call him "Rebbe" but he's more like a beloved figurehead than the center of their lives. Closer to the heart of the group it probably gets stronger,' Rosen had speculated, 'but that's totally guesswork.'

Ben was half dozing when the doctor came in an hour and a half later – the image of a surgeon emerging from a struggle in the operating room.

'Sorry,' he said tonelessly, not bothering with the part about having done his best. 'Next of kin?'

Ben showed his ID. 'We're looking. For now, absolutely no public word that he's gone. List him as guarded or whatever.'

'That official?'

'Yes it is. Let the OR people know right away, and nursing – we don't want any leaks.' No sense letting Kest know he'd succeeded in silencing Isaacs, if that had been his goal. 'We'll keep the guard here, too, for a while.'

The surgeon didn't look happy, but he didn't argue.

'He say anything?' No real hope of that.

'Not a word.'

43

When Ben got Lukas on the phone to tell him about Isaacs, the agent said, 'I got a call from Sid. He's frantic about this, doesn't want us to pull him out now, just when he's getting close to them. He thinks this is a religious deal all around. They're trying to convert him, or something, and he's sure that's the route to where we want to go. I don't like it, but it's headquarters making the call, not me, and they're saying he's experienced, as long as he feels safe let him stay. They really want the source of that hundred.'

'I'm going to catch a ride back,' Ben told him. 'We need to talk about this in person. Let's set it up for the morning.'

At home, he did his best to present a cheery face for Hannah, but he didn't do very well.

'Sweetie, I had a very hard day at work today,' he told her, a ploy that didn't often work, 'and I need some quiet time. Can you play by yourself for a little while?'

She pouted, but she went to her room. He poured himself a drink, not something he liked to do while Hannah was awake, but a little self-indulgence seemed in order.

The phone rang. He thought of ignoring it, letting the voice mail kick in, but he picked it up. It was Judith.

'I'm not sure how well I like this arrangement,' she said, her voice warm and seductive. 'A night or two a week doesn't seem enough.'

'I don't like it either,' he said. 'But I'm no fun tonight.'

'What is it?' she asked. 'What happened?'

'That . . . witness I told you about?'

'Yes?'

'He died.' It was safe enough to say: he hadn't let on it was connected with the bombing in Rockland County; he'd even been careful not to be visibly interested in the news accounts.

'I'll be right there.'

He thought he should say no, for no reason he could name. When she arrived he was glad he hadn't. He held her tight.

'It looks like this hit me really hard,' he said.

'Oh, Ben, I'm sorry. Had you been working with him a great deal?'

'Enough for him to be a real person, not just part of a case. I keep thinking it's partly my fault. He warned me it was dangerous.'

'You mustn't blame yourself that way.'

'It's hard not to. You tell yourself – I've got to get to the bottom of this, I've got to put these bad guys away. But at what cost?' He remembered Morgan's question – how willing was he to put people in harm's way? It was part of the job, after all.

'Was your witness a bad guy or a good guy?'

'He was a crook, if that's what you mean. And not always the most willing witness, either. But he was doing his best in his own reluctant way – even at the end.'

'Does it hurt your investigation to lose him?'

'It never helps to lose a witness.' His voice sounded to him like it was coming from a mile away.

'Is there any way I can help? Can I be a sounding board, or just hold you? I like to hold you.'

'Right now I can't think of anything I'd like more.'

Much later, as they were lying in bed on the edge of sleep, she put her arms around him again. 'I love you,' she said. 'I hate to see you troubled like this.'

It was a measure of how upset and exhausted he was that it took a long moment for her words to register fully.

'I love you, too,' he said but he wasn't sure she heard.

In the morning Ben assembled Lukas, Rogers and Ciampa.

'You set it up with Sid?' Ben asked Lukas when he came in.

'Yeah, for this afternoon. He keeps saying give him some more time.' Lukas's expression was comment enough on how concerned he was.

'I've got some news,' Ciampa said. 'Our forensics people found the legs of the detonating cap that set off the bomb – that's the connecting wires that stick out the bottom. We make them to be the same manufacture as a bunch that were reported stolen from a construction company depot in Brooklyn, along with a lot of other stuff. It's not proof, but if that's where it came from these people have a fairly major cache of explosives.'

'Along with the stolen guns and the assault rifles and so on,' Lukas said.

'If it's the same people,' Ciampa said, 'and at this point we're assuming it is.'

'The victim named Ari Benzvi as one of his murderers,' Ben pointed out. 'He's the Israeli student who signed for the assault rifles. That connects them well enough for me. Are we on him?'

'Nobody home,' Ciampa reported. 'We moved one of the pole

cameras to cover that house, but it's been dark, no activity that we could see.'

'What about Dov Winkler?'

'We have an address for him in Brooklyn. We're sitting on it, but he hasn't shown, either.'

Lukas had surveillance pictures of Asher Stern, taken outside his Brooklyn address – a tall, lean man with a gaunt face and a black beard, almost Lincolnesque. 'But so far I haven't seen him on any of the tapes from Centerville. And still no phone contact, either.'

'I said it might be a dead end.' No reason for the rabbinic leader to be connected to such things.

'One weird thing,' Rogers said. 'We've got a Centerville phone number that shows up a lot on everybody's phone records, incoming and outgoing. Real popular, but only kind of in bunches. Like a call comes in from one of the major players and then four go out. Or the other way. A call goes out and then whoever gets it makes a bunch more. And then days go by with nothing like that. Like some kind of part-time headquarters, maybe.'

'Whose number is it?' Ben wanted to know.

'That's what's weird. It's a woman's name, but all we have is that it's the same address as the home address for Joel Solomon, the rabbi gun dealer.' Rogers checked his notebook. 'Rebecca Diamond.'

'When you say you don't have anything . . .'

'No law enforcement record, no credit record for that name at that address, no motor vehicle record. Nothing at all in the last five years.'

'If she lives in Centerville she has to drive.'

'That's what we thought, and there are other Rebecca Diamonds listed in Rockland, but none of them is ours. So far she's just a cipher.'

'Could be a maiden name,' Ben suggested.

'Yeah. I was thinking the other way, that it's a married name and she never changed it at Motor Vehicles, but there's no other Diamond around there.'

'And it could just be a phony name,' Lukas said. 'If it's Solomon's address, likely it's his phone.'

'Any other news?' Ben asked the agents. 'Especially with an eye to getting some wiretaps in place?' That they were now dealing with the murder of a federal informant, presumably to keep him from aiding a prosecution, would make a major difference getting the Justice Department to move on an electronic-surveillance order – and they wouldn't have to mention counterfeit currency at all.

'I might have something,' Ciampa said. 'I brought some pole-camera tapes so you can get the cast of characters. And you'll want to see what's been happening the last two, three days.'

He showed them a collection of still frames duped from the pole-camera tapes. They were all there: Joel Solomon, the freight loaders who'd diverted the gun shipments, the freight loader's cousin they thought was a go-between, Alan Kest, Ari Benzvi.

'The one of Benzvi is from before the bombing,' Ciampa said. 'He hasn't been seen since.'

There were others no one had identified, among them a face Ben recognized.

'That's the street-patrol leader from Brooklyn.' He had Ciampa run the tape back so he could point the man out.

'Sure enough,' Lukas said, not pleased. 'I missed that.'

'Interesting that he's up in Centerville,' Ben observed. And to the ATF agent: 'You said something's been happening?'

'There's been a lot of movement. We think they're transfering some of the firearms.'

There were time-lapse pictures of station wagons going into garages, the doors closing, and the cars emerging minutes or hours later. In one, the camera had been aimed at a house and garage and had caught in a corner of the garage a pile of cartons that hadn't been there when the car went in. Ciampa stopped the tape and reran it to be sure everybody saw it.

'Those cartons are about the size and shape of the ones our informant described as holding assault rifles.'

'Whose garage was that?'

'Solomon's.'

'And he seems to be the center of something up there. Let's start getting this written up so we'll have a search-warrant application ready when we need it.' Ben could feel it all coming together. 'Anything useful from the camera at his synagogue?'

'Not that I saw. These same people all go there, but that's no news.'

'You have any of those tapes with you?'

'No, but I can get you some.'

'Good. The house, too. If nothing else, maybe we can get a look at this Rebecca Diamond, if she exists. And we need to keep an eye out for Benzvi and Winkler.' Belaboring the obvious, but it couldn't be overstressed. 'I want to have search warrants ready to go for their premises, too. Right now they're our best route into the heart of this.'

The drill now was to catch Dov Winkler and Ari Benzvi and squeeze as much out of them as possible. Then, depending on what they gave up, use that to squeeze Kest or Solomon, or both of them.

As always, the tension was between acting too soon – risking the loss of defendants because you didn't have enough information or whole prosecutions because you didn't have enough evidence – and being too careful about crossing t's and dotting i's and ending up with good cases against targets who'd fled. Or, if they were likely to destroy evidence, not even ending up with good cases.

'What about the counterfeit currency?' Ben asked Lukas after Ciampa left. 'Anything more from Israel?'

'Kiryat Yaacov looks like it's definitely central. The Russian – Rudovsky – made a trip up there a couple of days ago. Unfortunately they don't know who he saw there.'

'Why not?'

'Seems like he caught the National Police by surprise.'

'Maybe they should keep a better eye on him.'

'Yeah, that's what we tell them. The way they see it he's our problem not theirs. Israel may be better than most at helping out with counterfeiting cases, but they still have their own priorities. One thing that may help us there is that they knew who Ari Benzvi was right away.'

'And?'

'He's a Kiryat Yaacov boy, but we knew that from his records here. What we didn't know is that his dad's a rabbi over there, and he was one of the founders of Kiryat Yaacov, twenty-five years ago or so.'

'Any special kind of rabbi?'

'As a matter of fact, the chief rabbi of the whole town. How'd you know?'

'Just guessing, based on something from the same source that made me curious about Asher Stern. I think we're going to find that the reason Benzvi ended up in Centerville is that he's Asher Stern's nephew.' And the Rebbe's great-grandson, Ben didn't add.

'So maybe Rabbi Stern isn't such a dead end.'

'I'm not a hundred percent on this. Ask the Israelis who Benzvi's mother is, and if she immigrated from America.'

After the meeting with the agents Ben returned a call from Mary Harrell, the Deputy Assistant Secretary for Enforcement. 'We hear the IRS is giving you a clean bill of health. Nothing yet from the FBI, but I called a friend over there and he tells me they're going to be sending a positive report by the end of the week.'

'Thanks for letting me know.' A complication he didn't need right now.

Assuming Morgan and Nelson were in as big a hurry as they said, the nomination would be coming soon. Once it did, he'd be effectively off the Aljo case, traveling regularly to Washington to get acclimated at Treasury and to pay courtesy calls on members of the

Senate Finance Committee, the committee that reviewed Treasury Department nominations.

His first instinct was to turn the whole thing down, but he knew he couldn't. Not just because he'd been swayed by Harry Butler's opinion that the nomination could be so important in his life, but because alienating the Treasury Secretary would be as fatal to his staying with the case as moving to Washington.

Incredible, the difference timing could make.

44

Ciampa came in after lunch and dropped a pair of video cassettes on Ben's desk.

'You wanted to see the people at Solomon's synagogue. This is one from there and one from the house, too. If you're looking for this Rebecca, you'll see there are two women at the house with Solomon, one older, one younger with kids. I think the younger one has a husband – there's a guy who visits her and the kids. Only none of these people ever hold hands or kiss each other so maybe he's her brother – is that a religious thing, not holding hands?'

'Sort of,' Ben said, just as happy not to get into the laws of family purity.

He walked Ciampa's video cassette to the investigators' office and popped it into the tape player.

The Centerville synagogue where Joel Solomon presided was a nondescript brick building that had previously been something else, a small bank or a real-estate office. The building next to it, also a simple brick building, seemed to have been converted into a school.

The first frames showed a view of the two buildings from what must have been a telephone pole across the street. It all looked eerily deserted: like the tapes he'd seen stills from, the black-and-white images had been shot at one frame every four seconds, so normal speed played them back 120 times as fast. Cars went by too quickly to register, and even pedestrians were a blur.

For the next view the camera had been zoomed in to show only the entrance to the synagogue and the area immediately in front of the building. The doors were open and people were coming out. Ben slowed the tape, the motion still comically fast.

He recognized Solomon, a tallish man, slightly stooped, with gray hair and a small, pointed gray beard, dressed in a white ceremonial smock and a prayer shawl. He seemed to be greeting people as they left, like any clergyman after a service.

Ben ran the tape on frame-advance, one frame a second – jumpcut action four times as fast as life. Among the quickly shifting worshipers he recognized some of the principal players in the Aljo drama, though Alan Kest wasn't in evidence. There were many women, mostly in their twenties, thirties and early forties, Ben guessed – more women than men, which was unusual in an Orthodox Jewish congregation – and with the women, many children.

Ben let it play out, watching the ebb and flow, trying not to have preconceptions. Two of the women who had come out earlier were hovering in Solomon's vicinity, one older – past fifty-five or sixty – and one younger, perhaps thirty-five or so. With the younger woman were children, it was hard to tell how many because they kept darting in and out among the flowing skirts of the women, running off to play with other kids who might or might not be part of the family.

He put the tape back on normal speed as the congregation streamed off to enjoy the Day of Rest. The whole crowd vanished in a twinkling.

He fast-forwarded a couple of minutes' worth of tape to late Saturday afternoon – people arriving for the third Sabbath meal – then to the congregation leaving in the darkness after Havdalah closed the day. Again, Solomon was holding court, the older woman standing nearby, but this time the younger woman seemed to have a group of her own gathered around her.

Ben fast-forwarded to Sunday morning: a crowd noticeably smaller than Saturday's leaving the synagogue. Just men, no women. He slowed the tape to watch Solomon hurry toward the camera, walking with three men, all in conversation made more animated by the time-lapse urgency of the images. He was about to hit the 'play' button to speed things up further when something caught his eye. He rewound, hit 'frame advance', and picked out of the group a man who looked remarkably like Joshua Brauner. Froze the frame, then the next and the next, as the man approached the camera, his head turned partly away to make some important point to Joel Solomon, walking next to him.

One more frame and he was facing the camera. Joshua, no doubt about it.

Ben wound the tape back and let it run forward again at its madcap normal speed to get the body language. In the line of men, Joshua was clearly the focus, the others spacing themselves to have the best view of him as they walked along together.

Not quite believing what he'd seen, his mind unwilling to go the next step without more information, Ben stopped the tape and replaced it with the one of Solomon's house. He used the time-date numbers in the corner of each frame to find the matching moment of the day and let the tape play until he saw a blur of people approaching the house. Backed up and played it slowly.

There they were, coming home together, Rabbi Solomon and Rabbi Brauner. The door opened before they reached it and four kids streaked out, piling all over Joshua like eager puppies while in the doorway stood the younger woman from the synagogue tape, arms folded, motionless enough in her pose of respect and adoration for her loving smile to be visible.

Ben turned off the tape player.

For what seemed to him to be a long time he didn't have any thoughts he could identify. Just the image of Rabbi Joshua and his wife Rivka – Rebecca, in English – and their children.

'Rivka, my jewel,' Joshua had called her, 'her worth more than rubies.' But he must have been playing with Ben when he said that. Rivka was his jewel not just because of the Biblical valuation put on a capable wife, but because she was, or had been in her pre-teshuva days, Rebecca Diamond.

Ella knocked on the door, poked her head in. 'I thought you might be here. It's Mr Morgan, he says it's important. Line three.'

Morgan said, 'We just got word your nomination is coming through in the next few days. Congratulations.'

'Thanks.' Numb, unable to register it.

'I should warn you, it'll be low key. Not like being in the Justice Department, where the Associate AG gets a Rose Garden announcement with the President. All you'll get is a press release that nobody will notice except the people who care about such things. I'd like to start setting up appointments for you on the Hill. Say, starting Thursday.'

'That's great,' Ben said with an enthusiasm he didn't begin to feel.

'Good. We'll see you Thursday morning, then, and I'll try to get you in to see the committee chairman before the weekend.'

Just what he needed. Now he could go down to Washington and . . . lie? Or at least conceal.

Because if it was Rivka's phone that the conspirators had been calling, then didn't it have to be Joshua they were all talking to?

He couldn't believe it. It made no sense.

All these people, all these crimes, all connected to Joshua? How? Why?

He had to calm down, he was getting carried away.

Suppose it *was* Joshua everyone was talking to. Joshua was the successor to their Rebbe. Why wouldn't they want to talk to him? It didn't mean they were talking about illegal conspiracies.

But how could Joshua not have known what was going on if the house his wife lived in was the center of so much coming and going, if the garage in the house she lived in was the storehouse, even temporarily, for crates of illegal weapons?

And where was Judith in all this? She was close to Joshua, a lot closer than Ben had ever had a chance to become.

But that didn't mean she had any part in the conspiracy, even if Joshua did.

And if Joshua did, could that be behind Joshua's great interest in Ben Kaplan? Had he let himself be manipulated . . .

Ben's mind was spinning: he needed a steadying voice. But whose?

Not Harry Butler. He was too plugged into Morgan and Nelson, and Ben was his recommended nominee. If Butler smelled something rotten he might blow the whistle on Ben in self-defense. Not Freddi, either. He didn't want to burden her with information that would give her, too, a conflict between the personal and the professional.

Elliot Rosen. He was completely uninvolved in any of this, he knew some things about Stropkover theology, and law enforcement was familiar ground to him.

He called, got Rosen to make time for a conversation before a speech he was scheduled to deliver at six. Then Ben called home to say hello to Hannah, who reminded him that she was about to be picked up by her friend Ziporah's mother for a dinnertime play date he'd completely forgotten.

Zippy Klein was a new friend Hannah had made at Deborah's school. Ben had first met the Kleins at Joshua's Purim party: a couple about his age, warm and smiling. Nice people, clearly in thrall to Joshua.

'You know, sweetie, I'm thinking maybe you should stay home tonight.'

'Nooo! I want to go. You *said*.'

As he had. And what reason did he have now to say no? He was jumping to conclusions, inventing sinister connections where there might not be any. Maybe there was reason enough to suspect Joshua of knowledge or even complicity – but of being a threat to a five-year-old girl? And yet . . .

'Are you vulnerable?' Nate Morgan had asked him. 'Only through my daughter,' he'd answered.

'I'm sorry, sweetie,' he told Hannah. 'Some other time, okay?'

Elliot Rosen listened to him with increasing attention and concern.

'That's a hell of a situation,' he said when Ben was done. 'As far as what the religion says – if it's any help, Jewish criminal law has included an assumption of innocence since long before there was any American or English common law. So I'd say your first priority should be what it probably already is – find out more. And after that, your larger obligation as a Jew is the creation of a just world. 'Justice, justice shall you pursue,' Isaiah said. Another piece of advice you probably don't need.'

'It never hurts to be reminded.'

'Let's talk about Judith. That's the harder question. You said you want to marry her.'

'Yes, I do. I did. I don't know.'

'But you love her.'

'Same answer. I'm confused now. Doubting.'

'Doubting, sure, but how deep does it go? Have you considered what she'd have to do before you couldn't forgive her?'

'No, I haven't.' It was a good question, and a painful one. 'And I don't have any solid evidence that she betrayed me – just circumstances and suspicions.'

'Putting aside for the moment the more exotic parts of what Joshua Brauner teaches,' Rosen said, 'there's another theme you said he talked about, and that's the unity of two souls joined in heaven. I'd say if you think this woman could be that kind of life's companion you need to talk to her about this.'

'Talking to her is exactly my problem. There are implications for the case if I say anything to anyone. And for my career.'

'Is there any way to explore your suspicions without saying why you're concerned?'

Ben thought about it. 'I'm not sure there is.'

'Try to find one. Because you're clearly not ready to walk away based on what you know, but you don't know enough to stay, either. To find your way through this you have to have some answers.'

'And then deal with the answers when I have them.'

'True. And that may be the hardest part, because nothing says the person you're fated to be with is morally perfect. You'd better give some thought to what you're going to do if she's not.'

Ben closed his eyes. It was a decision he wasn't ready for.

'You can't decide how to handle this in the world until you can handle it in your own mind,' Rosen told him. 'You need to find a true and clear way for yourself. That's straight out of Proverbs – "More than all that you guard, guard your mind."'

45

The day's events and the conversation with Rosen had made one thing clear to Ben: until he knew more about Joshua's role in all of this, and Judith's, he was going to be seeing demons everywhere. Why else his overreaction to Hannah's play date? Did he really think the Kleins were going to teach her the value of a transgression for its own sake?

And what else was he worried about? Eliminating an informant might make sense, but targeting a prosecutor made none. Informants were unique: take one out and his information died with him. Prosecutors were as fungible as counterfeit hundred dollar notes: waste one and there was another ready to take his place.

In this case the next one would soon be in training. In hindsight, it had probably been a mistake to recommend Freddi. If Joshua ended up figuring in this, Ben needed to minimize his own connections with the Stropkovers. It would be hard to do that with Freddi, she knew too much about Judith and Joshua. Friendship might keep her out of it if she was a bystander, but if Aljo became her case she wouldn't hold back for a minute.

He and Lukas met with Sid Levy on the Red Hook waterfront not far from the ATF garage. The night was uncommonly warm for late March. They stood looking out over the harbor. The Statue of Liberty's torch twinkled in the last light of dusk.

'I've been mostly out of touch with Kest, the way you said,' Sid told them. 'But I had to call at least to say what a shame it was about our mutual friend Isaac.'

'And?' Lukas prompted.

'He sounded fairly broken up about it, actually. Wanted to know if I'd seen him or heard from him. I said the hospital would only say he couldn't have visitors. Kest wanted to know if I thought the police had moved him or something. Or if he was even alive.'

'You think he knows?' Ben asked.

'No, but at this point I think it's better for me if Kest isn't worrying about what Isaac might be giving up to the cops.'

'Sounds right,' Ben acknowledged. 'I'll have the hospital let the press know he died.'

'Did Kest give any sign that he had any part in it?' Lukas wanted to know.

'Not directly, no. But there's no doubt in my mind that he did. If those guys work for him, they wouldn't have done it on their own. Isaac mattered to him too much.'

'What about Winkler or Benzvi? Has anybody mentioned them?'

'Not in front of me. But it's like I've said, the people I've met around Kest don't talk much. I pick up what I can around the edges. There is one thing, though . . . something that Kest said that might have been a hint.'

'What kind of hint?'

'Well, Kest's kind of a funny guy. Studies hard, but he works hard at the store and, arthritis or not, he's strong as an ox. I said something to him about that once and he said, it takes strength to study Torah the way a man should. Then he quoted me from Ethics of the Fathers – "study alone without an occupation leads to idleness, and ultimately to sin."'

'Can't argue with that,' Lukas said.

Sid ignored the gibe. 'My point being, I looked it up, to see if it was real, and it's there all right. And the verse right after it says, "Beware of the authorities. They act like your friend when it's to their advantage but they don't stand by you in your hour of need."'

Ben thought it sounded familiar: something Joshua had said, maybe when he was criticizing the demonstrations about Menachem Siegel.

'You're saying the Rabbi was sending you a message?' Lukas said, interested now.

'Call it a friendly warning – a word to the wise so I wouldn't make Isaac's mistake. And the thing is, he kind of mentioned it again today, not that specific passage, just a general reference to taking comfort from those sayings.'

'Maybe you ought to take some comfort there yourself,' Lukas said. 'If he's warning you, take him up on it.'

'We've been over this,' Sid said in a weary tone. 'They hit Isaac right after he couldn't produce the hundred. Chances are it comes out of that, some way.'

'It wasn't long after Isaac introduced you to Kest that Kest asked Isaac for the hundred back,' Ben said. 'I'd like to be sure there was no connection.'

'Okay, look, we know they have to wonder about me, but like I said I haven't seen any sign that I need to worry, and believe me I know what to look for.'

'They're giving you extra rope,' Lukas said. 'See which way you hang yourself.'

'Or they could be isolating me, or using me to plant bad information. My point is, I don't see how it helps them to do me any damage.'

'Maybe they just don't like informants,' Ben said. 'It's been known to happen.' He quoted from the prayerbook: '*For the informers let there be no hope*. And they killed Isaac.'

'Look, I'm not about to do anything stupid. What I think is, is they want to use me somehow, maybe even get me on their side. And the main route to that is signing up for their version of the religion. I've put out some hints . . . So here's what I'm proposing. Let me blow my own cover. I tell them I'm working for the IRS or some such bullshit. And that I've seen the error of my slimy ways.'

'Is there even a chance they'll buy it?' Lukas asked.

'Yeah, I think they will, especially after Isaac, and this warning of Kest's. Scared straight, you might say. Remember, these people think they have a direct line to the capital-T Truth. All I'd be saying is I see the light, too.'

'It's way too dangerous,' Ben said. 'I can't say yes to that.'

'I'm not asking you to.' Sid turned to Lukas. 'See what they say at headquarters.'

Ben felt a surprising relief when he got home and saw Hannah, sullen and cranky as she was – punishing him for making her miss her visit with Zippy Klein. He'd been right to keep her home. No one might wish her harm, but for now he couldn't let her get any closer to her new Stropkover friends until he'd sorted out what was really happening.

In the morning he dropped her at school earlier than usual so he could take time for morning prayers, something he hadn't done in months, since the last anniversary of Laura's death. Binding the small leather tefillin box to his arm with its leather strap, a sign of commitment to God mandated in Exodus, he strained to surrender himself to the pull of rituals that had tied generation after generation of worshipers one to another for thousands of years, virtually unchanged. But the attempt to find some reservoir of faith untainted by the suspicions he couldn't banish from his mind felt hollow and forced, the ancient words dust in his mouth.

Lukas was on the phone, first thing. 'We're getting our notes together so we'll be ready for a draft of the Centerville search warrant applications. I wanted to remind you that we're also preparing operations plans for executing them. Not something we bother an Assistant with usually, but – special circumstances and all.'

The special circumstances being that Ben wasn't just an Assistant, he was about to be the boss of kicking doors. 'I appreciate it.'

'Something else – I got the answer from Israel about Ari Benzvi's mother. Name of Ruth Friedlander, emigrated from New York something like twenty-five years ago. That what you were looking for?'

'It means he's definitely Asher Stern's nephew.' As he'd guessed, before he knew that Joshua was part of all this in some still undefined way.

Something didn't fit. Benzvi stood at the nexus of the guns and the counterfeiting – signing for the illegal assault rifles and assassinating Isaac, presumably for Kest. Solomon, too, was involved with guns and with Kest. But now it seemed that Benzvi was closely connected to Asher Stern, while Solomon – based on the pole-camera tapes – was connected to Joshua. And Asher Stern was Joshua's sworn enemy.

'I got Benzvi's military record, too,' Lukas said. 'Guess what his specialty was?'

'Demolitions.' It had to be.

'This is your morning to be right.'

Ella stepped into the office and put a note in front of him: HRH.

'I've got the U.S. Attorney on the other line,' Ben told Lukas. 'But I want to talk some more about those operations plans, when we're closer to making a move.'

'I've decided to take your recommendation on the currency case,' Queen Victoria told him.

Damn. 'Terrific.'

She picked up on the hesitation. 'I thought that's what you wanted.'

'I do. I think she's a great choice. That's why I recommended her.'

'You've been holding out on me,' Freddi said when he'd briefed her. 'This isn't just a good case, it's a fantastic case. A bunch of Orthodox Jews in Brooklyn and Rockland committing financial frauds while they stockpile assault rifles and other illegal firearms, plus legal firearms and explosives, at the same time as they're printing counterfeit hundreds that are potentially almost undetectable, maybe with help or collusion from Russians in Israel, where there's also a whole village full of their friends. And now they just literally blew away our snitch.'

She took a breath. 'Wow. Are we talking Mideast politics here?'

'The Israelis don't think so, and I tend to agree with them. Undermining worldwide faith in US paper currency isn't going to help Israel.'

'And I don't suppose they need guns over there, either,' she acknowledged. 'Home of the Uzi and all.' She pondered it. 'Suppose it wasn't directly related to the government. Fringe fanatics, West Bank settlers unhappy with government policy – worried about defending themselves, maybe, if the government withdraws more troops.'

'But why stockpile guns *here*? They can't very well export the guns.'

'The Irish did. I had a cousin—'

'So you've told me,' Ben said. Merciless prosecutor though she could be, she relished stories of her desperado relatives. 'But I don't think we want to go there.'

He remembered Joshua's ferocity about the need for Jews to defend themselves against millenarian fanatics. Could Solomon be responding to that? Could there be two separate reasons for the guns in Centerville – some of them related to Alan Kest's criminal activities, and some to Joshua's passion for self-defense?

'Besides,' he said, 'we still don't completely understand how the guns are connected to the counterfeiting, and that's our principal focus. What we're worried about here is the counterfeit currency and where these people fit in that, and what they can lead us to.'

'True enough. Has the undercover been putting phone numbers for the targets in his reports?'

'Religiously.'

'Ha ha. But that's a big piece of getting our wiretap orders – having the undercover's report that Kest and company are doing illegal business over those lines. And you've tried every other way there is of getting the evidence we need, right? A snitch, but he's dead. An undercover, but he's getting limited information, and it may not be safe to leave him in . . . Pole cameras, even.'

'And a garbage search.' He told her about it – at this point she had to know.

'This is the alleged robbery with the demonstration and the security-patrol guy who almost died?

'Right.'

'The proper authorities know about this?'

'Everybody who needs to. But that doesn't mean we want to put it in the affidavit.'

'I can see that,' she said, 'but we won't have to. You may not know this about me, but I am the veritable queen of Title III eavesdropping orders.'

'I always thought one Her Majesty in the office was enough.'

'Think again.'

He talked to her about the agents on the case. 'I've already told them about you. You might want to get together with them tomorrow, get the case from their point of view – I'm going to be out of town all day.'

'Where to?'

'Taking Hannah to see Laura's folks in Florida, though they don't know it yet.' Because right now he wanted Hannah as far away as possible.

'Isn't this a little high-handed of you, Benjamin?' Some trick of the telephone made his mother-in-law sound forever young and innocent, no matter what she was saying. 'We do have lives of our own, you know.'

'I'd have given you more notice, but this is an emergency. Hannah needs to be someplace stable and calm and safe.'

'Safe!'

'I don't mean she's in danger. But there are things happening here that she might find disturbing.' True, but it was for himself, too: he needed to have a clear head, and no distractions.

'Hasn't poor Hannah had enough grief from law enforcement irresponsibility?'

'Edith, I don't want to argue with you. You and Bert are my first choice for this. I think you're best for Hannah and I know you must miss her, being so far away, but I can take her somewhere else if that's what you prefer.'

'No no, that's not what I was saying at all. You always were so quick to take offense.'

And you were always quick to give it, he didn't say. Laura had seemed to him a kind of miracle – that such a calm and rational woman could have sprung from one so thin-skinned and argumentative.

Ben had been avoiding Judith since he'd seen Joshua on the pole-camera tape, happy to trade messages, hurrying off the phone the one time they'd connected. Wanting to talk to her, not knowing what to say or how it would come out. He had no idea how he'd react to seeing her in class.

As usual he had to wait until the last minute to see. She walked in with two of her classmates, chatting busily enough not to look at him as she passed. His heart started pounding and his mouth went dry.

He was way off his usual rhythm, not least because the scheduled subject matter was testimonial privileges, the kinds of evidence that a criminal defendant or a party in a civil suit could keep out of court because it had been revealed in a confidential way to a doctor or a lawyer or a spouse. Or to a clergyman.

He caught Judith's eye as the class was breaking up. She stopped on her way out with the other students who had questions for him.

'If you want to talk about that report, I have a minute free,' he said to her.

'I'll wait.'

'You hungry?' he asked when the others were gone.

'For you. But we can have dinner as well, if you'd like.'

46

On Sixth Avenue he flagged a cab for them both.

'You're feeling daring,' she said as they started uptown.

'Up to a point.'

She leaned over to kiss him and he felt himself respond as if everything were the same. But he couldn't keep his misgivings from rushing in. He disengaged gently, sure she would sense his ambivalence.

'I had a chat with the Dean before class,' he said by way of diversion.

'What about?'

'My new job possibilities, and us.'

'You didn't!'

'It was way overdue.'

'What did he say?'

'He's very pleased. He likes it when his faculty take leaves for intersting jobs with impressive titles, as long as they come back.'

'About us.'

'Oh.' Exaggerated surprise, clowning he didn't feel. 'He's far from delighted, but he's way too much the gentleman to say so. He thinks you're an adult. He compliments us both on our taste, and he forgives us, on the condition that we live happily ever after, have great success in the law and promise to teach a course apiece forever and donate heavily.'

'He didn't say that.'

'Yes he did, and he wants you to finish the course with somebody else, as directed study.' He stretched out the details, leavened with anecdotes about the Dean, the whole cab ride home.

While Judith and Hannah greeted each other, he ordered dinner from a kosher Chinese restaurant nearby.

Hannah was excited about the trip to Florida until she understood that Daddy wasn't staying there with her. After that, there was explaining and cajoling to be done. When they'd finally kissed her good night he poured them each a glass of wine, and they sat down together in the living room.

Judith put her wine on the coffee table and moved closer on the couch to kiss him.

'Let's wait until Hannah's asleep,' he said.

She studied him. 'You're upset. About your witness?'

'Yes.' He was completely drained. 'About a lot of things.'

He reached for her, held her close. This was harder than he wanted it to be. He let go, took her hands.

'There are things we have to talk about.'

'That sounds ominous. Perhaps you should tell me what they are. The suspense isn't helping.'

'It's about Joshua,' he said.

'Oh.' She sat back, away from him. 'I suppose I should have expected this. But there's nothing between us. Nothing physical.'

Despite his exhaustion and the stresses of his day, his professional instincts kicked in, in time to keep him from reacting visibly. He sat watching her, saying not a word.

'I know he wants more,' she went on. 'But I've never given him the slightest encouragement, if only because I admire dear Rivka so much. She really is an angel. I know she believes everything Joshua does is in search of purification for his body and his soul, but I'm still an old-fashioned girl, and I don't want it to be with me. So whatever you think of me, or whatever anyone's told you . . .'

For a moment, relief overwhelmed caution. He hadn't realized how jealous of Joshua he was. 'What do I think of you? I think you're wonderful.'

She smiled tentatively. 'I told Joshua this would happen. It's no secret for some of us that the women who have truly entered into the mysteries Joshua teaches consider it a religious privilege to complete their monthly trip to the mikvah by being with Joshua – to join with him in their purity to follow the true meaning of what he calls the Torah of Emanation, the Torah of the Higher World.

'I was worried that there were too many people in his inner circle who knew that he wanted me to share that mitzvah with him, but didn't understand that it wasn't something I could do, not even if my level of faith were higher. I was concerned about what someone might say to you, and what you might think. That was part of the reason that Joshua arranged the wedding for us. He wanted to make it clear to you where my heart was and that we had his blessing.'

Chilled as he was by the world he glimpsed in her words, Ben couldn't deny her desire to reassure him. He touched the plain gold ring on her index finger, the one Joshua had given him to use for the wedding ceremony. Saw her again in her white dress under the canopy at the moment he had slipped the ring onto her finger.

'It was a wonderful moment,' he said, clinging to that memory as if it could sanctify what he had heard.

'As genuine as any wedding I ever expect to have,' she said quietly.

For a moment they were silent. *What would she have to do before you couldn't forgive her?*

Sitting here, looking at her, he felt oddly doubled, prosecutor and lover in one skin.

'Speaking of weddings,' he said, 'it's a funny thing that I've never seen Rivka or their kids.'

'You ought to spend a Shabbat in Centerville.'

'Does she live up there?'

'Part of the year. And Joshua is sometimes there and sometimes not. I think he was there this past weekend, after the retreat.'

'So she's alone with the kids most of the time.'

'It's a bit like being married to a sailor or a traveling salesman,' Judith said. 'She gets to have extra fulfillment when he's at home.'

'But with four kids it's got to be hard for her to be there all alone.'

'There's a rabbi there who looks after her. He and his wife have a separate flat in the house.'

That fit with what he'd seen on the pole-camera tapes. He said, 'You know, we've never talked about how you came to know Joshua, and to be his student.'

'Will that make this easier somehow?'

'You said my understanding your faith was important.'

'It is, very. And Joshua is a big part of it. I first met him at Oxford. He was a guest rabbi there, just as he was at OY that Shabbat you first met him.'

She talked about her earlier encounters with different approaches to Judaism, from the cosmopolitanized Mediterranean observance of her childhood through the celebratory kinds of prayer she'd learned at Oxford from the resident Hasidic rabbi.

'The rabbi at Oxford was a revelation, but until Joshua there was always a piece missing,' she said. 'There was something about Joshua that spoke to my soul, and that feeling stayed with me. I corresponded with him for almost two years about what I should read and where I could find services consistent with his teaching. The reason I decided to come to NYU wasn't only because the program is so good, but to be near Joshua and learn from him. And he's been very generous in teaching me, so I've come a much longer distance than I thought I could in so short a time.'

'Does that mean you're in the inner circle of learning and practice? I'm impressed.'

'It's nothing to be impressed about, and I haven't progressed nearly that far. The first time you and I talked about this, I said I wasn't sure yet how far I wanted to go.'

'You've come a lot farther than I have. All this about a hidden Torah – it sounds fascinating, if a little . . . special.'

'I do find some of it unexpected. But I've never felt any pressure to accept a teaching until I was ready.'

'And you don't have any trouble reconciling the kind of practice you just told me about?'

'Well, yes and no. But it's not something sordid. You have to understand that. Not one of your tabloid horror stories of sexual exploitation.' She touched his hand. 'I wouldn't be part of that, even at a distance.'

'No, of course not.' He couldn't resist the impulse to reach out to her, hold her for a moment.

'Does that answer your questions?' she asked.

'Here's one more,' he said. 'This Torah of the Higher World – is it just about sex?'

'No, it's the entire Torah, but different somehow, as if the same letters were in code instead of Hebrew. It often has to do with transgressing or reversing the commandments of the regular Torah.'

'In particular ways besides sexual?'

'What sort of ways do you mean?'

He could feel the danger. He needed to know more but didn't know where her loyalties lay, despite her declaration of fidelity. 'Like, reversing the laws about dealing honestly in business, for instance. Tax fraud, say.' If this went bad, at least he'd be backing up Sid's play. 'I'm not sure what . . .'

'Yes you are. You have something in mind.'

'You're right. I apologize for not being more direct.' He didn't like this, didn't like lying to her. 'It's just that I'm about to go through formal confirmation hearings for the job in Washington. I have to know if there's anything in Joshua's teachings that might cause people to misunderstand my connection to him. Not necessarily something he does, himself – even if it's his followers, or the rabbis who lead his congregations, if people might think he encourages it.'

'Why? Do you think they're some kind of criminals?'

Have you compromised the case in any way? That was going to be the US Attorney's first question, and a lot of other people's. If he had, until now it had been out of ignorance. He no longer had that shield, flimsy as it was. But he could hope that these same relationships that might have damaged the investigation might now be turned to advantage.

Judith wasn't content with his silence. 'You do think they're criminals, don't you?'

'That's not the point. It's just that all this emphasis on transgression, and what you were just talking about—'

'Don't blame me! This is something you had on your mind. You brought me here to talk about this. To betray Joshua.'

He was speechless.

'Answer me!'

'You're right, I am worried about some of Joshua's followers. But I'm not accusing Joshua of anything.'

She backed away from him again, farther this time. 'How long have you thought this way?'

'I only just found out these people have any connection to Joshua at all.'

'Oh, yes, no doubt you expect me to believe that. That you haven't been hunting him all along, and using me. The way you have been tonight, pretending to be interested in *me*, in my search for a way to express my faith. As if you cared.'

'I do. I do care.' It sounded feeble to him in the face of her hurt and indignation.

The intercom rang.

'That'll be the food,' he said.

'I'm not hungry.'

'I am.'

'Well, that's fine, because I'm leaving.' She went for the closet to get her coat.

He grabbed her arm to keep her from going. She pulled, but he held her.

She pulled harder. 'Please! Is this what we've come to?'

He let her go and answered the door, was aware that she was putting on her coat. As he paid for the food he was sure she'd dart out into the hall, but she didn't. He closed the door and took the food into the kitchen. When he came back she was still standing there in her coat.

He took her hands. 'Will you come inside and talk to me? I need us to be honest with each other. Except for Hannah that's all there is in the world that matters to me.'

In silence she let him take her coat and lead her back inside.

'I want us to be honest as well,' she said, 'but I do think we should have our dinner first, for the sake of our tempers.'

They ate slowly, not talking much. When he looked at her she was intent on her plate, as if the answer to their problem was written in the vegetables and slivers of meat.

'What do you want to ask about?' she said as they cleaned up.

'I need to know if Joshua knows about what these few people are doing.' No harm in revealing that. Kest had to know he was a target, or why had he killed Isaacs? 'If they come to him for counsel, maybe to find out if their transgression is a proper part of the cycle of descent and ascent that he teaches, or this Higher Torah.'

'Why? Why do you have to know that?'

'For my own peace of mind. And because if he is giving them

advice, it's going to come out. If I know, then I can protect myself, and I may be able to help Joshua, too.'

'What can these people be doing that could harm you just because you are learning about Torah and haShem from Joshua?'

'A man was killed. Innocent people were hurt.' He said it without thinking, too many kinds of outrage behind it to stop and think where it would lead.

It startled her. 'Your witness? That had something to do with Joshua?'

'I don't know.'

'But . . . people close to him.'

'Yes.'

'And you think Joshua knew about it.'

'I don't want to.'

'But you're afraid he might have?'

'All I know is that these are people who follow him. Who think of him as the Rebbe's heir. I understand that Joshua isn't the kind of Rebbe whose followers look to him for every significant life decision, but I don't know how it is for Stropkovers in the innermost circle, assuming these people are.'

'I don't know the answer. Can you accept that? That sort of thing isn't what Joshua confides in me.'

'What *does* he confide in you?' The old jealousy coming back.

'That would be confidential, wouldn't it?'

He was silent in the face of her anger, waiting for it to subside.

'There's something else, isn't there?' she said.

'Yes.'

'About me.'

'Yes.'

She crossed her arms over her chest and closed her extraordinary eyes. 'Go ahead, then.'

'Have you talked to Joshua about what we discussed in class?'

'Yes, I often told him about your classes. He was interested as soon as I told him about you.'

'When was that?'

'The first day. Before the first day – the day I saw your name in the course bulletin.'

'You told him?'

'Yes, because it was a significant discovery for me, because I'd truly been having fantasies about you in the time since we'd met in London. And he was interested. I asked him whether it was kosher to think of a coincidence like that as somehow made in heaven. And he said yes, especially when it comes to men and women. Do you know the word b'shert? It's what I was saying about two souls matched up in heaven before they ever came down to earth.'

'Do you think that's what we are? B'shert?'

'Don't you?'

He thought of Laura, wondered if anyone got to have two matches that were both fated in that way. And of Rosen – *nothing says the person you're destined for is morally perfect.*

'I want to.' He knew it was less than she wanted, but it was as much as he could manage. 'You said Joshua was interested in me.'

'Yes. As soon as I mentioned you.' She hugged herself tighter. 'This is making me very uncomfortable. I keep thinking there's something you're looking for that you're not telling me about. It's as if you're accusing me.'

'I'm just trying to understand.' But of course there was a potential accusation in this. He'd said things in class, used examples from the Aljo case – well enough disguised, he'd thought at the time. But he hadn't known that he had in his audience someone connected to his targets. Someone who was talking about him to the man who was their spiritual leader. 'It's important.'

'I've told you as much as I know.' She looked away from him, her expression as bleak as her voice.

She'd shut the door. If there was a way to reopen it he wasn't thinking clearly enough to find it. 'Maybe we should go to sleep. It's getting late.'

'All right.' She walked to the bedroom stiffly, holding herself apart.

In bed she turned away from him, curled up at the far side of the mattress. He lay on his back staring up at the ceiling, searching for answers.

47

When he woke up, she was gone. Just like after the wedding ceremony, he couldn't help thinking. Only this time Joshua wouldn't be waiting to explain it all to him.

Had Judith left his bed to report their conversation to Joshua? Asking the questions had been a gamble, and if that was where she was headed, Ben supposed he'd given up more than he'd gained. Why? Out of a need to believe in her? Yes, but something else, too. He'd been testing her: her love, her loyalty. It hurt to think he'd felt the need.

And if she had told Joshua, what would he learn from last night that he didn't already know? That Ben was after some Stropkovers? That he suspected them of tax fraud?

He still couldn't grasp the reality of what Judith had told him about Joshua – that, and Joshua's clear connection to Joel Solomon, and so to all the others, even supposing it was only as their spiritual leader – couldn't reconcile any of that with the Joshua he thought he knew.

Hannah was disappointed she couldn't say goodbye to Judith, but getting ready to go to Grandma's kept them both too busy to dwell on it.

The safety demonstration on the plane reminded Hannah of a fire drill they'd had at Deborah's school.

'Was it like they have at your other school?'

'No! It was fun.'

'What kind of fun?'

'Just fun.' Propagandizing. 'We went in a special place that was safe.'

'Outside?'

'No, silly. Inside.'

'Inside? Where?'

'I don't know.' Hands spread wide as if to say: how could I? 'A funny room with no windows. Some of the teachers were yelling at their class to make them sit down. Not Mrs Geller. She's nice.'

'Why didn't you tell me about it before?'

'You weren't there. I forgot.'

His punishment for going to Washington. 'What made you think of it now?'

'The yellow mask. They had a mask for your nose, only not yellow. It was for smoke.'

'How do you know?'

'Mrs Geller said. She said fire makes smoke. Everybody knows that. She said it's bad to breathe, like a million billion cigarettes. They let us try it on.'

Gas masks? He'd been struck by the passion of Joshua's concern, but what did Joshua think he was preparing for?

'Daddy,' Hannah said as they taxied to the gate, 'are you going to come and get me soon?'

'Yes, I am. I don't want to be without you a minute more than I have to. I miss you already.'

'That's silly. I'm right here. But I really want you to come soon.' Very emphatic.

'Is there a special reason?'

'Passover. Mrs Geller said it's coming soon.'

'Yes, it is.' He'd lost track of it: it couldn't be two weeks away.

'I have to be with you. Grandma and Grandpa don't like it when I'm Jewish.'

Never underestimate a five year old, Ben thought. 'I promise I'll come get you in time.'

He'd already called Nate Morgan to say he couldn't be at the Treasury building before the afternoon, blaming it on the Aljo case. The flight north from Florida felt like a Twilight Zone episode – Ticket to the Unknown. The sense of unreality didn't leave him on the cab ride to the Treasury Building or even when he was sitting in his office, waiting for a summons from Morgan, trying not to think of this as his last time here.

He was roiled by the question of how much, if anything, to reveal to Morgan. Professional responsibility and a desire to play it straight at Treasury called for him to be farther from reproach than Caesar's wife: he should tell all and withdraw from the case right now. There was the remote chance that if he did that he could save his position here.

But he cared too much about finding the truth to risk losing touch with the case. It was a need compounded of warring impulses – to banish all his suspicions by absolving Joshua completely, or to punish Joshua for his treachery by nailing him as thoroughly as anyone could be nailed.

The immediate problem was that he had to say *something* here: too many people knew too much about his association with Joshua to pretend he had nothing to disclose.

* * *

He tried to make some phone connections while he waited. He'd already called Judith fruitlessly from all three airports he'd been in; he picked up the phone with not much hope. Once again he got nothing – no Judith, no voice mail, no answering machine. He missed Lukas, who'd beeped him; and Ciampa, who'd beeped him twice; and Freddi. The only person he reached was Elliot Rosen. He hoped this wasn't a sample of his luck for the day.

The phone rang. Morgan: 'Sit tight, I'm coming up.'

Ben got up and paced, struggling to put his thoughts in order.

The chief of staff arrived, looking more lined and weary than ever, a man with weighty matters on his mind. 'We've got a lot to talk about, about your confirmation process from here on.'

'There's something else I'd like to cover first.'

'Really.' Morgan settled back on the antique-style couch. 'I'm listening.'

Ben started with a recap of the Aljo case: financial crimes, then the counterfeit hundred and the need to find its source. The ATF connection that took the case in a new direction. 'Not so surprisingly, the targets all have something in common. In this case it's geographical proximity and membership in a religious group.'

'What does this have to do with us?'

'There's a rabbi who wrote some books that I've read, and about two months ago he came to the synagogue where I belong and gave a speech. I was introduced to him at the reception after the speech, and since then I've spoken with him a few times, and I've been to weekly services where he was presiding, and a couple of discussion groups and a spiritual weekend he led.'

'Let me guess – he's got something to do with the religious group your targets are part of.'

'It looks as if he may.'

'Could he be involved in the criminal behavior?'

'So far we have no evidence he is.' That was true enough, but it made Ben uneasy. 'We also have no evidence he isn't.'

'Why didn't you know this sooner?' Morgan wasn't happy.

'I could take you through it a step at a time, but the short form is, first, there was no great reason to see these crimes as coming out of any religious motives and, second, the group has two opposing factions, and when the connection first came up it pointed pretty clearly at the other branch.'

'Do the others working the case know about this?'

'The man's name has never come up in the investigation. In fact, if I hadn't already made his acquaintance, it might never have. There are rabbis enough who *are* involved not to be looking for more.'

Morgan didn't hide his exasperation. 'All right, we can talk around this till we're blue in the face and my question is still going to be, Why do I care? Let me put it this way – if the whole world knew everything there was to know about you and this rabbi, would it matter to the US Department of the Treasury?'

'No.' Ben took a moment. 'I can't see why it would.'

Morgan studied him. 'You'll have to talk to your boss in New York about this, too. I suspect she may want you to take yourself off the case.'

'I'm already on my way off because of the consulting you want me to do. There's a very talented prosecutor who's begun working on it. She's drafting Title III orders and catching up on the history and getting to know the agents.'

'All right,' Morgan said. 'I'm going to need some time to decide what to do. My instinct is to put the nomination on hold for now. No one's going to think about that twice, if it doesn't last too long. If I have more questions I'll ask them. Meantime, there's no point your hanging around.'

It could have gone worse, Ben told himself, though he didn't underestimate the severity of Morgan's dismissal. He guessed the outcome would owe a lot to their need to get this nomination through the Senate quickly, though that could cut against him if they decided this would cause problems in the Finance Committee. The next hurdle would be Secretary Nelson's reaction, if Morgan decided to take this to him, though Ben was betting he wouldn't. And Queen Victoria's, which he couldn't put off past tomorrow.

He tried Ciampa again from a pay phone at the airport.

'Glad you caught me,' the agent said. 'We've got some developments. Word has it Winkler and Benzvi are in the wind. I want to get into Dov's apartment right away. I was going to ask Ward to put in the warrant for us, but I wanted to run it by you first.'

Another courtesy he could attribute to rumors of his elevation. 'Can you do it without the whole world knowing?'

'An entry like this, guns and explosives, we've got to be equipped to protect ourselves, and that means heavy vests and helmets. We'll go in as Brooklyn Union Gas investigating a midnight leak, and hope the neighbors don't look too close.'

'Okay. I'm sure Freddi can help you with whatever you need. You can tell her we talked.'

It was happening. He could feel the surge of anticipation that always went with setting the final stages in motion, closing the trap. But this time under the excitement was a chill of fear.

48

Elliot Rosen was working late at the Jewish Life Study Center, the rabbinic think-tank where he was a visiting Fellow. He had a tiny office, long and thin, not much bigger than a walk-in closet, with a narrow counter running the length of one wall that held a computer and unstable-looking towers of books and papers.

'They keep promising me a bigger office.' Rosen, in shirtsleeves, looked more like a harried middle manager than a scholar of the spirit. 'And this' – a hand waved at the chaos – 'is because I have to give a paper at this conference on Sunday, and I'm nowhere near ready.'

He pulled a stack of journals off a chair for Ben. 'But I'm glad to have a reason to take a break. We're still working the same problem?'

'If anything it's gotten worse.'

'How so?'

Ben repeated what Judith had said about women in the innermost circle joining with Joshua in their purest state as a way to obey the Torah of a Higher World.

'That's really something,' Rosen said. 'To hear that in New York at the edge of the twenty-first century.'

'It's pretty extreme.'

'Well, no it's not, actually. It's probably based on some of those ideas we were talking about the other day. Historically it's been called Redemption Through Sin.

'That sounds sort of scary.'

'Yeah, it does. As far as I know there hasn't been much of that lately, not at the level you're talking about, though some fairly prominent rabbis indulge in milder forms of it.'

'Like what?'

'Eating a ham and cheese sandwich on Shabbat once a month. Or even every Shabbat.'

'Why?'

'Mostly it's a way to cast the Law into relief. And for some people it can be to give yourself a sin to atone for. Did she name the Higher World this Torah was part of?'

'Emanation, I think is the word she used.'

'That's kind of what I expected. I did my research thesis on mysticism and heresy, and what I learned is there's a lot more mysticism in Jewish belief than most people today realize. This is one of those, a belief in four or five levels of existence, from the most mundane to the most heavenly – and the idea is that each of these "Worlds" has its own distinct reading of the Torah.'

'Judith said something that sounded like that. The same letters on the Torah scrolls, but a different meaning somehow?'

'Right. And in one version of the belief there's a higher World than ours – called the World of Emanation – and its Torah is a kind of opposite to the one we know that rules the World of Creation, which is our world.'

'So "no" means "yes"? That kind of opposite?'

'Yeah, essentially, if you take it all the way.'

'Is this related to the idea of transgression as a route to God?'

'That's actually a lot less extreme, though it might be good training, if you were going to get to Redemption Through Sin in stages.'

'Which is how the Stropkovers do things.'

'Apparently.'

'Joshua's attitude toward transgression seemed to be such a positive aspect of his teaching,' Ben said. 'He was very relaxed about it – just something that could be atoned for. And he made the atoning itself seem like an attractive prospect, not in any self-flagellating way.'

'And that much is basically consistent with the mainstream Jewish view. But violating a commandment intentionally in order to be able to repent is another matter. And doing wrong purely for the sake of doing wrong is right off the charts, even though people have preached it for centuries.'

'That sounds like something I've heard, too.'

'The motive is to go so completely against the prohibitions of the Law that the evil lower depths get overloaded and purge themselves completely. Like when you swallow something that makes you vomit – a lot more comes up than just the emetic. Serious heretics can find support for it in the Law, even though it's a misreading. The Talmud actually says that a transgression committed for its own sake is greater than a commandment performed for a reason other than its own sake.'

That was it. The textual basis of the second study session he'd been to.

'How far does any of this go?' he asked Rosen. 'Is criminality included, or is it limited to sexual transgression?'

'It's about violating any of the Biblical commandments. I doubt that breaking the secular law would count for much by itself. You'd have to be breaking some religious laws while you were at it.'

* * *

When Ben got home there was a message from Judith: 'I'm sorry to have disappeared without a word. I was upset that you could think of me the way you seemed to, without trust. I know some of what I said must be difficult for you, and confusing. I'm doing my best to understand your point of view, but I want to give us both more time to think.'

He called: no answer. He listened to her voice over and over, berating himself for not having thought out in advance what he was going to say last night, for having driven her away. It wasn't as if he had any evidence she'd betrayed him intentionally. Talking to Joshua about him, she could just have been innocently answering what must have seemed to her to be innocuous questions asked by a man she trusted.

Ben had trusted him, too. How deep had the betrayal been? How badly had he let himself be fooled? Stop, he told himself: you're getting ahead of the evidence.

He pulled his mind from it, from all speculation. They were on the verge of answers: somewhere out in Brooklyn Ciampa and a team from ATF, dressed as employees of the gas company, were waiting to break into the apartment of Dov Winkler. And after that, there'd be the question of how to deal with Centerville.

His beeper went off. Ten thirty, too early for Ciampa to be calling. It was a 703 area code – northern Virginia near Washington – but he didn't recognize the number. Somebody from Treasury? Or could it be Judith? What would take her to Virginia?

It wasn't Judith, it was Mary Harrell, the Deputy Assistant Secretary for Enforcement. 'I've been having some conversations with ATF that I wanted to discuss with you.'

'Sure. What's up?'

'They've submitted operations plans for search warrants on your case, the one we discussed. But there's another Assistant's name on the warrant application. Fredrika Ward?'

'She's been working on the case with me. Taking up the slack as I get ready to move down there.'

'Oh, okay. I looked at the tactical plan. They've covered all the major contingencies, but it looks like a delicate operation, a group of neighboring private homes. I wondered what you thought.'

Ben's danger flags went up. Why was Harrell calling him about this? Clearly she didn't know about the nomination being on hold. That made sense: Morgan wouldn't tell her until he'd decided how to play it.

'I'm going to need to respond to ATF about these plans,' she pressed. 'Secret Service, too. There's a high level of concern at both agencies because it's a religious group. I didn't want to go ahead without talking to you.'

She was trying to draw him into a decision he had no business being part of, because she didn't want to endorse something he'd disapprove of or disown when he got to be her boss, especially not on a case he'd been supervising as prosecutor.

But all his authority at Treasury was in the future, so even if he'd had no association with Joshua this would be treacherous ground for him. Offering his opinion on a plan that worked would gain him nothing, but if he made the wrong call he'd get a hundred percent of the blame.

'I'm glad you called me,' he told Harrell, truthfully enough: he was glad to have a heads-up that the planning had progressed this far. 'I'll make some calls and get back to you tomorrow morning.'

He called Lukas. 'You're getting ahead of me,' he told the agent. 'I hear you and Andy Ciampa have already sent the operations plans for the Centerville warrants to your headquarters.'

'That's why I was calling you all day long, to let you know.'

That might be true or it might be Lukas thinking fast. 'This is a lot sooner than I expected,' Ben said.

'It's what we were talking about, getting ready in case something breaks in a hurry. ATF was already working on the tactical plans for their own Centerville case, and Ciampa's pushing hard to speed things up. With a bomb killing and all those guns being moved, he figures they're the dog and we're the tail for now.'

'We can straighten that out in the morning. Has Ciampa hit Winkler's place yet?'

'In a couple of hours. But there's another reason I was calling besides the ops plans.'

Or the only reason. 'What's up?'

'You remember that question you asked me – what did our Swiss friend's father do when he was a big-shot banker?'

'I do.'

'Well, the answer is he was in charge of his bank's foreign deposits. Especially deposits from Germany and Austria and points east.'

'Including the Big War, you said.'

'Right. So I asked if he handled any particular deposits. And the answer is yes, from Germans and Czechs and Poles – Nazis and Jews alike. The governments, too.'

Ben was silent.

'So you asked the right question,' Lukas said. 'We're getting our Israeli colleagues to make friends with him to where they can reminisce about the old days. But I know what we're going to hear. Dieter has a big weight of guilt for what Daddy did with all the gold teeth and the stocks and bonds belonging to depositors who forgot to file a change of address when they moved to Auschwitz.'

'Just the kind of guilt that'd make him easy prey for a Russian con man who's suddenly an observant Israeli Jew.'

'So maybe we're about to solve the mystery of where our friends learned how to make OV ink. One thing we can pretty well count on, now – that hundred-dollar note came from Israel, and Kest was lying to Isaacs about getting a briefcase full in return for some computers.'

'That's progress. Let's get together in the morning,' Ben said. 'Ciampa, too. We ought to talk about those operations plans.'

49

Ciampa and Lukas were hanging out by the coffee maker when Ben got to the office in the morning. He took a cup for himself and they gathered around his desk.

'How'd it go with Dov Winkler?' he asked Ciampa.

'Went great. We told the neighbors we were looking for a gas leak, they didn't bat an eye. Nobody home, like we figured. One surprise – it looks like two people were living there, and from what the neighbors said the second one was Benzvi, probaby part time.'

'You think they're gone for good?'

'Most likely – what they left behind they could live without. We got the dogs in and they lit right up. Definitely traces of explosives. Better than that, we found some tags in the trash that came off a brand new leather case for a laptop. We're guessing they'll match up with the fragments of the case from the bombing. And little bits and pieces of wire insulation, a few other items of corroboration like that. They're our guys, all right.'

'Any idea where they are?'

'A receipt from a travel agent would be nice, but so far not a thing.'

'I hear you and Frank have your operations plans for the warrants in Centerville all worked out.'

Ciampa looked at Lukas.

'I told you he's got friends in Washington,' Lukas said.

They went down the hall to a conference room. Ciampa used the chalkboard to sketch a rough map of the southeastern corner of Centerville.

'We've got the synagogue up here on the right, then there's the highway' – running along the left edge of the board – 'and down here' – bottom center – 'the residential area in question.' He added more streets to the map, including one leading down from the synagogue. 'Most of our targets are around this dead end near the bottom.' He drew in some squares and rectangles for houses. 'Either around this circle at the end of the street, or in the houses with adjoining backyards. Kind of like a compound.

'We figure the best time is Saturday morning. Everybody's out praying, all in the same place. Nobody's home except a few women and little kids, old folks, sick people. We're going to pull in extra female agents to come in behind the SRT's and deal with the women and kids.'

He sketched in where the ATF Special Response Teams would be deployed and how they'd move in from the highway ahead of the other ATF and Secret Service agents and the state cops who'd be enlisted for perimeter control.

'We've already made our arrangements with the state troopers. They're cool with it. We figure to block access from the direction of the synagogue and hit these three houses, the ones where we've seen crates of guns or verified delivery of illegal or stolen weapons. The way the geography is, in order to do it right we also need to isolate these others just past them over here.'

As Ciampa sketched it out, it seemed like a well-constructed plan – ample personnel, strong perimeters, good provisions for intelligence and communications.

'Saturday?' Ben said. 'You're not talking about tomorrow, are you?'

'Next week,' Ciampa told him. 'That's pushing it some, though. I was saying, the search-warrant affidavit is based partly on seeing those crates in the garage and on the most recent deliveries, and we can't let that get too stale. We can do it during the week if we have to, wait till people are off praying or going to work, but it's not as good as Saturday, when everybody's on foot, nobody's using the telephone. That's a big one, because it's a close-knit community and we figure somebody's going to spot us on the way in, and we're better off if they don't pick the phone right up, which Frank's rabbi tells us on Saturday they won't.'

'You brought your rabbi in?' Ben asked.

'Sure did,' Lukas said. 'Anybody who can tell us what to expect is somebody we want to talk to.'

'What if you do get spotted?' Ben asked.

'In the first place we do our damnedest not to be,' Ciampa said. 'But if we are, we have a couple of fall-backs.'

They spent the rest of the morning going over the contingencies. When they were done, Ben called Harrell at Treasury.

'I've just been over the plans with the agents, but I'm still dealing with this as a prosecutor, so I can't be overseeing it at the same time from a Treasury point of view – especially with no official status down there.'

'I can appreciate your position. I'm not asking you to exercise authority you don't have, but I do feel uneasy putting my name on it, precisely because you *are* involved.'

'Then I'd say take it to Nate Morgan if you think that's appropriate, or kick it back to ATF and Secret Service.' Leaving it squarely in her court. 'Of course, if you have specific problems with it, I'd like to know about that, for my purposes, here.'

'I suppose I could pick some nits,' she said, in full retreat. 'You always can. The way things stand, though, I'm inclined to go with the agents' professional judgment.'

Much as Ben didn't want to talk to the US Attorney about Joshua, he really had no choice. Victoria took the news with her usual blank expression, though he saw deeper creases at the corners of her eyes than he'd have liked.

'I have two questions,' she said. 'One is, have you compromised the case in any way?'

As he'd predicted. 'No. Absolutely not.' True or not, playing it this way he couldn't afford to waffle.

'All right, I'll take that at face value for now. The second question is, have you gained any information that might be helpful?'

'There's this – if I hadn't already known the man I wouldn't have been able to recognize him on the surveillance tape.' Expanding on the point he'd made to Morgan. 'We'd have no reason even to think he might be involved. And at this point we still don't know that he is.'

'Have you talked to the people at Treasury about it?'

'Yes, I have.'

'And?'

'The first reaction was fairly mild, but they're going to hold the nomination announcement until next week – in case they think of any questions.'

Her eyebrows lifted a barely perceptible fraction of an inch. 'Well, this isn't the best news. I'll give you credit for not holding back, and I don't intend to convict you of anything by association – or the rabbi, either, I suppose.'

That was good, but he was sure there was more.

'I think you ought to withdraw from the case as quickly as possible without causing any drama,' she said. 'You can stay on it while Freddi gets up to speed, but I want that to be soon. No fuss, just you're too busy with the Washington thing will do. When do you expect to hear from them?'

'Soon, I'm sure.'

'And I'm sure you'll let me know right away.'

It was a dismissal, but he hesitated. The conversation had left him with a question. She anticipated him.

'You want to know if you still have a job here, in the event the one in Washington evaporates.'

'Yes.'

'Well, pending some indication that you've behaved improperly I don't see why you couldn't stay. But I don't want to jump to any premature conclusions.'

He hadn't completely dodged that bullet, but as with Morgan, it could have been worse. It was vital now to have it be seen that he was on the right side, to blunt the doubt that came with even a minor connection to a man who now had to be one of the investigation's major subjects.

And it was time to treat Joshua just that way, to find out how he earned his money and how he spent his time, to go over his phone calls and his bank records and his credit-card bills and all the other mundane elements of figuring someone out.

The phone calls. That had been in the back of Ben's mind waiting to pounce ever since he'd seen Joshua on the pole-camera tape. Joshua Brauner had made at least one phone call to Ben Kaplan. From where? How long would it be until someone recognized the home number of an Assistant US Attorney on his target's phone records?

He couldn't get over how thoroughly Joshua had gulled him, and in how many ways.

To calm himself down, he called Hannah. She seemed fine, excited about discovering shells and pretty rocks on the beach and watching the birds. He hoped it would last.

Lukas called at three. 'Time for our meeting with Sid.'

Ben packed up his briefcase for the day, thinking about how to handle the undercover, hoping Ciampa had fooled Dov Winkler's neighbors as completely as he thought.

They met Sid by the sports complex on the piers. They sat in Lukas's car, rain drumming on the roof, tinted windows open only enough to let in some air.

'ATF just tossed Dov Winkler's apartment in Brooklyn. I'm worried that may make things more dangerous, get them more on their guard.'

'I'm just asking for this one more weekend,' Sid protested. 'One more Sabbath with them. If I can't make the breakthrough I want, forget about it, I'm out. But if I do, man, believe me, it's going to be worth it. I'll be right on the inside.'

'What's so special about this weekend?' Ben asked him.

'They invited me to a kind of retreat. Very serious spiritual deal, twenty-six hours with a dozen other people, no sleep beginning to end, a lot of bonding. It's a trust thing, kind of an initiation' –

Congratulations, Suzanne had said, *on being one of us*.

—'The perfect place for me to break down and confess my guilty secret.'

'Awfully damn risky,' Lukas said.

'Did they tell you who'd be running this retreat?' Ben asked.

'Kest, as far as I know.'

'Have you heard any talk about a rabbi higher up than Kest?' Dangerous ground, but he had to know.

'You know, there *is* somebody they bitch about. Higher up, I don't know, but he's got some kind of authority. I just overheard it once or twice, kind of sarcastic, like he's so head-in-the-clouds he doesn't always get what it takes to live in the world.'

'You get a name?' Heart hammering.

'I've heard two – Nehemyah and Ben Yosef. Nehemiah, and the son of Joseph. But I'll bet it's the same person.'

Not Joshua. Ben was surprised, and relieved. Could he have read it wrong? But overheard talk about an unworldly higher-up named Nehemiah the son of Joseph was no evidence that Joshua was or wasn't part of it.

'But you still think Kest is the boss . . .'

'Of the business stuff. And of the illegal stuff, I'm almost a hundred percent sure. That's what I want to find out. And if this Nehemiah is giving him grief, maybe that's who I ought to be talking to.' He looked at them both. 'Another reason to stay in.'

'Here's what I think,' Lukas said. 'I think you're a guy who's got to go out and climb every mountain he sees, good weather or bad. And this time around *I'm* the fucking St Bernard. If it was my call, I'd say no.'

'What did headquarters say?' Ben asked.

'They said ask you,' Sid told him. 'They'll give it the final thumbs up or down, but your opinion'll make a big difference, being the one who knows best what the case needs.'

That was bullshit, Ben thought: more people trying to draw him into Office of Enforcement decisions before he had the job. He thought of Isaac Isaacs, of sending him out to do battle against his will. This was the opposite – Sid wanted to go, Lukas wanted him to stay.

'It's Kest who invited you?' he asked Sid.

'Yeah.'

'I know something about that kind of Shabbat retreat,' Ben said, measuring his words. 'I was on one that sounds a lot like what you were describing. It can get very intense. The one I was on was studying, praying, meditation, and no sleep, plus wine Friday night and schnapps Saturday noon, then wine again for seudah shlishit' – the third meal – 'and Havdalah. You're surrounded by people the whole time—'

'So it's probably safe unless they're *all* out to get me.'

'Where's this weekend take place?' Lukas asked the undercover.

'Brooklyn, I assume.'

'Not Centerville?'

'Could be. We're meeting early enough to make the trip in time.'

'If it's Centerville, maybe you ought to go, after all,' Lukas said. 'As long as you've got some way to stay in touch.'

'I told you I can't wear anything on my body. And I won't be carrying my bag around, either.'

'We'll give you a shoe phone,' Lukas joked. 'Something high tech like that.'

Sid checked his watch. 'We'd better get moving.'

50

At home Ben found two telephone messages. The first was from Florida: 'This is Edith. Just a second, here's a message from Hannah. Go ahead, honey.' Then Hannah's voice. 'Hi, Daddy. It's nice here. Can I keep Shabbat here? Grandma and Grandpa don't want to.' Edith again, 'We were hoping to drive up to Orlando for the weekend as a treat for Hannah but she turned very difficult about it so I'm afraid we're staying here. Please call so we can talk about this.'

He put the answering machine on pause and called immediately. 'Is Hannah still upset?'

'She's in her room and she refuses to come out. Not even to eat. We tried to take her to the movies, but she insists that she absolutely will not get in the car until after dark tomorrow. Does your religion really require five year olds to deprive themselves this way?'

'In the first place it's not deprivation. And it's not *required* until she's twelve. But kids are encouraged to try observing some of the rules, and not riding in a car and not watching television or using the phone are things kids can do fairly easily.'

'We just want her to have a good time when she's here. We see her so infrequently. If you could explain to her it's because we love her.'

'You can ask her to come to the phone, but it's after sunset so I doubt she will.'

He was right. 'Tell her I love her very much. I'll call back after dark tomorrow. And the most loving thing you and Bert can do is just let her do what she wants.'

The second message was from Judith. 'I miss you. I'll call you after Shabbat.'

He dialed her number even though he knew that, like Hannah, she wouldn't answer. Whatever Shabbat she had planned, she'd already embarked on it.

He had a momentary, shocking image of Judith in the white silk dress as Sabbath bride with Sid Levy as groom, Joshua presiding with a smile. Forced it from his mind. He was torturing himself for no reason.

* * *

He made himself have some dinner and started to look at the books on mysticism Rosen had given him. This time he quickly found himself absorbed in the vivid and unexpected images and legends.

The phone rang. He leapt for it, had to remind himself Judith wouldn't be using a phone.

It was Lukas, sounding as close to agitated as Ben had heard him.

'We need an emergency Title III order. And we're gearing up to move on the search warrants, too.'

'Whoa. What's happening?'

'We're monitoring the pole cameras twenty-four hours now, and we've got some kind of summit meeting at Rabbi Solomon's. Including Winkler and Benzvi.'

'Who else?'

'Kest, the firearms guys. A whole convention of people we're interested in. And Sid.'

'You're sure he's there?'

'We saw him go in. And he's wearing a tracker.'

'And you're sure this isn't the religious retreat he was talking about?

'If it is, it's a damn funny coincidence all the retreaters are people we think are committing crimes. Like they're making him a member of the club.'

'He said "initiation." What do you propose to do?'

'First thing, we want to tie into the phones.'

'No hurry for that. They won't use the phones till tomorrow night.'

'Unless they break a rule or two.'

Ben couldn't argue with that. After his last conversation with Elliot Rosen, he had no way to know what the Stropkovers considered kosher behavior.

Lukas said, 'We want to get some kind of bug in there, too, before they get done talking to each other.'

'How do you propose to do that?'

'We'll try to put something in from the outside, under cover of darkness. Down the chimney, or under a door. I'll admit it's not ideal.'

'Then what?'

'Depends on what we hear.'

'It seems like an awfully big risk for not much hope of return.' Like the garbage run, he was tempted to say. 'These people aren't naive about security.'

'Look, Sid's in there.'

'That's exactly what worries me – that you'll spook them somehow. Endanger him just by your presence.'

Lukas didn't argue. Instead, he said, 'We may need to yank him out of there. You have that arrest warrant for him, right? David Gershon.'

'Ready and waiting.' It was an emergency strategy – if the undercover was in danger you could break into the premises with a warrant to arrest him in his undercover role as a bad guy. That way – theoretically – you could get him out without compromising the operation. 'But you really want to go in and get them *all*, don't you?'

'Andy Ciampa's the one who's pushing it. He sees his two bombing suspects in there and he wants to nail them.'

'I thought we had bigger fish to fry here. You willing to lose your precious lead?'

'There comes a time when you roll everyone up and squeeze as hard as you can. They killed Isaacs, they're moving the guns, something's about to break. We may never have a chance like this again.'

'You can't be serious. You move in on these people with them all together like that, you've got instant Waco.'

'We're not stupid. All we're talking about for now is increased surveillance and trying to hear what they're saying. Building up our intel for when we *do* move. The rest of the plan is the same as we talked about, except we want to consider bringing these people in for questioning tomorrow on their way home from praying, after we've done the searches.'

'For questioning?'

'If we have to arrest some, we'll do that, too. We'll need to draft up some warrants just in case.'

'That's a lot for a Friday night. You sure about this?'

'I'm sure.'

'Hang on, I'll conference in Freddi, if she's not out on a date.'

He tried, got voice mail.

'Not home,' he told Lukas. 'I'll beep her and get right back to you. Just sit tight for now.'

'Don't worry, I know how to keep it in my pants. But the first order of business is getting that eavesdropping order from Washington.'

'That's why I want Freddi in on this. It's her specialty.' And he didn't want his own name on the application.

He beeped Freddi, and when she didn't call back at once he beeped her again. And again.

'What's this thing you have about Friday nights?' she wanted to know, answering the third page.

He told her about Lukas's call.

'Hooee. Okay, I'm at a restaurant, I can't do it from here. Let me get someplace better, like the office.'

'Lukas sounds pretty crazed.'

'In that case . . . maybe I can get it underway from here. For some dumb reason I have my little computer thingy right here in my bag. Can you get me on the line with Mr Lukas?'

'Coming right up.' Ben conferenced Lukas in and listened while they went over the details together.

'Let me know,' he said to Freddi when she got off the phone to call Washington.

Ben wanted to be out in Centerville, but for the moment all he could do was wait for Freddi to call back.

This was Solomon's house they were talking about – and if Solomon's then Rivka's, and so Joshua's.

And Judith? Was Centerville where she was this Shabbat? She'd spoken with obvious affection of Rivka. How much connection to all this did she have?

'Have you compromised the case in any way?' Victoria had asked him. 'No,' he said, because he'd felt he had no choice but to say that, and because he hadn't wanted to consider the effect of all Judith might know, if she'd passed it on to Joshua. And yet, it wasn't her fault that he had told her things he shouldn't have.

Unless it *was* her fault. Maybe it wasn't just a matter of her innocent answers to Joshua's not-so-innocent questions. Hadn't she accused Ben of using her to get at Joshua? Maybe that idea had come to her so quickly because she knew Joshua had used her to get to Ben.

And why not? Joshua couldn't have known at the beginning that Ben was stalking Aljo, but his interest would have been aroused anyway just learning that an influential person in law enforcement had turned up in his world. What better than to get close to such a person?

Especially with Judith right there to make the connection and follow it up. To get even closer than Joshua himself could. And he'd have seen the need for that the moment she'd reported Ben's use of a garbage search as a classroom example, right on the heels of the incident in Alan Kest's driveway. And who could say what extra hints Judith had gotten from Hannah, talking about Daddy and his unusual visitor, and their interest in news of the Brooklyn excitement.

Joshua must have been beside himself when he realized what he had. Judith, too. Because they were close, Joshua and Judith, no doubt about that, whatever the truth of her disclaimers about sex between them.

And how easy to embody the idea of redemption through sin in the sexual antics she'd staged – as he now saw it – in order to enthrall him so completely. So she got both to serve her Rebbe and at the same time to act out his distorted ideas of approaching haShem and rebuilding the world.

And Hannah, what about Hannah? That was the worst. To expose her to the hope of a new mom, and in the service of what? His own unrecognized sexual frustration and the total blind gullibility it had produced once he'd opened himself up to it? Rosen had challenged him to think of what Judith might do that he wouldn't be able to forgive her for, and here was the answer – hurt my daughter, play on my daughter's vulnerability as a way to fool me.

How was he going to salvage this? How was he going to keep it from reawakening in Hannah all the symptoms that she'd been gradually putting behind her, and all the pain they expressed?

Freddi called him just before nine: she had the eavesdropping order. She'd already called Lukas to tell him about it.

'I almost wish they'd turned you down,' Ben said. 'This idea of planting a bug is crazy.'

'Lukas tells me he's trying to arrange a power outage for the streetlights so they'll have some darkness, but I think he's beginning to see that the downside's too serious.'

'Let's hope so.'

51

Ben was on the phone as soon as he got up on Saturday, aware of how upset Hannah would be if she knew. He made sure Freddi was going to be at the office to handle emergency warrants, and he packed up a laptop with a modem and a printer so he'd be able to receive and generate documents at Centerville.

During the night Lukas had given up on the idea of putting a bug into Solomon's house – Joshua's, as Ben now thought of it. From the outside all seemed quiet, he reported: no sign the people in the house were aware of looming trouble, or that Sid might be in danger.

'You're assuming he's okay, then?'

'I keep telling myself we got through two Saturdays all right with him out of touch. The problem is – the cast of characters is completely different this time. I'll be happier when they go out to pray and we get a look at him.'

'I'd like to be up there by then, myself.'

'There's an ATF guy on his way up. He'll swing by and get you. Ciampa's leaving you in my care – he's too busy to be babysitting prosecutors.'

The ATF guy was a Public Information officer, full of anecdotes and lore, and resentment for the black eye Waco had given the agency. 'The worst part is, it was the FBI that really screwed the pooch. But, hey, we made the first mistake so we take the blame for the whole thing.'

Lukas met them at a tiny strip mall on the highway that formed one boundary of Centerville. There was a dry cleaner and a kosher pizza parlor and a pharmacy, all closed for the Sabbath. A diner, looking more permanently closed, had a construction dumpster by its side wall.

'That's where friend Isaacs got bombed,' Lukas said. They were sitting in his car.

Ben looked again: what had seemed an everyday sight was suddenly cast over with evil.

'I'm getting worried,' Lukas told him. 'Nobody's left the house yet. What time do they usually start praying?'

'It varies. Eight thirty, nine, nine thirty. Ten would be late.'

'Well it's past nine thirty and nobody's left the house.'

'Just the houses you're watching, or the whole town?'

'We only know what we see on the pole cameras. The people who went home from Solomon's last night came back real early, and a whole bunch of new folks have arrived from the houses right around, to where it's likely fairly crowded in there. There are a couple of dozen people over at the synagogue, but nobody we recognize.'

'Not Solomon or Kest.'

'Nope, they're both at Solomon's.'

Ben sat in silence a moment, preparing for what he had to say next. 'There's a piece of information I just picked up,' he said. 'That house probably isn't Solomon's, except in name. The real owner is likely to be another rabbi – Rebecca Diamond's husband, if I'm right.'

Lukas was intrigued. 'Where'd this come from?'

'The pole-camera tapes. I recognized him.'

'What!'

'Rabbi Joshua Brauner. He's the figurehead of a group that follows the teachings of a rabbi from the Old Country, and Kest and Solomon seem to be part of it.'

'And you *know* this figurehead.' In the close confines of the car, Lukas's indignation was an almost physical presence.

'Not well. And until now I had no idea he had any connection to Kest, or any of this.'

Lukas looked at him hard. After a moment, some of the tension drained away. 'And you say Jews aren't clannish! How deeply is he involved, do you think?'

'Yesterday I wouldn't have guessed he was remotely connected. Now, the way they're all at his house – his wife's house – you have to figure he's got some part in it.'

'How well do you know this guy?'

'We've had some conversations about religion.' Ben gave him an edited version of what he'd told Morgan and Victoria. 'And he was the leader of the retreat I was talking to Sid about.'

'Holy shit!' The look of suspicion returning.

'It's like an all-night bull session. I heard some interesting theology, got some advice about my personal life you could probably read in a self-help book. What I was exposed to wasn't exactly sinister, though I can see why they'd use an event like that to make new people feel more part of the group.'

'And what about this rabbi? He's not this Nehem—Whatever Sid was talking about?'

'That's definitely not his name.'

'You said figurehead. Is that it, or is he the boss?'

'It's not a formal hierarchy. I'd say he's more like an elder statesman than a bishop. From what I've seen, people do go to him for advice, but I'm not sure that goes all the way to committing crimes.'

Lukas started the car. 'There's somebody you ought to talk to.'

The trees in Centerville had looked winter naked in the pole-camera images, but seen in person on a bright April day they wore a haze of green and yellow buds. Ben saw not a car moving on the narrow, sidewalkless streets bordering lawns already turning green. Some of the streets were chained off. He expected bands of indignant young men in white shirts and dark trousers to emerge from some house or behind some bush and block their way, as he'd heard happened in towns like this when people tried to drive through on the Sabbath.

There was no chain blocking the road at the T-intersection where they pulled up behind a telephone company vehicle – a panel truck with dark smoked windows and a squat cylinder on its roof that looked like some kind of ventilator. Beyond it was a telephone-company equipment truck; a lineman was working at the top of the pole.

Off to the left Ben saw a pleasant street, thickly lined with trees that even in earliest spring were dense enough to block most of the view to either side. The street ended in a wide paved circle off of which led four driveways, just like on Ciampa's rough map. Only one house was clearly visible: a real-life version of the house identified as Solomon's on the pole-camera tapes. Joshua's house.

Lukas reached into the back seat for a couple of hard hats with telco markings. 'Congratulations,' he said. 'You just became a repair supervisor.'

Getting into the surveillance van Ben had to duck past one of the small cameras hung on pan-and-tilt mounts near windows temporarily covered with ballistic padding. He and Lukas sat on an upholstered bench that ran along one side atop densely packed high-tech equipment. Lukas introduced him to the incident commander, the ATF Assistant Special Agent in Charge of a regional Special Response Team – a big man named Healey with an impressive gray moustache and eyebrows almost as bushy who was sitting almost knee-to-knee with them in a swivel chair that gave him access to the floor-to-ceiling racks of electronics and monitors on the van's other wall and the cameras mounted to look out the turret Ben had mistaken for a ventilator.

'Ben's been the prosecutor on the case,' Lukas said. 'And he's in line for an enforcement job at Main Treasury.'

Healey held out a bulky hand. 'Good to meet you.'

'Ben turns out to have some personal acquaintance with some of these people, and how they think.'

'Really.' The eyebrows went up.

'It was just as big a surprise to me,' Ben said.

'I figured he could give us some insight,' Lukas said. 'Maybe even talk to the guy for us.'

'I don't know about talking to anybody,' Healey countered, 'but we could sure use information.'

'Why don't I just tell you what I know about him, and you can ask me questions.'

'Let's get my negotiator in here first.'

On cue, a phone rang. Healey picked it up. 'Yeah?' he said, and listened awhile. 'Is it being handled?' he asked, said 'Okay, keep me posted,' then hung up.

'We've got press.' Disgusted.

'How?' Lukas asked.

'Could be somebody in the next town alerted them, over by the school where we've got our staging area, but I'd say it was those folks in there.'

'Why them?' Ben asked.

'Because this one reporter says there's going to be a statement from the house. So who the hell did she hear *that* from?'

He picked up the phone again and made a couple of quick calls. In response there was a knock on the door and a tech squeezed in to sit at the console on the van's front wall.

'Jeff's off the pole,' he said. 'The camera's ready to go.' He played with the knobs and buttons and a monitor came to life: a clear color image of the dead-end street. He muttered into the mike at his mouth, and the camera – controlled, Ben guessed, from the other truck – zoomed to show the house at the end of the street.

Healey said, 'What I don't see is how they got word out to the press. They didn't use any of the lines we have wires on, and the cellphone scanner didn't pick anything up.'

'They're not supposed to use the phone at all,' Ben commented, 'or anything that needs electricity, not until at least a half-hour after sundown.'

'Yeah, well, they had to use something. So if it's a sin to use electricity on Saturday, we've got some sinners in there.'

There was another knock, and another ATF agent wedged his way in – the negotiator. They sat in the crowded van and Ben recited what he knew of Joshua Brauner's life story and his religious philosophy, again detouring around the issue of transgression and repentance, wary of the misunderstandings an idea like redemption through sin was sure to cause. The negotiator interrupted now and then to ask smart questions. When Ben wrapped it up, the negotiator said, 'Do you think he's directly involved in the crimes, or is it just his . . . people?'

'I was saying to Frank, he has to at least know about it. There's a phone here in his wife's name that the conspirators all call, and we've seen crates of guns in this house, and his wife and kids live here at least part of the year.'

'But we're just deducing here,' the negotiator said. 'We've got no actual evidence of it.'

'No. Not yet.'

'Heads up,' the tech said. 'We've got somebody coming out of the house.'

52

Joshua came out onto the open front porch of the house. The tech muttered an instruction and the remote camera zoomed to a medium close-up.

On the monitor, Joshua looked serene and in command. He was dressed for the occasion in a long coat of white silk over loose white trousers, as if he were about to offer the congregation's prayers before the Holy Ark. He wore a cylindrical, white-satin cap embroidered in gold and a large prayer shawl over his shoulders like a fringed white cape with black stripes. His beard glinted with fiery highlights in the midday sun, and his eyes looked penetrating and intense, almost unnaturally blue.

He started with a prayer in Hebrew and then English: Praised are You, O Lord, who blesses his people Israel with peace.

Then he was silent. When he began again he was speaking softly, obviously confident that someone out there had equipment good enough to pick up what he was saying, and that shouting wouldn't help.

'Shabbat shalom, Sabbath peace, to all of you who are watching,' he said. 'I won't take much of your time. This is just a plea to be left alone.'

He was facing the ATF vehicles, not fooled by their telephone company camouflage, but because he didn't know the camera was atop the pole he wasn't looking at the lens. Instead, he seemed to be conversing with some unseen listener. On the monitor it produced a strange but powerful feeling of intimacy.

'A great sage of the past taught that we should each and every one of us keep busy with the Law and with the practice of good works and in that way we would not come to harm. All of us here try to live by that principle.

'And by our example of studying the Law and practicing good works we've made a new friend. In only a short time, he's seen that we offer far more than the secular society whose servant he had become. He's offered to join us on our journey, and let me assure those who sent him to spy on us that they have no reason to fear that he's been hurt or coerced.'

He turned toward the house just as the door opened and Sid came out. Like Joshua, he was wearing a white prayer smock, this one much simpler, and a prayer shawl. It was hard to tell on the monitor but Ben thought he looked tired, under strain.

'Zoom in, zoom in,' Lukas was saying, but the image stayed the way it was, and the tech said, 'That's it.'

'Hi,' the undercover said, looking almost directly at the camera. 'I want to say hello again to my wife and kids, so they can see me, and let everybody know I'm okay. Frank, if you're out there, tell them at headquarters I quit.'

He turned, traded glances with Joshua, and went inside.

Joshua took a moment, then resumed. 'I spoke of a journey, because it's the destiny of the people for whom I speak to fulfill their ancient Covenant with the God of Abraham, the God of Isaac, the God of Jacob and restore themselves to the land of their ancestors.

'The prophet Jeremiah tells us, "cursed be he that does the work of the Lord with a slack hand." And my portion of the Lord's work was assigned to me by my teacher Reb Yaacov Moshe – Jacob Moses – of blessed memory, just as an earlier Joshua was instructed by his teacher, the greatest teacher of all, Moses, the receiver of the Law, to lead his people into the land of redemption and peace that was promised to us by the Lord.

'We can't allow ourselves to be hindered by mistaken attempts by the civil authority to interfere with this holy journey. Indeed we must declare our independence of any such authority and respectfully state that the Law of the Eternal, Lord of Hosts, must prevail. There can be no law higher, there can be none even equal.

'Though we are called the People of the Book, and justly so, we have at times in our history also been a warrior people. If that is our role in this moment, we will accept it, but we will do nothing to seek it out. We wish to be left in peace. We wish to leave in peace, to seek our destiny in peace.

'Until now, we have sought only to live quietly and practice our religion and prepare as we thought necessary to defend ourselves from danger. We are ordinary people, with the ordinary desire to be left alone to live our lives in peace.'

'Live your life in *prison*, asshole!' the tech muttered.

'I ask you once again,' Joshua was saying, 'in the Name of the Lord of Hosts – let us leave this place undisturbed and in our own time.' Then he, too, turned and went inside.

The phone in the van rang. Healey picked it up, listened, gave it to Lukas, who listened a longer time.

'None at all?' he said and listened some more.

He handed the phone back to Healey. 'Let's get some air,' he said to Ben.

'They monitored a phone call right before the rabbi came out,'

Lukas said as they walked to his car. 'Sid called his wife and kids. No code words, no sign of coercion. No all-clear, either. But it may have been scripted.'

'What about when he came out?'

'Same. No signals, no hidden meanings. You don't think he seriously converted, do you?'

'It seems like a stretch.' The last thing Ben wanted to do was overpraise Joshua's seductiveness.

'Sid said he was trying to convince them he was going over to their side. But if this was part of his act, why no signal, up or down?'

'Maybe the whole business was scripted.'

'There are hand signals. There are things he can do.'

'He could have been afraid to do anything that might blow his cover.'

'Just so it wasn't a little drama Brauner dreamed up for us so we wouldn't feel pressure to get Sid out of there.'

'Are you really going to stop feeling that pressure?'

'Not for a minute. But I'd like to think Sid was getting over on them the way he wanted to.'

'Let's hope.'

Lukas opened the car door and sat sideways in the driver's seat, feet on the ground. 'Brauner couldn't have been clearer if he sang "Let my people go." Sure, rabbi. That is, if you leave out murder – self defense! – and whatever he meant to imply by his little declaration of independence. And the counterfeiting. I bet that's why they want to go to Israel – to be with their phony money. Is that how Brauner was, the times you saw him?'

'Not really. The Joshua Brauner I've seen is a bouncy, warm, energetic guy, or else very intense. That kind of removed coolness he had, that's new to me.'

'What do you make of it?'

'I don't know, frankly. There's something going on. Maybe it's an act, or maybe the pressure is getting to him and that's how he protects against it.'

'You think he's flipping out?'

'I don't know about that.' Though it could be, he supposed. 'I've heard him talk about Jews needing to arm themselves against crazies wanting to ignite the apocalypse. It's the one time I saw him get carried away. So when he finds out there's an army of federal agents and state police on his doorstep . . .'

'Well, if he's all wound up like that, then I give him extra points for style,' Lukas said. 'No yelling, no ranting and raving, the soul of reasonableness. I'll bet it's a big PR plus for him, as against jackbooted thugs like us. That's probably why he called the press, so we'd have to be careful with him.'

'How much is that going to matter?'

'You kidding me? Since Waco and the Montana Freemen, you get a situation like this, public perception is going to be everything. They have to be quaking in their boots at headquarters right now. And ATF even more. Thanking whoever they thank that this is out here in the country, not in the Big City, at the same time they're wishing it could be northern Siberia instead. Maybe you should be glad you don't have that Washington job yet.'

Lukas leaned into the car for the phone and called his New York headquarters. Ben leaned against the fender and breathed the spring air and tried to make sense of what was happening. Thought of Judith, maybe right there at the end of the street, not a hundred yards away. What was she thinking? Did she know he was out here?

Lukas finished his call and got out of the car. 'I've got to talk to ATF about setting up a perimeter. Normally we don't bother prosecutors with the details' –

A polite way of saying, We'd rather be dead and in hell than let an Assistant listen in.

—'but seeing as you're going to be dealing with this kind of thing pretty soon, maybe you want to be a fly on the wall, see how it feels on the front lines.'

'Sure,' Ben said, surprised.

'No opinions unless they're asked for,' Lukas told him.

Healey unfolded a small table from the van's wall so he and Lukas could spread out a map of Centerville and debate their options. It quickly became clear that the planning hadn't covered this contingency: everyone they wanted, gathered in one place at one time, but with access to an arsenal of unknown size, and no way for the forces of good to take them by surprise. Plus an undercover to worry about.

'We're not even thinking about a direct assault on an armed building when they know we're coming,' Healey said – it was the central mistake ATF had made at Waco.

'We haven't got the personnel, anyway,' Lukas said. 'Not for that.'

'That's the truth. We've got enough for Plan One, which just went out the window, and enough to establish a much tighter perimeter here – Plan Three – complete with roadblocks. Make sure we catch anybody who tries to get out of the area, and we can debrief them at the school.'

They left the techs to staff the surveillance van and Lukas drove them to the school past the roadblocks already set up to keep the press out and civilians away. While Healey got the operation organized, Ben called Freddi to fill her in.

'What about your girlfriend?' Freddi asked when he'd wound down. 'Wasn't she a follower of Brauner's?'

He didn't answer.

'You okay? Was that the wrong question?'

'I don't know where she is at the moment,' he said, in a voice so artificially flattened it made him think of Joshua.

'Do you think she's in there with them?'

'I don't know,' he said, the weight of it finally hitting him. 'I don't know. She's just disappeared.'

'I'm sorry,' Freddi said, sounding like she meant it.

53

Once everyone was getting into place, Lukas took Ben back out to the car, slapped a red gumball on the dashboard and, siren wailing, drove them down the empty left side of the road past a long line of fuming motorists. Beyond a reinforced state-police roadblock, the road leading to the inner perimeter was lined on both sides with parked cars – dark sedans with radio antennas and state police cruisers.

As they progressed there were more vehicles, and groups of troopers were hanging out, along with some men in sport jackets – state police detectives? Though there was no longer any need for complete secrecy, Ben thought they were being careless about revealing their strength and deployment to whoever might be watching from the nearby houses.

Further in, they passed more serious-looking vehicles: a communications truck with state police markings, a state police special equipment truck, and two large unmarked vans that Ben guessed might be ATF's, even a truck from the NYPD Emergency Services Unit. Here, the men and women walking among the vehicles wore bulletproof vests under windbreakers with big POLICE and ATF logos.

The two trucks with telephone company markings were still at the intersection, but most of the view down the street was blocked by a wall of seven-foot-high ballistic shields made of a dull black composite material intended to stop bullets, arrayed across the road to protect the federal agents and state troopers behind them.

'What do you think?' Lukas asked him.

'Impressive.' Ben wondered how it looked to the people on the business end of it.

'Treasury law enforcement at work, with an able assist from the state, and some equipment support from the city.'

They were interrupted by the insistent clacking of an approaching helicopter. Lukas scanned the sky for it.

'I didn't think we expected air, yet.'

The helicopter came into view over the trees – white with green markings: a big number six in a circle.

'Shit,' Lukas said. 'That's press.'

He banged on the door of the surveillance van where the ATF

incident commander was conferring with his state police counterpart. Healey poked his head out.

'I know. We sent out a bulletin establishing a no-fly zone, but nobody cooperates any more. The state police have some choppers on the way to chase them off.'

'It's going to be a real circus,' Lukas said.

Having been to the front lines, Ben was shuttled back to the high school. As a prosecutor he had no role here but support, and the intensity of his personal interest wouldn't have bought him a better seat even if he'd been willing to admit to it.

As the afternoon progressed, more agents and troopers arrived. The brass were arriving, too, state police down from Albany and federal agents up from New York: Tim Ahl from Secret Service and the Special Agent in Charge of ATF's New York office.

TV monitors showed the views from the pole cameras. There was no movement visible at any of the houses. Curtains were drawn across all the windows, and no one ventured outside.

It was all deceptively peaceful except at the staging area, where the state police were trying to manage the demands of a growing horde of television and print reporters frustrated at being kept away from the action. An apparent armed standoff involving observant Jews forty-five minutes from the press capital of the world, the city with the largest population of Jews outside Israel, was a public-information nightmare of a magnitude that the operations planners hadn't foreseen.

As the battle lines went up between law enforcement and the reporters and camera operators eager for access, Ben worried that the effort needed to control the movements of eager journalists was absorbing the police and federal agents more than the operation itself.

At four o'clock, after fruitless attempts to reach someone in the surrounded houses by phone, the state police incident commander walked around the wall of ballistic shields and stood in full view of the houses at the end of the street. With a bullhorn, he introduced himself and apologized for any inconvenience the law-enforcement deployment might be causing.

'We don't want to frighten anybody, but it's my duty to inform you that we have evidence you are harboring fugitives and holding contraband. We have federal warrants here for the seizure of the contraband, which includes weapons and explosives, and for the arrest of the fugitives.' He named Dov Winkler and Ari Benzvi and – despite Sid's apparent defection – David Gershon, his undercover persona. 'We ask you to cooperate with us in making these people available and opening your doors for the orderly execution of our search warrants. We can do this quickly and painlessly, with very little disruption to your lives. And we'll do our best to respect your needs and not disturb the peace of your Sabbath any more than absolutely necessary.'

As expected, there was no response. Everyone went back to waiting.

Watching them put up the black barrier to block the street, a section at a time, Alan Kest had imagined the police drawing up their forces behind it, unseen. The frustration and anger he'd been feeling all day was building past his ability to contain it, and the police announcement made him erupt.

'Look out there,' he said to Benzvi loud enough for everyone to hear. 'This is all because you murdered Isaac.'

'Not murder,' the Israeli defended. 'Execution.'

'The police say murder. That's why they're out there. We can't fulfill our destiny with police on every side.'

'Who are you to tell us what we can do! You, the one who nourished the viper in our bosom – and now you bring this other snake. A policeman. A man who lied to us so he could put us in jail, or worse.'

This time Kest held his peace. *Do not try to calm your enemy in his anger*, the sages taught. And he had only himself to blame. He should never have told about Isaac not returning the note. He had spoken in the spirit of repentance, but . . .

Benzvi seemed confused by the silence. 'You're a stupid old man,' he shouted in exasperation.

'And you're an arrogant, foolish boy,' Kest couldn't resist saying. 'It's a shame on the memory of your blessed great-grandfather, may his teaching endure, that you should try to lead us further into this danger.'

Joshua had been watching and listening. The Israeli turned to him.

'Rebbe, what should we do?'

'Rabbi Kest is right,' Joshua said. 'We can't fulfill our destiny surrounded this way. We have to free ourselves. After Havdalah we can talk of it again.'

As night shrouded the scene and darkness made the atmosphere more tense, Ben could summon no convincing reason for them to let him stay. He accepted a ride back to the city with the same PI officer who'd brought him out.

'Interesting that you had the state police make the announcement to the people in the house,' Ben said.

‘We’re trying to stay in the background here, as far as the public. The people in the houses, too. ATF’s got such a nasty image, especially when it comes to religious groups, and the worst thing you get from a state cop is a traffic summons. So we figure they’re a less alarming adversary, easier to surrender to.

‘It’s a total press mess already,’ he continued. ‘And this is barely the beginning – when there’s a feeding frenzy like this, nobody’s safe. And some genius in Washington already decided there’s a burning need for us to distribute our tape of the Rabbi’s little speech. I suppose they think he’ll look like a kook, but, shit, there are people who still think Vernon Wayne Howell spoke directly to God, and this guy looks a whole lot saner – and cleaner – than Mr Howell a/k/a David Koresh ever did. Makes a whole lot more sense, too.’

At home Ben found a telephone message from the US Attorney and one from Elliot Rosen: ‘If that’s your guy on the news we have to talk.’ Nothing from Judith.

He called Hannah first, hoping she was awake and not too upset he hadn’t called sooner.

She came right to the phone. ‘Daddy, I want to come home.’

‘Why? What’s wrong?’

Hesitation, and then a stage whisper. ‘Grandma hates me.’ He could hear that she was on the verge of tears.

‘Oh no. Why do you think she hates you?’

‘Because my mommy was her little girl—’ The words cut off in a sob.

‘Yes, and now you’re her little girl—’

‘Nooo. It’s my fault my mommy died.’ Now the tears, a torrent.

Oh Lord. ‘No it’s not. Of course it’s not. Who told you that?’

‘Grandma.’ Barely audible amid the sobs.

‘Oh, sweetie.’ He wanted to put his arms around her. ‘Your mommy was hit by a car. That’s not your fault.’

‘Yes it is.’ Great gulp of air. ‘She was saving me.’ More tears, then, in a kind of singsong, repeating a rote lesson: ‘So I have to be very good all the time or else it isn’t worth it that my mommy died.’

‘Oh no. No no no.’ How did you contradict that? Any argument he made now would be repeated to Grandma and no doubt countered, only making things worse. ‘Hannah, sweetie, I love you very much. Can you put your grandma on, please?’

Teary yell of *Grandma*, footsteps, and the familiar sweet voice that this time made him shudder with anger. He brushed by the niceties.

‘Something’s come up here, and I need to have Hannah back.’

‘Oh that’s a shame. We’re having such a good time.’

‘I may not be able to come down myself but I’ll send someone as early as I can arrange for. Monday, probably.’

'First it's an emergency to bring her here, now it's an emergency to take her away. I don't know what she's been telling you.'

'I just need to have her back here with me.'

'If it's about her mother's death, she's old enough to learn how to behave in adult company, and I think she's old enough to understand that she has a responsibility—'

'Edith, she's five years old, and I don't want to argue with you about this. I need to have my daughter with me. And I'm asking you, out of consideration for all of us just leave the subject of her mother's death alone. I'm going to make arrangements and I'll call back.'

He was lucky enough to catch Vashti at home. When he'd worked things out with her, he called Hannah again.

'Sweetie, Vashti's coming down to get you day after tomorrow. I want you to be back here with me.'

'Can Judith come instead? I want Judith to get me.'

'She can't, sweetie, I'm sorry.'

'Does she hate me, too?'

'No, no. No, she loves you. But . . . she had to go away for a trip.'

'When is she coming back?'

'I don't know, sweetie, she didn't tell me.'

'She isn't coming back!' He could tell how tired she was, and at a distance of fifteen hundred miles he wasn't sure how to cope with it. 'She's never coming back, like my mommy!' Another torrent of tears.

Edith took the phone. 'I'll try to put her to bed. I can see why you want to have her back with you.' She hung up before he could comment.

Shaken, he called Rosen and left word, then he returned the call from his boss.

'I hear you had some excitement,' she said.

He told her about it.

'If they want somebody up there tomorrow, it should be Freddi, not you. This is getting too dramatic and public for you to be there. And what kind of objectivity can you have at this point, making decisions that may involve people's lives? You've got other work you can be doing.'

He'd gotten home from Centerville too late for the early news. At ten and again at eleven he skipped among the local reports. Centerville was the lead story everywhere he looked. They all showed clips of Joshua's speech. Uniformly, the image and the sound weren't as clear as they'd been in the survellance van. He thought some clever press officer might have degraded the quality in duping the press copies, hoping to make Joshua less compelling.

A state-police spokeswoman made the vaguest of references to financial crimes and firearms theft and the murder of a federal witness, and answered questions about specifics with generalities. ATF, still working hard to maintain the lowest possible profile, had no comment.

Most of the usual inane anchor-reporter dialog touched the obvious bases of Waco and Ruby Ridge and the Montana Freemen, and expressed general ignorance of Rabbi Joshua Brauner and whatever group he led. The more enterprising reporters had ambushed rabbis on the way out of Havdalah services and come up with a few willing to pontificate at great inaccurate length on who Brauner and his congregation might be and what they might believe. No one had yet gotten Asher Stern on camera, but Ben doubted that would last past morning.

When the news was over he called Judith, let it ring as long as he could endure the no-one-is-answering computer messages from the phone company. After that there was nothing left to do but go to bed. The coming days were not likely to be easy ones.

He lay awake wishing for sleep, imagining Judith in the Centerville house watching out the window while Joshua gave his speech, waiting for him to return to her. And Rivka and the four kids waiting, too. Then he imagined their idyllic menage dazzled and deafened by stun grenades, torn apart by bullets from MP-5 automatic carbines like the ones ATF used.

54

Rosen called in the morning.

'Your rabbi was saying some interesting things,' he told Ben. 'Starting with an allusion that unless I'm nuts was a definite reference to the coming of the Messiah.'

'Come over and let's talk about it,' Ben said. 'I'm very interested.'

'Okay. I've got to give the benediction at a temple breakfast, then I'm all yours.'

Waiting for Rosen, Ben called Suzanne and Mark Altman, and Zippy Klein's parents. He got no answer either place, and none at Judith's. He explored radio and television, found only Centerville. With the end of the Jewish Sabbath, the reports went, the authorities were hoping to establish communication with the people in the houses, a fringe religious group whose history the reporters were only beginning to learn.

On television, the scarcity of news plus the need for visual excitement yielded replays of the worst images of the FBI assault on the Branch Davidians at Waco five years before. Armored vehicles with horror-movie snouts broke holes in the building's walls. Flames devoured everything. A voiceover by an artificially panicky newscaster speculated, with perhaps more relish than she intended, on whether this standoff, too, would end in flames and death.

For filler some stations broadcast tape of local zoning and tax disputes between Centerville and the non-Jewish neighboring community, and interviews with people in the area. Not just the Stropkovers but all the Jews of Centerville were damned as interlopers, people with no thought for the history of the area where they had bought up so much land and imposed their own institutions – just as the churchgoing old-timers were accused of inflexibility, selfishness and intolerance.

Rosen seemed almost a different person in his neat business suit, white shirt and tie. 'My official rabbi clothes,' he said. 'Mind if I take off the jacket and tie? They're killing me.'

'Please do,' Ben said.

Rosen accepted a cup of coffee, settled onto the couch.

'I'm really stoked about this,' he said. 'The way he buried hints here and there. You know the part where he quoted Jeremiah cursing people who do the Lord's work with a slack hand? That's only the first half of the verse. The rest is, "cursed be he who withholds his sword from blood."'

'Ouch.'

'Right. Serious. And just the kind of generalship you can expect from the Lord of Armies. That's the aspect of God he kept invoking, Lord of Hosts. *Hosts* – that's not "folks who do a lot of entertaining," it's *really big armies*.'

'I didn't even notice it. You think it's important.'

'I do. I don't know who the message is for, but this Rabbi Brauner doesn't strike me as a man who throws around scriptural passages without knowing what all the implications are.'

'You said there was something at the beginning about the Messiah.'

'That teaching he quoted, that we should busy ourselves with the Law and the doing of good deeds and that way not come to harm?'

'Right . . .'

'Well the kind of "harm" he was talking about is what's called the "birth pangs of the Messiah."'

'Birth pangs?'

'Yep, and everybody gets to have them. It's a legendary period leading up to the appearance of Moshiach. There are all kinds of theories about it, none of them pleasant – drought and famine and strife, great sinning, the Law forgotten. The rabbis in the Talmud offer various prescriptions for avoiding it. And one of them – attributed to, I think, Rabbi Eliezer – is exactly what Joshua said.'

'That's weird, because the little I heard him say about this coming so-called millennium was very disdainful of the whole idea. And especially of the people who calculate a messianic appearance by a secular calendar.'

Rosen was nodding at that. 'That's not surprising. There's this major debate in the Talmud about when the Messiah will come and two of the rabbis basically put a curse on anyone who tries to figure out the exact time by using Biblical pronouncements or prophecies – so and so many years from such and such an event. "May their bones be blasted," or words to that effect.'

'But you still think Joshua was talking about the Messiah.'

'I do. Because there's also a theory that says to claim you know who the Messiah *is* and his time is *now* isn't the same as calculating when in the future he might arrive.'

'Reasoning that could warm a lawyer's heart.'

'And very Talmudic.

'But how would Joshua know – *think* he knew – that Moshiach was here?'

'Not by signs and portents,' Rosen-said, 'because the prevailing view is there won't be any. It's just, you know when you know. You see the effects – the people return to Jerusalem, there's an increase in Torah learning and Sabbath observance. The problem is, there are people who say that all those things are already happening right now. So the major missing piece is that the Holy Temple has to be rebuilt on its original site. Which is one part of the story that isn't happening. Though didn't you say your suspects were doing business with a cattle breeder who does genetic engineering?'

'Not only that – he's a fundamentalist who's talked about breeding a Biblically significant herd.'

'If they're trying to breed a perfect red heifer, then maybe they do have some idea about rebuilding the Temple. Maybe that's why Brauner's talking so much about Israel. You can't rebuild the Temple in upstate New York.' Rosen shook his head. 'I don't know, maybe we shouldn't get carried away with this. A word here, a word there. It doesn't necessarily add up to anything.'

'Joshua talked about Jews having to defend themselves against Christian apocalyptic violence because of the so-called millennium. Maybe that's what the references are.'

'Could be. Most of the really horrible stuff in the New Testament Book of Revelation is actually straight out of Jewish end-time mythology, especially the parts that say war is going to play a big part in the coming of the Messiah.'

Ben didn't see hard-headed Treasury agents like Lukas and Ciampa responding to this kind of speculation. He beeped Lukas anyway. It seemed a long time before there was a return call.

'No news,' the agent said. 'Situation unchanged.'

'Communication?'

'None. We shout at them with a bullhorn, call on the phone, nothing. Looks like Brauner's said his piece for now.'

'How's Freddi doing up there?'

'Staying out of the way, like she should. She's kind of a distraction, anyway. That's one fine woman.'

'True. But you wouldn't want her prosecuting you.'

'I'm ready to believe it.'

'Listen, have you got your rabbi up there? Or any others?'

'Hot and cold running.'

'Have they looked at Brauner's speech?'

'Over and over.'

'Did anybody talk about messianic imagery, or any references to bloody swords?'

'I don't think so, but I'll confess to tuning most of that stuff out.'

'Ask them. Ask what Jeremiah says after the warning about doing the Lord's work with a slack hand. And ask them about the birth pangs of the Messiah.'

'Say that again?' Lukas said and, when Ben did, said, 'You're kidding me, right?'

'I wish I was.'

Lukas called back less than an hour later.

'Talk to the rabbis?' Ben asked him.

'Was that a practical joke?'

'Not hardly. Why?'

'They looked at me funny. A couple of them didn't want to talk about it. There was one who thought it was a clever reading of the speech, to think about those things, but he doubted Brauner had it all in mind. *Our* guy gave me a long lecture full of scripture I didn't get most of and then basically told me not to mess around with what I didn't understand. Anyway, that's not why I called. I got a bulletin from Israel. Our Swiss chemist turned up dead.'

'That's bad news. How?'

'Gunshot to the head, execution style.'

'Any leads?'

'Nothing yet. Our office in Cyprus is going to tell the Israeli National Police there might be a connection with the Russian we're interested in.'

'You think that's who did it?'

'There were some cuts and bruises that the Israelis say look like he was being persuaded to say things he didn't want to.'

'Like chemical formulas?'

'Seems likely. That's why we think it's Rudovsky. That makes two murders for this crew.'

'With Isaacs, you mean? Different people, different jurisdiction, different motives.'

'Not the way I see it.'

'Any word about Sid?' Ben asked.

'We're still taking Joshua at his word on that.'

'That Sid switched sides?'

'That Joshua believes he did. Now that it's Sunday we're going to give Sid a while longer to communicate, then we may have to think again about going in to pull him out. This time the arrest warrants can have his real name on them.'

Ben wondered if Sid had really fooled Joshua, or if Joshua was fooling Sid – and the world – by pretending to be fooled? At least Joshua seemed to understand that keeping Sid alive and well offered some protection. There was a limit, though, to how long he'd be able to rely on that.

Thoughts of Joshua and deception led inevitably to thoughts of

Judith. The more Ben went over their history together, the surer he was that she'd been playing him like a pipe, from his lowest note to his highest. And he'd known nothing, only the touch of her fingers and the pleasure of her breath.

It was a paradox. She'd betrayed him, had used him, maybe unwittingly, but used him nonetheless. And if she'd used him she'd used Hannah, which was far worse – inexcusable. Yet he ached for her. He couldn't make the anger real enough to extinguish the longing. Maybe because he still could tell himself she, too, had been manipulated and used, by Joshua. That Joshua had fastened on him as a target of opportunity and encouraged Judith to get close to him without letting her know he had a hidden motive.

And what about the others? he wondered, the good people he'd met and come to care about who worshipped with Joshua and revered him. Had they been manipulated, or were they all willing accomplices?

He called Judith again, again got no answer.

He walked up West End Avenue to the townhouses that held the school Hannah had tried and the synagogue next door to it. Shades were down and curtains pulled over all the windows. The buildings almost looked deserted. He tried the doors; they were locked.

He went across town to the Stropkover synagogue on the East Side. The doors there were locked, too, and there was no sign of anyone around. He walked to Suzanne's and asked the doorman if they were home.

'I haven't seen them.' He rang upstairs, got no answer. 'I guess they're out.'

'Were they around yesterday?'

'You know, I couldn't tell you. I don't really keep track.'

He wanted to go home, but instead he headed downtown. Third Avenue in the lower Fifties was deserted, all the offices and stores closed for Sunday. He walked up the sidestreet and stood staring up at the house where Judith was staying before he mounted the steps and rang the bell. He heard the chimes echoing in the empty house. Rang and rang and rang, then sat on the stoop knowing no one would come but for a long time unable to leave.

He went back home to call Florida. Hannah was frantic with fear and confusion. She'd been watching television with her grandparents, had recognized a picture of Joshua on the news and gotten excited. Once Edith and Bert had heard that the man of the hour was someone Hannah and Ben knew, they hadn't been able to get enough of the news and commentary. They'd subjected Hannah to a Sunday full of public affairs programs devoted to richly imagined biographies of Joshua Brauner, guesswork history of the Stropkover movement, and speculation about fringe religious groups and the possibility that Centerville would turn into another Waco, speculation complete with the same kind of footage Ben had seen in New York. Or so Ben pieced together from what Hannah told him.

All his attempts at reassurance didn't allay Hannah's fear that something very bad was going to happen to Joshua, or stanch her incessant and unanswerable questions about Deborah and Dina and the new friends she'd made at their school, and especially about Judith.

55

Ben went to the office Monday feeling like a condemned man. He had to remind himself that no one else knew what was weighing him down so heavily. Queen Victoria and Freddi Ward knew only the merest part of it, and as far as the rest of the office was concerned, he was on his way to bigger and better things. For now though, there was nothing more important to him than the standoff at Centerville, and he couldn't do anything about it.

He tried to keep his mind on case-intake work. It was late morning before he remembered to call Nate Morgan.

'I hardly imagined when we talked about the rabbi that he was going to be on TV day and night,' Morgan said.

'I didn't either.'

'I'm told you gave ATF some help.'

That had to mean Mary Harrell was briefing him on the case. 'I had some information they thought was useful.'

'As long as you're part of the solution, and as long as this doesn't end with your rabbi shooting at our agents, I'm content not to see it as a problem. As long as *you* don't.'

'I don't. But I'm willing to wait and see what happens before we go ahead – to be sure nothing like that does happen. And he isn't *my rabbi.*'

'Point taken. I appreciate your being careful. And there's no harm leaving your nomination on hold a little longer – if it's only a *little* longer.'

Unable to stay out of it, he called Freddi.

'How's it going up there?'

'More waiting.'

'You're in good company.'

'In the abstract, maybe. You're welcome to the company I actually have. Agent Lukas seems to think he's charming.'

'Charming? Frank?'

'That's what I mean.'

'He's a good agent, though, if you can get past the attitude.'

'He's been asking about you,' she told him. 'What your status is, are you out of the loop. I told him we're both on the case, only I'm going to be taking over because you're expecting a new job, and you're not out of the loop at all.'

'Thanks.'

'Sure. I don't think he knows which way to jump. Doesn't want to get on your wrong side because of the Washington job, but he's uneasy about your knowing Brauner.'

And what do *you* think about that? Ben didn't ask.

After what Freddi had told him, he was surprised to get a call from Lukas.

'More news from Israel.' The agent sounded unexpectedly cheery. 'They went to pick up the Russian and have a chat about the chemist. Rudovsky was gone, but they tossed his house in Jerusalem and found some sample vials of printing ink. We won't have test results for a week but Cyprus says it sounds like the real thing.'

'So it does all tie together over there.'

'It sure looks that way. And I'm betting it all comes back to your friend Rabbi Brauner. At this point there's zero chance his disciple Rabbi Kest just got that phony hundred in exchange for some computers. It came in the mail from Israel. This has got to be all one international organization.'

'Except that the real action's all over there. Isaacs' sample is the only sign they might circulate the notes here. So if you've got the source at the Israeli end, the real source, where they're actually producing the OV ink and the notes, I'd say that's what we ought to be concentrating on. And that makes the people here secondary.'

'You know, all of a sudden you sound just like a man trying to get his friend off the hook.'

It made Ben a lot madder than he was ready for. 'Listen, I don't know what you think but I'm trying to save lives – *agents'* lives. And the lives of people whose only stake in this is their spiritual wellbeing, people who had no idea what they were dealing with. If we can roll up the counterfeiting operation on the Israeli end, we can take the pressure off, here. Get Sid out of there and let the rest of them have a chance to run – to Israel, wherever. The murder suspects aren't going to get anywhere, and we can confiscate guns and explosives as well from empty houses as occupied ones—'

'Suppose they take the guns and bombs with them?'

'Where? How far can any of them get? The problem is we're all stuck in some kind of rote response. Okay, we're surrounding the houses while we figure out what to do next – at least we're not kicking doors first and then pondering the magnitude of our mistake while we sift the bones out of the ashes. But there have to be other ways to skin this cat.'

Lukas was silent.

'Fuck it,' Ben said. 'Why am I wasting my breath?'

'Hey, hey, hold on! You're not wasting your breath, you're making sense – but that's only if they can get the job done in Israel. Because, with the chemist dead, Rudovsky is our only clear link to the operation over there, and if they let him get away then we're really fucked.'

Ben couldn't think of a counter-argument.

'And we still have to hang onto all these rabbis,' Lukas concluded. 'Because my gut still tells me the head and heart of it all is right here.'

It was a raw day, cool with a threat of rain, but Ben wanted to be out in the air. At noon, he clipped on his beeper and forwarded his calls to his cellphone, so he wouldn't be out of touch.

The phone warbled as he crossed the plaza toward the Municipal Building. It was Freddi. 'Hey, you want to come up here, get into the real action?'

'What's happening?'

'We're negotiating. They've got a lawyer talking to us, and Rabbi Brauner gets on the line himself now and then. He really does want to take his people to Israel, and he understands he may have to give up something to do it.'

'Sid?'

'They're treating him like one of their own. Not a word about using him as a hostage or a bargaining chip.'

It was more than he'd hoped for. 'You think they'll come out?'

'Or let us in. And one prosecutor isn't going to be enough to handle everything, not if we need to take statements and cut deals. I've already got a couple of paralegals coming up. They'll bring you, and you can ride back with me.'

The paralegals, two young women from Major Crimes, spent the trip in a state of agitated glee at the prospect of seeing Joshua Brauner, whose speech they'd both watched over and over on the news and whom they both found totally fascinating, Ben gathered from what he could hear of their front-seat chatter over a booming CD. Fascinating and sexy.

For himself, he kept trying to combine Freddi's breakthrough with the pictures Lukas and Rosen were painting

Nothing in Joshua's speech announced that he'd been part of the criminality, except perhaps the implication that Isaacs' murder had been community self-defense. Maybe, despite Rosen's millenarian imaginings, Joshua had talked some sense into Kest and the others. Lukas might be right that the Russian was only the operational boss of the counterfeiting effort and the real power was here, but that didn't mean it was necessarily Joshua.

It would be no small trick, keeping the pressure on whoever came out of the surrounded houses in just the right way to produce the maximum useful information, not just a handful of plea bargains for Isaacs' murder and some federal gun-law infractions. But for the first time there was a chance they'd be able to piece together some real answers.

The high-school parking lot had filled up beyond capacity with state police cars, unmarked vehicles, TV station vans topped by camera cranes and microwave dishes, and a motley flock of cars. Standing by the vehicles, looking ready to mount up and ride, were small groups of reporters and camera operators and occasional pairs and quarters of troopers and agents.

Inside the school there was an even greater sense of expectation. Crossing the gym to the corner that was partitioned off as a control center and headquarters, Ben spotted Asher Stern on the bleachers with two young men dressed, like their rabbi, in black suits and fedoras. Stern, silent, had a fierce, inward look; his disciples, for all their scholarly mien, kept their eyes on the movement around them with the alertness of bodyguards. Sitting separately were three bulky men in Hasidic garb, deep in argument. Hot and cold running rabbis, as Lukas had said.

He found Freddi on the phone. Her cheeks were flushed and her eyes bright. She hung up and turned to him. 'It's set. The lawyer's letting them in to execute the warrants – five minutes.'

56

Sid Levy shifted on the narrow cot that was the only furniture in the cramped, icy room, trying to get comfortable enough to sleep. If he got any kind of opening he'd need to be as alert and rested as possible, and the two nights since the sleepless marathon of Friday and Saturday hadn't provided much in the way of recovery.

When he first met Joshua Brauner and saw that he, not Alan Kest, was the real boss here, Sid had considered just keeping his mouth shut about who he really was and hoping to make it through the weekend. But at some point just before dawn, after being up all night praying and meditating, the Secret Service part of his consciousness had slipped out of focus and he had emerged from meditation into the rhythms of the morning affirmation of God's Oneness with nothing else on his mind. And it was then, between the dawn prayers and the more formal Saturday morning service, that Joshua had come to talk to him, and the truth had simply come out, not because he'd gone over to the enemy but because under Joshua's level gaze maintaining the lie that Sid Levy was David Gershon simply seemed pointless.

Lying awake, hearing the squeak of a wooden chair as the guard outside the door did his own best to get comfortable, Sid tried to convince himself that whatever his motives, however muddled he'd been at the time, he'd only been carrying out the plan he'd agreed on with Kaplan and Lukas.

Joshua didn't seem surprised by the news, embraced him and congratulated him on putting aside the lie and the pretense. Nothing more was said about it until, after the additional Sabbath service and the blessing over wine, they were having a sort of Yiddish brunch around tables in the living room and dining room, the house crowded with people who had been arriving through the morning.

The men who had started Friday night together were at a separate table in a study at the back of the ground floor. Joshua asked Sid to introduce himself to the others by his real name, and when he did a major battle started. The argument took the form of a discussion of religious principles, the sort of thing that was appropriate to a Sabbath afternoon, but the subtext was clear enough. He had unwittingly walked into the middle of a war over the death of Isaac Isaacs, mostly between Alan Kest and a muscular, cold-eyed young man with an Israeli accent who seemed to exist in a space all his own, as if the others were all allowing him extra room.

By admitting he was a federal agent, Sid gave the Israeli explosive ammunition, and Sid's crediting Kest with opening his eyes to the truth proved to be weak armor. The Israeli – Ari Benzvi – clearly had the upper hand with Joshua, and Sid saw that he might be on the edge of a death penalty himself.

He'd gained some ground by letting them know a surveillance team was out there and by making the call home and the little speech on the lawn, but when the law-enforcement presence became oppressively visible, pressure in the house built to near bursting.

When Joshua had agreed with Kest that they couldn't fulfill their destiny surrrounded by police, rage and frustration had reddened the Israeli's face, though he'd said nothing.

'But justice must also be served,' Joshua had added. As it is written, "And you shall root out evil from your midst."' He'd ordered Kest and Sid put under guard and taken away.

They hadn't allowed him much in the way of rest since then. There had been interrogations that were part of a trial, he was sure, though whether his or Kest's he couldn't tell. And now he was alone in a small dark room, awaiting his fate.

He wondered how many were left in Centerville, and how they were dealing with the cops and agents surounding them. If there was going to be a firefight, he supposed he was better off out of it.

Ben sat with Freddi and waited, both of them staring at a video monitor that showed the waiting agents – their ATF and POLICE windbreakers bulked out by the flak jackets underneath – and the houses beyond.

'Tell me how you did it,' he said, trying not to be jealous.

'It wasn't hard once we got started. He wanted some assurances we couldn't give him about not arresting anybody right there when we went in, but we worked it out. He seems like a reasonable enough guy.'

Ben knew better than to agree. 'I'm glad it worked out.' He was surprised by how tight his voice sounded.

'Have you heard from Judith?' Freddi asked, clairvoyant.

'Nothing.'

'Maybe you'll be seeing her in a few minutes. On TV, anyway.'

On the screen a single figure emerged from Joshua's house – a middle-aged man in a gray business suit.

'That's the lawyer.'

He crossed the lawn and in the middle of the paved circle he met the lead agent. They traded a few words, then the agent beckoned and his team came out from behind the wall of ballistic shields and followed him to the house at a trot, weapons ready.

A speaker crackled. 'We're at the house. Everything's quiet. We're going in.'

The ATF Special Response Team split up, two agents moving to cover the front door and two the back door of the house while the others went inside behind the lawyer.

The picture went static. Ben had to remind himself to breathe.

Nothing.

'Shouldn't they be coming out?' someone said behind him.

Nothing.

The two agents covering the front door rushed into the house.

Ben and Freddi looked at each other.

The team leader came out with the lawyer, both men gesticulating broadly, obviously arguing.

'Something's wrong,' Freddi said superfluously. She reached for the phone, thought better of it.

Again, agents took up guard positions at the front of the house. A pair of vans raced into view, bouncing across the lawns. The vans pulled up flanking the house and agents from a second SRT boiled out of them.

'Something's *very* wrong.'

The monitor went blank. Someone had decided the video feed should be cut off, a way to limit information leaking to the press.

They waited in an agony of ignorance – five minutes, then ten. The phone rang and Freddi snatched it from the receiver. Listened, her face going pale.

'No,' she said sharply. 'No, that can't be, I was just talking to him. He *has* to be there. No, I'm not suggesting—' Listened again. 'All right.' Sounding defeated. 'I'm standing by.' She hung up slowly, turned again to Ben, her face bleak.

'They're gone,' she said in a voice he could barely hear. 'Nobody home.'

There were, it turned out, no adult men under seventy in any of the houses within the perimeter, and only one woman, who was taking care of three infants and an epileptic four year old. There were nine other children under twelve, and three seniors: two women and a man clomping around in shoes too big for him – Sid Levy's shoes, with a tracking device in one heel. They were all immediately claimed as clients by the lawyer who'd escorted the agents to Joshua's house.

'He was *there*,' Freddi insisted to Ben when the initial turmoil had calmed down. 'He had to be, because we had wiretaps and cellphone scanners and all the rest of it, so we knew he wasn't calling in from somewhere else, on call forwarding or anything like that. There was no other signal coming into the house or going out of it. He had to be there, talking to me on the phone. And five minutes later he's gone without a trace, and all the others with him.'

Ben had the antic thought that he shouldn't feel too bad having been deceived by a man who could disappear at will, taking with him somewhere close to two dozen companions.

Freddi said, 'They appear to have told the kids their mommies and daddies were flying away with Joshua on a holy chariot, but the smart money's on a tunnel.' She made a skeptical face. 'I don't know, though – it'd have to be a long one, and they all had to be past the perimeter by early this morning, when we really tightened things up. And that still wouldn't explain how Rabbi Brauner managed to be there on the phone until the very last minute.'

'Teleportation. There's something like that in the mystical tradition, I think. Great sages who travel out of their bodies into the heavenly realms.'

'This one took his body with him.'

57

Ben sat in on the briefing for the law-enforcement brass. Healey ran down what the agents had found, turned it over to Ciampa, who described the room-to-room search.

'The dogs definitely found traces of explosives in the garages and basements. Other than that – some crates in one garage where we were expecting to find assault rifles were full of food.'

'As far as the tunnels, the dogs helped out there, too,' Ciampa was saying. 'Initially there was no sign of any route of escape, but they sniffed a booby trap behind a blind door built into the paneling in the basement of the principal house. We'd have found it, but not so quickly. The bomb squad came in and they found a device containing a small amount of military explosive—'

Healey leaned forward to interrupt. 'We're recommending that this information be considered classified, and completely embargoed from the press.'

'Right. The one device that they've actually used so far was conventional industrial explosive, so we're sticking to that for the public. The device that we found appeared to be intentionally non-lethal, and we think it was a demonstration – here's what we *could* have done to you if we'd wanted to – as a way to slow us down, which it did.'

Beyond the symbolic booby trap at the tunnel entrance, no weapons or explosives had been found. ATF and the state police were following out the tunnels, which appeared to interconnect three of the four houses around the circle and one of the two with adjoining backyards. Only one of the tunnels they'd found extended past the perimeter, running under the street where the state police were set up on the south side of the compound.

The people who had stayed behind were refusing to say a word or to consider any deal, though they'd been told they'd be charged with concealing and harboring fugitives and aiding their flight, even conceivably as accessories to capital murder. Because Joshua had been so emphatic about leading his followers to Israel, watches had been mounted at all airports within any reasonable distance.

Throughout the reports and speculation, Ben heard an undertone of nervous self-justification. It occurred to him that if Joshua wasn't found, there'd be a lot of hard questions asked – and teleportation wasn't going to be a good answer.

A good thing, he thought, that he'd been in New York and Freddi had been here when Joshua and his people slipped through the federal fingers. Assistant US Attorney Benjamin Kaplan, former acolyte of the disappearing Rabbi Brauner, would have been far too tempting a scapegoat.

He rode back to the city with Lukas and Freddi, each of them wrapped in a glum silence. Ben suspected Lukas was brooding about Sid Levy, Freddi about evaporated glory as part of the team that had talked a score of armed religious fanatics out of a barricade situation.

For himself, beyond his worry about Sid, he was still seething at being so completely used and betrayed. He tried to focus his anger on Joshua and not his own gullibility.

Lukas caught Ben's eye in the rearview mirror. 'That stuff you told me to ask the rabbis about?' the agent said. 'You believe in it?'

'Why?'

'I went back and talked to the rabbis again, and guess who was there. Rabbi Asher Stern.'

'I noticed that he was there. What did he have to say?'

'He's a piece of work. He makes a big fuss about not saying anything negative about anybody, but what he does say, if you asked him does Brauner breathe fire and eat babies, he'd probably tell you "not all at the same time," so as not to sound uncharitable. So he's a hundred percent happy to believe Brauner is out to get his sword bloody.'

'Let's go with it for a minute,' Ben said. 'If Brauner was looking to fight, why sneak away?'

'Wrong battlefield, not prepared, wrong time, enemy too strong . . . You want some others?'

'No, that's fine. Then maybe he's really on his way to Israel. That fits better with the messianic references.'

'So far at the airports we've stopped a grand total of two groups with Centerville addresses,' Freddi reported. 'Four adults and nine kids, nobody we're specifically interested in, and none of them will say a word.'

'Headed for?'

'Rome and Athens. Which could easily mean Israel.'

Lukas said, 'None of the people we ID'd as being in the house with Brauner have shown up at their homes in Centerville or Brooklyn, or where they work.'

Checking the obvious locations had been the first order of business. Lukas and Ian Rogers had been at the center of the effort, providing the addresses they had for the Aljo conspirators, while Ciampa contributed ATF's case information. Agents from both agencies had gone out, with cooperation from NYPD. They'd found nothing – no one home, two of Aljo's three stores shuttered as if for the Sabbath. The locations were all staked out, in the event any of the fugitives showed up.

The only exception had been Alan Kest's parter in Aljo, Joseph Ohry. Agents had found him at the store in Brooklyn, uncooperative except to say he hadn't seen or spoken to Kest since the Rebbe's death and the break with Asher Stern. He just ran this one store and let the accountants make sure he got his share of the profits.

Freddi said, 'I keep wishing we had a better idea of who all Brauner's followers were, but it's not like we can roll up to the synagogue door and demand a list of members.'

'Are you covering the houses of worship?' Ben asked.

'I don't know,' Lukas admitted. 'My mind doesn't naturally go that way – look for bad guys at church.'

By the time Ben got home Monday evening, word of the disappearing rabbi and his equally insubstantial congregation had spread. Speculation about it had become the new national pastime, or so it seemed to Ben, checking the news. Opinions on what had happened in Centerville and what it meant were varied and colorful, with supernatural explanations by far the most popular, especially among people who'd picked up a smattering of Kabbalah, centuries-old mysticism that had become a craze among millenial seekers of all faiths.

He was expecting a big greeting from Hannah, back from Florida with Vashti. He didn't get one.

'Poor thing, she's tired,' Vashti said. 'She went in her room soon as we got in and hasn't been out since.'

He went in to talk to her but she wasn't interested and he wasn't going to force it. As he was leaving she said, 'I want to go to school.'

'In the morning. Janice'll be glad to see you.'

'Not that school! Deborah's school.'

'I know, sweetie, but we talked about it, and you know you have to go to regular school.'

He thought about Deborah's school – Joshua's – and about the adjacent synagogue, and that gave him an idea about something Joshua might make a detour for on his way out of the country.

He called Lukas. 'If Brauner and company are really on their way to Israel, they're not going to leave behind their Torah scrolls. It's a big deal to desecrate them, so you definitely don't just leave them lying around.' He remembered Hannah telling about a class visit next door to see the Rebbe's Torahs. 'Some of Brauner's come from the old country, brought over by their original Rebbe, and that makes them even holier, and completely irreplaceable. I'm not saying he'll go back for them himself, but whoever does might be worth following.'

'Good idea. Thanks.' Before Lukas got off he said, 'We know how he did the trick with the phone calls.'

'How?'

'The techies tell me he was sending a digital audio signal on the TV cable, changing frequencies every few seconds to keep it undetectable, then decoding it at the house and converting it to a regular analog signal they could feed into the phone line. It's all computerized switching so there's no audible delay. The result being you get what sounds like Brauner talking on the phone from the house, only he's really somewhere else – and we have no way to detect that he's not actually present at the location.'

'And nobody would notice?'

'Seems not, but I'm just repeating what the techies told me. The point is – he could have left there any time after he came out to make his little speech and we wouldn't have known.'

Ben got a call from Lukas later that night. 'I have some more news,' the agent said. 'I know I'm supposed to be calling sexy Freddi with my bulletins, but this is one I need you for. They found Alan Kest.'

'That's great. Has he said anything about Sid?'

'He hasn't said anything at all.'

'Where'd they find him?'

'Centerville. In one of the tunnels. About three feet underground.'

'Oh, shit. Killed how?'

'Ritually strangled, whatever that means.'

Ben didn't want to know. 'Any word from Sid?'

'No, but I'm seriously worried, and I haven't got clue one where to start looking for him.'

'Any idea of the motive for killing Kest?' Ben asked him.

'That's why I'm calling you. Why would Brauner kill his number one crook?'

'Rodef.' The word was out before Ben knew he was thinking it.

'How's that?'

'Someone who's out to commit murder, or rape – there's a religious obligation to save them from committing a sin so horrible, even if the only way to do it is to kill them. And some rabbis extend it to a person who's endangering the whole community.'

'You figure they're laying it all at Kest's feet?'

'Well, he gave the bogus hundred to Isaacs, if they know about that, and that's what really got us going. In any case, he was Isaacs' mentor, and Isaacs betrayed them. And Kest's the one who accepted Sid at face value.

'The only problem is,' Ben said, reconsidering, 'he'd already done those things, so it was already too late to stop him. The law I quoted is about future danger, not past acts.'

'However you slice it,' Lukas said, 'I sure don't like how they deal with traitors. I'm worried about Sid . . . And Kest dead makes another link to the counterfeiting plant we've lost. Brauner and the rest of them had better show up somewhere, and soon.'

58

Vashti had the morning off after her round trip to Florida. Ben got Hannah ready for school, fed her breakfast, and escorted her out the door.

As they crossed West End Avenue, she pointed and said 'Look, Daddy.'

A few blocks to the north the broad avenue sloped sharply upward, offering an unbroken view of a carnival of police activity.

From the distant top of the hill down to its low point at 96th Street the usually rapid morning traffic had been choked to a single downtown lane, with uptown traffic diverted to Broadway. Blue police sawhorses blocked off the other lanes; parked behind them were blue-and-white police cars and equipment trucks. Men and women in the darker blue of police uniforms were pulling more sawhorses from a flatbed truck and setting them up in what looked like corridors for pedestrians. It was still rush hour, and the grand old apartment houses that lined the avenue and the townhouses on the side streets were pouring commuters and schoolkids out into the gray morning to be confused by this unexpected obstacle course.

'It's by Deborah's school,' Hannah said, more intrigued than alarmed. 'What are they doing?'

'I don't know, sweetie. Something with the traffic.'

'Is there a bad person?' It had taken him a long time to convince her that the police, who had killed her mommy, were really there to protect good people from bad ones.

'Light's changed.' He took her hand to cross the side street, away from the police action. 'We have to get you to *your* school before you're late.'

When he'd delivered her safely to a smiling teacher, he walked back uptown. Instead of heading for the subway station entrance on Broadway, he stayed on West End.

He paused to watch from in front of the public school at 96th Street – it seemed as if the cops up the hill were hurrying everyone along, not giving anyone time to linger. A TV-news remote truck crawling along in the line of cars pulled up by one of the cops directing traffic.

The driver leaned out to ask a question, but the cop waved him on impatiently.

As Ben continued to observe the scene, he noticed that the tempo was different at the top of the hill – 99th Street and beyond – where he saw a bigger, denser clot of blue uniforms and a small crowd of civilians as well, with the civilians being passed along toward Broadway only in ones and twos, and slowly. A checkpoint of some kind?

A mother dropping off her children at the school stopped next to him to watch.

'You know what it is?' she asked him.

'No, do you?'

'Radio says it's some crazy Jews. Look at that – cops turning the whole city upside down being careful. Sure beats me why they don't bust down the door and shoot their sorry asses, like they do it uptown.'

Ben approached a heavyset cop leaning against a sawhorse blocking the sidewalk just past 96th Street and showed his Justice Department ID. 'Do you know if there's anyone here from Secret Service or ATF?'

The cop waved him by. 'You want to talk to the captain. She's up there by the command post.'

There was a vehicle parked halfway up the hill that looked like an enormous RV in police blue-and-white, the only thing in sight that could remotely be a command post. Ben folded his wallet open and hung it from his jacket pocket with the ID showing and headed that way.

The duty captain was a woman with a cherubic face and a no-nonsense air, standing outside the vehicle talking with a couple of detectives. She glanced at Ben's ID when he introduced himself and said, 'How can I help you?'

'Is this about people in the school and synagogue down the block there?'

She looked at him, waiting for more.

'If it is – if it's related to the people in the standoff in Rockland over the weekend – then it's my case.'

'Hang on a minute,' she said, and knocked on the door of the vehicle. 'Somebody for the fed,' she told the cop who opened it.

Ciampa poked his head out. To the police captain he said, 'He's okay,' and to Ben, 'Come on in.'

Inside, the vehicle seemed even bigger. Comfortably wide, it was long enough for two separate office sections – each with counter-like desks along both walls and a built-in sitting area, the two sections separated by floor-to-ceiling cabinets – plus a roster board on the wall facing the door and an open area behind the driver's seat.

'Frank's on his way,' Ciampa said. 'You got here quick.'

'What's happening?'

'Our bad guys turned up. In the wee hours yesterday, we were still sitting on our butts up in Centerville, the precinct down here got a call, a prowler or some other unusual activity, so they sent a radio car. They looked around, went and knocked on the door. There were folks inside but they weren't coming to the door. This was at the school. So the police called for backup and got access to a roof where they could see the back of the building and the garden, and they sat on it, wait and see who came out. Which no one did. So they went up to knock again, and somebody, looked like a rabbi, came and told them to go away and the cops said can we come in and look around, we heard there were prowlers. So the rabbi said no, we're fine.

'Next thing was, the end of the day, we'd notified the PD we thought somebody might come by for the Bible scrolls, so the precinct detectives were surveilling the location and canvassing the neighbors, and somebody put it together with the prowler call that morning. And they started hearing about how a lot of people showed up at the school building Sunday carrying suitcases and such, enough of them to where some of the neighbors thought it was funny, especially when nobody came to school on Monday morning. So the PD let us know and we brought over a bunch more surveillance photos and don't you know it, we got hits on one of the bombers and on Rabbi Solomon and the head rabbi – Brauner. And one "maybe" on Lukas's undercover, a woman who said there was a man who looked like he was hurt or sick or drugged. More or less fits the general description except he had a hat brim covering a lot of his face.'

'We've got to assume that's him.' Ben needed to believe they'd brought Sid here, and not left him in a hole somewhere to be discovered the way Kest was. 'Hurt how?'

'Just, being helped along by a man on either side. So he could have been under duress.'

'And Brauner's in there, too?'

'So say a couple of the neighbors who were out walking their dogs when he pulled up around dawn on Sunday with three pals and unloaded some crates and hefted them into the school.'

'Crates?'

'I see we're thinking alike, here. But we don't know for sure it was the guns.'

'This was dawn Sunday? Two days ago?'

'So they say. It looks like he left Centerville earlier than we thought.'

Ben pondered it: Joshua had fooled them all, and badly, in

Centerville – it was hard to credit that he'd just let himself be caught here like this.

Ciampa said, 'I thought Ward was supposed to be taking over the case.'

'She will be. Do they know about this at my office?'

'Isn't that why you're here?'

'I live down the block. I saw the activity on my way to work. Any contact so far with the people inside?'

'We haven't tried. The PD didn't put all the pieces together till fairly late last night. Then the first plan was to set up surveillance maybe on the apartment house rooftops where they wouldn't see it and follow anybody who came out of the buildings to go to the store or wherever, then pick them up out of sight of their buildings and see what they could tell us about what was going on in there. But with all that activity yesterday morning, cops banging on the door and sitting on the place, there was no way to just kick the door and catch them by surprise. And with major explosives to worry about, evacuating the neighbors had to be high on the agenda. They got started seriously establishing a perimeter in the last hour or so, and they want to be all set up before they try and make contact.'

'Who's got the inner perimeter?'

'NYPD Emergency Services. New York, once we're in the middle of the city like this we turn it over to the experts.'

There was a knock on the door. The driver opened it and Frank Lukas came in.

'You sure called this one,' he said to Ben. 'You have any idea what it is?'

'None. But it looks like a pattern. First he gathers the faithful in Centerville, now he's gathering them here.'

'Why not just run?' Lukas said.

'Maybe he *is* running, and we caught him before he got away. Assuming he's even in there any more.'

'True,' Lukas agreed. 'The neighbors saw him Sunday morning, right? And he's a guy who knows how to turn invisible on his way out of places. He could be anywhere by now.'

Much as he wanted to stay, Ben had to get downtown. Leaving the mobile command post he noticed a patrolman at the sawhorse barrier under siege by a short, dark-haired woman.

'You don't understand,' she was saying, 'I have to talk to someone. I have to.'

'Okay, ma'am,' the police officer was saying. 'If you'll just calm down.'

'Can I help?' Ben said. The woman looked familiar, he wasn't sure from where. Probably someone from the neighborhood.

'Who are you?'

'I'm Assistant United States Attorney Benjamin Kaplan.'

'Oh.' Despite her plump cheeks and a healthily rounded figure, the woman looked drawn and distraught. 'Are you in charge?'

'If you'll tell me what's on your mind, maybe I can help.' Abruptly, he remembered where he'd seen her before. At Joshua's East Side congregation the weekend he'd stayed at Suzanne's.

'You're here for the people in the shul, aren't you?' she asked, her agitation increased now that she had a more receptive audience. 'I know those people in there. There are children.' She was looking at him intently. 'You have to be careful, please.'

'Why don't we go somewhere we can talk?' he suggested.

He brought her to the command post vehicle and left her with Lukas and Ciampa while he went out to get somebody from the Emergency Services Unit. He wanted to hear what the woman had to say, but only with plenty of other people around to distract her from him. He came back with a sergeant from ESU and a detective from NYPD intelligence.

The woman seemed reassured by all the attention she was getting. 'They're all in there,' she said.

'Do you know how many?' the intel detective asked.

'I don't know exactly how many, but families.'

'How do you know about this?'

'We were supposed to go, my husband and I. He called us.'

'Who called?'

'Joshua. Joshua Brauner, our rabbi, our spiritual leader. He said he was gathering the most faithful in his congregations. A special retreat, he said—'

Ben traded glances with Lukas.

'We have prayer retreats sometimes,' she was explaining, 'sometimes right here in the city.' Her eyes sought out Ben, as if he would be the most likely to understand. He steeled himself against worrying that she recognized him, doing something dumb like putting a hand over his mouth. It was probably just his Jewish name—

'You said there are children,' Ciampa said. 'Do you know how many, or what ages?'

'Boys over thirteen and girls over twelve. That's what he told us. He said the younger children should go to the caretaking families from our congregation. We have a system for that, for when the grown-ups are away, like on retreat.'

'But you didn't go,' the detective said.

'My husband said we should, even with what happened in Centerville. He said he wasn't surprised Joshua could disappear like that, and reappear where he wanted, that the great rabbis could do that. But I wouldn't go. I was afraid for the children – we have a twelve year old and a fifteen year old. I wasn't going to let him take them.'

'Did the rabbi have a reason for you all to gather like this?' Ben asked. 'Did he say why you were all going to have this retreat?'

'He was having dreams, he said. He saw things in the dreams, and the meaning was to gather everyone here for Passover because there were great things happening in the world. But I told my husband it didn't seem right. That if Joshua really did all the things they were saying on the news, and he was endangering people in Centerville, then how did we know it wouldn't happen again?'

'Did Joshua say what the great things were, that were going to happen?' the intel detective asked.

'All my husband told me was "great things."'

'Did that mean something particular to you or your husband?'

'No. I mean, yes, in a way. Joshua sometimes spoke about the danger in the world because of people who were arming themselves to fight a battle against the Devil in the year 2000 or 2001. And that some of them called Jewish people by the name 'false Jews' and said people who pretended to be Jews were soldiers in the army of Satan and had to be annihilated. And Joshua said we had to be ready to defend ourselves from such people, that it would be a terrible time but full of a kind of greatness, too.'

'You think that was what he was talking about, here?' the detective pressed.

'I don't know.'

'Defend yourselves how?' asked the ESU officer.

'They had guns. And they did target practice.'

'They? Just the men?'

'Men and women. I did, once, but I was no good at it.'

'Did your husband follow the rabbi's instructions?' Ciampa asked her. 'Did he go to this gathering?'

'Yes. He went and he cursed me for not going with him. And he took our son.' She began to sob, as violently as a child, her whole body shaking.

When she'd calmed down, Ben asked if she knew who else the rabbi might have called.

'I don't want to get anyone in trouble.' Sniffling.

'We're trying to keep them *out* of trouble,' the ESU officer assured her.

Ben said, 'The more we know, the better we can reason with them and help them see why they should come out. And the less likely we are to say the wrong thing.'

'I only know some of them.' She named four families, then hesitated, offered two more.

The first people she'd thought of were Suzanne and Mark Altman.

Ben knew he shouldn't be surprised, tried to find solace in the fact that Deborah and Dina and Sara and Naomi were off somewhere else being cared for, not barricaded in the building with their mother and father.

The cops persuaded the woman to stay and go over her story again so they could be sure they had everything right, and to get the specifics of the caretaking program and whatever else she could give them. Ben and the two Treasury agents left them to it.

Walking toward Broadway, Ciampa said to Ben, 'Frank was saying you told him something before about Brauner's waging a war, something about the Second Coming? Was that what she was talking about, the "great things"?'

'Could be. Only for Jews it's the *first* coming.'

'Bad enough,' Ciampa said. 'That was no picnic, either. And I don't want somebody making me out to be any Roman centurion.' He pondered the possibilities. 'I'm not believing this,' he said. 'We've got women in there, we've got teenagers, we've got a religious guy who's worried about the year 2000 and who's preparing for some great event. Please tell me this isn't another Koresh at Waco. Not my case.'

59

Downtown, Ben was one of a half dozen Assistants and paralegals who found their way to the investigators' office to watch the Secret Service/ATF/NYPD press conference, broadcast from the main briefing room at Secret Service's World Trade Center headquarters. It was short, and as businesslike as the efficient, high-tech room it was held in:

After noting that the suspected criminals – barricaded in two adjacent buildings housing a synagogue and a school – had been joined by a large number of people not implicated in any crimes, Tim Ahl announced that the NYPD, in particular the elite Emergency Services Unit, had accepted a request from the federal agencies to isolate the suspects and assist in their apprehension.

'There's nobody better to contain this situation or to bring it to a swift and successful conclusion. The officers of the Emergency Services Unit know the city, they know their job, and they've got more experience doing it than anybody else in the world.'

'We appreciate the faith Secret Service and the Bureau of Alcohol Tobacco and Firearms have placed in us,' the ESU commanding officer responded. 'Praise from organizations with the ability that they demonstrate daily is high praise indeed.'

The backpatting festival produced a chorus of groans and jeers from the handful gathered in the investigators' office to watch.

The first questions, about the people in the buildings and their beliefs, were disposed of quickly: they belonged to a group of observant Jews thought to be followers of a deceased rabbi from Eastern Europe. Anticipated law-enforcement strategy was described as aimed at avoiding violence and preventing casualties. Neither Tim Ahl nor the ESU boss would say how long they expected the situation to last or speculate about the exact number of people in the buildings, or their ages, or their state of mind.

One reporter wanted to know how much disruption this would cause to the city's normal life.

'Not any more than necessary,' the ESU commanding officer said. 'We're sorry there has to be some temporary dislocation for people who live in that immediate neighborhood, but that's inevitable, and we'll keep it to an absolute minimum. We're called Emergency

Services because we deal with emergencies – one of our most important missions is saving lives, and what we want most here is to see this to a successful, and by that I mean peaceful, conclusion.'

'Then why are you all out there in flak jackets carrying automatic rifles?'

'We're dealing with people we have reason to believe may be armed. We owe it to ourselves and the community to be properly equipped, no matter how much we want to have this incident end quietly. We went out on over fifteen hundred warrants in dangerous situations last year, and some years we've done close to two thousand, and only on a tiny percentage of them were we forced to fire our weapons. It's a record we're proud of and we intend to maintain.'

Freddi came to see Ben when she got back from the press conference.

'How did it go?' he asked her.

'Fine, I suppose. I stayed demurely in the shadow of our sovereign, who no-commented everybody with that smug look of hers that says, "I have enough evidence to send these people away unto the third generation."' She raked her fingers through her hair, a gesture that had once reminded him of a movie star but this time seemed awkward and nervous. 'I'm worried that your friend Judith could be in there with them. Have you heard from her?'

He wondered what she was trying to get out of him. 'Not since before Centerville.'

'So she could be in there.'

'Is this leading somewhere, or is it all preamble?'

'I'm sorry, it's this damn case, I don't know why it makes me so tense . . . Look, I know this isn't easy . . .' She raked at her hair again. 'All right. No preamble. This school they're holed up in, it's the school Hannah was going to for a while, isn't it?'

He started up out of his chair in anger but caught himself, both hands on his desk for steadiness, lowered himself back to sitting. 'Why?'

'I probably shouldn't be telling you, but – the building plans they got are old, mostly the original blueprints, whatever had to be filed. Some construction permits, too, but nothing in the last twenty years. They're convinced there must have been major alterations and they need somebody who's been inside, and so far they're striking out. The woman whose family is in there with them is from across town; she's only been there once or twice and claims not to remember anything about the layout. If Hannah went to school there, even for a few days—'

'*I've* been inside,' he interrupted.

'When?'

'A few weeks ago, when Hannah kept saying she wanted to go there all the time, I got a tour.'

Freddi sat down and reached into her briefcase for a legal pad. 'Tell me about it.'

'How about we go see the ESU intelligence people, or the tactical planners? This isn't the kind of thing you filter through third parties.'

The police were setting up a rear command post in the gym of the public school at West End and 96th. Ben and Freddi were stopped at the door for ID and to state their business, then left standing there.

A few partitions had been set up to section off the open space. Technicians were wiring up phone lines that ran to a phone-company truck parked on the side street. There were about two dozen cops, many in the white shirts and blue ties of high-ranking supervisors, talking on the phone or conferring over long tables spread with papers or maps or architectural drawings. At the far end of the room, at a small table under one of the basketball hoops, sat two men in Hasidic black, watching it all with bemused curiosity.

The white-shirt lieutenant the two prosecutors had come to see apologized for keeping them waiting and led them to the table that held the building blueprints, found chairs for them.

'Ms Ward says you've been inside,' he said to Ben.

'Right.'

The cop pulled a blueprint out from under a couple of others, slid it toward Ben. 'Can you read that?'

'I get the general idea.'

'Okay, use it for reference and take me on a tour.' He gave Ben a marking pen. 'If you see something you know is wrong, mark how it is now. You don't have to worry about messing this up, it's a copy.'

Ben studied the architect's drawing. He'd expected it to be outdated; he wasn't prepared for it to be completely wrong. At first he had trouble relating it to anything he'd seen.

'You have a clean piece of paper?'

'That different?' the cop asked.

'That different.'

'Use the back.'

He described what he remembered, sketching it out roughly as he went – the classrooms and small auditorium on the garden and parlor floors, the office and dining room and kitchen on the next floor up, then another floor: classrooms and the teachers' lounge. On the top floor, another classroom and the big, open room where the Purim party had been, that Joshua had told him was used for phys ed.

'Okay, anything else you can think of?'

'There were a lot of cartons of food in the office near the kitchen, and stacked along one wall in the dining room. When I asked about them I was told they were for the kids – school lunch stuff. It was more than they usually had around but they'd gotten too big a bargain to pass it up.'

'Okay, that's good, that's helpful. You have any idea how much food, how big the cartons were?'

Ben estimated the size with his hands. 'Oh, and one other thing. There's a room in there somewhere that's like a bunker or an old-fashioned air-raid shelter. No windows.'

'How big?'

'I don't know.'

'You didn't see it yourself?'

'No. I was told about it.'

'Who told you?'

'Just . . . one of the parents.' He couldn't help glancing at Freddi, seeing her eyes narrow – imitating Victoria, he thought.

'Lieutenant, will you excuse us for a minute?' she said.

'Sure. Why don't I go get some coffee.'

'It was Hannah, wasn't it?' Freddi said. 'The one who told you about the shelter.'

'She's five years old, Freddi. You know her – you know how fragile she still is. I'm not exposing her to this.'

'There are people's lives at stake here.'

'What are you suggesting? Bring her here? Let her have a little chat with the lieutenant so his people can go in and blow Rabbi Joshua away? And maybe Judith, too. And then explain to Hannah how it wasn't her fault, the way it wasn't her fault the police killed her mother?'

'We can get a child psychologist, someone who knows how to ask little kids questions.'

'Great. Like the ones who help them remember how their teachers practice Satan worship?'

'You're being ridiculous.'

'I won't take the chance with her mental health' – unwilling to talk about how upset Hannah already was at Judith's disappearance – 'and the police don't want answers from her that might be unreliable.'

The lieutenant was back with his coffee. 'You have anything more for me?'

'Not just yet,' Freddi told him. 'But we think we may have another source.'

'I have to tell you,' the lieutenant said, 'this is going to make a big difference. We try to be ready for surprises, but the men going in there need at least an idea of what they're going to see, or we could have a real disaster.' He shook Ben's hand. 'We really appreciate it. If there's more, especially about that bunker room, we need to hear it.'

'They have gas masks,' Ben remembered.

'They do?'

'I don't know how many or how recent or sophisticated, but they do have them, and they do drills with them, grown-ups and kids, both.'

'That's not what I wanted to hear,' the cop said. 'But if this goes bad you just probably saved some lives.'

They walked out of the school together, paused on the sidewalk where sawhorses sheltered them from the in-and-out traffic of police officers and from curious bystanders.

'I could have just blurted it out about Hannah for everyone to hear,' Freddi said. 'And then you'd be dealing with the police about her and not with me. And you heard what the lieutenant said. They're the ones whose lives are going to be on the line, if it comes to that.'

'Right – if it comes to that. But we don't know it will. That's another reason I don't like this – you want to risk Hannah and you don't even know if it's necessary.'

'Once we *know* it's necessary, it's too late to start debriefing her.'

'My point exactly. Nobody's *debriefing* my daughter.'

They stood there in angry silence.

'The only thing I can suggest,' Ben said, 'is that I'll ask her about it, see what I can learn from her myself.'

'How will you know what to ask?'

'It seems fairly straightforward. If you want, we can get the questions from ESU. Just like the psychologist would.'

'Aren't you the one who said this kind of thing couldn't be done through third parties?'

'That's how we're doing it with Hannah, if we're doing it at all.'

Ben turned away from Freddi to break the tension and for the first time noticed a crowd a block to the north, just above the base of the hill. They were gathered around a man standing with his back to the continuing police action so it would form a backdrop for the TV cameras ringed around him. It was the Reverend Walker, they discovered when they went over.

'. . . these same people,' he was saying. 'The very ones who only had to tell a single lie and the police came out in force to disrupt the lives of who knows how many innocent young men? Why? Because those young men were black, and the ones who told the lie about them . . . well, we know what they were. And what does it turn out but these liars were thieves and killers all along, and now they're holding a whole neighborhood hostage. And what are the police doing? Are they doing what they'd do in an African-American neighborhood, sending in the troops to bash down the doors and shoot up the place? Scare babies and hurt innocent people? No, they're not. They're disrupting traffic to make a safety zone and they're sitting on their butts and talking nice. I say it's an outrage!'

'This isn't going to make anything easier,' Freddi observed.

'No, but you can't really blame him.' Here was the garbage search back to haunt them, to put pressure on them when it was least needed. And he knew from his encounter in the morning that Reverend Walker's indignation would find a ready audience.

60

Doing pushups to keep himself from getting stiff and stale, Sid Levy heard the door to his room being unlocked. He got up and sat on the bed.

It was two kids, a boy and girl, the boy with a shotgun, the girl with a tray of food. The boy told him to lie flat on his stomach while the girl came into the room and put the plates on the floor, then retreated, carrying the tray with her.

Good technique, he thought. Someone had been training them, the Israeli probably. He had an air of the army about him.

'Hey!' he called before they could get the door closed.

'What?' the girl asked.

'If you could please ask somebody to feed me more often, I'd appreciate it.' This was the first food he'd seen since Centerville. 'And water. I'm really thirsty.' His last drink had been from the tap when they took him to relieve himself.

'Sorry,' the girl said. 'I'll tell them. But we're very busy.'

He made himself eat slowly, hard as that was, knowing that if he didn't he'd get sick. There wasn't much, but he savored it all: rich chicken soup, a goulash-like stew, some tough bread, tea. The plates were paper, the tea in styrofoam. There were no utensils, but he managed without them, and there were napkins to wipe his hands when he was done.

Finished eating, he went back to sitting on the floor by the door, head resting against the wood, his listening post. He'd been trying to piece together a sense of the comings and goings in the corridor. Occasionally he'd heard a conversation. He'd decided that whoever was holding him was under siege and maintaining military discipline with no real dissent so far beyond the kind of grumbling that was to be expected. He'd heard brave warrior talk when the guard changed outside his door, and some banter of the form 'Why don't they just kill him and get it over with?' which he chose to think of as youthful bravado and not a sign of anything imminent.

But he knew it had to be based on something, and that he had to think of a way to survive. Or, if he couldn't manage that, at least a way not to go quietly.

* * *

It was a rare treat for Ben to be home early enough to join Hannah for dinner, even though the pleasure this time was dimmed by his ulterior motives. He'd planned to wait till afterward to bring up Joshua's school, but Hannah had school stories of her own. Her nemesis Bobby G. lived on the block with Deborah's school, and he'd told scary stories about being awakened in the dark and hurried out of his house by strange men with guns.

In the course of reassuring Hannah, Ben got her talking about her memories of Deborah's school – how it was different from her regular school and what she'd liked most about it and what they did there and where they did it.

After they left the table they played a game of drawing maps of the school, alternating who put in what door or window or stairway. Hannah quickly grew impatient with it, adding vast fantastical spaces to divert herself and tease him. Then she scratched it out and drew another building next to it.

'What's that?'

'Judith's house.' Drawing away. 'That's my room.' A big square. And another next to it. 'And Judith's room.' And then a little box across the page. 'And *that's* Daddy's room.'

'Hey! How come I get such a small room way over there?'

'Because. You made Judith go away, and now she's never coming back.'

It was still light out, benefit of the first days of Daylight Saving time. He suggested they go out for a walk, adding the bribe of a double-chocolate ice cream cone. It was way more than she could eat, especially after dinner, but they'd long ago made a game of the inevitable dripping, melting goo. Slower to develop in on a raw April evening than in the July sun, it still caused screams of delight as she tried to keep it from getting all over her.

When they'd picked a corner trash basket for the honor of receiving the remains, they started home again, to the accompaniment of a raucously honking fire truck which they had to stop and watch roar by, lights flashing – headed downtown, away from the site of the standoff, to Ben's relief. It was an opening to talk about the fire drill at Deborah's school and where it was and how they got there.

'It had funny stairs,' she said. 'The girls went down this way and the boys went down the other way. And we had the Torah over us to protect us.'

'Is that what they said?'

'No, silly, it was *there*.'

'What do you mean?' he was going to say, having trouble with the idea of a teacher holding a Torah scroll aloft as the kids passed beneath it and down the stairs. But he could see she was running out of patience, and the information he needed was about geography, not symbolic defenses against fires that weren't happening.

At home again, he got out the building blocks she never played with – a gift from Freddi, with some idea about gender-neutral toys – and they made a rough model of the windowless room. The stairs were indeed odd, if Hannah was at all accurate – they appeared to be within the room, starting from a small landing right at the door and going down steeply to the right and left along the wall, as if the door was almost at ceiling level. Like stairs to a basement, he thought, though he'd never seen any built quite that way.

'Do you remember how to get there?'

'Down the hall and then a door and another hall.'

'Do you remember where?'

A definite shake of the head.

'Where did you start?'

Another shake of the head.

'Do you remember what you saw when the fire drill was over and you came out?'

'No!' A sweep of her little hand knocked the blocks across the room.

'Okay,' he said. 'No more questions. Thank you very much. This was a fun game.'

She was already at her toy chest, bent over it so her top half was completely inside.

They'd asked Ben to report in person, easy enough with the public school less than five minutes' walk. He hesitated to leave Hannah downstairs with the talkative Mrs Brunello, knowing their conversation would turn to the neighborhood's most exciting event, and then to the fact that Hannah actually knew the magical disappearing rabbi. It was a kind of local celebrity that would do neither Hannah nor her father any good. He started to call one of Hannah's school friends instead and realized that the same equation held, whoever she spent time with – and Mrs Brunello's range was narrower and more benign.

The command post at the school was noticeably more complete, and noticeably more crowded. There were more white shirts, mostly with gray hair above them, and more partitions, tables and chairs, making it look like a permanent installation. The cop at the table by the door was openly skeptical of civilian arrivals, the category she put Ben in until he showed his credentials.

Plenty of neighborhood residents were clamoring to get in: four already there when he arrived, five more in the few minutes he was waiting, all anxious to be heard by Someone In Charge. Small wonder

– there had to be hundreds of residents of the affected area, all with a full-strength New York sense of entitlement.

The lieutenant debriefed him, along with a captain – 'Pavesi' it said over his shield – and a lieutenant in a blue shirt: not a desk jockey. The two Ben hadn't met before wore the round, blue-on-blue ESU patch with a profile of an antique white-wall-tired rescue truck. They all asked him questions, calmly but thoroughly. He tried to give concise, clear answers, and drew diagrams where he thought they would help. Not surprisingly, they were most interested in the fire-drill room and the gas masks. Carefully, he avoided saying anything that would tell them who his source might be.

'What did you guys do?' he asked Hannah after he collected her from Mrs Brunello's.

'Nothing.'

'You didn't talk about anything?'

'No.'

She didn't look up from playing with her beanbags. He bent to kiss the top of her head, the same cornsilk hair as her mother.

The day had tired Hannah enough to fall asleep over her toys. He put her to bed, pondering how he was going to take care of her while the standoff between Joshua and the police continued, just up the block, a constant threat of upredictable disruption. There had been a time when the need for a second parent hadn't seemed so incessant, but now he couldn't see how anyone managed alone through a crisis. He wondered if he could coax his mother to come East for a week or so – without her new husband.

The late news was led off by the mayor, a rebroadcast of a press conference at City Hall. The crowd gathered around him included Arthur Goldstein of the Joint Jewish Council, the Police Commissioner, the ATF Special Agent in Charge and next to him, Tim Ahl, the Secret Service SAC. And, looking regal as ever as she tried to upstage the Manhattan DA, US Attorney Victoria Thomas.

The mayor, always definite if far from silver-tongued, began by noting that the city faced a difficult situation which was being addressed with the help of inter agency cooperation for which everyone involved deserved praise.

'We're confident this is going to end quietly. We want to remind everyone who's watching that it's our intention, without prejudicing anyone, to give suspected and accused criminals their full day in court. And that we have respect for everyone's religious convictions.'

He praised the residents of the Upper West Side for their patience and cooperation, and called for the rest of the city's citizens to benefit from their example and especially to refrain from inflammatory rhetoric – a clear reference to Reverend Walker – 'while we let this situation work itself out.'

The press conference coverage was followed by video taken from the station's traffic helicopter and from the roof of an apartment house across West End Avenue: images of a police presence running all the way around the block. Besides the video, the station had photographs made with extreme telephoto lenses, clear enough to show the faces of ESU cops behind a wall of freestanding ballistic shields like the ones at Centerville.

The live updates Ben saw all originated blocks away from the action, some of them taped in the temporary shelters – bright school gyms or synagogue vestry rooms, nothing like the permanent shelters for people with no homes to go back to when the excitement was over.

After encouraging the neighbors to complain about their disrupted lives, the reporters asked how they felt about the people they'd seen at the besieged school and synagogue over the years. Nice, religious, quiet, and respectful were the words used most. Good to their children. Everyone who'd had any contact with Stropkovers seemed confused by this turn of events. Some thought a mistake was being made.

There were rabbis on the news, too, better informed than the ones Ben had seen during the Centerville standoff. At the same time as they urged calm and reason, they took care to distance themselves from Joshua Brauner.

So far there was no word from inside the houses, and no follower of Joshua's who was not part of the barricaded group had come forward as a spokesperson.

Flipping channels, Ben was stopped by a report on one of the more tabloidy stations: the press had finally caught up with Asher Stern. 'I won't make any specific comments about Joshua Brauner. But over the centuries we've seen many self-deluded rabbis appear, some very learned and prominent, who misled their followers into one heresy or another – including, tragically, encouraging false messianic hopes. And to mislead people in this way is one of the worst crimes in Jewish Law.'

Freedom of speech, Ben thought, but somebody ought to tell Stern he wasn't helping matters.

The last segment Ben caught featured the ESU bosses Ben had met at the command post. The blue-shirted lieutenant, Walter Brown, turned out to be in charge of ESU's Apprehension Tactical Teams. He was eager to make clear, as much for Joshua's benefit as anyone's, Ben guessed, that Emergency Services was as much a rescue force as a SWAT organization – all EMT certified, some licensed as nurses or even doctors – not people to be afraid of.

Pavesi, the ESU captain, appealed to the people in the houses to respond to the soundtruck announcements about bringing the children out, along with anyone else who wanted to leave. He also had a request for the news people who were interviewing him: 'We've cut off the cable service to those buildings, but they still have televisions and we don't know what they can receive. If you had a husband or a boyfriend on the front lines, would you want somebody to be beaming a TV picture of his position and activities to a potential enemy?'

'That's a very warlike image, Captain,' one reporter challenged. 'Aren't these American citizens, most of them law abiding and many of them women and children? And all of them presumed to be innocent?'

'Yes they are, and that was just a manner of speaking. But I think it makes the point.'

61

The phone startled him. For an instant he had the irrational hope it might be Judith. He went to pick it up, feeling dislocated and a bit crazy.

'Hello, Benjamin. It's Joshua.'

He felt a spike of shock and then everything around him went still. 'Hello, Joshua.'

He was hyperaware of his own slow, regular breathing. He felt uncannily calm, and very clear. Could he record this? On the answering machine? No – it would make a click or a beep if he turned it on. He would have to try to take notes.

'I need your help,' Joshua said. He sounded the same as always, no audible tension in his voice.

'What can I do for you?'

'I need somebody to tell these people outside that they're making a mistake.'

'What mistake?' Ben had no training at this. All he had were his instincts and what he knew about dealing with white-collar criminals and their lawyers, in situations where he almost always had the upper hand.

'We're no threat to anyone. We've done nothing that isn't in self-defense. I told you once, this is a dangerous time for Jews. I'm responsible for many souls. Many. As it is written, "the myriads of Ephraim, the thousands of Menasseh." I'm not ready to repeat the mistakes our people made in Europe sixty years ago, when millions were led away to die. We see what's coming and we choose to arm ourselves in our own defense. But we're peaceful people. You know that, you must know that.'

'I want to believe it, Joshua, I really do.' Struggling to control the mixture of loathing and fascination Joshua's voice aroused. 'And what better way is there for you to show you're peaceful than putting down your guns and opening your doors?'

'And then your friends the police will come in and take away our guns and carry us all off to prison, and we'll be defenseless.'

'You know, it's amazing,' Ben said: 'The police talk about my friend Rabbi Brauner and now here you are talking about my friends the police. Maybe we should all get together, me and all my friends.'

'Don't be bitter, Benjamin, it doesn't become you.'

'I mean it, Joshua. You're not as terrible as some of them want to think you are, and it goes the other way – these aren't the forces of evil out here. Their job is to protect the people of the city, and you've got them worried. You're armed with dangerous weapons and explosives in the middle of a densely populated urban area. You have to admit that's worrisome. But if all you're trying to do is get your people to Israel, I'm sure that can be arranged.'

'Have they fooled you that completely?'

'I'm not saying everybody can go. There have been crimes committed, and the criminals have to answer for them.'

'We will all answer for our crimes before a Judge both sterner and more merciful than any who serves the United States. But even for the purposes of This World, there must be other ways besides surrounding us with men in body armor and Nazi-style helmets carrying machine guns, evacuating the entire neighborhood and mounting snipers in the windows and on the rooftops.'

'Joshua, how can I make you see – the problem is, you think you need to defend yourself, and so do the police.' Ben narrowly missed saying "so do *we*." It was trickier than he liked, avoiding anything that would seem to align him with the police. 'And as far as that goes, no one out here has bombed a Stropkover to death, or strangled one.'

'Are you going to tell me the secular courts don't have anyone executed? And is their law higher than ours?'

'Dina d'malkhuta dina,' Ben said for want of another reply: the law of the kingdom is the Law.

'Up to a point. Not if it conflicts with the Torah or threatens the community.'

For a moment, Ben was without a response.

'Benjamin, I'm asking you to make these people understand one simple thing. We want only to be allowed to leave in peace. All of us, together. We're not going to live on a comet, we only want to go to Eretz Yisroel, to prepare properly for what will come.'

There was an intensity in the words 'prepare properly' that brought Ben a memory of the dying Rebbe's blessing – *prepare for Messiah the son of David.*

'False messianic hopes,' Asher Stern had said. Ben didn't want to go there, and yet he knew there could be vital information to be gained . . .

'What is it you're preparing for?' he asked evenly.

'Only what we are all preparing for, whether we know it or not.'

'And do you really need to be in Israel?'

'So it is written, so the sages tell us. We must return to Galilee and Jerusalem.'

'No one wants to keep good people from going anywhere they want to go. I can't promise anything, but I'm sure if you were to let the people with you leave, the children and the women especially, that we could find a way to help them to get to Israel. They can't do that in there with you.'

'There are a lot of roads to Israel.'

'Joshua, the people out here don't know you the way I do, and they think it's dangerous to leave you alone because if they do someone's going to get hurt.'

'It won't happen unless they make it happen.'

'We have to make them see that. Can you accept that much?' He waited but there was no answer.

'Joshua, I'm just down the block from you, you know that. Let me go to the police command post and tell them we're in touch. Let me talk to you from there, so they can hear.'

There was a long silence, then Joshua said, 'Rabban Gamliel of blessed memory, a great sage, taught us in these words – "Beware of the authorities. They do not befriend anyone unless it serves their own needs. They appear as a friend when it is to their advantage but do not stand by a person in his hour of need."'

It was the passage from Ethics of the Fathers that Sid Levy had found, prompted by Kest. He needed to ask about Sid, wanted to be careful how he framed the question. Before he could, Joshua was moving on.

'Benjamin, my friend, my brother,' Joshua said, 'I called you because I want to believe you're the exception to Rabban Gamliel's view. Judith tells me you are, and she's a remarkable judge of character. She's the one who urged me to make this call. She joins me in the hope that you can make our position clear to the police.'

Ben's tongue was frozen. Judith *was* there. The artificial calm that had sustained him fled.

Joshua waited while Ben regained his voice.

'All I want is to have this end without conflict,' Ben said when he could. 'If you can express some of your concerns and your motives to the police, it could be a step in convincing them to let you leave, the way you want to.'

'Don't you think they're listening to this conversation already?'

'Not on my end.' But he couldn't be a hundred percent sure about that.

Joshua was silent again. 'All right. In the morning. Go there in the morning and tell them I'll call the number they keep shouting at us, but only to talk to you.'

Ben tried to think of what to do next, but he couldn't get his mind off Judith, there with Joshua. He had to fight free of it. If the police had monitored the call, on Joshua's end or his, they'd wonder why he wasn't calling to report it. To focus himself he got a pad and made notes on the conversation. Then, finally calm enough, he picked up the phone to call the police.

'What was I supposed to do, hang up on him?'

They were debriefing him in a second mobile command post, brought up to keep the negotiating team close to the tactical people. A police lieutenant named Anderson, principal hostage negotiator for the incident, was doing most of the talking.

'Due respect,' he said, 'you have no training, you could have sent him over the edge in a minute, saying the wrong thing.'

'I didn't, though, did I? I had a long conversation with him, I opened a dialog when so far you haven't said word one to him. Let's look at the positive side of this. I didn't call him, he called me, and we've got some progress.'

Anderson, a compact man with hooded eyes and a thick scar down one cheek, seemed to have been assembled without the module that produced harsh emotions. 'What you have to understand is that Joshua Brauner needs to talk to us,' he said with bland confidence. 'He'll have to, because he has to talk to somebody.'

'He's got a telephone – he can talk to anybody he wants,' Ben said. 'So you ought to be glad I'm the one he picked. At least you know whose side I'm on.'

'Do we?' Someone from police headquarters, borough commander or chief of department, Ben hadn't registered the title. 'By my personal rule book, anyone as close to these people as you are ought to be out of this by now.'

'Hey!' Lukas was in the crowded command post as Secret Service case officer. 'Give the man a chance. He's put more hours of time and more thought into this case than all of you put together.'

'Can we all calm down, please?' interjected Pavesi. 'Let's talk about the things we know. This man Brauner may walk like a rabbi and talk like a rabbi but right now he looks a lot more like a cult leader, and we have to be aware that a lot of these cult leader types are emotionally disturbed. And when we're dealing with someone like that we have to be very careful.'

'I'm all for being careful,' Ben said, 'but I'd hope for a more precise view of this than just "emotionally disturbed." That covers an awful lot of ground. Let's remember he lives in a country where federal agents assaulted a religious group with tanks, and a big-city police department not that far from here burnt down an entire city block going after some folks holed up in a townhouse. Even paranoids have real enemies.'

'You're right – there's crazy and crazy,' Pavesi acknowledged. 'But people always have somebody they'd rather talk to than us. *I've got six hostages here, you want them to live, get me the President on the phone.* The point is, we can't put them in a position of power like that.'

'But this isn't that. He's already talked to me, he's used me as a way to communicate with you. Why make this into an issue with him if it doesn't have to be one? Isn't there a rule about staying with whoever starts the communication and developing that relationship?'

'Yes there is, but if it's not a pro then his main job is to move the hostage-taker over to someone who is.'

'And if they won't talk to anybody else?'

'Our experience is, people in this situation, they'll talk to you, eventually,' the hostage negotiator said, the continued reasonableness of his tone a contrast with the angry scar that twisted one side of his face. 'This rabbi's got a whole thing worked out about why he's doing this, and it's no good to him if nobody knows it.'

'From what he said to me, he has only one point he wants to make,' Ben said. 'That he sees what he's doing now as self-defense and he wants to go to Israel. For the rest of his message, if there is one, you're not his audience. This isn't like the MOVE standoff, in Philadelphia, where they were broadcasting their beliefs to the neighborhood, or even Waco, where Koresh would have preached to anybody.'

'We know all about MOVE,' said Lieutenant Brown, the ESU Apprehension Team commander. 'We're not about to burn down the neighborhood. That's not the point here.'

'And it's not the point I'm making,' Ben countered with a fervor fueled by his fears of law-enforcement overreaction. 'I'm saying that if you have the wrong idea about what he wants, because you think it's the same as what somebody else wanted, then you're going to make mistakes.'

The police boss from headquarters bridled at the word 'mistakes.'

'I hear you're in line for a big law-enforcement job in Washington,' he said, 'so I guess sombody smarter than I am thinks you're right for this kind of work. Okay, that's fine. In two years, when you've been at it awhile, we'll sit at your feet. But right now, do us all a favor and remember you're still an amateur.'

'Maybe I'm coming at this wrong,' Ben said. 'I'm not at my most tactful when I see the possibility of basically good people being goaded into bad acts that could get them killed, and a lot of cops and agents, too.'

'That's harsh,' said Brown. 'We're not here to goad anybody into anything.'

'Our philosophy is always to use the minimum force consistent with the situation,' Pavesi said. 'I'd rather bore them to death than go in shooting. Especially with kids in there.'

That was what Ben wanted to hear, but he suspected Pavesi knew it, so he wasn't sure how much to credit it.

After he'd collected Hannah from Mrs B. for the second time that night, he went to his bookshelves and took down Joshua's books and the books Rosen had given him. If Joshua was going to insist on keeping up this dialog, some homework was in order. Ben especially wanted to know more of what Joshua had written about the Messiah, and about war.

62

West End Avenue still carried a single lane of traffic, Ben noted as he headed up the hill in the morning. The rest of the roadway was dense with police vehicles.

A new element was the gut-shaking, head-pounding rattle and clatter of jackhammers. They played in chorus, loudest on the blocks closest to the standoff. Ben remembered a photograph he'd seen of an earlier New York: a street being dug up and in front of the hole a sign – DIG WE MUST FOR A GROWING NEW YORK. This digging was likely to have other purposes.

Anderson was waiting for him, wearing lightweight headphones and a graceful boom mike hovering in front of his lips. With his scar, buzz cut and cold, hooded eyes he looked like the world's most sinister switchboard operator.

'Has anybody decided what we're going to do?' Ben asked.

'We think it's best if I answer,' Anderson said, reasonable as ever. 'That's what I'm here for. Then we'll see what happens.'

It was just Ben, Anderson, Pavesi and a tech in the negotiation command post. Everybody else from the night before would be listening in the tactical command post just up the block.

They all came to attention when the phone rang. Tape reels started turning. Ben put on a headset.

'Rabbi Brauner?' the negotiator led off. 'This is Lieutenant Anderson of the NYPD.'

'I called to talk to Benjamin Kaplan,' Joshua said in Ben's earphones.

'Well, I can't do that for you right now, Rabbi, but I'll be happy to talk to you myself, I think we've got some things we can work out here, and you want to be talking to somebody who can produce results for you, wouldn't that be better—'

'You're saying you don't have respect for Benjamin Kaplan's word?'

'No no no, I'm not saying anything like that. But I know you understand we all have ways of doing things, and one of our ways in the police department is that we can't give authority for our activities to people outside the department. So you could talk to Ben Kaplan, sure, but that'd just be talk. And I know from what he told me that you want to get your people out of there safely, so I'm the man you want to talk to because I can help you with that, protecting your people, getting them out okay and on the way to wherever they want to go, so you don't have to worry about self-defense the way you were saying to Ben.'

'He told you about our conversation?'

'Yeah, he did, because that's the best way to help you out and that's what he wants to do. And that's what I want to do, too. So let's talk about how we can give you some assurances that we mean what we say and get you all out of this with as little fuss and bother as possible.'

'If he told you about our conversation then he told you I only want to talk to him. Please put him on the phone.'

'I will. I'll do that. But I need to let you know some things about how we operate because I think we both want the same result here' – there was a click on the line – 'Rabbi? Rabbi? You there?'

The tech at the console was shaking his head.

'Shit! Try and get him back.'

The tech dialed, and the phone rang. No answer.

Anderson pulled off his headset and microphone. 'He'll call back.'

'You think so?' Pavesi asked.

'He wants to talk.' Anderson turned to Ben. 'He's got at least one line we haven't identified, the one he used for the first call to you. We'll need a recorder on your line in case he does it that way again.'

Ben had to bite back a completely unexpected 'no' that followed a flash image of Judith calling him, a hope he hadn't realized was so strong.

'Sure,' he said. 'Only, maybe we can put a switch on it so I can turn it on when he calls. That way you don't have to be monitoring it all the time.'

'Appreciate the thought,' Anderson said, 'but here's what – chances are, the call comes in you're going to be kind of agitated. And you don't know how it's going to start, and by the time you know it's Brauner you're already into it, concentrating on every word, and maybe you forget to throw the switch. I know you want to protect your privacy, but we'll have somebody good on the wire. If it isn't relevant, they'll switch off right away.'

'Okay, that's fine.' Ben said. He couldn't help being impressed by Anderson's technique.

Ben stayed in the negotiators' command post: Anderson wanted him there if Joshua called, even though they still weren't planning to put him on the phone. Like students cramming in a college library, he and the negotiator sat next to each other at the narrow desk that ran along one wall, both of them reading the works of Joshua Brauner, both making notes on what they read.

The morning was punctuated by debates among the police brass about how to get Joshua communication again. They gave Ben a better idea of what was happening on the inner perimeter. There were two of Lt Brown's Apprehension Tactical Teams on duty, not quite twenty men, prepared to go in and get Joshua and the others out the moment they got the order. As Joshua had charged, they were supported by snipers stationed on rooftops and in apartments across from the buildings where Joshua and his people were.

Ben could hear the jackhammers again – from what he'd overheard he'd concluded they were mostly cover noise, a diversion while tiny holes were drilled through the brick walls of Joshua's domain. Through these holes, expert Technical Assistance cops in the adjoining buildings would insert microphones and perhaps tiny cameras.

Even over the racket of the jackhammers Sid's ears were tuned to the door being unlocked; he thought it would be the kids with more food. It was the same boy with the shotgun who told him to lie on the bed and face the wall, but the footsteps he heard next were heavy boots.

Strong hands grabbed his wrists and pulled them behind him, handcuffed them too tightly.

'Hey!' he couldn't help shouting.

He was hit hard across the back of the head. 'Shut up.'

There were two of them. They pulled him to his feet. One was the Israeli – Benzvi. He was dressed for war: fatigues and combat boots, a Sam Browne belt with a big pistol under the flap of his holster. The other one Sid hadn't seen before. He was in fatigues, too, but he had the look of an accountant or a stockbroker who worked out a lot. They pushed him up against the wall and stood close, menacing him. The boy with the shotgun stood in front of the closed door, his eyes wide.

'What are they going to do?' Benzvi said into Sid's face.

'Who?'

Benzvi sucker-punched him. He doubled over.

'The police. What are they going to do?'

He forced himself to stand up. 'I don't know.'

Benzvi backed up a step and open-handed him across the face.

'What are they going to do?'

He kept saying he didn't know, because he didn't, and Benzvi kept hitting him. He rolled with the first few blows, but he was quickly too dazed to anticipate them in time. Benzvi was wearing rough leather gloves and the blows were beginning to take skin with them.

'I'm not police,' Sid managed to say finally. 'Don't know what they do.'

'Bullshit,' Benzvi said and punched him in the gut again. 'Will they attack?'

'Don't know,' Sid said when he could and as the Israeli raised his hand again added, 'Don't think so. No attack.'

His knees were giving way. The stockbroker caught him and pulled him upright, braced him against the wall.

'They won't attack?' Benzvi said. 'Why not?'

'Want you alive.'

'Why?'

'American way.'

The stockbroker held him, Benzvi hit him. 'No jokes.'

'True. No attack.'

'Why?'

'Waco.'

'What?' Another open-handed blow, this one harder, to the temple. Sid reeled, saw double.

'What's Waco?'

Could he not know? Sid tried to think straight. He could feel the blood dripping down his face, and now it was getting into his eyes. He shook his head, blinked. The stockbroker grabbed him by the hair and wiped his face roughly with a towel, then let go and shoved so he lost his balance and crashed to the floor.

Lying there he heard the mutter of voices and for a while the questions and the hitting stopped.

The stockbroker propped him sitting against the wall.

'What would make them attack?' Benzvi asked.

'Don't know.'

This time when Benzvi hit him it bounced his head against the wall.

'What would make them attack?'

'If you're worried,' Sid managed to say, 'just surrender.'

Boom! And the same question, again.

'Hurting kids, if they knew.'

'What else?'

'Nothing. Nothing else. They'll wait.'

Benzvi hit him again, not so hard this time – a reminder. 'What else?'

He couldn't figure out what to say, couldn't think at all. There was nothing left to do but embrace the pain, welcome it, hope for it. Pain is good for you. It was hard to hold onto the thought, or the idea that

Benzvi would have to get tired eventually. He heard himself sobbing, and then he was unconscious.

At one o'clock Joshua still hadn't called back. Pavesi invited Ben to take a lunch break with them. It was chilly and damp out, drizzling by the time they left the sandwich place on Broadway and headed over to the grade school.

They sat down at a table full of ESU cops. Except for the police command post in the gym the school was empty, the local school board and the city's schools chancellor having agreed to start Easter vacation here a couple of days early.

Conversation over lunch centered on Joshua Brauner, how long he might be able to hold out, and what his personal agenda might be. Ben was happy to plead ignorance to most of the questions they asked him – making clear that his contact with Rabbi Brauner had been limited. He did better answering questions about the crimes that had led to this impasse: they knew it was his case. He was intrigued to find that the cops saw it mostly as ATF's investigation – guns, explosives and a bombing murder. They were aware of financial crimes and something about counterfeit currency as reasons for Secret Service's involvement, but they didn't attach a lot of importance to that part of it. Lukas and Tim Ahl had to be working overtime to keep the counterfeiting so low profile.

They were just finishing up their sandwiches when the door opened and an ESU boss came in followed by two burly detectives and another man and a woman. There was a scurry around the table to gather up the deli paper and crumbs.

'No, no. As you were, as you were,' the ESU boss ordered and Ben realized that the man who'd come in behind the detectives was the mayor.

His Honor wanted to know Anderson's impressions of Joshua. Did he sound sane? Reasonable? What kind of demands was he making? No demands yet, Anderson said – leaving out the clear demand to speak to Ben Kaplan.

'Well, stay in touch with him,' the mayor said. 'If you have to promise him things, promise him things. Nobody said you have to deliver. Whatever it takes to get those people out of there.'

The mayor went over to the deployment map on the wall to recommend improvements in the ESU front-line positions, then left as abruptly as he'd arrived, forging on to a first-hand look at the troops in the field despite dissuading noises from his police guides and the increasing drumbeat of rain on the windows.

'That was our CO,' an ESU sergeant told Ben. 'Inspector Burke. You've got to wonder how he keeps a straight face.'

63

Burke came back only a few minutes later, brushing rain from his uniform.

'He's out there getting into a heavy vest.' Shaking his head. 'I told him, Mr Mayor, you don't want to be putting yourself in harm's way, there's nothing to see anyway. But he's like a kid out there. I left him with Pavesi and Brown, good luck to them.'

He turned to Ben. 'You're Kaplan?' Held out a hand. 'Junior Burke. There's been a lot of talk about you, you probably know that.'

'I gathered.'

'I hear good things from Secret Service' –

Ben didn't know whether to be surprised or not.

—'Going by the book, you shouldn't be here at all, but we've decided to risk letting you talk to Brauner, as long as it's a hundred percent clear to you what side you're on. You have any questions about that? Any doubts?'

'No.' Ben took a good look at Burke – a whippet-thin man with a medium-brown complexion and penetrating brown eyes – and decided the way to get him to keep Ben Kaplan around was to be open and complete, at least up to a point. 'It's true I know some of those people. Not well, but I do know them. It may be more important that they know me. I have to assume that if they're in there with Brauner, they're loyal to him, and that's likely to mean they mistrust anybody out here. There's a chance they'll cut me some slack that maybe they wouldn't for a stranger. As far as my emotional issues that might get in the way, the biggest one I can think of is the undercover I've been working with, getting him out of there in one piece. And the good news is, that's likely to get everybody else out intact, too.'

'And the religious part of it?'

'Has nothing to do with it.'

'All right,' Burke said. 'I'm going to take a chance you're smart enough not to do anything stupid.

'I only have one instruction for you – don't promise anything by way of tactical changes. I've heard negotiators say, "You want us to pull back, okay we'll pull back." But the real answer is likely to be, we won't pull back in any meaningful way. We may make a show of it, give something small, pull a couple of trucks out of their line of sight, but if it comes to going in, we need to be in position.

'That said, we're not going to make the Waco mistake of threatening and bullying and running tanks up and down and all the rest of that. If he's looking for the apocalypse we're not giving it to him.

'But we can't do the Montana Freemen thing, either. This isn't the middle of nowhere, and the only way we can cover the perimeter here and be ready to move is by keeping people on full alert twenty-four seven, and no way can we maintain that for three months. We've got to get some kind of trust established, try and talk them out, but we also have to be alert for our opportunity.

'We've got a lot to think about here, ways we integrate the tactical approach with negotiating, balance maintaining control with establishing trust and appearing to listen and understand. And never mind what the mayor said, we don't do business that way.

'My point is, you don't want to promise something you don't know you can deliver, because it ruins the trust, if you have any. And at the same time we can't let our tactics be determined by somebody who's sitting here trying to score points for being a nice guy. Because at the end of the day, it's going to be on us, and we have to determine our own battlefield.' Burke's eyes locked on Ben. 'You have to understand that, a hundred percent.'

He understood. Understood it could mean tear gas and concussion grenades and a hail of bullets. Depersonalizing the bad guys to justify tactics that would keep cops alive. He understood, too, that those same cops would be putting their lives on the line to save Sid Levy and a lot of other people they didn't know who weren't cops, kids who had been placed in danger they didn't understand, good people who'd been badly misled . . . He understood above all that there was a vast potential for disaster here, for mistake and overreaction, and that to have any effect on it he had to be on the inside. 'I do understand,' he said, 'and I'll keep it very much in mind.'

'Okay,' Burke said. 'If you're going to talk to them, you've got to know that we've turned off their gas as a safety measure, and the electricity, too. We have to do these things, in any situation. We have to keep the place lit up brighter than day, from the ground and from the air, because we can't afford to have them sneaking around in the shadows, plus there's the noise from our helicopters and our generators, and the jackhammers we use for sound cover, and all of that probably makes it hard for them to sleep.

'People say, you don't want to make it an us-against-them situation. But we're not the ones doing that, they are. And it's not our job to make their lives easier.'

Ben said, 'It's likely to take a long time for the discomfort to get them. From what I saw in the school building they're fairly well supplied.'

'We know that, and it's a problem. They have a gasoline-powered generator, too, which is a double problem. It keeps them in electricity, and it's a real hazard to us and them if they're storing any quantity of gas to run it. But those aren't your worries. Your worry is to keep Brauner talking, get him to feel his relationship with you is a relationship with us, and as soon as possible move him over to one of our guys, like Lt Anderson. In the meantime, lieutenant, if you'll be so kind as to give Mr Kaplan a more complete rundown on the rules of your profession, we'll all be grateful.'

The principles sounded simple enough; in practice they were harder to apply, as Ben learned before the day was over. The phone rang at four thirty, catching everyone by surprise.

'Headphones,' Anderson said to Ben, who was already reaching for them.

'I'm going to answer,' Anderson said, 'but I'll let you talk if he insists.' He gave the tech the high sign and the ringing stopped.

'Anderson,' he said.

'Put Ben Kaplan on,' said a voice Ben was almost sure was Mark Altman's.

'We can only do that for Rabbi Brauner,' Anderson said agreeably.

'Put him on.' An order.

'All right, but listen a minute – we want to communicate with you, we want to make this easy, so let's try and talk reasonably to each other. You want me to respect you, and that's fine—'

'Ben Kaplan.'

Anderson pointed at Ben.

'This is Ben Kaplan,' Ben said into his microphone.

'It looks like the rain isn't stopping,' he heard Joshua say.

'That's what the forecast says.'

'Your police friends are getting wet.'

Ben sighed. 'You keep talking about my police friends. I said it last time – if they're my friends, how can they be your enemy?'

'Because you've blinded yourself to who they really are. I don't blame them for it any more than the sheep can blame the leopard. They're simply doing what police do. Was that the mayor I saw out here?'

'It was.'

'That was very unwise. If we were the dangerous fanatics the police seem to think we are, we could have killed him in a minute, never mind all his ill-fitting protective gear.' A pause. 'But there are no killers here.'

'Tell that to Isaac Isaacs,' Ben said before he could censor it.

'Whatever judgment he suffered, he brought it on himself.'

'What about repentance and redemption? Isn't that what you preach? Couldn't Isaac have repented and become a better, purer person for his sin? Approached haShem all the closer?'

'Some things you can't repent.'

'And Alan Kest?'

'A misleader and a sower of dissension. A rodef, endangering every one of us. It was too late when I understood he'd become a slave of the sitra ahra – the Other Side – the kind of Jew who provides fodder for the rantings of Samael.'

The Other Side, Ben knew about – source of the Evil Inclination, domain of the Adversary. Samael was a new name.

'Joshua, can't you see you're endangering these people as much as Alan Kest ever did? They could all walk out of there right now and go safely about their lives. Go to Israel, if that's what they want to do. But you're holding them hostage.'

'Benjamin!' Full of fatherly reproach. 'You know better than that.'

'Joshua, you've got innocent people in there, you've got children—'

'Not children. Adults.'

'Adults for religious purposes, for obeying the commandments. But they're still kids. You know that.'

'No one is here who doesn't want to be.'

'Including Sid Levy.'

'Your former spy? Yes, him, too.'

'His family and friends were kind of taken by surprise. They'd get some peace of mind if he could call them. Just to reassure them.'

'Of what? That he's here voluntarily? He's already said so on the phone to his wife, and for your cameras. Why should they doubt that? We don't kidnap people and brainwash them. Everyone here is content, and the ones who wanted to call their relatives and friends before they came have already done it.'

'Even if you've convinced them they're content to be there with you, *you* know they're all hostages for a few people who have committed bad crimes. At least send the kids out. They didn't do anything to earn this. If you'll tell us how many, we can have Sabbath-observant families ready to care for them until this is resolved and they can all rejoin their parents.'

'The young people are such a joy to us, Benjamin. And Passover is coming! Such a happy holiday, to sit around the table and talk about being delivered from slavery and receiving the Law from the Holy One, praised be His Name. A holiday especially for young people.'

'We found a lot of Passover food in Centerville,' Ben said. 'That's something you should talk to Lt Anderson about. I'm sure he could help you with it.' A token effort to move Joshua over, as they'd told him to.

Joshua ignored it. 'How is little Hannah? Judith talks of her so fondly. She sends her love to both of you.'

Her love. Bitter gall. A flash of anger battling with longing and loss. *Careful,* Ben warned himself: if Joshua goaded him into an unconsidered response, it could do damage he couldn't foresee.

'This must be hard for Hannah,' Joshua said.

'I wish I could believe you cared, but you're the one who's causing it. And tell me those kids in there with you aren't having nightmares.'

'Dreams. We should talk about dreams. I've been having interesting dreams.'

'Tell me about them, and maybe I'll understand better.'

'Benjamin, Benjamin, how hard is it to understand that all we want is to be allowed to go on our way, together?'

'Does everyone in there feel that way? Suzanne and Mark, too? And the Kleins?' Not real questions: camouflage for himself.

'Everyone. But I'll send your greetings to your friends. And you tell the police they're wasting their time and the taxpayers' money. Tell them the reason I called was to make an offer. If we can leave in peace – all of us, and within twenty-four hours – we'll disarm our explosives and leave them behind.'

'You'll have to talk to Lt Anderson about that—' Ben said before he registered the click of Joshua's breaking the connection.

'Who's Hannah?' Anderson asked him.

'My daughter.'

'And who's Judith?'

He'd known that would be coming, as soon as Joshua mentioned her name. 'Judith? She's someone who worships at one of Brauner's congregations, just like Suzanne and Mark and the other people I asked him about. And she's also a student of mine, in the evidence class I teach at NYU, and she's become friendly with my daughter – again, just like the other people I mentioned.'

'That's all?'

'Actually, she's the one who introduced me to Brauner.' See – nothing to hide: I'm full of harmless anecdotes. 'He was guest rabbi at Ohevei Yisroel, where my daughter and I usually go for Friday night services, and Judith happened to be there to see him, too. We ran into each other on the way in, so we sat together and that's how she started to get friendly with Hannah. At first I thought she was just buttering up the professor, but now I think it's genuine—'

'Okay. I got it. Is it a problem for you, having her in there?'

'I want them all out safely – all the people in there I know, and all the ones I don't know, too – without any violence if we can possibly arrange it. But that's what we all want, isn't it?'

64

After everyone who needed to had heard the tape of Ben's conversation with Joshua, there was a meeting to discuss it. Number one on the agenda was Joshua's offer: was it a threat or a bluff? If he was offering to disarm his explosives, did that mean they were armed now? And what was the tacit 'or else' if they missed the deadline?

'Don't forget the booby trap at Centerville,' Lukas said. 'He's good at symbolic gestures. We don't know what he's really got in there.'

'We know what was stolen from the construction site,' countered a detective from NYPD intelligence. 'The bomb that killed your informant was real enough, and he's got his bomb builders in there with him.'

There was never any real chance the offer would be accepted. The question was, how to play the rejection: Take a large part of the twenty-four hours before replying? Ignore the offer entirely? Or use it as a way to open negotiations on other subjects – get Joshua talking, get him accustomed to adjusting his terms and making concessions?

And finally, was there a way to get any more information from Joshua about his implied threat, and if not, how could it be prepared for if things went badly?

'Let's get some coffee,' Ben suggested to Lukas when the meeting broke.

Down the hill from the action was a Salvation Army residence, its ground-floor dining room a temporary aid station for the neighborhood's dispossessed, a place to sit and eat and just be out of the weather. In one corner of the broad, open dining room was a stand with coffee and donuts, marked NYPD. Ben poured himself some coffee, skipped the donuts. Lukas took two. They sat down at a table in the corner of the room, where they'd have some privacy.

Ben sipped at the hot coffee, watched Lukas tear into a donut, thought he should have taken one himself.

'Any word from Israel?' Ben asked.

'No sign of the Russian yet. They tell us they're looking.'

'Do we have any leads to the counterfeiting plant without him?'

'He's got to be dealing with one of Brauner's people over there, but we don't know who. We're trying to get the National Police to pay some attention to Kiryat Yaacov, especially the people there who are on our phone lists. And now that we know about Benzvi, we might want to focus on that family.'

'So the basic answer is the Russian is all you have.'

'Right. That's why we need to get something out of the people here.'

'I'm worried about Sid, too,' Ben said.

'Yeah,' Lukas said, 'I didn't like the way Brauner weaseled out of that. If Sid really fooled him, why not let him make another call?' Lukas considered Ben a moment. 'You have something in mind.'

'I do. Something that might help with both problems, but it's not something I can suggest, myself.'

'I'm listening.'

'Okay – this depends on your ability to keep track of people, but . . . we want Sid out of there, and we need somebody to lead us to the Russian or the counterfeiting plant—'

'Oh no.' Lukas wasn't having any. 'Forget about it.'

'Wait. Hear me out. If we let them all go, we get Sid back, and we can put a tail on the ones we really care about. Brauner first and foremost, Winkler and Benzvi, Joel Solomon, and a couple more if we can get a sense of who's near the top. This Nehemiah that Sid was talking about. And there are bound to be people in there who are scared enough by now to talk to us when they come out.'

'Where did I hear this bullshit before?' Lukas said. 'Last time you were saying we have good leads in Israel so we can afford to go easy on these folks, maybe let them go. Now it's we *don't* have good leads in Israel so let's let them go. Have we got a pattern here?'

'The only pattern I see is, I'm trying to make sure we find that counterfeiting plant and the people who run it.'

Lukas took his time finishing his donut. 'I just don't get you. When we started I asked around about you. Everybody kind of figured, you lost your wife to a police action, and then there was some kind of lawsuit, so you were going to be a wimp, or worse, about anything that had the potential for violence or getting out of control. I'm the old-fashioned type – I believe you can't cook up a good investigation without breaking some eggs.

'So I was watching how you worked, and then I hear you're maybe going to Main Treasury, and that made me pay more attention to how you dealt with agents. When you turned down a chance to ride along with us – to be out in the field with the kind of agents you were going to be responsible for – that put me back to the rumors.'

Ben didn't bother to protest.

'But you could've done a lot worse when Rogers made a mess of that garbage run,' Lukas acknowledged. 'You've protected the investigation since then, and you didn't grandstand about your new job in Washington. And I convinced myself the reason you didn't ride along was what you said – you figured it was my job and you didn't want to get in the way. So, I was okay with all that – on a provisional basis.'

He took a bite of his second donut and washed it down with coffee.

'Now this – you keep wanting to let them go. All that work, and a pile of luck, too, and we've got them all in one place, and this time they're not disappearing. There are people in there responsible for two murders, one of them somebody who worked for us. We've got an undercover in there to worry about. We can't just let them walk away.'

'I thought finding that counterfeiting plant was the most important part of this for you. Hell, for the Treasury Department. For national security.'

'I never said it wasn't.'

'You're having trouble on the Israeli end. And Kest . . . he's past being any help.'

'Yeah, and like I said we've got a whole houseful of people here, and some of them have to be involved in the counterfeiting, your friend Brauner number one among them. The way it works, we have them – we squeeze them.'

'You can't squeeze them if they're dead. And what about Sid? You willing to have him get caught in a firefight?'

'No, that's true enough. But if he's fooled them . . .'

'Right. So the big moment comes and they do what? They give him a gun and say, "Here, Sid, you're point man." You going to hope the police snipers can tell which one is him, or Lt Brown's shock troops? Or maybe *my friend Brauner* will give him a name tag so we know not to shoot him.'

Lukas just stared.

Ben got up to go. 'This is scary stuff, Frank. You're right, I have no stomach for people dying uselessly, especially when there's a better way. I know this much – major decisions are being made by the cops, and they don't even know what this is really about, because so far nobody's given them a clue these people are connected to anything that matters beyond the walls of those buildings.'

When they reconvened, Burke asked for Ben's impressions of the conversation with Joshua. He focused on the reference to Samael and the Other Side. 'If we want to find out what Brauner thinks he's doing, we ought to follow that up.'

'Trying to get away with murder is what he's doing,' said the chief of department, 'and he thinks he can confuse us like he did those poor bastards in there with him. But mumbo jumbo is mumbo jumbo.'

'Yes and no,' said the ATF boss. 'We've got a fringe group of a recognized religion here – the theory is work within the framework of the religious belief, if you can.'

'It's a trap,' an intel detective said. 'Once we get into unraveling Brauner's theology, he's got us where he wants us. He can spin it out however he wants, change it as he goes along, bluff and stall, get us worn down and confused.'

'I don't think he's inventing any of this.' Ben looked for assistance to the two rabbis who'd been brought in to analyze the religious content of what Joshua had said, both of them regular advisors to the police on the needs of New York's many vocal Jewish communities. 'Can you tell us anything about Samael?'

'These are deep matters,' one of them said. He had a round face, with a flowing red beard and sidelocks between his Hasidic black coat and his widebrimmed hat. 'Very deep. Samael is the heavenly prince whose dominion is Edom – which is Rome, and also all the nations that were arrayed against the nation of Israel since ancient days. He is also called haSatan – it means the Accuser – because according to the legends he stands before the Throne of Heaven and accuses the Children of Israel, enumerating their sins. An important angel. And the defender of Israel before the Throne is the great angel Michael. And this debate between Samael and Michael stretches from the Exodus until the wars of Gog and Magog in the time of the King Messiah.'

Lukas shot a sharp glance at Ben.

'Messiah!' Ciampa said. 'I told you – it's another guy who thinks he's Jesus.'

'Shit. Do we have to worry these folks are going to commit suicide in there?' the chief of department asked no one in particular.

'What about it?' Burke asked Ben. 'Did Brauner strike you as suicidal that way?'

'Not in the contact I had with him, but that's not exactly a professional diagnosis. And who can say what he'll do under this kind of pressure? That's what worries me. He seems to be having more moments when he's not connected to everyday reality. I can't say it won't get worse.'

It was an opening for Lukas to suggest letting them go, but he didn't say a word.

Ben went home to have dinner. He'd been worrying since Hannah's return from Florida about what to do to shield her from all that was happening. He'd decided his only safe ally was Vashti, and she'd been happy to offer Hannah a temporary home.

For the occasion, she'd set the table with flowers and colored napkins and paper plates for three.

'How come it's a party?' Hannah wanted to know.

'For the fun of it. And we're all eating together. Vashti, too.'

Hannah was full of animated chatter. A large part of her morning at school had been an assembly to help the kids understand the excitement that was upsetting the daily life of so many of them.

When Hannah ran out of stories and questions, Vashti rose to the occasion with tales of her neighbors and her kids. 'Do you want to come and stay with us?' she asked when she had Hannah giggling over the fun they all had in Queens. 'We live near the big airport, too, and we can go watch the planes take off.'

Ben wouldn't have guessed that would appeal to Hannah, but apparently Vashti knew things about her that he didn't: she loved the idea.

'We can? Can I, Daddy?'

'Sure. If that's what you want. And if it's okay with Vashti.'

'If you promise to be very good,' Vashti said with great seriousness.

'I promise.'

'Good,' Ben said. 'Then that's settled.'

'But I can't stay for Passover,' Hannah announced to Vashti. 'We're having Passover with my best friends Deborah and Dina and Judith, aren't we, Daddy? Is it soon?'

'It's not till the end of the week,' Ben said. Two days away, but he didn't want to make it seem too soon, not now.

He went out to Queens with them to make the separation easier. He carried his beeper and cellphone, but the trip passed in peace, out and back.

When he got home he took out his books again. Even among the books Rosen had loaned him, he found nothing about Samael.

Restless, he went out into the cool night, enjoying the mist in the air, last vestiges of the day's rain. He walked to a bookstore on Broadway and stood in the aisle reading the titles of the books in the Judaica section. He picked a few and checked the indexes. In a book about mysticism he found *Samael, see Satan.*

He skimmed the text and got a better sense of what to look for. He collected an armload of books with references to Samael and related topics and carried them to an empty chair by the broad window looking down on Broadway.

He quickly became fascinated by what he was reading – vivid legends and tales full of demons and evil, totally unlike the gentle stories of sages and scholars, pious men and fools he was familiar with.

He read about Samael in many incarnations, of which Samael

haSatan – a name that seemed to mean Adversary as well as Accuser – was only one. And over and over he encountered the idea that to weaken the Other Side it was necessary to cooperate with it – variations on the theme Rosen had called 'redemption through sin.'

Reading further, about the birth pangs of the Messiah and the messianic age, he found famine and pestilence, war upon war. And not one Messiah, but two: a Messiah descended from King David, and his precursor the Messiah from the line of Joseph – the warrior messiah.

Dizzy with it all, Ben took the two most relevant books to the cash register and went home to ponder what might be going on inside the school and the synagogue – and inside the mind of Joshua Brauner.

65

When Ben checked in at the office in the morning, Ella said he should call the boss.

'See about getting the PD to put in a line for you here,' Victoria told him. 'If this is going to drag on, it doesn't make any sense for you to be sitting around on the West Side waiting for the phone to ring.'

He returned a call from Nate Morgan, who wanted to know what was going on. 'We can't send you up to the Hill while these people you know are playing Waco games.'

'At least so far nobody's shot at anybody,' Ben said.

'How do you think it's going to come out?'

'I'm hopeful.'

'And I hope you're right,' Morgan said. 'But we can't keep this nomination on hold forever. I think it's fair to tell you that we've begun to look in other directions. We want this to come out well for you, and for everyone, but we have to protect ourselves.'

With the threat of an explosive end to the standoff weighing on him, Ben's impulse was to tell Morgan to shove his job. He kept his mouth shut.

At the mobile command post Anderson told him they'd decided to try opening communications based on Joshua's offer to disarm his explosives. He and Anderson spent some time role-playing scenarios for the call. Then ESU sent out the robot they were using to patrol the street in front of the synagogue and the school and had it announce that a phone call was coming.

The first time they tried the call, all the lines were off hook. They sent out the robot again. Ten minutes later Joshua called.

'We're ready to leave here.'

'Good,' Ben said. 'I knew you'd see that was best for everyone.'

The simple beginning turned into a knot of misunderstandings and word games, with Joshua increasingly insistent on his fear that the police were not to be trusted.

Finally, his tone changed from passion to portent: 'I'll say this much to the police who are listening to us, this much and no more – lift your siege so we can meet our destiny in its proper place, in Galilee and Jerusalem, and in its proper season. Otherwise, the results are on your head.' With that, he hung up.

A muscle in Ben's arm jumped, then jumped again. Great, he thought: now I'm twitching.

Anderson took his earphones off. 'He's sharp. And it's important to him to make everything our fault. You notice that? He didn't do anything except what other people forced him to.'

'The results are on your head' was echoing in everybody's ears when the tactical bosses gathered to debrief the call. The threat made a frightening addendum to Joshua's earlier talk of explosives.

They learned nothing new kicking the rest of Joshua's words around. Burke asked if there was any special significance to Brauner's wanting to meet his destiny in Galilee and Jerusalem.

'This is a man who is talking of matters relating to the time of the Messiah,' said the red-bearded rabbi. 'Galilee and Jerusalem are mentioned in such legends.'

'Is it possible that he's referring to the Messiah descended from Joseph?' Ben asked.

'Yes, perhaps,' said redbeard, startled. 'Those places figure in the stories about him.' The rabbi – Goffman was his name – seemed uncomfortable with the subject even though he'd brought it up himself. He let it go immediately when the chief of department pushed it aside as more mumbo jumbo.

The major issue was whether this latest call ended the possibility of negotiations based on Joshua's original offer. There was already a strong faction in favor of a preemptive strike. Ben had to remind himself that he was there on sufferance, and in no position to weigh in against police overreaction. Gradually, the debate swung in favor of holding out hope for a talking cure, pale as the chances for further dialog seemed.

When they took a break, with five hours left until the deadline, Ben went for a walk to consider his options. He'd wanted to say more about the wars of the Son of Joseph, but he didn't know enough yet.

He walked over to Riverside Drive, past the access road, blocked off to serve as a staging area. Among all the equipment and the impatient cops in battle gear was the ESU bomb truck. Its bulbous, metal-mesh blast-containment cage, an incongruously festive shade of salmony pink, loomed over the scene, a reminder of how serious all this was.

A scary context for talk about arguing angels and a warrior messiah.

But in Hebrew the Son of Joseph was Ben Yosef, and the warrior messiah, Son of Joseph, was also called Nehemiah in some of the prophecies. Ben Yosef and Nehemiah were names Sid Levy had heard from Alan Kest, talking about someone in a position of religious authority, someone who was out of touch with ordinary reality.

According to legend, the warrior messiah opened the way for the Messiah everyone knew about and talked about and waited for – the one called Son of David. And Joshua had said his task was to prepare for Messiah, the son of David.

Ben had taken that preparation to mean encouraging Sabbath observance and the dietary laws. But preparing the way through worship and observance couldn't compare to initiating the reign of the Son of Joseph. If Joshua spoke of himself as Nehemiah and Ben Yosef, and there was every reason to suppose he did, it all fit together with appalling immediacy.

The Son of Joseph was supposed to appear in Galilee and Jerusalem, and wage terrible battles. Ben's great fear now was that once Joshua was convinced he couldn't get to Israel properly armed and prepared, he'd trade the Galilee and Jerusalem for Centerville and New York.

Crossing West End Avenue on his way back to the command post Ben almost bumped into Lukas.

'Something on your mind?'

'Joshua Brauner.'

'There's a surprise. Anything in particular?'

'I think he's going to provoke an attack.'

Lukas stopped. 'Why?'

'I think he has to. He's always talked about defense. These aren't people who'll attack the police.'

'Why fight at all, why not just wait? Hope for public pressure, or some legal trick . . .'

'If it goes on too long, he'll lose his hold.' A made-up reason.

'You think he's suicidal enough to prefer outright war? It doesn't go very well with arming in self-defense.'

Ben dropped it. He couldn't say anything to Lukas about his warrior messiah theory without a lot more to back it up, not after their last conversation.

66

In the negotiation command post, Anderson was going through the line sheets from Joshua's phone calls, making notes. The negotiator seemed tense and abstracted in a way he hadn't before – his resilience pressed out by the weight of Joshua's threat.

His arm still twitching, Ben tried to read the books he'd bought the night before, looking for more evidence for his theory about Joshua, or something to debunk it.

For all Rosen's talk of blasting the bones of anyone who calculated the time of the End, Ben found plenty of opinions on the time and manner of the coming of the two messiahs. There was even an extended argument between a pair of the Talmud's sages concerning not the year or the century when the Age to Come might begin, but the day and the month. According to the one whose view was preferred – Rabbi Joshua! – the day of the *final* redemption would be the same as the day of the *first* redemption – which was to say: the first day of Passover, marking the deliverance from Egyptian bondage – because 'good things are brought about on a good day, and bad things on a bad day.'

Could the expectation of Passover as the time of the coming of Moshiach be behind Joshua's increasing urgency?

Ben needed another opinion. He thought of redbeard – Rabbi Goffman – because he was already part of the process. But he'd seemed uneasy with the subject, and Ben didn't know him well enough to get past that. Ben called Rosen instead and arranged to meet him for dinner. Assuming it all hadn't blown up by then.

Mid-afternoon, Ben found his eyes closing. He shook his head to clear it, with no success. Anxiety, he thought: sleep as a defense against the fear of what might happen if Joshua's four-thirty deadline wasn't met. He kept rerunning the conversations with Joshua, picking out the threatening parts and the parts that sounded mad.

He went outside again to get some air. West End Avenue seemed oddly still, as if hushed in anticipation of what was to come. It took him a moment to place the reason: the single lane of traffic had been closed off, so there was no movement on the avenue except police officers hurrying from one station to another.

* * *

He went back to the command post and sat with Anderson and the tech, nervously watching the clock. By four o'clock everything was buttoned up, the Bomb Squad on full alert. Even the forward Apprehension Tactical Teams were hunkered down behind something solid. Visual information was purely by remote camera and the robot roving up and down across the street from Joshua's buildings.

The digits on the electronic clocks seemed to slow as the deadline approached. There was no communication from Joshua, and no report of any unusual activity. Four thirty came, and went. As the minutes continued to pass in silence, the tension began to dissolve, but the alert wasn't canceled until six.

Ben couldn't shake his fear of what Joshua might do once he decided he couldn't meet his destiny next Passover in Jerusalem, if that was what he'd meant by 'in its proper season.' What if he thought that this Passover, here, was all he had?

Had that been the point of today's deadline – one final attempt to get away from here before his hand was forced? Setting the deadline this afternoon left him time to orchestrate whatever he had in mind for this Passover, if the ultimatum failed. Not that he had to act tomorrow night – the Talmudic Rabbi Joshua had said only *on the day*, and the 'day' in question stretched from sunset on Friday through the first hour of darkness Saturday night. So this Rabbi Joshua had a good part of the weekend to play out his drama. *If* that was what he was up to.

Ben felt even more pressed by time than he imagined Joshua did. He needed to warn the cops about this soon, but he needed to be prepared when he did. It would be a hard sell, and he'd only get one shot.

He took a break at six thirty, armed as always with beeper and cellphone.

'I'm going to grab some dinner,' he told Anderson. 'But I'll stay in the neighborhood.'

In the time he had before he met Rosen at seven, Ben called Hannah at Vashti's and listened to stories about the fun she was having and the trip to the airport that was planned for tomorrow, when school was closed for Good Friday.

'We talked about Passover in school. When are you coming to get me?'

'In the afternoon, after you come back from the airport. Maybe Vashti'll bring you home, because I have to work all day.'

'Deborah's going to say the four questions with me. We practiced.'

'Oh, sweetie, I don't think they're at home.'

'I want Judith to hear me say the four questions.'

He could hear an edge of panic in her voice, as if she were already anticipating loss and abandonment. Or was it just him, his own pain, his own sense of confusion and emptiness?

'We'll go to Justine's. You had a good time last year. And you can say the questions with Justine.'

'No! She's no fun.'

'Well, you and Vashti have a good time at the airport and I promise we'll have a special treat for this Passover.'

'What?'

'It's a secret.' Hannah liked secrets and surprises. Not the kind that this Passover promised.

He and Rosen went to a restaurant in the neighborhood. It was crowded with people seemingly unconcerned about the drama less than a mile away, though Ben thought the chatter was brighter and louder than usual, and at some of the tables he saw TV crews and journalists.

He left most of his food untouched while he bounced his theories off Rosen, pressing for a a definite conclusion Rosen was hesitant to give.

'The question is,' the chaplain said, 'How much distortion is Joshua willing to work in the legendary timetables? There are two clocks running. One is – get the Son of David to appear, with a pre-announcement by the prophet Elijah, during Passover, preferably the first day. The other is – there's supposed to be a breathing space between the death of the Son of Joseph and the arrival of the Son of David. Forty days, in most accounts. Joshua can act out one of those timetables this year, but not both.'

'Based on what he's been saying about feeling rushed, my guess is that the Passover deadline is the one that matters to him.'

'What scares me about all this,' Rosen told him, 'is how plausible it all is, predictable, even. Ever since the destruction of the Second Temple, there's been a plague of false messiahs. They come in clusters every few hundred years.' The law-enforcement chaplain drew lines in the condensation on his beer glass, his face dark with worry. 'It scares me how much free-floating belief is abroad in the land these days. And there's more and more as the calendar digits roll over.'

Ben spent another hour at the command post waiting for a communication that wasn't coming. He went home exhausted. Cumulative effects of the past days, he thought, and relief that nothing had happened so far. He fell into bed, clothes and all, and was immediately asleep.

Something woke him with a dream still vivid in his mind – a grown-up version of the one Hannah had once told him about, a line of people waiting before a high throne to be judged by a man he couldn't quite see – Joshua? By the side of the throne stood a woman holding a sword that steamed with the blood of a man she'd just beheaded, and behind her was a wall of marble down which cascaded a sheet of blood—

The doorbell rang again, shattering the images. He got up, rubbing circulation into his face. As he navigated the dark apartment, he had a muddled sense that something was wrong. The doorman was supposed to call from downstairs. Guests couldn't get into the building without being announced, and the neighbors wouldn't come calling without an invitation, not even Mrs B.

His first thought was that he'd slept through his beeper and the telephone and someone from the command post had come to get him. He checked the beeper, still on his belt: it showed no messages. Then he thought, *Joshua sent someone*. The thought was so alarming he turned toward the kitchen for a knife, the dream image resurfacing and it *was* Joshua on the throne of judgment. He pushed it from his mind – it was only a dream, he couldn't let it spook him.

Through the peephole in the door he could dimly see the figure of a woman, hunched and shadowy, a kerchief over her hair.

Still wary, he opened the door—

Incredibly, it was Judith. She looked drawn and dazed. Her hair was tangled where it had escaped from the kerchief, and there were long scratches on her forehead and her arms, streaks and smudges of dirt on her clothes and on her face and legs. She looked as if she'd been dirtier and had tried to wipe herself off.

She stepped past him into the apartment. He stood there, without the wit to close the door. She did it for him, stood with her arms folded around her. She was wearing a thin sweater and a long wool skirt.

'You must be cold,' he said, inanely.

She nodded, eyes closed. She seemed to be shivering.

'Wait here,' he said – more inanity – and went to get a blanket to wrap her in.

'You look exhausted.'

'We have to talk,' she said.

'Okay. Let me draw you a bath first and heat up some soup. You can sleep that long.'

'Okay. But will you make some coffee, too?' With the blanket tight around her she followed him to the bedroom and lay down.

'Wake me.' She was asleep before she could say more.

He put up coffee and soup and drew the bath and tried not to think about the ancient Israelite Judith, whose story he'd looked for fruitlessly in the Bible and finally discovered in the Apocrypha – a beautiful Judean woman in the beseiged hill city of Bethulia who left her home to enter the camp of Holofernes, the enemy general, beguiled him and diverted him and lulled him until, stuporous with food and drink, he was insensible to her using his own scimitar to sever his head from his body.

Ben still had every reason to believe Judith had betrayed him. Even if she wasn't here to act the role of Judith of Bethulia, he would have to be careful. Especially because the strength of his reaction to her hadn't diminished.

He woke her when the bath was ready.

'You okay by yourself?' he asked, knowing there was no way he could help her into a bath.

'I'm fine.'

He left her alone and went back into the kitchen, where he wouldn't have to hear the sounds of her getting out of her clothes and into the steaming water.

After ten minutes he went to knock on the bathroom door.

'Out soon,' she said.

'I'll leave some clothes on the doorknob.' He found a clean pair of jeans, a T-shirt and a heavy flannel shirt to go over it, wool socks.

She appeared a few minutes later, still damp, her hair twisted into a thick wet rope. His clothes were too big for her but she'd folded the cuffs and looked, with her face scrubbed clean, like a teenager. In the light, he could see that her scratches and bruises were superficial, the result, he guessed, of her escape. Because one way or the other she had escaped – either from Joshua and the police, or just from the police.

She looked gaunt, he thought. She had probably lost a little weight, but it was in her face that the strain of the past week showed most.

She drank the chicken broth with an avid hunger. He gave her more, and she slowed down.

'Good,' she said, wiping a drop of soup from her chin. She held out the bowl. 'More.'

Just like Hannah, he couldn't help thinking as he ladled out more. He gave her bread and she happily used it to sop up the soup.

He watched her eat, then poured her the coffee she'd asked for and gave her a plate of Hannah's cookies to go with it. 'I'm afraid the cupboard's sort of bare.'

'This is fine.' Her eyes were shining and the color was back in her cheeks. 'We eat, but the rations are short. Joshua says he wants to make the food last as long as possible.'

Intent as he was on her, he registered what she'd said: if Joshua was rationing food to last as long as possible, maybe he wasn't planning anything dramatic just yet.

67

When she was finished eating they went into the living room and sat on the couch.

'This is all so normal,' she said. 'In the middle of a world gone mad. Inside, with Joshua, he tries to pretend it's normal – like a Sabbath retreat with more people – but how can it be normal when men with machine guns are standing guard everywhere where anyone might come in?'

He'd have to ask her about the guns, about Sid, about so much, but he wanted to see how she was playing this. He imagined himself standing guard and knew he'd see anyone leaving, as well as anyone coming in. Reason, by itself, to be wary of the fact that she was here.

He touched one of the scratches on her leg. 'How did you get these?'

'Getting out. There's a long tunnel, and some of the others know about it but only Joshua knows it's been finished. Actually, it hasn't been, not really. It's so narrow most of the way, there's barely any opening at all. It's cold and dark and terribly frightening, and there were rats. I thought I would die from lack of air. I wanted to turn back, but I couldn't. Someone had to let the outside world know what it's like.

'It's terrifying how calm everyone seems, full of enthusiasm and a sense of shared effort that's only just beginning to wear off and let reality peek through. And there was no one else who would come out but me. The others are either afraid of Joshua or blinded by him. They don't see how bad it is – even with Joshua the way he is – or how much worse it will be.'

'Tell me what you mean – "with Joshua the way he is." How is he? What's he doing?'

'All day and into the night he talks about the Age of Moshiach and the Ingathering of the Exiles. And about preparing the way. And he tells us his dreams.'

'What kind of dreams?'

'Frightening ones. Great clouds of fire in the sky, sucking up the air and drying up a huge river, but then the water returns and engulfs the cities of the wicked, like Noah's flood. In one dream he saw lions prowling the streets of Manhattan, one of them gnawing on the rib of a living man. A tower where he could see the whole world and half of it was a wasteland full of skeletons and the other half was covered in serpents. That's how he knew we had to come here.'

'The city of towers, by the river.'

'Yes. And he talks about the wrath of God and calls haShem the devouring fire that will wipe out our enemies when Moshiach comes. He tells stories about Joshua the warrior king who defeated all the nations in the land haShem promised to Moses and the People of Israel.

'He talks and talks, and sometimes it makes frightening sense, and sometimes he just seems to be rambling. Especially when he's telling his dreams.'

'Didn't he used to do those things before?'

'Not like this. He's changed. As if the tremendous pressure he's been under has transformed him somehow.'

'Made the cracks wider?'

That brought a momentary look of reproach, then her face crumpled. 'I'm afraid.'

He squeezed her hand, struggled against the impulse to comfort her. If he got any closer he'd be lost. He said, 'It's hard to imagine Joshua as anything but positive and hopeful.'

'He is, still, but it's different. Darker. He talks about false messiahs – some who were charlatans and crazy men, but also the great sages and wisemen who thought they were Moshiach, and who might have been, for their great learning and wisdom and the generosity of their souls, but their era wasn't ready for them. I can't tell if Joshua thinks he himself is the messiah for this generation or if, as he tells us, he believes he's only preparing the way.'

'How are the others taking it?'

'Most, especially the men closest to him, are excited, looking forward to the great events he speaks of. He spends a lot of time with the young people. I think he frightens some of them, even the older ones, but most of them look up to him so much it frightens *me*. A few of the mothers want to keep their children away from him, but he insists that they come to all the prayer services. And he holds special prayer vigils for the men standing guard.'

'What are they guarding against?' He thought about having her talk to the intel cops, but he didn't want to interrupt the flow, didn't know how she'd react to the suggestion. And he remembered that the ancient Judith had won her way into the enemy camp by promising valuable information from behind the city walls.

'Joshua's always talked about the dangers of the Western-calendar millennium, and the fanatics who believe they have to rid the world of Jews in order for their Jesus to come again. He says now that those people are the vanguard of the nations that will be led against us in the time of Moshiach. He hadn't expected that war to come yet, or the first threat to come from this direction, but he says that's what this is. That the police are manifestations of the sitra ahra – the Other Side. The armies of . . . Armilus? I'm not sure of the name – as often as he says it I can't get it to stay in my mind.'

But it had stayed in Ben's mind, reading about it: Armilus was the anti-messiah born of Samael and a woman of stone, destined to vanquish the Son of Joseph and kill him.

'Does he say anything about how it will all come out?'

'Only that we have to be ready to fight, to make an example for the rest of Israel and the other nations. That the harder we fight the sooner the battle will end and Moshiach will come, the sooner our own souls will be redeemed and the sooner we will have our places in the World To Come.'

'Does that mean the battle is going to end well?'

'Oh yes. He says if we are strong and fierce and pure the police will stop opposing us.'

So he wasn't telling them everything. 'And it doesn't scare people?'

'Some. Mostly the women. Either the men aren't frightened, or they're hiding it. Of the men there's a group he calls his Sixteen' –

That, too, was in his reading: the Son of Joseph going into battle with sixteen champions at his side.

—'They're like a palace guard. He keeps them apart from the rest of us, except to organize fighting groups and give orders.'

She talked about jealousies among the members of the different congregations, rivalry for Joshua's attention, growing strain between the generations.

'It started out like a game, hiding so no one would know we were there, many of us coming in through secret back entrances. It's hard to believe some of us have been crowded in together for five days now and the police have been laying siege to us for three.'

'How many are you?'

'I think there are close to fifty adults and perhaps fifteen children between thirteen and twenty.

'Suzanne and Mark?'

'Yes. Mark is Joshua's closest lieutenant among the Sixteen. And Suzanne is important among the women who aren't suited to fighting. She helps Rivka the way Mark helps Joshua. They're responsible for everything domestic and for daily social and religious discipline.'

'Women fighters?'

'Yes. Joshua tells tales of the great women warriors from the Bible, like Deborah and Yael' –

And Judith? Ben wanted to say.

—'And some of the women and the children – especially the oldest children – are among the most enthusiastic. But there's uneasiness now as well. Rivka has begun to talk among the women about protecting the children, in case the police don't see the truth so quickly and let us go. For the first time, I've heard her question Joshua's decisions in public – not yet in any serious way, but she's a woman of principle, under the gentleness.'

'Where do you fit in all this?'

'I don't. Joshua wanted to give me command of the young women, but I'm no warrior. I'm afraid I disappointed him.'

He was glad she could manage even that much irony, unsettling a picture as she was painting – despite the rifts, it sounded much more martial and unified than the mad con-man guru with mostly reluctant followers the police seemed to be imagining. Much more dangerous.

'Does no one understand how crazy this is?' he asked.

'I think some are coming to see it, at last. But Joshua has been building this for more than four years, since the Rebbe had his stroke, and these are his prize disciples. I thought Mark was the best hope for moderation, he's strong and sensible. But he's losing his place to this horrible . . . boy . . . from Israel, who's a fanatic. And Joshua listens to him because he's the Rebbe's eldest great-grandson. His mother brought him up to believe the Rebbe was Elijah, destined to bring Moshiach.'

'How long has he been here?'

'I don't know. He came when he got out of the army.'

'That seems young to have so much influence.'

She hesitated a long time. 'There's a rumor that Joshua is his father.'

Ben took a moment to digest it. It fit what he knew, added just the right spice to Joshua's story of his thwarted romance with of the Rebbe's granddaughter.

'Are transgression and the Hidden Torah still part of what he's teaching?'

Judith smiled sadly and for a moment he saw the deep fatigue behind it.

'All of that's over for now.' Again the hint of irony in her voice: 'I don't know why I say "for now," it's likely to be forever. He keeps repeating the same verse, *A redeemer will come to Zion, to those who turn away from transgression*. In the past he preached that in order to turn away from transgression you first had to be fully engaged in it. Now, only the turning away matters. Sex is only for married couples when the woman is pure. The rain has been good for us – fresh running water for the mikvah so the women can purify themselves. Joshua has even talked of taking a new wife from among the young women, at the Shabbat wedding ceremony if he has one.'

'But he's already got a wife.' He didn't have to ask who Joshua had in mind for the next one.

'Yes. He'll either declare the thousand-year rabbinic prohibition against polygamy at an end, the timing is close enough, or he'll divorce Rivka.'

'Why?'

'He says it's to bring the Shekhina' – God's living presence – 'to dwell among us. He repeats the teaching in the Kabbalah that when a man unites with his wife in holiness the Divine Presence is between them. And he says there's no sex more holy than on Shabbat or on a wedding night.'

Into the uncomfortable silence, Ben said, 'Is he making plans for Shabbat?

'Yes. As I said, it's as if everything were normal.'

'And Passover?'

'Only what you'd expect, with tomorrow the first night.'

'He hasn't tied it in with his talk of great events?'

'Only that we'll be remembering the ancient redemption from slavery at the same time as we anticipate the coming redemption from exile and the rebuilding of the Holy Temple. "Good things happen on good days and bad things happen on bad days," he says. As a way to encourage us.'

It chilled Ben to hear it from her. It was one thing to theorize, another to have what amounted to direct confirmation. He needed to get away from it and come back. And there was so much else he had to ask about. 'At Centerville, Joshua brought out a man he called a converted spy. Do you know what's happening with him?'

'Joshua's been keeping him in a closed room under guard. Joshua spoke of a trial, and the death penalty. They've done it once, to Rabbi Kest. It was awful.'

'And you think this trial will be soon?'

'Yes. For Rabbi Kest it was three judges, because there were so few of us, but now Joshua says they need twenty-three men who are the most qualified by knowledge of the Law. They were selecting them when I left. Everyone was there. That's how I could get out without being noticed.'

Ben's beeper went off. He checked it, knowing what it would be. 'Joshua wants to talk to me.'

She stared at him. 'Will you go?'

'I don't have much choice.' He got up to call the negotiating team.

Anderson answered. His twelve-hour-long tour was over, but he was still at the command post.

'Brauner wants to talk to you from here,' he told Ben. 'Says it's important.'

'On my way.' He reached down to touch Judith's cheek. 'Will you come with me?'

She drew back. 'Why?'

He sat next to her, took her hand. 'This call has to be about you. The police will know you're here. They'll want to talk to you.'

'No.' Panicked. 'I won't do that.' She hugged herself, shivering.

'It's okay, it's okay.' He pulled her to him, stroked her hair.

'I came to tell *you*,' she said into his neck. 'You can tell them.'

'All right.' He stood up again quickly, as much to protect himself from her warmth as to be on his way. 'Will you be all right? You can sleep. I won't be long.'

She took his hand, pressed it to her face, kissed his palm the way she had that first night . . .

'Promise?' she said. 'Promise you'll come back soon?'

'I promise.'

68

'Benjamin, my friend,' Joshua began. 'I told you it would go hard if your masters in the police and Secret Service and the Bureau of Firearms disdained my offer. But it isn't yet too late. Just now I fell asleep and dreamed a dream. I was on a grassy slope with the great sages of the past, all standing in an enormous circle, praying. Suddenly the moon raced by over our heads and then a second moon, larger than the first, and the earth began to shift in its orbit and the ground beneath us buckled. And when everything was still again I was alone, no longer in this body but in the body of a great wild ox cropping the grass, and standing by me was Reb Yaacov Moshe, our Rebbe of sainted memory. And he reminded me of my destiny, which is to prepare his people for Moshiach Ben David. And he sent a message, his own message for the soldiers of Armilus who besiege us. The message was, "Thus speaks the Lord – Set my people free that they may serve Me." You who are listening now, and you who will listen later, heed the voice of a man of great wisdom and holiness, companion of the great angel Michael, the Advocate of Israel. *The Lord says, Set my people free.*'

There was so much passion in Joshua's voice, and the message was so different from the accusations about Judith Ben was expecting, that he was momentarily without words.

Anderson motioned to him to speak. He snapped himself out of it.

'It's in your hands, Joshua. It's always been in your hands. The Holy One, praised be He, gave human beings free will, and when we exercise our free will we collaborate with haShem in the continuing creation of the world. You say so yourself, in all your books.'

'Don't patronize me, Benjamin, not now. It isn't yet too late to turn away from evil, not even for the police. I'd hoped talking to you I'd have someone who'd understand, who could interpret me to the nations. I fear I was wrong.'

'Joshua, you don't need interpreters. You need to speak plainly of mundane things, and you need to listen. Those are people you love, in there with you. And they love you and rely on you. You don't want to hurt them. I know you don't.'

There was a silence, not long, Joshua's silence this time. Then he spoke, a new note of disdain in his voice.

'Benjamin, my misguided friend. You think you're being the good, upright defender of the laws of Edom, but you can't see how it twists you. You yourself sent a man to betray me, at the same time you were pretending you respected me. You think I don't know that? You sent someone to inform on his own people, a foolish, foolish man. He was warned and he continued and now he'll suffer the fate he deserves, according to the judgment of the court.'

Ben began to protest but Joshua was still talking, strident with certainty. 'Ulamalshinim *la hi tikvah*, we pray every day. For such as he, *let there be no hope*.'

'Haven't enough people died, Joshua?' – a trial and the death penalty, Judith had said – 'There has to be a better way to prepare for Moshiach. What about the Ingathering of the Exiles, going to Israel—'

'Don't preach to me, Benjamin! Even now you deal in betrayal. You think I don't know? No hope, Benjamin, no hope. In This World, and the World To Come. You think you have everything you want now, don't you? But you're wrong.'

'No, Joshua, you're the one who's wrong.' He had to keep this from getting to be about Judith. 'I didn't send anyone to betray you. The people I'm interested in are criminals. I never imagined they had anything to do with you. I always thought you were what you presented yourself to be, a wise teacher, a righteous man seeking a path to the spiritual rebuilding of the world.'

'And now? Now what do you believe I am?'

'That depends on what you do next. You have so much in your power, the lives of so many people – the myriads of Ephraim, and the thousands of Menasseh, as you put it.'

'No, I have nothing in my power. Unless you can persuade your forces to allow us free passage, nothing I can do will change the outcome.'

'What outcome, Joshua? What are you telling us?' Ben asked, but there was no one on the line.

'He was talking about the undercover,' Anderson said, half to himself. 'That *is* what we were hearing.

'What? What were you hearing?'

'We finally got something interesting on our bugs – it sounded like a trial, we thought it might be a trial of the undercover, but what we could hear was so full of side issues and questions that had nothing to do with informing or spying or anything like that we weren't sure what it actually was.'

It shook him, even though Judith had told him about it. He tried to be relieved that now he could make his point without bringing her into it.

'When did this start?'

'I just heard about it maybe half an hour before Brauner called for you. I don't how long it's been going on.'

'I need to talk to somebody about it.'

'No problem – they're going to want to debrief about this call anyway. There's a bunch of them on their way.'

There was nothing for Ben to do now but tell them everything he suspected, and hope he could make it plausible.

'I think Brauner wants to provoke an attack,' he said when the tactical commanders and their advisors had all crowded into the mobile command post. 'Provoke an attack or lure you in somehow. I think this trial may be part of it.'

'Why would he do that?'

'Because he thinks he's a legendary warrior who has to wage war against the enemies of the people of Israel.'

'Of whom do you speak?' Rabbi Goffman asked in the silence that followed.

'The Anointed Son of Joseph.'

'Ah yes, as you have said before.' Goffman seemed no more happy with the subject than he had the first time.

Ben wanted to avoid the word Messiah. Ciampa had already decided that Joshua thought he was Jesus, and it wasn't a good image to encourage. There were too many cartoons of shaggy-haired men carrying THE END IS NEAR signs, too many images of gibbering schizophrenics claiming to be Jesus. It would be dangerous to pigeonhole Joshua that way. Crazy he might be, but it was a subtler and more devious madness than believing he was God, or God's Son, and it wouldn't necessarily interfere with clear thinking on the tactics of urban warfare.

'I wasn't ready to say anything about this when the possibility first occurred to me,' Ben said. 'I've learned more about it since then.' He ran down the evidence that Joshua thought he was the Son of Joseph, preparing to wage war against the forces of Armilus.

'Rabbi?' Burke asked redbeard.

'Yes, all of that has been written of, as he tells it.'

'So you're talking about mass suicide by cop,' the intel detective said. 'Like Waco.'

'If that's what Waco was,' Ben said. 'But no, it's not like pulling a gun on a cop and hoping he'll shoot you. And it's definitely not about Brauner's taking his followers to a higher spiritual level via death. If I'm right, what he wants them to do is fight – fight to *win* – not necessarily die.' Though as things stood fighting and dying were likely to go together.

Again, the cops looked to Rabbi Goffman, who nodded grudgingly. 'Yes, if Rabbi Brauner actually believes himself to be Moshiach ben

Yosef making war against the army of Armilus, then he must fight a great battle and he must have a victory, and then he must be slain.'

'A victory?' Burke asked.

'Yes, that's part of the teaching, for those who believe these things.'

'You don't.'

'What I believe is not of interest. But Rabbi Brauner spoke of himself as an ox, and that is part of the belief. As it is written of the tribes descended from Joseph, "he has horns like the horns of the wild ox; with them he gores the peoples." This is understood by the sages to foretell the coming of the Anointed One from the house of Joseph. And the Torah verse continues with mention of the myriads of Ephraim and the thousands of Menasseh, as was spoken of in the telephone conversation. These are Joseph's sons.'

'So you think there's going to be a provocation,' Pavesi asked Ben. 'To get us into battle.'

'He's got to lure you into a place where he can beat you,' Ben said, 'Even if it's only in a limited way and for a little while.'

'And this might be it.'

'Yes. And there's a real chance he's aiming for a specific window in time. I think if you can hold out for the next few days, a big piece of his delusion will be proved wrong, and the whole structure in there will begin to come apart.'

'What's this window in time?' Inspector Burke wanted to know.

Ben talked about Passover, about the opinion of the Talmudic Rabbi Joshua that the messianic age would begin on the same day as the deliverance from Egypt. Fearing as he spoke that redbeard would shoot him down, on the grounds that there wasn't enough time for the Son of Joseph to do battle with Armilus and then lie dead in the streets for forty days as legend predicted, and still have Elijah announce the Son of David for *this* Passover.

But Rabbi Goffman simply listened, nodding sagely, and when Burke turned to him said only, 'There is such a discussion in the Midrashic writings, as he says.'

'And do you think Brauner would provoke us to attack him, to get this to happen sometime tomorrow or Saturday?'

'About that I cannot say. HaShem has not given me the power to look into other men's minds, for which I am thankful.'

The ESU commander turned to Ben. 'What exactly are you suggesting?'

'There are two ways I can see to handle it. Either be prepared to wait out any provocation, or else – he needs a victory, so let him have one without giving him a chance to win it by killing cops.'

'How do you propose we do that?'

'Let him go—'

'Not in this lifetime,' the chief of department said.

'—Get ready to follow the people we think are criminals and then withdraw completely. Make it a condition that they give us back the undercover first. We avoid a bloodbath, plus there could be significant investigative value for Secret Service.'

Burke looked to Tim Ahl.

'Maybe. But my concern right now is the undercover.'

'Can you think of better way to get him back?'

The intel detective, at the far end of the command post, leaned forward to say, 'I have a major problem with this trial being to provoke us. We only know about it because of the bugs, and he doesn't know we put them in. So how can it be a provocation?'

'How do you know he doesn't know?' ben challenged. 'Does it take that much for him to be aware he's vulnerable along his outside walls?'

'Mostly, people don't think of it that way, that we'd drill holes in the side of a house. They figure the walls are solid, and the jackhammers are another way to annoy them, not to cover up some other noise. But even suppose they *are* worried about bugs. It's a long way from thinking somebody might have bugged you to staging a show trial for the bugs you think might be there.'

'What about cameras?' Ben asked. 'How much of this can you see?'

'I don't think that's in your need-to-know,' the chief of department said.

'The important thing is,' Burke said, 'I'm not prepared to treat this trial as anything but real. So let's talk about this phone call, which I have to say sounds spooky to me. Dreaming he's an ox but it really means he's this doomed warrior.'

'It's a very specific dream,' said a woman Ben hadn't seen before, standing in the open area behind the RV's driver's seat with Pavesi and one of the intel detectives. Her long silver hair, multicolored dress and heavy necklace of amber beads led him straight to the stereotype – West Side Shrink – though he didn't think of them probing the workings of criminal minds, and absent ones at that. She said, 'I think we have to consider that what he described might not be a dream at all but rather a confabulation for the purpose of reinforcing a power dynamic within the group, or perhaps with respect to an adversary.'

Seeing blank looks all around, she sighed and said, 'He made it up to make a point.'

A light blinked on the communications console. The tech connected a line, and Anderson answered, grunted a few times, and turned to the others. 'They've got a verdict. Guilty. Sentence is death.'

'Anything about when?'

'Not so far.'

'They're sure about the verdict?' Burke asked.

Anderson checked. 'Yeah.'

'We may have to go right in if we're going to save him,' Burke said.

'Excuse me,' Rabbi Goffman said, smoothing the red beard and moustache. 'If they are following the halakha – the religious law – then there is no need to hurry, this minute.'

'Why not?' Pavesi asked.

'There is a rule in the Talmud that if there is a guilty verdict in such a criminal trial, then the judges must next continue to deliberate overnight, and then in the morning they must vote again and see if anyone has changed his mind from guilty to innocent.'

'You're saying they can't execute him tonight?'

'If they are following the rules.'

'If you listen to the tape could you tell?'

'Perhaps, with the help of haShem. I'm willing to try.'

69

While Rabbi Goffman verified that the trial was according to religious law, the ESU bosses and the intel cops left for the school command post where they could review their assault plans with Lt Brown, the head of the Apprehension Tactical Teams. Ben was eager to get home and see if Judith was willing to help convince Burke and the others of the danger ahead.

As he left the negotiation vehicle, Lukas walked with him. In the moonlit brightness beyond the police floodlights the avenue still gleamed with the last of the rain, spuriously calm. The police sawhorses and the elephantine command-post campers, the Technical Assistance truck, even the cops patrolling the outer perimeter with its fringe of press trucks and milling reporters and camera crews waiting for something to happen – it all could have been for a political convention or a visiting head of state.

'How sure are you about this?' the agent asked.

'How sure?' The question was treacherous in its simplicity. Lukas's would be only one voice in a heavy debate about whether to try to rescue Sid Levy – balancing the life of one man against the casualties that would surely be suffered in an assault. But Lukas was the case agent: his voice would carry extra weight.

And it was Ben's sense of the mood tonight that the cops were eager to move. Joshua had made a fool of ATF and the state police, and the NYPD wasn't going to let him do the same to them, whatever Pavesi might say about preferring to bore Joshua to death.

'You mean, am I life-or-death sure?'

'That's what I mean.'

There it was: Did he argue for leaving an agent to the mercies of his captors? An agent who had insisted on having him as a contact, whom he'd worked with closely.

'Come with me,' he said. 'There's somebody you have to talk to.' It was the only way. He'd never get Judith into a roomful of armed cops, but she might talk to one agent – a man whose name she already knew, even if it was only from having heard Ben complain about him.

* * *

They were intercepted by a pair of ESU cops heading up the hill from the school.

'Kaplan?'

'That's me.'

'Captain Pavesi wants to see you.'

'I'm in a hurry. I can be back in a half hour or so.'

'Cap's in a hurry, too. Let's go, it won't take long.'

The intel and ESU cops had a fresh set of drawings of Joshua's school building spread out on a table.

'Take a look,' Pavesi said. 'Anything you see that looks wrong?'

Ben pushed down the roiling need he felt to get back home to Judith. Lives could depend on his taking his time with this.

'Nothing wrong that I see,' he said finally. 'It's all consistent with my memory.'

'This is as much as we got from the people we could convince to talk to us,' Pavesi told him. 'If there's anybody else who might know something, especially about that bunker . . .'

'Maybe there is.' He didn't know how Judith would react, and first he wanted her to talk to Lukas. 'Let me see what I can do.'

'I'll send Harris with you,' Pavesi proposed – the intel detective who'd been at all the briefings.

'No. This guy'll spook if he has any idea there are cops around. If I can get him to come in I will, but don't count on it.'

Turnabout. Ben had been on the other end of this one often enough: an agent's sources were the agent's, and that was how it was.

'This the same person we're on our way to see?' Lukas asked as they walked down West End.

'Yes.'

'Who?'

'Somebody from inside the buildings.'

'Somebody got out? How?'

'You'll hear in a minute.' Ben was too wrapped up in his thoughts to say more. Could he be wrong to think the trial was Joshua's way to get the cops to attack? Everyone seemed convinced that Joshua wouldn't think the walls had ears, and they were probably right that he wouldn't stage a phony trial unless he *knew* about the bugs. But if the trial was real, it could still be a provocation.

Judith had talked about it, about a probable death penalty for Sid Levy. Could that be the real reason she'd struggled through the tunnel? That Joshua had sent her to bolster the provocation? After all, Joshua had manipulated him before, and used Judith to do it. So there was a real chance he was bringing Lukas to talk to someone who'd been planted on them.

But if she was Joshua's emissary, why hadn't she painted a picture more calculated to tempt the police into attacking – a community in disarray, good people and children endangered, faulty defenses – just as Judith of Bethulia had misled Holofernes and his captains? She'd done the opposite: described a disciplined martial society, organized and alert. But letting Judith get out to tell what she thought was the truth was just the kind of indirection that Ben was coming to think Joshua might relish.

Lukas at his side, Ben hurried into his building with a quick wave hello for the doorman, who was getting ready to go off duty, talking to his late-shift relief.

'I want to go in first and prepare the ground,' he told Lukas in the elevator. 'This is somebody who's already refused to talk to the police.'

'But he talked to you.'

'Right.' There'd be time to correct the gender later.

Ben fumbled his key in his eagerness to get into the apartment. He rushed through to the bedroom, a hundred urgencies propelling him.

'Judith?' he called. 'It's me, Ben, I'm home.' Not wanting her to be scared by unknown noises.

The bedclothes were jumbled. It took him a moment to see that she wasn't there. Not in the bed or the bedroom or the bathroom. Or any other room.

The answering machine was blinking: one message. He pressed 'play', heard Rosen's voice, fast-forwarded – only Rosen. He called his office voice mail, skipped from message to message, heard nothing relevant. Raced back out to the hall.

'What's wrong?' Lukas asked.

'Gone.' Ben kept poking the elevator button.

In the lobby, the two doormen were still talking.

'Did you see my friend leave?' Ben asked.

'Yeah, a while ago. I put her in a cab. Listen, was that all right, sending her up before? She said she wanted to surprise you . . .'

'No problem. You didn't happen to hear what address she gave the cabby?'

'No, I sure didn't. Why? Is everything okay?'

'Fine. I just . . . She was alone, right?'

'Yeah.' Looking at him with more interest. 'You sure it's okay? I mean, she didn't take anything?'

Ben forced a laugh. 'No, nothing like that. I guess we got our signals crossed, is all.'

'Sure,' the doorman said, imagining . . . Ben couldn't guess what. Nothing half as dramatic as the reality.

Lukas rode back upstairs with him.

'She?'

'Yeah.'

'Who?'

'A friend.'

Together, they combed the apartment. There was no sign of a struggle. In the bathroom hamper Ben found the clothes he'd given her to wear, and hers were nowhere to be seen.

The note was on the front hall table. Lukas found it. It said, 'I love you. Hannah, too. Good bye.'

'Want to talk about it?' Lukas said.

'Not really.'

'Well, I do. It's damn well about time you started being straight with me. You hid that you knew these people, this crazy Brauner. Now you've got an informant, he this he that, and it turns out it's your girlfriend.'

'I brought you here to see her, didn't I?' Ben was furious, fear about Judith and the impending horror feeding his anger. 'Does it occur to you that it took a lot of trust to do that, and maybe I ought to get some coming back my way?'

'It *occurs* to me you've got a conflict big as a house, negotiating with a barricaded group at the same time you know your girlfriend is in there and you're not telling anybody. This is a hell of a time to be thinking with your dick.'

'Name-calling isn't the answer, either. We've got people on the verge of a shooting war.'

'You're not helping much—' Lukas cut himself off. Began again, calmer. 'Did you learn anything from this woman?'

'Let me tell you what she said, and then let's see if we can figure out what to do.'

They went into the living room, and Ben gave Lukas a condensed version of the visit from Judith.

'You don't have any idea where this tunnel is?'

'None.'

'Shit,' Lukas said. 'You think she was telling the truth?'

'I did, when she was telling it.'

'But she went back. I'd say that changes things.'

'*If* she went back.' But he knew she had – it was the only reason to put those clothes back on.

'Where else?'

'I don't know. But, yes, if she went back that makes it more likely he sent her.' It hurt to acknowledge this newest evidence of betrayal, but its implications were too important to ignore. 'That just supports my opinion that the trial is a provocation. But I'd still think it was, if only because of the way Joshua rubbed it in our faces in the phone call.'

'Assuming any of this is true, wouldn't he do more than just tell us about a trial he didn't know we could hear?'

'He will. I don't know what – find a way to fool us into thinking his guard is down, maybe.'

'And you're saying we should just sit on our hands, no matter what.'

'Yes, I am.'

'And they're really going to put you in charge of agents? Making policy.' Lukas laughed, short and bitter. 'The retirement fund is about to take a major hit.' He looked at Ben as if seeing a stranger. 'You just want to leave Sid to their tender mercies, and that's your policy decision?'

'Look, Frank, this isn't easy for me. Sid is my responsibility as much as anybody's, and I care about getting him out of there. I really do. But there's too much at stake here for the decision be driven by guesswork about the fate of one man, especially a professional who went into this with his eyes open, aware of the risk.' Ben knew he wasn't helping himself with Lukas, but this was too important to pull any punches. 'We don't even know he's alive at this point. From what they said in the briefing they never heard him once during the trial.'

'If he's dead, why have a trial at all?'

'Same reason. To get us worried about him exactly the way we are. Or else it's Brauner's way to justify to his own people an execution that's already occurred.'

'Bullshit.'

'All right, it's a reach. But if Sid *is* alive, how do we know his guard doesn't have instructions to kill him the minute an assault starts? My point is, *we don't know an assault will save him*. We do know it'll kill cops and civilians. And another thing – *we* know Sid, *we* see him as a person, *we* care about him. All he is for the cops is a pretext to do what they want, which is to go in there and clean house.'

Lukas thought about it. 'All right, there's something in that. But we still can't leave him there.'

'If we're going to get him out, if it's not already too late for that, it's got to be by negotiation.'

'And how do we do that? All Brauner does is call, rant, and hang up.'

'He won't hang up if we start by saying, "Yes, you can leave."'

'Shit. Still on that.'

'It's the only way. Let them all out and pick them off one at a time.'

Lukas shook his head. 'It might make sense, if it made sense. We let these people go, they're going to scatter all over God's creation, and we're not going to be able to tell one from the other.'

'I don't believe Secret Service and ATF together can't do better than that. And even if a few slip through, what do we lose?'

'The counterfeiting plant. Plus a couple of guys who killed a federal informant.'

'We've still got leads in Israel. We can push harder there. When we get deeper into Brauner's phone and financial records we'll have more. And as for the murders, how different are they from mob hits? You want to risk how many cops killed, and how many people who have nothing to do with murder or currency counterfeiting, for the sake of what?'

'You seriously think the cops are going to let these people go, or that we are? We were talking about policy? Okay, here's a fast policy lesson – policy isn't just for today, it's for tomorrow and all the tomorrows after that. Let these people go now and every asshole who gets in trouble with the cops will be be staging a standoff and saying "You let the Jews go, now let me go."'

'It doesn't have to go that way,' Ben said, knowing it wouldn't help. Worry about setting precedents sometimes led to bad decisions, but it was the way the world worked.

Lukas was quiet for a while. 'Do people really believe this kind of stuff? Enough to put their lives on the line, and to kill other people?'

'Go ask that question in Ulster or Bosnia, for starters. Or India.'

'What I'm asking is, do Jews think like that?'

'This isn't about thinking anymore. A lot of people would say it isn't Judaism anymore, either. Whatever it is, the hard core already killed Isaacs and Kest, and these people that Brauner's assembled are the ones he trusts most to follow him. He's been building them up for a battle with the forces of evil, in one form or another, for a long time. And ask yourself this – if these people were any other religion at all, would you doubt it for a minute?'

Lukas didn't answer. Wearily, he stood up. 'Even if it was possible to let them go, you know why it won't work? Because it's not what Brauner wants. What your girlfriend said about the bomber being Brauner's son? He'll never turn him over, and he'll never let him be taken. That's why he's keeping the rest of them holed up in there even though we've offered to let them go to Israel.'

'It's only a rumor about Benzvi. We don't know it's true.'

'But he *is* the holy Rebbe's great grandson, right? And that's reason enough by itself.'

Ben had no answer for that. It was a worry he'd had himself.

Lukas said, 'So that means we're going to have to go in and get them sooner or later.'

'All I'm saying is, *later*. It could save a lot of lives. Maybe including Sid's.'

Lukas headed for the door. 'I've got to get back.'

'Maybe I ought to come and tell the others what I told you.'

'Do you think anybody's going to listen to you at this point? I don't know if they're listening to *me*. This is ESU's show, they listen to their own. I'll pass along what you got from inside, but they're going to decide how much is real.'

'Frank!' Ben called after him.

'Yeah?'

'Burke told me the most important thing to ESU is they have to determine their own battlefield. Ask him this – if they let Brauner lure them in, then isn't he the one choosing the field of battle, and the terms, not them?'

'Good point. And even if you're a hundred percent right you said they've got at least until the holiday starts tomorrow. Maybe we can get this figured out by then.'

Ben sat in his easy chair, staring at the note from Judith for he didn't know how long, fighting his sense of futility. Lukas was right. He had nothing new to add, and they weren't listening.

The phone rang. He bolted for it. It was Rosen.

'Didn't you get my message?'

'No, I—' It was too complicated. 'No, I didn't.'

'I found something else. It was tickling my brain while we were talking so I looked until I found it. It says in the Talmud that Elijah can't announce the Messiah on the Sabbath or a major festival like Passover, or even right before. He can't interrupt preparations for the holiday. Passover's tomorrow night.'

'So you're saying it's too late for Joshua? He can't wage his war in time?'

'Either that or he's got to move right away. And I mean *right away*.'

'Good things happen on good days,' Ben quoted. 'We've got to do something.'

'And soon.'

'I may need some religious support. Can you get over here?'

'Already there. As soon as I came up with this I headed your way. This is me on a cellphone seeing if you're home.'

70

Leaving to meet Rosen downstairs, Ben used his cellphone to beep Lukas. After five intolerable minutes of waiting for Lukas to call, trying to focus on what Rosen was telling him, Ben said, 'We can't just stay here. Let's get over to the command post and find a way to make them listen.'

'Can we get some support first?'

'I don't know who.' Tim Ahl, Queen Victoria, Nate Morgan – the more powerful they got, the farther they were from the center of things and the harder it would be to explain the problem. Among them only Ahl had heard any of the talk about Joshua's invoking messianic legend. There was no route but the direct one.

The phone rang.

'What?' Lukas.

'It's tonight. It has to be tonight.'

A silence, then, 'You really think so?

'Absolutely. I'm telling you, if we can just hold out . . .'

Another silence. 'Damn.'

'Something's happening.'

A much longer silence. 'Where are you?' Urgent, now.

'Home. I've got somebody with me, the FLEOA chaplain who helped with Isaacs.'

'Good. Bring him. Walk up West End on the east side of the street. I'll meet you.'

Ben and Rosen met Lukas coming the other way at 95th Street. From the duffel bag over his shoulder he thrust an ATF windbreaker at the chaplain. For Ben, Lukas had a snug personal bulletproof vest and then, over that, the thick bulk of a heavy vest. A Secret Service windbreaker went over that.

'Let's go.' He turned to walk back up West End, making good time up the steep hill.

'Sorry I don't have a vest for you, rabbi, you won't be able to go the whole way, so talk to me now. You think Ben's right about this Messiah business.'

'Yeah, I do. It's straight out of the Midrashic writings and the Talmud.'

'I don't need the footnotes. Just so you don't think this is crazy.'

'Hell yeah, it's crazy. But everything he's said so far is a hundred percent justifiable if you believe the legends.'

'Big if.'

'Why? Millions of Christians believe Revelation, and that's a whole lot wilder, even though it's based on a lot of the same stories. And they *really* believe it, right down to the seven-headed beasts and the locusts with men's faces and the teeth of lions.'

'I still have trouble with this being Jews.'

'Try this,' Rosen said: 'The general who led the Jewish revolt against Rome, a hundred years after Jesus, fought the best legions of the Roman army to a standstill for three years. And a big reason his followers were so fierce was they believed he was the Messiah. The greatest rabbi of the age said so.'

'All right,' Lukas said, 'I take your point. Let's see if we can convince anybody else. Here's what's happening. They've been following some activity in the buildings with bugs and cameras, and they think they've got a time window, or they will when these people change the guard for the night shift, which they think is going to be in the next hour.

'I know for a fact that nobody so much as hinted to Wally Brown about any of this religious stuff. I'll probably get my ass in a sling for this, but I think I can get you in to talk to him at the forward observation post. Figure you'll have five minutes, max. Just make your case, if he has questions answer them. Rabbi, I'm going to want you standing by outside the heavy-vest area. If Lieutenant Brown wants some corroboration I'll try to get him to talk to you.'

They were at the first police barrier. Lukas flashed his shield. 'They're with me.'

The cop at the barrier gave them an odd look, but he passed them through.

The staging area on West End Avenue was lit by a spill of light from a pair of helicopters beaming searchlights down on the school and synagogue, as they had at random intervals every night. There seemed to be more activity on the street, a greater sense of purpose. There was an enormous ESU truck Ben had never seen before, easily ten feet tall, with a rack of floodlights atop it at least twice as big as any other he'd seen deployed.

Further up, Ben saw a massive armored personnel carrier wearing dun-colored camouflage paint as if it were ready for desert warfare.

'They're serious.'

'Oh, yeah. The MALT truck – Mother of All Light Trucks – goes up the street with the APC. They get your attention.'

'How's the real force arriving?'

'That they don't tell me.'

They came to another barrier. This time it wasn't as easy. There were two cops in personal vests, each carrying an MP-5 automatic rifle. One held them there while the other listened to Lukas explain their mission then went off to consult someone up the chain of command.

It was long minutes before he came back with a lieutenant whose name bar said Walton.

'What can I do for you?'

Lukas went through the litany again, embellished this time with references to Lt Brown and Captain Pavesi.

Walton made a radio call. Ben hoped it wasn't to anyone within earshot of the chief of department.

'I need some ID,' Walton informed them.

Ben had his Department of Justice ID; Rosen showed a badge that looked as official as Lukas's. Whatever it was, it satisfied Walton. He led them up along the outside line of sawhorses past the blocked-off street, then back around to an armored bus just to its north.

He poked Rosen's shoulder. 'This is as far as you go. You can stay in the bus, or go back the way we came. Anything else, you need a heavy vest and a helmet.' To Lukas, he said, 'Where's your helmet? And his?'

Lukas pulled two Kevlar helmets from his duffel bag.

'They're not much good to you in there,' Walton said.

Lukas motioned to Ben and Rosen to get into the empty bus. 'Wait here. I'll be back.' He strapped on his helmet as he left.

'Holy shit,' Rosen said, momentarily giddy. 'This is really happening.'

'Oh yeah,' Ben said, not quite believing it himself. It felt very different from Centerville, at the periphery of the standoff. The night and the chill air of early spring had something to do with it, and the purposeful movement of armed men all around them, the massing of vehicles and *matériel*, the menacing clatter of the helicopters overhead. But there was something more: the growing certainty that within hours, or perhaps minutes, lives might truly be lost. This was not the sparring of a courtroom, it was not the intellectual and political conflict of tactical planning. There was nothing abstract about it, or conditional.

71

Lukas poked his head in the bus door. 'Let's go,' he said to Ben. 'Rabbi, you sit tight.'

Surprisingly, the agent didn't head back toward the besieged street but up the avenue away from it. There was an alley midblock between two of the big apartment houses. Lukas – carrying an MP-5 now, a sight that did more to worry Ben than to comfort him – led him down the alley to a tall wrought-iron fence that had been breached. There was a cop in a heavy vest and helmet standing guard at the opening. He nodded to Lukas and waved them on.

Past the fence they were in the rear garden of the first townhouse on the block. They crossed it to where a wooden stockade fence about six feet high had also been broken through.

'In here,' Lukas said as they entered the second garden.

He led Ben by an open glass-and-wrought-iron door into the garden-floor apartment and threaded his way through it to the front door.

'Okay. This is one of those brownstones where you come out under the stoop. We have to go around to the street and up the stairs. It's all visually blocked from the buildings across the street. They can't see us, but it's not completely hardened. If they decide to pepper the front of the building at random . . .'

'I get the idea.'

'So we just move quick and quiet.'

'I'm right behind you.'

Their way lit by the fringe of the helicopter floodlights, they emerged into the night behind a right-angled wall of tall, black ballistic shields like the ones Ben had first seen at Centerville. Overhead and over the building's stoop was an awning of black canvas randomly draped with ballistic blankets. Lukas skirted around to the front of the stoop and up, taking the outside stairs three at a time, in complete silence as far as Ben could tell over the pounding of his heart.

They were quickly inside the building. Like all the townhouses on this side of the street, it had been completely evacuated. Lukas led him up the stairs to the top floor.

The windows in the front apartment were covered by pull-down shades that added a silvery cast to the floodlit scene outside. One-way viewing, Ben guessed. He could see the synagogue and the school, diagonally across the street.

There were three big cops in the room, made bigger by their battle gear. Not just heavy vests and helmets but radios, handcuffs, ammunition, sidearms. MP-5s and individual ballistic shields were stacked against one wall.

Lt Brown separated himself from the others. 'This better be good.'

Ben talked fast, but he'd had time to think and he did what he could to make his words count.

'You're sure about this?' Brown asked sharply.

'About the theory, yes.'

'And you have a rabbi who agrees with you who knows something about law enforcement.'

'Yes.'

'We're going to have to give this some thought. And I want you out of here.' His radio crackled, words Ben didn't understand. Brown checked his watch.

'I wish you'd been earlier. You have a heavy vest, right? All right, we've got something scheduled, and I can't have you out in the street for the next little while. So for now just try to stay out of the way.'

He ushered them back away from the window. 'We're trying something with the robot, and we don't know if it's going to draw fire. We've been running it up and down, making announcements, and this time we're going to run it straight at them, try and get in closer, to test their reaction and to get them wondering what we're doing. At the same time we want to get a more detailed infrared picture of the buildings – Technical Assistance put a special camera on it for that. They get that picture, we don't.'

Two small television monitors were angled into the room on a butcher-block kitchen counter across from the windows. One showed what the robot saw; the other showed the robot and the street, seen from a camera mounted on the windowsill.

The robot trundled out from behind the ballistic shields and rolled down the street, turned sharply and accelerated toward the townhouse where Hannah had briefly gone to school.

The sound of a gunshot startled them all. The robot's-eye-view picture wobbled.

'Hold your fire!' Brown barked into the microphone at his collar. 'Hold your fire.' And then: 'Can we get a better look?'

The picture changed as the robot stopped and its camera swiveled upward, panning the façade. Blank windows.

Brown turned to Lukas. 'I'm hoping that was just some nervous kid' –

On the screen, the robot had resumed its course toward the building. Ben could hear through the closed window that it was making an announcement, but he couldn't get the words.

—'but I want you two out of here. We've got a diversion waiting to get underway. This may change the schedule.'

Ben said, 'But Lieutenant, that's just what they—'

'I heard every word you said,' Brown interrupted. 'I'll talk to my bosses about it, and you go talk to them, too. But you're out of here, right now.'

Before Ben could respond, an explosion rattled the windows. They all ducked down.

Brown's radio crackled: 'Explosive device midblock. Broken windows on our side of the street, shrapnel damage to buildings, blew some ballistic shields over. No injuries apparent. Blew the fucking robot away.'

'What was it?'

'Grenade launcher, maybe. Forward observer number four saw a flash in an upstairs window, east building, the same one the first shot came from.'

'Anybody else shooting?'

'One burst from our side, reflex reaction. No return fire.'

'Okay, good.'

Ben looked at the monitors. One was blank, the other showed a wide view of the street. Two cops in heavy vests and helmets carrying individual shields were scuttling into the street to set up the fallen ballistic shields. Down the block from where Ben had last seen it, the robot lay on its side, one tread half blown off, the rest of it unrecognizable.

'Time to go,' Brown said. 'Get over to the command post if you can, someplace we can talk on the radio if I need to.'

Lukas led Ben down the stairs to the front door. The agent ducked through into the outer vestibule to check the front stoop.

'Okay, let's go,' he said. 'Stay close.'

He scuttled down the stairs, gun in front of him ready to fire, Ben right behind him. As they reached the bottom and started around toward the door to the garden-floor apartment Ben heard sharp reports like loud gunfire and the crash of breaking glass above him.

'Down!' Lukas shouted and threw him against the side of the stoop.

There was a loud explosion directly above them and the stone stoop shook. Debris hit the awning and the street.

Lukas shoved him toward the apartment door. 'Get out of here. There's nothing you can do.'

Ben hesitated.

'You're in the way, go on.'

Beyond the ballistic-sheild barrier there was the roar of automatic weapons fire. An explosion knocked two of the ballistic shields askew. Beyond them billows of white smoke glowed with overhead light that suddenly dimmed as the clatter of the helicopters changed pitch and faded. Ben thought he heard a man scream.

'Go on!' Lukas shouted at him.

He turned to go and chaos erupted around him. Ripping noises, noises of impact, a whirring in the air he couldn't identify, flying pieces of stone and concrete and something else. Ben felt tugged first to one side, then another.

'Ah shit,' Lukas yelled and then he fell, dropping the submachine gun.

Ben ran to him, ducked over as if that would provide some protection from whoever was firing blindly at the building.

Lukas was clutching at his thigh, his expression glazed.

'Fucker hurts. You see blood?'

Ben looked, saw a dark stain spreading rapidly over and around Lukas's fingers. 'Some.'

'Pulsing?'

Ben didn't get it at first.

'*Is it?*'

'Oh. No – not arterial.'

Lukas relaxed a fraction.

Ben felt as if they were in a temporary pocket of calm. Whoever had been shooting in their direction seemed to have turned his attention elsewhere.

'Let's get you out of here,' Ben said. He bent and reached down, put Lukas's arm around his neck. 'Hang on.'

'Get out of here, yourself. I'm okay.'

'Fuck you,' was all Ben could think to say. He reached his free arm under Lukas's back and lifted, not very far. 'Shit, you're heavy.'

He let go of the agent and stood up. The fight was raging outside. He heard someone on the stairs, going one way or the other. He grabbed the MP-5 from the ground. He remembered an FBI picnic, years ago, a table with all kinds of guns on it and you just stepped up and ripped off a few bursts with each one – the high point of the day's entertainment. There was a cocking handle . . . Lukas had already pulled it. Ben checked the receiver for a safety, a fire-selector. Found them. Conveniently, the full-auto position was engraved in red. He selected it. It all seemed to take forever.

Holding the gun in one hand, he bent next to Lukas. 'If you can hold on, I can drag you.'

'Okay.'

Lukas grabbed Ben's arm with both hands and Ben pulled.

There was motion toward the street, a shadow in the new gap between the ballistic shields. Ben let go of Lukas and took a step away from him, crouched low, the gun out in front of him pointed toward the movement. It was going to be a cop, it was going to be a cop . . .

He couldn't tell – cop or not. Just a black figure silhouetted against the remaining police lights, with some kind of automatic weapon that was scanning back and forth looking for a target.

God, what if it's a cop. I can't shoot a cop.

Something, he didn't know what, tightened his finger on the trigger without his willing it. The first burst missed but the second bounced the silhouette back out of sight.

'Jesus,' Lukas breathed.

'No vest, no helmet,' Ben said, giving voice to what he had not consciously seen.

He put the gun down and, with strength he didn't know he had, lifted Lukas and carried him into the apartment and down some hallways to a room with a bed, went back and grabbed the gun.

There was noise from the other end of the apartment, heavy footsteps, the beam of a flashlight. Reinforcements. Ben went out into the hall to meet them.

'Hold it!' a voice ordered.

Ben froze.

A tall man in police blue, vested and helmeted, sergeant's stripes on his arm, appeared from the back of the apartment. 'It's okay – they're ours,' he reported to the men behind him. Then, alarmed: 'Officer down.'

The word passed back along the ranks and the sergeant went straight to Lukas. 'Where?'

'Left thigh,' Lukas managed. 'Missed the artery.'

'Good for you.' He bent to examine the wound, had to pry Lukas's hand off it.

'Pressure,' Lukas said.

'Good man. That's what you need. Let's get a bandaid on it. O'Hanlon!'

A half-dozen other men were in the room now, all labeled POLICE. One came over and pulled out a first-aid kit, started to cut away the blood-soaked pants and put a sterile pressure bandage on Lukas's leg.

'What's happening out there?' the sergeant asked Ben.

'A gun battle – and grenades, I think. There's a barrier at the front of the building, so you can't see much. Some of them are out of their buildings. One got as far as here.'

'He still out there?'

'No, don't think so. I, uh . . .' Unable to make the words, Ben hefted the MP-5 he was still holding.

'Right. Good work. You know the way out?'

'I'm not—' Ben stopped himself. He'd do Lukas no favor pointing out that he didn't belong here. He was wearing a heavy vest and helmet and carrying a submachine gun, and the sign on his back said SECRET SERVICE. 'Yeah, I know the way.'

'Let's go then.'

Ben led them to the open front door. The sound of gunfire was constant now. Ben guessed maybe five minutes had passed since the first explosion, maybe less.

'Lt Brown and the A-team were based on the top floor, front,' he said. 'You have to go around and up the steps to get there. I don't know what the status is. I think the first explosion was in there somewhere.'

'Yeah, first floor.'

Another explosion rocked the street in front of the building. They all ducked back.

Ben heard a loud clanking and grinding, and what sounded like a badly muffled truck engine. The armored personnel carrier.

'That's our guys,' the sergeant said. He passed the word that they'd be going up the stairs to the apartments above and to assume the location was held by bad guys.

'Staying or coming?' the sergeant asked.

Judith was out there in the buildings across the street, Ben was sure. And Sid. Full of adrenaline as Ben was, fully armored and with a gun in his hand, he was ready – eager – to go in after them. But he wasn't trained in the tactics the cops would be using, couldn't provide the kind of backup these men expected and deserved. Zeal wasn't enough. And there was Hannah to think of.

'I'll stay here,' he said. 'With my partner.'

'Okay,' the sergeant said. 'I put in a call for medics. The wound doesn't look bad. Shock is his real enemy for now.' He turned to the men who'd come through the apartment with him from the rear garden. 'All right, let's move out.'

72

Aaron, the kid with the shotgun, had marched Sid across into the other building, up three flights of stairs and into a broad, open room with mirrors on one wall and rows of mattresses on the polished wood floor. It was crowded with women and kids, some armed, some not. Just in front of a two-piece partition that blocked off a rear corner of the room, two young teenage girls were holding each other, sobbing.

They'd left Sid behind the partition, lying hog-tied next to four Torah scrolls covered in red velvet, complete with filigreed silver breastplates and crowns.

They had spared one of the rear-guard fighters to keep watch over him – a girl no more than twelve with a shotgun that looked like the one Aaron had carried. He thought it would probably knock her over if she fired it, but it was the right weapon. From eight feet away, the distance they'd stationed her at, she couldn't miss.

He tried to get the girl to talk to him, but she wouldn't respond, and then it was too noisy to talk. The roar of gunfire made her flinch, and as it continued she began to shake, but she kept the shotgun pointed at him. One of the women still in the room beyond the partition – Rivka Brauner, Sid realized – looked in on them to be sure the girl was all right. She glanced at Sid; he couldn't read her eyes.

He tried to follow the battle by the intensity of the firing but there was no information in it. Then he heard the door open and people pouring back into the room beyond the partition. Sobbing and crying, and somebody trying to establish order. Loud sounds of gunfire that had to be coming from the hall. Shouted orders. The door slammed.

Lukas was in and out of consciousness. The background arpeggio of gunshots and the intermittent roar of the APC were a kind of torture for Ben, as if he were hearing in the metallic, mechanical sounds the tearing of flesh and the screaming of human mouths.

The medics came, finally, strapped Lukas to a stretcher and headed out. Ben followed behind, retracing the route that had brought them here, the sounds of conflict diminishing behind him. At the hole in the wrought-iron fence, a cop stopped him.

'Kaplan?'

'Yes.'

'They need you back there.'

'Sorry?' He didn't get it.

'Lt Brown wants you. Go back and someone'll meet you.'

Brown was downstairs in the parlor floor front apartment. Even by the reflected glow of searchlights on the buildings across the street Ben could see it was a mess – the bay window blown out, the wood-paneled walls splintered, the ornate, fourteen-foot ceiling cratered.

'Looks like you were right,' Brown said to him. 'They sucked us right in.'

It had started with the explosions, first one in the front apartment beneath Brown's command post and then a dozen more, bombs launched mortar-style at the snipers and the other forward positions. Then crude smoke bombs, pillars of white rising in front of the two townhouses, and the doors opened and men poured out into the smoke, firing machine pistols, carbines, shotguns. Brown had thought they were all men, but among the dead they had seen women, too.

A suicide charge, and the single A-Team left in front had kept to their cover and returned fire when they could, outnumbered at first because the other two teams were in back of the buildings, teed up for the assault that Brown now had to trigger early.

Not that moving up the schedule would have worried him if he'd had time to worry. A firefight was unlike anything else – you waited, tense and worse, forever, feeling like a rat was gnawing your intestines. Then for a sudden few seconds, minutes at most, you were plunged into it – more action than the wildest sport, a state of mind as altered as any the drugheads yearned for, your life – your *life* – and everyone else's depending on things that were happening too fast to know what they were until they were over, pure clarity and total unreality all at once.

Brown had been planning a commotion of his own out there in the street, the APC already grinding its way over the brow of the hill for a frontal diversion he now didn't need. 'Go, go, go!' he'd shouted into the radio, and the A-Teams waiting in back had gone.

In front, some of the attackers had made it to the ESU side of the street and police reinforcements were finally pouring into the fight. The din of gunfire was a mad elixir, adrenaline for the overadrenalized.

On the monitor Brown was using to watch the rear assault, men were scrambling up ladders and into windows. It looked good and then abruptly it didn't. A man was thrown back off a ladder, another slumped over a windowsill – half in, half out.

'10–13! 10–13!' the radio blasted. 'Officers down!'

Then an explosion blew out the back door of the school building as men crowded through.

'They just let us come ahead, then ambushed us once we were fully committed,' Brown told Ben. 'Goddamn fucking mess.'

'How bad?'

'Bad. We lost those two killed right away, going in the window, and three wounded by the booby trap—' He broke off abruptly. 'This isn't over yet. We've got two pockets of resistance, one in each building, and we don't have any idea where Brauner is—'

'He wasn't leading the charge?' Ben asked.

'No. Should he have been?'

'I guess not.'

'I'm just hoping he didn't get away again,' Brown said. 'We figure he's got to be in that bunker you told us about. You sure you don't know where it is?'

'You've got everything I know about it.' Then Ben remembered: 'There's a tunnel.'

'Yeah, Lukas told you? We think we found the mouth, dynamited. We figure they did it to cut off retreat. And we don't know where the other end is. So if he left that way, he's gone, just like Centerville.'

'I don't think he'd do that, leave these people to fight and die without him,' Ben said. He hadn't thought about the tunnel – what Lukas might say about it.

'I hope you're right, because we have to find him. The holdout ambushers on the top floor of the synagogue building we can deal with okay, but the other group is a real problem. It's kids – teenagers – and they've got a bunch of women in with them, and they claim they've got the rest of the explosives and they're ready to blow us all into the next world unless Brauner tells them not to. They had an adult commanding officer, but he's dead, and now they're barricaded in on the top floor of the school building, saying things we don't understand. Religious stuff. You're the only one who's talked to these people . . .'

'I'll do what I can.'

'Good. Just so you understand it's not a hundred percent safe up there. If they set off the explosives . . .'

'I don't think they'll do that, not if we don't panic them into it.'

It was what Brown obviously wanted to believe. Ben almost believed it himself.

'All right,' Brown said, 'let me give them a heads-up over there, and we'll go.' He walked across the room, dialing his cellphone.

Ben stood by the window, looking out. The street was empty except for an armored car painted police blue and the armored personnel carrier, which was clanking and grinding in the narrow street to put its back to the synagogue stoop. The ballistic shields had been scattered like Hannah's toys on a bad day. One helicopter had returned to hover overhead, the battleground's cold private sun.

'Sir,' one of the ESU cops said to him, 'you probably don't want to stand by the window like that. They still have access to a couple of upstairs windows.'

Brown came back. 'Okay. Let's give it a try.' He indicated the gun Ben was still holding. 'You want to keep that?'

Ben had an image of the man he'd shot at, jerked backward by the bullets. He shook his head and handed the gun over.

They trotted diagonally across the street sandwiched into a flying wedge behind three A-Team cops carrying individual ballistic shields, skirting the bodies still lying where they'd fallen. Ben, trying not to look, couldn't help but see. A man, spreadeagled on his back, one hand still clutched around a rifle, eyes open, face twisted – Len Eban, from the Shabbat retreat. Again, the image of a silhouette with a gun, reeling backward. Ben kept going.

Passing the armored personnel carrier, Ben glimpsed a couple of ESU cops in battle gear hustling out of the synagogue building with a stretcher, lifting a wounded cop up into the safety of the APC for evacuation.

Inside the school building they hurried through hallways full of cops, past battle-trashed classrooms and offices and up the stairs, Ben fourth in a line of five, right behind Brown. They stopped at a landing just before the top floor, already crowded with armored cops.

'There's one door that's the only access to most of the floor,' Brown said. 'It has a window in it, so they can see out into the corridor, and we can see whoever's standing right by the door, in front of a curtain they've rigged as a visual barrier. The glass is no obstacle for us, but like I said they've threatened to blow themselves up, so we need to talk them out if we can.'

'How many are in there?'

'We don't know who's in the bunker and who's here, but we're figuring there's at least twenty people here, kids and women, maybe as many as thirty.'

'Who's doing the talking?'

'One of the kids – a girl about sixteen. I think her name is Nahama' – stress on the middle syllable – 'Is that a name?'

'Hebrew, probably.'

'Right. And there's a boy, too – Aaron – same age or older. They don't always agree, but she seems to be the mouthpiece for now.'

'Have they shown any sign they might try to break out?'

'Not since they sealed themselves in after their adult commander got shot. I think they're too scared and confused to do anything aggressive for now.'

The cop who'd been trying to act as negotiator got the girl to come to the door where she could see Ben standing in the hallway guarded by two cops with ballistic shields. She was just tall enough to be comfortable looking out the window in the top half of the door. He saw dark curly hair, dark eyes and pale skin: she looked like a kid playing grown-up, none too confidently.

'Who are you?' she said.

'I'm Ben Kaplan.' Stepping forward.

'You're some kind of cop?'

'No, I'm not. I'm just dressed like this because of all the guns and shooting. I'm a friend of Mark and Suzanne Altman's.' He'd decided on the way up not to mention Judith, unsure what effect her escape – and return? – would have had on her status. 'And I know Rose and Morty Klein, too. My daughter is friends with their daughter Zippy.'

'I don't believe you,' the girl in the window said.

'It's true – ask them. Have them come and take a look, if they're in there with you.'

She turned away from the window. He heard muffled sounds of conferring, saw shadowy figures behind the curtain. A roomful of kids, really – girls as young as twelve. What if it were his own daughter in there, Ben couldn't help thinking, something he couldn't dwell on or it would paralyze him.

Nahama came back. 'What do you want from us?'

'I don't want anything from you. I want to help you see there's no reason to lock yourselves in, this way.'

'We're staying here until we see Joshua,' Nahama said. 'Our instructions were to protect the Torahs and to keep ourselves from being captured, no matter what.'

'Nobody wants to capture you.' He didn't know that, didn't know if they'd shot any cops before they holed up in here, but for now it didn't matter.

'If you don't want to capture us, then why are all those police out there?'

'Because you're in there with guns and bombs, and helpless people you're threatening to kill.'

'No we're not. Who said that?'

'Didn't you threaten to blow yourselves up if the police tried to come through the door?'

'Or through the windows, or the floor or the ceiling. Or try to gas us, or anything. It's all wired, and we know what we're doing, so don't try anything.'

The last part had the rhythm of a rehearsed speech, but there was an edge of panic in it, too. It scared him.

'It's okay, don't worry. No one's doing anything. But don't you see that sounds like a threat to kill people?'

No answer.

'Is Rivka in there with you?'

'Why?'

'What does she have to say about all this?'

'It doesn't matter. Rivka isn't Joshua's wife anymore.'

As Judith had predicted. Did that mean she'd gone back to a wedding?

'The only person we want to talk to is Joshua. He told us he was going to find Armilus and fight him. And we should wait until he came back for us.'

'He didn't say how long you should wait?'

'Forever, if we have to. Where is he?'

'We don't know.'

'You're lying.'

'No. He's disappeared.'

'If he's disappeared that means he's gone on to meet Moshiach, and we'll wait for him however long it takes. Unless he sends Eliyahu haNovi' – Elijah the Prophet. 'That's what I told the man before you. He didn't know what I was talking about.'

'It's too close to Passover for Elijah,' Ben said. 'He can't announce Moshiach while we're preparing for the holiday.'

'We're all ready. We have everything we need, matzos and all. He can come to our seder.' She grinned nervously. 'He can even drink his wine.'

'Is your mother there with you?'

She didn't respond. The curtain behind her moved and Ben saw a taller figure, heard a drone of speech. He wondered if the microphone ESU had in the hallway was picking up any of it. Nahama turned and snapped something at whoever was there, a hiss as Ben heard it.

'Does your mother approve of all this?' he asked.

'Leave my mother out of it.' Angry, or defensive.

'I thought Joshua wants to take everyone to Eretz Yisroel,' Ben said, 'the land that haShem promised to the children of Israel.'

'Yes. And he will. We're ready for that, too.'

'It says in the Torah, "Honor your father and your mother, that you may long endure in the land haShem promised you." How can you fulfill Joshua's desire to endure in the land haShem promised if you don't honor your mother?'

'But Joshua told us, a teacher deserves more respect than a father. So it must be the same for a mother.'

'It says in the Talmud,' Ben said, reaching for what he'd heard at the study session a lifetime ago, 'that where profaning the Name of haShem is concerned *a teacher is paid no respect*. And not honoring your mother is violating an important commandment and violating a commandment is profaning the Name.'

'Where does it say that, about a teacher is paid no respect?'

He tried to remember which volume of the Talmud it was . . . 'In Berachot.' He hoped she didn't ask any more questions.

'How do I know you're not making that up?'

'It's a lot to make up, on the spur of the moment.'

'I don't know,' she said.

'All I'm saying is, your obligation to Joshua is to follow the commandments – that's how you respect him best – and the commandments say listen to your mother.' Hoping the inverted commandments of Joshua's Hidden Torah were beyond what teenagers were taught. 'And it's a positive commandment for the other kids to listen to their mothers, too.'

Silence.

He said, 'There has to be a better way for all of us to carry out Joshua's wishes than sitting on a stack of dynamite.'

'I don't know. I have to talk to the others.'

'Okay. I'm going to go down the hall a little way. If you need me, just call.'

'You're doing okay,' Brown said. 'You think she'll go for it?'

'I don't know.'

'I think she's really scared, looking for an excuse. I just hope the others are feeling the same way.'

They sat waiting on the stairs. A TV monitor showed the doorway as seen by a camera mounted on the newel post. From down the corridor the microphone sent them raised voices, male and female.

'Not all of them feel that way, it sounds like,' Brown observed.

The argument subsided, then rose again, louder. Ben made out only stray words: Joshua, liar, stupid, Moshiach. Torah, mitzvot. No, and never, and forbid and – loud and definite – Yes I am!

Then shrieking and all at once *No!* and *Stop!* and *Aaron!* and a gunshot. Screaming and wailing. Someone saying ohmigod over and over.

The cops were on their feet, weapons ready. The monitor showed the door, nothing else. They could hear crying, and what sounded like reproaches, and then a hoarse male voice shouting, 'Shut up, shut up, will you all just *shut up!*

After a tense minute of silence came the same hoarse voice: 'Yo! Cops! Kaplan!'

Ben looked at Brown, whose brow creased in thought before he nodded.

Ben went out into the hall with the two cops he was coming to think of as his guardian angels, their ballistic shields protecting him like the wings of the fierce carved cherubim decreed for the Ark of the Covenant.

'My name is Aaron,' the hoarse voice said. The new face at the window was a tall, slender young man with fair skin and high color in his cheeks, a thin wisp of a beard. 'I'm in charge here now. You can talk to me.'

'Is Nahama okay?'

'You don't have to worry about her anymore. You were talking to her about honoring our mothers and fathers, right? And profaning the Name?'

'Yes.'

'Well, come and hear. This is what Joshua teaches about honoring fathers and mothers: The commandment to keep the Sabbath holy was given to Moses *before* the commandment to honor parents, to show us that keeping the Sabbath is more important. So if your father tells you to do something that would profane the Sabbath, you have to dishonor him by disobeying. But nobody makes their own decisions about what's permitted or forbidden on the Sabbath – you need a rabbi for that. So you're supposed to listen to the rabbi over your father. Or your mother. And *that's* the word of haShem. So don't tell me to listen to my mother instead of Joshua. Joshua is the only person I'm listening to and I don't want to hear more except if it's from him.'

73

'The kid's crazy,' Brown said. 'We're in big trouble.'

Ben didn't say no.

'We've got to find Joshua.' There was real urgency in Brown's voice. 'You sure you don't know where that bunker is?'

'You said you looked for it.'

'We've been through the building twice. All except this floor, and I figure if he was up here, they'd know it.'

'Let's take another look.'

They went through the school building top to bottom, found classrooms converted to dormitories and other signs of the school's recent use and everywhere the debris of battle, but nothing that could have been the windowless room Hannah had described, or the stairway leading to it. Yet Ben was sure she'd been telling the truth. He was missing something, but what? *Down a hall then a door then another hall . . .*

'Is this building connected to the other one?' he asked Brown.

'Sure is. In the basement and on the parlor floor.'

'Let's look at that.'

'I thought it was in the school building.'

'So did I.'

On the floor plan, the layout in the basement didn't look right. The parlor floor looked possible.

Ignored while the kids argued whether to listen to their mothers and the mothers argued whether to fight or surrender, Sid labored to squeeze himself into a ball tight enough to force his feet through the loop of his arms so that his hands would be in front of him. Straining against the ropes, he rubbed his wrists bloody, made it worse scraping his shoes over them.

When he heard the shot, he didn't realize at first that it had been a way to end the arguments, but then he heard the wailing and Aaron's shout for silence, and some other male voices, the older teenage boys, Sid guessed, sounding like they were rounding people up and shusshhing them. He heard Aaron call for the cops and then for Kaplan. Kaplan! What was he doing here, now?

Whatever the reason, it meant that Aaron would soon be focusing on his cop hostage, and Sid didn't want to be helpless. Fingers slippery with blood, he picked urgently at the tight knots around his ankles with the piece of spring wire he'd worked out of his mattress his first day in the little room and sharpened into a weapon. He could fight with his wrists tied if he had to, but not hobbled this way.

Down a hall, then through a door and down another hall.

The second hall led to the synagogue sanctuary. Ben paced up and back in the sanctuary aisle, remembering the time he and Hannah had come to services here with Judith. But this didn't seem like the right place for a narrow stairway that went down into a hidden chamber.

He went up the steps at the front of the low stage that took up the far third of the room, about three feet above floor level, walked past the reader's table to the Holy Ark, and turned to look back out over the stage to the pews.

He walked back across the stage and down the steps and suggested to Brown that they go for a quick look around the floor beneath – the one at garden level.

'You think it's under that stage?'

'Could be.'

Unlike the observation-post townhouse across the street, this one had an inside stairway connecting the parlor floor and the garden floor. Downstairs they found a room filled with round tables and chairs – the space where he'd had that first Shabbat dinner with Judith and Joshua, where Hannah had met her friends Deborah and Dina . . .

Further back, roughly under the sanctuary stage, was a kitchen and a storeroom and an office with French doors that led to the garden. They all had ceilings much lower than the dining room.

'You really think they're up there?' Brown asked him, looking at the ceiling.

'It's a lot of empty space. It could be six feet high.'

'That's pushing it.'

'Okay. Five. Five and a half.'

'Where's the access?'

'Good question.'

They went back upstairs and examined the sanctuary from the aisle between the front pews and the stage.

'A hatch under the rug?' Brown guessed.

'No.' Hannah would have remembered that.

Ben went up onto the stage again and stood contemplating the wood-and-marble paneled rear wall, punctuated by the Holy Ark. 'We had the Torah over us to protect us,' Hannah had told him.

Feeling like a heathen desecrating the Temple, he approached the Ark and pulled the tasseled rope that drew back the curtain, then opened its ornate doors. The white-satin-lined enclosure, where once had rested the Torah scrolls, swaddled in red velvet and adorned with ornate silver breastplates and crowns, stood empty. 'Our instructions were to protect the Torahs,' Nahama had said: it seemed she'd meant that literally. Ben wondered if custody of the holy religious objects might hold Aaron and the others back from incinerating themselves.

He stood contemplating the empty Ark – a recess about four feet high starting about four and a half feet from the floor – higher than usual, he thought. It would be awkward for a short worshiper to take the heavy scrolls from their niches for the weekly Torah reading. He stepped back and examined the marble facing around the opening.

He closed the Ark doors. Held a finger to his lips and pointed at the Ark. Brown looked at him with skeptical eyes, then at the Ark again. Looked up and nodded: he'd seen it. In the marble veneer beneath the curtain was a fine vertical centerline: the base of the Ark was a pair of flush doors.

Brown beckoned him to the back of the sanctuary.

'If that's it, it's not going to be easy. We don't have an entry procedure for a four foot-high door on top of a five-foot-high room.'

'You can look in, though.'

'We can try to put a fiber-optic camera in there, sure – but we can't look around corners.'

Aaron was making a kind of speech, something about having to kill Nahama because she was in league with the devil, but some of the others were trying to shout him down.

While he listened, Sid tried to work at the knots on his wrists, but he knew there was no way he could untie them. If he got a chance to make a move he'd have to do it this way. Meanwhile he had to hope that anyone who looked in wouldn't realize his hands hadn't been in front of him all along.

For the first time since they'd dumped him here, he inched toward the partition. He needed to get a look at what was happening out there.

A cop from the Technical Assistance Response Unit arrived in the sanctuary with the fiber-optic camera, accompanied by Inspector Burke and Captain Pavesi.

Brown got off the phone with the cops upstairs in the school building. 'It's gone quiet up there,' he reported. 'There was some yelling but it's calmed down, for now. I don't know if that's good or bad.'

Burke was looking at Ben, not happy. 'Does it ever occur to you just to stay where you belong?'

He's going to pull me out of here, Ben thought, but he let the comment go by, and so did Burke.

The TARU cop wanted to hear what Ben knew about the fire-drill shelter in order to anticipate what obstacles the camera's thin optical fiber might encounter. It seemed likely to Ben from Hannah's description that the stairs were directly below the Ark.

Moving carefully, aware every moment that they were all vulnerable to gunfire from below, one of Brown's cops put a heavy vest in the floor of the Ark and the tech expert climbed up into it and began snaking the optical fiber through the Ark and down. It was a slow, delicate job.

They all watched the monitor set up at the back of the sanctuary as the fiber-optic lens made its way down through the darkness below the Ark. The screen brightened slightly as the lens descended between shadowy forms the tech cop interpreted as two walls enclosing what might be stairs.

The lens stopped against a stair tread and the tech cop pulled it back up, inserted a long, slender wand alongside it and tried again.

'I wonder what they're doing down there,' Brown said in a hushed voice.

'If there's anybody there,' Burke said.

'Have to be.'

The lens began moving again, past the edge of the stairway and into an open area alongside it – brighter but still dim.

'Holy shit,' Brown breathed.

Leaning forward to study the monitor, Ben could just make out two people in the bunker. Closest to the lens was a man who had to be Suzanne's husband, Mark. He was sitting at an odd angle, back against the wall, his head thrown back against a dark splotch on the wall. His hand was by his side, holding a pistol.

'Suicide,' Brown said. 'You recognize him?'

'Mark Altman. He was one of Brauner's closest lieutenants.' Poor Suzanne, Ben thought, and those four little girls.

'Who's the other one?'

Ben had to look hard at the image. 'That's Joshua Brauner.' He was lying on his side in the middle of the room, eyes closed, wearing a white prayer gown like the one he'd been in when he made his statement at Centerville.

'Joshua? Our Joshua?'

'Right.'

'Oh shit.'

'There's somebody else, too.' Burke pointed. 'Right at the edge of the screen.'

Ben looked, saw only a shadowy form at the margin of the round image.

The ESU officers and the TARU expert conferred, decided the doors could be opened without fear of attack.

'Booby traps,' Brown remembered.

They called in one of the bomb-sniffing dogs that ATF and the Bomb Squad had waiting. When it didn't react to anything near the Ark, ESU rigged the doors with long cables so they could be opened from across the room. When the doors were safely open, they lowered in a viewing device with a lens that could see the length of the low-ceilinged room. They lowered a microphone in with it.

There was a third person at the far end of the bunker, a woman curled up on a thin mattress, indistinct in the dimness. Ben thought she might be naked.

'You know her?' Burke asked.

'Her name is Judith Zilka.'

74

Ben watched the monitor as Brown and another ESU cop went down stairs that looked just like what Hannah had described.

Brown bent over Joshua, looking for a pulse. He shook his head.

The other cop went to Judith, his body blocking the camera's view of what he was doing.

'Lieu, can you check this one?' he said, and Brown came over to try, fingers pressed to her neck.

He nodded and spoke urgently into his collar mike. 'We've got one breathing down here. Unconscious, and beat up real bad. Strap welts on the body, blunt instrument on the face and head—'

Ben closed his eyes against a wave of dizziness.

'Aaron!' came a sudden cry from the side of the room.

It was a boy sitting cross-legged on the floor at the far edge of what Sid could see through a slender gap between the partition's panels. The boy's white shirt and face were streaked with blood. There was a girl lying with her head and shoulders in his lap, and his arms were around her. Her blouse was so red Sid didn't immediately realize that was where the blood came from.

'It wasn't enough to kill her, was it?' the boy said, in lower voice, now that he had everyone's attention. 'You had to say all those bad things about her, didn't you?'

'Hey, Jacob, take it easy. I know you're upset, but it had to be—'

'Shut up, Aaron,' Jacob said, his voice lower still. He let go of the girl with one hand and pulled something from his lap. 'Remember who I am, Aaron?' he said. 'Trustworthy Jacob. Religious Jacob. Reliable Jacob. None of you knows who I am, only Nahama knew—' He started to cry, clutching whatever it was, something black and solid, a cellphone or a radio, Sid thought, but it couldn't be that because there was a tension in the room that there hadn't been before, as if no one were breathing.

A stocky boy about fifteen drew a handgun and began sidling toward Jacob, who was still sobbing, bending to kiss his girlfriend's cold, bloody forehead. The girl sitting nearest them was watching with wide eyes, cringing backward from the approaching boy.

'Stop!' Jacob said, his head coming up. He held the device overhead, his thumb poised over a red button, and Sid knew what it had to be.

'Drop the gun and go lie down over there,' Jacob pointed the detonator for emphasis.

Nobody moved.

'Do it,' Jacob said, 'or I'll send us all straight to Heaven. I'm a believer, remember? I believe we're all going to be resurrected in Jerusalem after the Last Judgment. And my soul wants to be with Nahama's. So do what I say, or yours will be, too.'

'You're sure that's the rabbi?' Brown asked when he came out of the bunker.

'Definitely. He's dead?'

'Oh yeah.'

'How?'

'That's for the ME, but one thing – somebody shoved a nail into the back of his skull, looks like it goes up into his brain.'

'Jesus,' Burke breathed. 'One of *them*?' The two others in the bunker.

Brown shrugged: who knows? 'The woman's been beaten within an inch of her life. I don't see where she'd have had the strength. And the guy had a gun – why use a nail?'

'Some kind of ritual?' Burke ventured, looking to Ben.

'Not that I ever heard of.' But he did remember, vaguely, a story from the Bible – an Israelite heroine, not Judith of Bethulia, killing an enemy with a tent stake driven through his temple.

His thoughts were derailed by the urgency in Brown's voice—

'What the hell do we do now? We've got a dozen kids ready to blow themselves to kingdom come, and their moms with them, if they don't see this clown.'

'Then let them see him,' Ben said, the words just popping out.

'You can't be serious.'

'Let me think about it.' His eyes still fixed on the dim image of Judith, Ben didn't expect to be able to think at all, but his mind was surprisingly clear.

'I need a rabbi,' he said. 'There's the one who warned me about this, he's waiting in the bus on West End.'

'Suppose you fill me in, first,' Burke said.

'They say they want to see Joshua, they won't do anything until they do. I think we should bring him there and show them.'

'You *are* serious,' said Brown.

'Yes.'

'You don't think it'll freak them out knowing their rabbi's dead?'

'Young Aaron is plenty freaked out already, and we're never going to be able to bring him the live Joshua he wants. I don't see what else we can do but bring him the dead one.'

'I wasn't too happy letting you talk to the girl,' Burke said, 'and look how that ended up.'

'He was doing great,' Brown countered. 'He had her convinced.'

'This isn't the same,' Ben said to Burke, not ready to deal with the fact that Nahama's willingness to listen to him had probably cost her her life. First he had to keep the boy who'd shot her from killing anyone else.

Burke wanted him to use a photograph: 'This is a murder. We like to have Crime Scene take a look before we disturb the body.'

'They'll never believe a photo. We'll end up having to use the body anyway, and we lose the impact of surprise – they'll have time to rationalize it away before we can show them the real thing.'

'All right, let's get your rabbi,' Burke said, 'and meanwhile I'll think about it.'

'It might help to find Rabbi Goffman, too,' Ben said. 'I think he may be better for this.'

'Jacob, there must be a better way,' Rivka Brauner said softly.

She was sitting not far from him – the only one now, everyone else was huddled in the middle of the room, on Jacob's orders.

'Suicide isn't what Joshua wanted, Jacob. You must know that.'

Hearing her calm voice seemed to take some of the wildness out of Jacob's eyes, and his own voice was calmer: 'Rivka, please, don't instruct me about Joshua's intentions. Didn't you oppose him when he cleansed the sin of your rival?'

'Cleansed? With a whip?'

'And didn't he divorce you? Nahama was right, you don't speak for him anymore.'

'You've known me all your life, Jacob. You've gone on trips with Joshua and me, lived in our house. How can you say I don't know his mind?'

'I don't want to talk about it. The sages teach us that a man causes himself evil if he talks too much with a woman. And Shimon, the son of Rabban Gamliel, said he who increases words increases sin.'

'He also taught that the world stands on three things – truth, justice and peace. And Rabbi Yismael said, "There is only One who judges alone."'

Sid thought she was taking a big chance, trying to get the boy to give up the detonator. Aaron, though disarmed for now, had allies who were eager to seize power again, and everyone was too on edge with fear and grief and fatigue to be sane about risks and consequences.

Waiting for the rabbis, Ben watched the Emergency Services cop use his EMT training on Judith, checking for obvious wounds, anything that needed immediate attention, trying to make her more comfortable. 'Be careful,' Ben wanted to shout, but he held his peace. Seeing her this way had banished for now his confusion about her actions and her motives. He just wanted somebody to get her to a hospital, but they'd told him no wounded civilian would be moved until the area could be made safe for medical personnel. And that had to wait until the final standoffs were resolved.

Pavesi came back with Elliot Rosen, wearing a heavy vest now. 'The other one's on his way.'

'Some mess,' Rosen said. 'You okay?'

'I'm fine.'

Ben filled him in on what was happening. As they talked, Task Force cops came in to cordon off the area in front of the door to the bunker with crime-scene tape. Ben looked around for Brown, didn't see him.

The ESU lieutenant arrived a minute later with Rabbi Goffman in tow. Ben introduced the two rabbis – one clean-shaven, in jeans and turtleneck, the other with a full red beard and sidecurls, in his usual black suit and a round-brimmed black hat – and brought Goffman up to date. Where Rosen had seen the possibilities of Ben's plan right away, the Hasidic rabbi was, as Ben had expected, skeptical, though he seemed ready to see Joshua as a misleader.

'The teaching this boy quoted does not mean we *always* listen to rabbis before fathers – that way lies much profanation of the Name. The Talmud does tell us that sometimes we honor a teacher before a father, but this is in a passage about the duty to ransom captives – if your father is a captive and your teacher is a captive, you must ransom your teacher first.'

'There's a duty to ransom parents?' Ben asked.

'Yes.'

'What about others? Captives who are just part of the People of Israel?'

'Yes, those as well.' The rabbi was smiling. 'And now you are going to remind me it is my obligation to help ransom these captives here.'

He stroked his beard in a way that reminded Ben of Joshua, steepled his fingers and pondered.

'If we wish them to believe Joshua died in battle with Armilus, and to remind them that according the prophecies the Son of David will come and bring him back to life, first we must be sure Joshua truly taught he was Moshiach ben Yosef.'

'He spoke of Armilus, of Galilee and Jerusalem, he called himself Nehemiah, he had a personal guard of sixteen handpicked warriors—'

'Sixteen? That, too? You didn't say so before.'

'Sorry. I thought I did.'

'So maybe,' Goffman said. 'Do you know if he also taught that he must die at the hand of Armilus?'

'No, but it makes sense to take the legend and the prophecy whole.'

'So there is a risk.'

'Worth taking,' Ben said. 'It's all we have. And I think you should be the one to do this, if you're willing. Rabbi Rosen is Reform so they may not listen to him.'

'He's right,' Rosen chimed in despite his obvious disappointment. 'I don't have the weight for it.'

Again Goffman pondered. 'All right, but first, with help from Above, I need to think how I will do this, what I will say.'

'You think this is going to work?' Burke asked him.

'Im yirtzah haShem,' he said, with less confidence than Ben would have liked.

'If God wishes,' Rosen translated.

Burke turned to Brown. 'You have a report from up there? What are the kids doing?'

'We're getting more sounds of arguing, but too far from the door to make it out. They tried to slide a microphone in under the door a while ago and somebody shouted into it that if they tried anything like that again everybody would be real sorry, and then he stomped it. That's all. But I'll tell you, I'm worried – we've been away a long time since Aaron sent us for Joshua, and it's not going to take a lot to set him off, especially if he's under pressure in there.'

'All right,' Burke said. 'It's crazy but let's do it.'

75

'Aaron, come and hear,' Ben said. 'It's Ben Kaplan.'

He waited, tried again.

The slender face with a wisp of beard and a hint of sidelocks appeared in the door, watching in silence.

'I have somebody who wants to talk to you,' Ben said.

'I told you, only Joshua.'

Ben heard a commotion behind him – Brown's voice: *I can't let you do that* – and turned to see Rabbi Goffman coming toward him. The rabbi had taken off his flak jacket.

'Hello, Aaron. My name is Baruch,' he said. 'Baruch Goffman. I'm a rabbi, too, like your Joshua, and I bring you joyous news of him.'

'Why can't he bring the news himself?'

'Because he has fulfilled his destiny as he prophesied, and the destiny of the People Israel. He has fought the great demon Armilus and died a glorious death.'

'No! I don't believe you.'

'To fulfill the prophecy, as it is written, "And the land shall mourn, every family apart." And why does every family mourn? The sages tell us, "they mourn the slain Messiah." Thus it must be, if Elijah is to announce the Son of David.'

A long silence. Ben wondered if this was going to work. He backed away to the stairwell to keep from confusing things.

The silence continued. Goffman stood calmly where he was, as if panicky, murderous eighteen year olds were an ordinary part of his day.

'How do I know you're not lying?' Aaron demanded, no cleverer than the girl he'd shot.

'I can show you a picture.'

This at Burke's insistence, though Ben knew it wouldn't work, and Goffman offered it with no enthusiasm.

'You think I'm stupid? You can't fool me so easy.'

'Then I have something better than a picture.' He beckoned and the two cops who were carrying the stretcher with Joshua strapped to it moved up into the corridor.

'I can't believe we're doing this,' Brown said.

The cops held the stretcher so Aaron could see who it was.

'Joshua! Oh, God! Don't be dead!'

'He died a glorious death,' Goffman said. 'I must tell you more about it and what it means for all of us, but I can only do that if we are face to face. It is disrespectful to keep a rabbi standing here like this.'

Hearing this, Brown rounded on Ben. 'What the fuck! We said if they *insisted*. He's volunteering!'

'I didn't expect this—'

'Taking off the vest was bad enough—'

'He's made his play. We can't call it back now.'

'There goes my fucking pension,' Brown said.

'I want Joshua,' they heard Aaron say. 'Before you can come in, I want Joshua with us.'

'Of course. You can send people out to carry the stretcher. No one will bother them.' To the cops he said, 'Put it down, please and go away.'

They turned to Brown, at the top of the stairs: 'Lieu?'

'Okay, leave it there,' Brown said. That much was part of the plan.

'It's good we took time to mike the stretcher,' Brown said to Ben. 'But I still don't like the rabbi going in there.'

On the monitor they saw a boy and a girl come out and the door close behind them. Goffman stayed near them, a human guarantee of safe passage as they went to lift the stretcher.

The door started to open again to accept them—

There was shouting and a shot and the door slammed shut, the sharp noise blending with the thudding impact of struggling bodies against the door.

'Down!' Brown shouted, but there was no explosion.

Another shot, and then a yell: 'Police! Police!'

Brown was up. 'Go! Go! Go!' – and over his shoulder to Ben, 'Not you!' – as he and his men poured up the stairs and into the hall, their own shouts of 'Police!' a counterpoint to shouts and cries from beyond the door.

On the monitor Ben first saw only their backs, then a quick confusion of motion as they shoved the rabbi and the two kids out of the way and galloped around and over the still form of Joshua, bursting the door open ahead of them. Once they were past the door it slammed closed again, leaving only the abandoned stretcher with Rabbi Goffman standing next to it, and an ESU cop herding the two would-be pallbearers away from the door. The sounds of conflict were almost drowned out by shouted orders – too harsh and overlapping to make out any single word.

Ben called out his name as he walked into the hallway, to keep from spooking the cop, who swung his MP-5 in the direction of the new motion, then registered who it was.

'We ought to get this out of the way,' Ben said to Goffman, bending to lift one end of the stretcher. The rabbi took the other end and slowly they carried Joshua the length of the hall.

'You okay?' Ben asked when they put the stretcher down. The uproar behind the door had faded to relative silence.

The rabbi nodded, offered thanks to God. 'Is this what you wished to happen?'

'No, I wanted what I told you, that you would tell them that according to the sages Joshua had to lie unburied for forty days until Elijah came to announce the Son of David, so the right thing for them was to come out and live a life of such purity that Elijah would come early.'

'I hope that is what you truly intended. I would not have come to provoke violence.'

It was a while before Brown came to the door. 'We're secure. Rabbi, thank you. You were great.' He called Ben in. 'Somebody here you need to talk to.'

They moved through a narrow corridor past a galley kitchen and a bathroom. Where the room opened out, the broad, open space Joshua had showed him – part gym, part dance studio – had been converted into a dormitory, most of the floor lined with mattresses.

Not far inside the room a body lay on the floor partly covered by a blood-stained sheet. Nahama, Ben guessed. There was a boy sitting next to the body, holding her hand; his shirt and pants were streaked with blood.

The room's other living occupants – about a dozen women and as many teens – sat on the floor in ragged rows at the far end of the room, in front of a cloth partition like the mechitza that separated men from women in the sanctuary, guarded by Brown's Apprehension Tactical Team. Ben glimpsed Suzanne and Rose Klein, arms clutching their knees, the picture of exhaustion. Face down on the floor, hands cuffed at the small of his back, was the lanky figure of Aaron.

Ben's attention was drawn by a long table nearer the door, where ESU cops were giving first aid to two wounded teenagers and a thin, unshaven man with the hollow-eyed look of not having slept in too long. His wrists were bandaged and there were scabbed scrape marks on his face. It took Ben a moment to recognize him.

'Sid?'

The undercover stared blankly. 'Kaplan?'

Ben stepped closer. 'It's good to see you.' Understatement of the year. 'You had us worried.'

'Not as bad as I had *me* worried.' The undercover looked Ben up and down, motioned him to turn so he could read the SECRET SERVICE on Ben's windbreaker.

'You get promoted?' A weak grin. 'Or maybe *de*moted.'

'Promoted, definitely. I'm trying to live up to it. What happened?'

'Got lucky. Kid with the detonator had a crush on Nahama. Real pissed off at Aaron, threatening to blow us all sky high. Brauner's wife talked him into giving her the detonator instead, said she'd help him punish Aaron.' He winced as the ESU cop butterflied a long gash on his forehead. 'Fucking Aaron almost killed me.'

'You jumped him?'

'When he was wailing about Joshua, and everybody was watching the door for the body to come in. It was my first real chance and I didn't know when I was getting another one.' He waved the ESU cop away. 'Enough. Let me out of here.'

'You sure you can walk okay?' the cop asked him.

'My friend here'll help me. Ready to go?'

'I am, if you are. Is he?' Ben asked the cop.

'If he goes real slow and easy.'

Ben checked with Brown.

'Take him out in the stairway for now. I'll give you the all-clear when you can go down.'

Sitting on the stairs, leaning back against the wall, the undercover told his story in fragments.

'It was Rivka who saved us, even though she gave Aaron back the upper hand. At least she had the detonator. She was working on building a quiet revolt, especially among the women. So there was this moment of uncertainty when Aaron said that Joshua was dead and the body was coming in. Nobody knew what to think or do. Just the fact that he was dead paralyzed some of them. Even so, one of the kids took a shot at me when I went for Aaron. He must have flinched – the range couldn't have been six feet.'

Sid stopped talking and wiped sweat from his forehead, held his hands out in front of him. 'Still shaky,' he said, then: 'I still can't believe you did that – bringing up the body like that. Fucking amazing.' He leaned out to look down the hall. 'That really is Joshua.'

'It really is.'

Brown came out to tell them that the holdouts in the other building were in custody: the sound of the battle breaking out here had automatically triggered a go-ahead for the planned assault over there.

'It's all clear now,' Brown said. 'You can go on down.' To Ben he said, 'Get him to the medics, and then if you'll just hang out down there a minute, I'll be right with you.'

With the battles over and the mopping up begun, Ben's first

thought was to find out about Judith – make sure she was getting care, was on her way to the hospital. He asked the medics he left Sid with, but they didn't know.

Against the flow of the bomb squad on its way in, Lt Brown came downstairs with Rabbi Goffman and assigned a cop to escort him back beyond the perimeter.

'You know, Rabbi,' Brown said, 'you scared the hell out of me pushing Aaron to let you in the way you did, but it worked out fine, thank God, and you were terrific calming everybody down, just now. My men and I are really grateful.'

'I'm glad if with God's help I could keep even one person safe. If I can do anything more, to help these people or with anything else, please call.' He fished in his jacket pocket and handed Brown a business card.

Before he left the rabbi turned to Ben. 'You were a member with these people, for some short time?'

'Just on the fringes. My daughter and I belong at Ohevei Yisroel.'

'Really? A very fashionable place I'm told, and I'm told also that the rabbi there has a good heart. But it would be an honor for me, if you wish to, if someday we can discuss together the teachings of Joshua Brauner – may haShem protect us from the misleaders – and help each other understand the right and wrong of it.'

'It would be my honor,' Ben said. 'And my pleasure.'

Brown walked Ben across the street to the parlor-floor apartment downstairs from the forward observation post. With the lights turned on, it was even more clearly the site of an explosion, debris everywhere, but the upended chairs had been righted and arranged in a rough circle with the couch, a heavy easy chair and some chairs from the dining room.

ESU cops were sitting and standing around – Inspector Burke and Captain Pavesi and three of Brown's A-Team sergeants, and the squad leader of Brown's snipers.

'Everything under control?' Burke asked Brown.

'Looks that way.'

'Cap and I are going to the hospital to check on our guys. We'll leave you to figure out what actually happened tonight. There's a big thermos of coffee in the kitchen, and some cold drinks, too.'

Ben took some coffee: he had the feeling that otherwise he might crash any moment. Brown grabbed a can of cola, and they both went back in to sit down with the others.

'Let's start from the beginning,' Brown said. 'We were all set up to go in the back, and we were preparing our diversion out front, and all hell broke loose. Johnny?'

The sniper leader talked about the homemade bombs that had

been launched, what he'd seen of where they came from and where they landed.

'Do we know what they were using to launch them?'

'Shotguns,' said one of the A-Team sergeants. 'We found one rigged with a stand so it worked sort of like a mortar. Not all that accurate, but more than good enough.'

They went on from there, everybody adding details, trying to build an overall picture. To the early talk Ben could add only his quick view of one of Joshua's warriors out in the street not long after the first bombs were launched.

Sid Levy came in, further bandaged, and Brown gave him his chair. The undercover had been locked away most of the time, he said, but he'd overheard enough to have the impression that there were two main fighting groups, with only a small volunteer force involved in the frontal assault on the police. The two commanders were an Israeli called Benzvi and an American whose name was Mark. Ben gave the cops a quick summary of what he knew about the two men.

'When Joshua didn't come to give the word, or Mark, either, there was a lot of confusion, from what I saw,' Sid said.

'It was someone in the synagogue building who started it,' said one of the A-Team sergeants.

'Benzvi, then. A stone killer.'

When they got to the endgame they heard from the sergeant of the A-team that had cleared the holdouts in the synagogue building. Cops lowered on ropes from the roof had slammed flashbang stun grenades through the windows, then followed them in quickly enough to keep the last six of Joshua's Sixteen from carrying out their threat to kill as many cops as they could before they died.

'Butch and Sundance,' Brown joked, but Ben was thinking of Masada.

Then it was Brown's turn, and Ben's, to talk about the final standoff, and here Sid could give them some of what they'd missed from the outside.

'It was close, real close,' he said. 'Some of those kids had really been indoctrinated, way worse than the grown-ups. It made a major difference that Ben came in with religious justifications for cooling things off – it gave the kids and mothers who were less convinced about the extreme stuff something to work with.'

'It also got Nahama killed,' Ben said.

'Yeah, but that was the real breakthrough. It was Aaron killing one of his own, not some soldier of the evil Armilus. And Aaron couldn't sell the idea that she'd been taken over by the devil, because she was the most popular kid there.'

When Sid talked about the conversation between Rivka and Jacob,

Ben was startled to hear him mention Judith. Sid barely knew who she was, had met her briefly at Centerville before they locked him up. 'It was harder for Rivka because people thought she was talking against Joshua from jealousy.'

As they went back over the details, making sure they had the night's events as clear as they could, Burke and Pavesi arrived from the hospital with news that the wounded cops were all expected to survive.

'We've got three dead, besides,' he said. 'This is maybe the worst single event in the department's history.'

The cops all contemplated that in heavy silence.

'We've got a lot of wounded on the other side, too,' Burke said. 'A couple of women and some teenagers. I don't know about them, except for the woman who was in the bunker.' A glance at Ben. 'She's unconscious, and they don't know if there was brain damage, but the docs are saying they think she'll recover, enough so maybe she can tell us what the hell happened with Brauner.'

By the time they'd done a quick review of the action with Burke and Pavesi and talked about how to present the story at the upcoming briefing for the bosses, day was breaking.

'Well, anyway, we've got one good hero for the media,' Burke said, wrapping it up. 'How about it counselor?' turning to Ben – 'The man who negotiated with the mad rabbi and the last holdouts, saved an agent's life, found the secret bunker, and masterminded the final diversionary tactics – not bad for a rookie. The least we can do is get you a little ink and some TV exposure.'

Burke was needling him, but Ben wasn't willing to let it go by even as a caffeine-fueled joke.

'I'm glad I could help,' he said, 'but I'd just as soon we kept that part of it to ourselves. I've got a five-year-old daughter to raise, and we live right in the neighborhood here. The best reward for me is being able to go out of my apartment in peace, and being sure my daughter won't be bothered at school. You've got plenty of fallen officers who can be all the heroes you need.'

'That's the sad truth. We've got way more heroes than any of us want. All right, you've got your wish – so take off and get some sleep. The chiefs'll be unhappy not to have you at their briefing, but if they can't contain their disappointment we know where to find you.'

Exhausted as he was, Ben was still too wired to sleep. He walked home in the hazy light of dawn and went upstairs. The pots and dishes from Judith's supper were in the sink. Her note was on the hall table.

He put the note in his desk drawer, not ready to throw it out but knowing he couldn't leave it where Hannah would see it. He washed the dishes, remembering how he'd felt after that first Sabbath dinner Judith had shared with them here, how he'd wanted to kiss the lipstick mark on her glass. Only this time she wouldn't be knocking on the door.

He had to call Vashti before Hannah started hearing about Joshua Brauner's apocalypse. And she was expecting to go to a Passover dinner tonight. He didn't see how they could do that and avoid constant conversation about the past night's incredible events. He'd have to start talking to Hannah about all of it this afternoon, anyway – reminding her that sometimes people got sick in a way that changed how they thought and acted. They'd talked about that before, when she'd been confused and frightened by some of the neighborhood's more flamboyant homeless people.

He told Vashti to say he'd be coming out in the afternoon to visit for a little while – she'd have to be in on the official version of the story. Until then, he said, keep Hannah away from any source of news: she could watch the airplanes take off as they'd planned, but not from inside the terminals where TV monitors would be dinning every ear with the details of the Jewish War on the West Side.

And maybe the better part of valor for tonight was just to have a quiet family Passover for two.

It wasn't going to be easy with Hannah, and it would take time, just as it would take time for him to decide what to do about Judith. But all that was in the future. He called the office to say he wouldn't be in, set the alarm for three in the afternoon, arranged for a car service to take him to Vashti's and finally tumbled into bed.

76

He went to see Judith in the hospital on Saturday. Looking down at her still form, the breathing and feeding tubes, the wounds and bruises on her face, hearing vital-signs monitors beeping and pinging in the background, he felt again the impact of the days he'd spent watching Laura in her coma. Watching and hoping and knowing all the hope in the world wasn't enough.

When he got home he called the dean of the law school to tell him a student had been caught in the mess on the West Side and was in the hospital. 'I was thinking you might want to notify her family. It's Judith Zilka.'

'I'm sorry,' the Dean said after a silence. 'You okay? Is there anything I can do?'

'I'm holding up all right. I should be able to finish out the term without any problem. But we'll need to talk.'

'When you're ready.'

'And about Judith – she'll need a good lawyer.'

For the next days the news was all about the shootout on the Upper West Side. There were many versions – Crazy Rabbi was a popular one, but so was Spiritual Leader Cracks Under Millenarian Pressure.

Stropkovers from both sides of the schism, mourning ten dead and nineteen wounded, accused the police of having acted rashly and driven Joshua and his followers to desperation. Asher Stern surfaced briefly, demonizing Joshua and his closest followers while offering a welcome to the survivors, though he was curiously silent on the subject of Ari Benzvi, the suspected bomber who was not among the survivors or the bodies so far identified.

Most commentators seemed content to call the outbreak of violence an aberration, and to blame Alan Kest for masterminding the criminal behavior that had precipitated it – the financial crimes and illegal dealings in explosives and firearms, and especially the bombing death of Isaac Isaacs. Counterfeit currency never came up.

On the law-enforcement side, most of what Ben saw was NYPD's show, with federal agencies a secondary voice. The police had taken almost all the law-enforcement casualties – three officers killed and eight wounded – and the press was focusing on the incident as potentially by far the largest test yet of New York's death penalty law and the Manhattan DA's historical reluctance to employ it – assuming the shooters could be identified.

Reverend Walker expressed condolences but didn't miss the opportunity to note that in his neighborhood the death toll would have been much higher. There was an overflow of public introspection in all branches of the mainstream Jewish community, prayer sessions and healing dialogues at every congregation, especially OY, which announced a special remembrance as part of the traditional memorial service at the end of Passover, the first event of a planned week-long inter-denominational program on religious fanaticism.

When Ben visited Judith on the day she came out of her coma, the nurses told him not to expect much. She was propped up in bed, hands folded, gazing at the wall in front of her. He said hello, and she seemed to recognize him.

'Hello,' she said.

He tried to make conversation but she said no more. He pulled a chair next to the bed and sat there with her, troubled by questions of loyalty and betrayal at the same time he was remembering the brightness Judith brought to Hannah's eyes, and Sabbath dinners that felt like family; the smooth dips and hollows of Judith's body, her textures and fragrances and the electric connection he'd felt with her.

After almost an hour of silence – knowing he'd come here for some kind of resolution, yet with no idea what it would be – he reached out to squeeze her hand and said good bye.

'Will you come again?' she asked, barely audible.

'Of course.'

'How is Hannah?'

'Upset,' he said. 'Confused. We talk about it, but it's been very hard for her.'

'I'm sorry,' Judith said. 'She's a wonderful little girl.'

He nodded, not trusting his voice.

He was on leave from the office, granted by a visibly reluctant Queen Victoria. It gave him time to be with Hannah, and to try to make sense of the past weeks.

He was surprised to get a call from Nate Morgan.

'I wanted to make sure you were okay. They told me at your office you were home, and I've to got say, taking time off sounds like a smart idea. You don't have to feel under pressure from us, either. We can talk in a week or so.'

Ben hung up perplexed: could they still be considering him? They had to be, or why the call?

* * *

He kept going back to visit Judith, though she still spoke hardly at all. To pass the time he offered unsolicited commentary about the political craziness increasingly dominating the daily news reports, or else he sat in silence, saddened and confused yet unable to stay away. On his fourth visit he found an elegantly dressed, dark-haired young woman bustling around Judith's room, folding clothes into a leather suitcase and keeping up a constant stream of patter for a silent Judith, in a language Ben didn't recognize.

She stopped when he came into the room. 'Hello, I'm Miriam, Judith's sister.'

'Ben Kaplan.'

She seemed to know the name and relaxed a bit. She'd arranged for Judith to move to an inpatient rehab center out in the country, she told him. 'We've got to be careful about her, she's had an awful shock to her system, poor thing.'

Ben brooded continually about his own errors, and about Judith and whether she'd betrayed him and Hannah wittingly or not, and especially about what she'd done in those last hours, wanting to believe that the whipping she'd gotten meant she'd been telling the truth about why she'd escaped, but still baffled by her return to Joshua. Convinced she must have killed him, uncertain what had prompted it.

Freddi Ward came by to visit one night with fancy take-out food for the three of them.

'What's happening with the case?' Ben asked after he'd put Hannah to bed.

'I wasn't sure you'd want to talk about it.'

'Most days, I don't.'

'Well, to start with, figuring out who to charge with what is turning into an advanced seminar on prosecutorial discretion. Her Majesty's even cooperating with the DA.'

'Amazing.' Her usual style was to compete viciously with the Manhattan District Attorney whenever a big case involved violations of both federal and state law.

'And it's not going to be any easier if the survivors of Joshua's army plead some kind of temporary insanity – they were brainwashed and sleep-deprived and thought they were being invaded by Nazis, something like that.'

'Is that what you're expecting?'

'That's the rumor.'

'What about Brauner?' Ben asked her. 'Any sense of what's happening with that?'

'That's going to be interesting. The nail came from a crate of gas masks stored under the stairs in that bunker, and everybody in the building had access. Your friend Judith had motive and opportunity, and she had a smear of his blood on her hands, but there's no way to know how or when it got there, and the ME says the nail didn't kill him right away, he suffocated.'

'Suffocated?'

'That's what the man said' –

Could that mean Judith *hadn't* killed him?

—'and meanwhile Judith herself hasn't said a word, and her lawyer is taking the position she needs to recover before she can even consider giving any kind of statement. So for now at least, without an eyewitness or a confession, the DA doesn't have anybody to charge. How is she, by the way?'

'Judith? There doesn't seem to be any serious damage, and the cuts and bruises are healing, though the worst ones will take a while—'

'Not what I mean.'

'Emotionally? I don't know. She doesn't talk much. She seems haunted. Sometimes she asks for Hannah, and Hannah asks for her a lot, but I don't see how I can even let Hannah near her. It would just get her hopes up, and then the thought of putting her through another disappointment . . .'

'It's about you, too, though, isn't it? Avoiding disappointment.'

'I suppose it is. There's still too much I don't understand about what happened, and I don't know what I want.' It wasn't true, he knew what he wanted – Judith and Hannah and himself in a world where none of this had happened – he just couldn't have it.

He went to visit Judith at the rehab center, one exit past the turn-off to Centerville. Set in a valley amidst cliffs, it looked more like a luxury resort than a hospital.

They walked down a flowered path in the silence he was growing accustomed to with her, Judith progressing slowly with the help of a walking stick. Prompted by a dazzling flash of lightning and a crash of thunder, Ben looked for shelter, saw a gazebo down another path beyond pink splashes of azalea. They hurried there as fast as Judith could go and got under the roof just as the clouds burst.

They sat next to each other on the gazebo bench – Judith watching the rain pelt down around them, Ben watching her watch the rain, too conscious of the way the soft cloth of her dress hugged her body.

Unexpectedly, she began to speak, her voice strong but flat. 'Suzanne was here to visit. I didn't know what to tell her about how Mark died.'

'The police must have told her—'

'Only that he shot himself. She thought I'd know why.'

'Do you?'

She hesitated. 'He came looking for Joshua and saw us there and he wanted to kill me. He beat me with his fists and his gun, raving that he would seal the bunker and say Joshua had gone bodily to heaven to fight Armilus and left Mark behind as his general. That's all I remember, the hitting and the pain and then everything went black.'

Why was Mark trying to kill you? Ben wanted to ask, though he was sure he knew the answer.

After a while she began to speak again. 'Joshua was furious with me when I came back. He had the women strip me and then he beat me with a strap eighteen times. That's what the Talmud prescribes for those who can't survive thirty-nine. I thought I would die. And then he had them take me to the bunker and lock me in.'

'Why go back at all? You were safe.'

'I went to kill him. I was lying there in your bed and I saw I'd made a mistake to come out. I knew I had go back and kill him or everyone was going to die.'

His eyes burned and his stomach knotted, but he made himself speak. 'That's right,' he said as lightly as he could manage, 'you're Judith.'

She didn't smile. 'Joshua knew it, too. He thought he could do better than Holofernes, but he was wrong.'

There was nothing to say. He waited, knowing what had to be coming, wanting to hear but dreading it.

'When the whipping was over he made me go through a marriage ceremony,' she said. 'And then he went to prepare everyone for battle. I knew he was going to come back and consummate the marriage. To bring down the Shekhina for the battle, he said.' She was speaking in the same monotone, looking at her hands. 'I had a long nail I'd pried from a wooden case, and I tried to sharpen it on the concrete floor while he was gone. When Joshua came back he just ripped off the gown they'd given me. It hurt so badly where he'd beaten me. And then he turned away to undress himself. And I took the nail and I shoved with all my might so it went up into his brain through the soft spot at the back of his neck. I don't know if that killed him. When he fell I held his nose and mouth until I was sure he wasn't breathing. I had no sword. The real Judith used a sword.'

Her façade of numbness cracked, and she began to weep. She turned in on herself in a way that didn't encourage a comforting embrace.

'I hated him so much,' she said, her voice steady though the tears still streamed down her cheeks. 'He'd betrayed us all, perverted our faith. How could we know if *anything* we'd done when we were with him had been good or true? How would we ever trust anyone in the future? And still I couldn't get it out of my mind that everything about him was good and true and *I* was the bad one, even as I pushed the nail into him, even as I kept him from breathing.'

He didn't know how long he sat motionless in the echoing spell of her words before some need made him reach out and touch her hand.

They sat together until the sun forced itself through the clouds, but she didn't speak again until they were walking back to her room.

'I had to tell you,' she said. 'It was too important for me to let it be a mystery between us.'

'I'm glad you did.'

As they approached the residence building she said, 'My lawyer wants me to talk to the District Attorney.'

'That's probably smart,' Ben said, thinking – it's a solid story of self-defense and the defense of others: if her lawyer plays it right the DA won't want to touch it.

Nate Morgan called: the Secretary wanted to see him.

'I don't know what the Secretary has in mind,' Ben said, 'but I should tell you I've decided to withdraw my name.'

'Oh no you don't. I read the Secret Service reports – you're a genuine hero. The Senate is going to eat it up. And you're going to be great in the job.'

'And what about the fact that I was where I didn't belong, doing things that weren't mine to do?'

'Look, if somebody thinks you shouldn't have been playing agent, or that you had a conflict – what you did worked, and that's what counts. Though I *am* curious how you missed it that your rabbi was a madman.'

Ben hadn't ceased worrying about that. About his own need for the community and belonging that Joshua offered. His blindness in the hope of comforting belief, his inability to see past the pleasures of sex. He knew he could take no comfort in the fact that no one else seemed better able to define the border between faith and fanaticism, or the point where fanaticism turned dangerous, but it was the best answer he had for questions like Morgan's.

'Tell me what signs I should have looked for. A rigid need to make others conform strictly to your beliefs? The use of psychological or physical coercion? The impulse to punish physically or even to kill those who believe differently? Those things have all been part of almost every major established religion in the world, at one time or another.

'The simple fact is,' Ben told Morgan, 'that for nearly all the time I knew him, Joshua Brauner affected my life only for the better. He was tolerant and understanding, and I never saw him do anything that looked even close to crazy until it was far too late. Maybe I should have known sooner. I don't see how.'

'Okay. That'll do, for our purposes.'

But your purposes aren't mine, Ben thought, and said: 'I appreciate your confidence, but I still have to say no.' Wanting no part of the exposure or the disruption in his routine with Hannah that went with the job, not at all sure the hero card would survive the inquiries that were already being called for on all sides and the multiple prosecutions that were likely to follow. And if he stayed in touch with Judith, that would only complicate things more.

Saying no to the Treasury job hit Ben harder than he expected it to. How hard was brought home by a surprise visit from Frank Lukas.

'Rumor has it you turned down the job.'

'In the interest of the Service.'

'That's not how we see it. You impressed a lot of people, and a lot of people are grateful, starting with me. I owe you – not just for me, for Sid, too.'

'No, I owe you,' Ben said, knowing that Lukas was sincere, and knowing too that his message would have been different if Sid hadn't come out of it so well. 'It was an education working with you. And speaking of that, what's happening in Israel?'

'Rudovsky's gone, for one. Back to Russia, we think. The Israeli National Police claim they're cooperating with us in Kiryat Yaacov, but there's not much to go on there except rumors that some heavy machinery was moved in a few weeks ago and then hauled right out of there the day after the standoff started in Centerville.

'Sorry,' Ben said. 'I thought we were close.'

'We were. We found a machine in Kest's store they were using to make engraving plates, back in that shielded room of his. These were definitely the people, and we're going to stick close to their friends for as long as it takes. We don't have a choice, because by every indication that heavy machinery in Kiryat Yaacov was an intaglio press.' He paused. 'The truth is, we jumped too fast. We should have given them more room. Maybe we even should have found a way to let them go, the way you said.'

Ben could guess how hard that admission had to be. 'You'll catch the rest of them,' he said.

'Yeah, sure. Frank Lukas always gets his man. You sure I can't convince you to change your mind? I'd really like having somebody I trust in Washington for a change.'

'Maybe another time. And, meanwhile, you've got somebody here in New York.'

Ben was becoming increasingly uneasy in Judith's company. The silences had returned. She was vague and abstracted: the haunted quality he'd mentioned to Freddi only seemed to increase with time. He had to accept that all the wishing in the world wasn't going to heal her, and all his admiration for what she'd finally done wasn't going to banish his misgivings – for himself and for Hannah. He couldn't help feeling some relief when Judith told him her sister had convinced her to go back to England to convalesce, and the DA had said he wouldn't stand in her way.

On the Friday Judith was leaving, Ben decided it would be better to bring Hannah along to say goodbye than to have Judith simply disappear from her life.

He wasn't prepared for the rush of emotion he felt when he saw Judith sitting at the side of the VIP lounge in an airline wheelchair. Hannah ran to greet her, galloping across the lounge as if she was about to jump onto Judith's lap. At the last moment she seemed to remember that Daddy had said to be careful because Judith had been sick. She walked gravely the final steps and handed Judith an envelope.

'I made a "get well and have a happy trip" card.'

Judith took it with a smile. 'Thank you. Do you have a kiss for me, as well?'

Hannah nodded shyly and stood by the side of Judith's chair and reached to peck her cheek.

'You can do better,' Judith said. 'Climb up on my lap for a minute and give me a hug.' A small grin. 'Only not too big a hug.'

They went up to the observation deck to watch Judith's plane take off. Hannah recognized it waiting for a runway in a long line of jumbo jets.

'See, it's the one with red white and blue, right behind the green one.'

'You really do know all about this,' he marveled.

'I like airplanes,' she said. 'They're fun. Only sometimes they take away people you like, and that's sad.'

'Yes, sometimes they do. And it is sad.'

'But sometimes they bring them back, too,' she said.

He bent to give her a hug and a kiss. 'And it's easier watching them go when there's somebody you love who stays with you.'

He took her hand and together they watched until Judith's plane angled upward into a clear sky.

Still hand in hand they walked back through the terminal.

'Daddy, can we go and welcome the Sabbath tonight?' Hannah asked him. 'I want to sing the songs and say the grape juice prayer. Can we?'

'I don't see why not,' he said, feeling unaccountably hopeful.

AUTHOR'S NOTE

Readers of my fiction know that while my characters and stories are all made up, the world in which they exist is based closely on fact. In writing NO HIGHER LAW, I started with the desire to explore aspects of the American criminal justice system which, if not actually secret (like the grand jury of my previous novel), were at least not well known.

I was pointed in the right direction by John Sexton at the NYU School of Law, an institution so full of exciting people and thought it's worth a book of its own. He introduced me to Ronald Noble, now on the NYU Law faculty, who in turn got me fascinated with the little-known aspects of Treasury law enforcement.

By coincidence, I was already friendly with James Johnson, whom Ron had recommended to be a successor of his as Assistant Secretary of the Treasury for Enforcement. Despite his crushing schedule Jim (Under Secretary, at this writing) was responsive to my queries and enormously helpful. So was Raymond Kelly, who now heads the U S Customs Bureau but was Under Secretary for Enforcement when he let me in on what was for me the biggest law-enforcement surprise of my research – that unlike the FBI, which does everything by itself, Treasury's enforcement agencies are happy to call on local law enforcement when they're better suited to the job at hand. This is particularly true in New York, because the NYPD's Emergency Services Unit is second to none in its ability to deal with difficult confrontations.

The time I spent with the ESU, courtesy especially of Robert Giannelli and Richard Greene, and also of more members of the Apprehension Tactical Teams than I can name here, convinced me that Secret Service and ATF and Customs have the right idea when they call on ESU.

There is so much that is surprising and compelling in the abilities and activities of the United States Department of the Treasury that it would take a career's worth of novels to capture it all. Just as the merest example, who would guess that the secret inks that adorn U S currency are made in Swiss laboratories and factories (and shipped to the U S in huge barrels like the ones used to transport petroleum)? And though NO HIGHER LAW is set in early 1998, soon after the first wide circulation of notes featuring optically variable ink, a short year later real-world counterfeiters in pursuit of a new Supernote have already mounted an assault on that seemingly invulnerable bastion of authenticity.

Among the many in Treasury law enforcement to whom I owe gratitude are—

At ATF: Alex D'Atri, Joe Green, Chris Behn and SAC Jack Balass.

At FinCEN, whose powerful variety of research tools I could only hint at here: Stan Morris, Jim Erwin and Tom Eberhardt.

And of course the helpful folks at the Bureau of Engraving and Printing.

I had help, too, from the law enforcement community outside the Treasury Department, especially –

Karyn Carlo and Richrad Lopez of NYPD.

Jim Clemente and John Tann of the FBI.

My research extended far beyond the world of agents and prosecutors, and many people took the time and effort to provide assistance.

Nathan Lewin helped me bridge the gap between law enforcement and religion.

Joe DePlasco and Herbert Block put much of the story into the context of how New York really works.

I also got aid in that department from Martin Begun and Michael Miller, and from Vicki Ciampa, who introduced me to them.

Katharine Muir provided psychological insights and a clear-eyed reading of the early text.

Linda Imes reprised her role as confidant, source of introductions, and inexhaustible font of information and challenging questions.

Tina Bennett made an early suggestion that turned me in a direction I would not otherwise have gone, with fateful results.

Nahama Broner and Judith Wrubel were my early escorts into the world of Jewish renewal.

Michael Strassfield and Joey Krakoff provided different kinds of rabbinic support.

Special thanks as well to:

My literary mafia: Lawrence Block, Lynn Bundesen, Betsy Elias, Katherine Finkelstein, Bob Geller, Dan Kleinman, Judith Mintz, Gidion Phillips and Peter Stern.

Michael Rudell, Bruce Keller and Ken Burrows for listening to my publishing story and knowing what to do about it.

Everyone at The Virginia Center for the Creative Arts, especially Sheila Pleasants.

The theology in NO HIGHER LAW is all authentic, as are the quotations from the Hebrew Bible and the Talmud. Likewise, the rituals described are all essentially as they are practiced by members of at least some of the many kinds of Jewish congregations to be found in the United States and around the world.

Joshua Brauner's Messianic theories are all drawn from Jewish thought, some of it quite mainstream, though the more extreme forms of his ideas about a Hidden Torah and redemption through sin are largely associated with theologies that were thought of, even in their own time, as heretical. His Sabbath wedding ceremony goes beyond anything I know about in modern esoteric Judaism, but it pales beside the sexual practices attributed to various heretical Jewish sects of the past, especially some that followed in the wake of the false messiah Shabbetai Zvi.

But what is most consistent in all the varieties of Judaism I encountered is this – the movement towards spiritual renewal that is so evident in Christian America is no less operative in Judaism. And this phenomenon isn't restricted to the U S, or even wholly to Jews. Gentile celebrities make much of their study of Kabbalah, and in Oxford one of the most popular student associations is led by a Hasidic rabbi. Everywhere one turns, Jews are taking new pleasure in the rituals that initiate the Sabbath and generally increasing their practice of the commandments associated with living a Jewish life. Study groups like those visited by Ben Kaplan are proliferating, and there are several congregations in New York (and many other cities) as full of enthusiastic worshipers from all walks of life as is the fictional O.Y.

The Centerville I've described here is fictional, too, but there are communities just like it in the northern suburbs of New York City. There is a real Midwood in the real Brooklyn, inhabited by a variety of observant congregations some of whose members live in houses like Alan Kest's but none of whom follows Joshua Brauner or the equally nonexistent Stropkover Rebbe. The only person I've ever known who was actually from Stopkov, a real town in the Carpathian mountains, was my grandfather Aron Friedman, of blessed memory.